LÀNG CÂY TRE

A Novel

John Otis Nichols

Paperback ISBN: 979-8-9955022-0-3

Printed in the United States of America

This is a work of fiction. Names, characters, places, and incidents are either products of the author's imagination or are used fictitiously. Any resemblance to actual persons, living or dead, events, or locales is entirely coincidental.

Historical events, locations, and cultural references are incorporated for literary purposes. While certain historical settings and circumstances may be based on real events, the story, characters, and dialogue are fictional.

First Edition

Dedication

First, this is for my brother. Where did your courage come from?

To my friend, SPF **Robert Warren Parent,** KIA July 21, Thừa Thiên Việt Nam. I have cried countless tears for you. May you walk the green fields of Valhalla.

To Dave (Paps) Wingfield, it was an honor to stand beside you. I cannot imagine.

To Jimmy Fox, you are strong and courageous in your convictions.

To all who served in Vietnam, to every nation, on every side, and in every capacity.

To all who carried the burden of duty, who endured the heat, the fear and the loss.

To those who returned forever changed, and to those who never returned. You are not forgotten.

And to those countless innocent lives, men, women and children who suffered and who still bear the silent echoes of war.

To the families that still grieve today for those they lost. May all their sacrifices never be forgotten.

Ecclesiates 3:8 (King James Version)

"A time to love,

and a time to hate.

a time of war,

and a time of peace."

TABLE OF CONTENTS

ACKNOWLEDGEMENTS

Làng Cây Tre began as a personal project and remained so for many years before reaching its final form.

The author extends sincere gratitude to those who encouraged the completion of this work and supported the effort to bring it forward.

Special thanks are offered to Toni Tucker Locke and Mary Ethel Elam for their encouragement and support.

The author also acknowledges the use of ChatGPT as an editorial and research assistant during the development of this manuscript. Its contributions included language refinement, continuity review, and limited dialogue support, particularly in Vietnamese.

All content, structure, and final editorial decisions remain the work of the author.

AUTHOR'S NOTE

This novel is a work of historical fiction, but it is grounded in real places, real events, and the lived experiences of those who passed through them.

I served in Vietnam from August 1967 to August 1968. Like many who were there, I carried those experiences with me long after I left. Over time, reflection has changed the way I understand that period—not only the events themselves, but also the people who lived through them on all sides.

Làng Cây Tre does not attempt to recreate history in exact detail, nor does it seek to explain, justify, or condemn the war or those who served. Instead, it focuses on individuals—soldiers, villagers, and families—whose lives were shaped by forces far beyond their control.

The Vietnamese characters and communities depicted in this novel are fictional, but they are inspired by the resilience, dignity, and humanity of people I encountered and those I have come to understand more deeply over the years.

To those who served, I am proud to be among your number. You are far better than the image portrayed by so many. For those who returned, welcome home; and for those who did not return, you remain constantly in our memories.

Any historical references are used in the service of the story and should be understood within that context.

PROLOGUE

Genesis 1:1–5 (KJV)

> "In the beginning God created the heaven and the earth. And the earth was without form, and void; and darkness was upon the face of the deep. And the Spirit of God moved upon the face of the waters. And God said, Let there be light: and there was light. And God saw the light, that it was good: and God divided the light from the darkness. And God called the light Day, and the darkness He called Night. And the evening and the morning were the first day."

God reached out His hand and spoke the "Word" and heat exploded into the vastness of the empty expanse, filling what was to become the universe with trillions upon trillions of degrees of heat. There was opaque light, fixed in space, no sound—only heat. Space expanded at a rate far faster than what would later be known as the speed of light. In an instant, the heat began to cool, and in that cooling, the first particles began to form.

In that early heat, the first fundamental particles formed. As the universe expanded and cooled, protons and neutrons took shape, and electrons followed soon after. Within minutes, the lightest atomic nuclei formed, and when the universe cooled enough for electrons to bind to them, the first true atoms appeared—mostly hydrogen, with helium close behind. For a long time, the universe held no stars, only vast clouds of gas. Over hundreds of millions of years, gravity gathered that gas into denser regions until pressure and heat rose high enough to ignite nuclear fusion. The first stars were born, and with them starlight spread into the surrounding dark, their photons traveling outward across the widening cosmos.

Within those orbs of nuclear fusion, the first elements fused into heavier elements. Under the watchful eye of God, the elements necessary for life began to form. Over billions of years, each star grew as it consumed its nuclear fuel. When that fuel was exhausted, the star collapsed upon itself and exploded from the compressive force, scattering newly formed elements outward into the vastness of space.

After nine billion years, within a small arm of a spiral galaxy, a molten sphere of rock formed and began to circle a newly born star. The molten rock was relentlessly pummeled by asteroids, meteors, and comets, each carrying its own elemental cargo. Many of the comets bore water, frozen within them as they traveled through space. When they struck the molten surface, water vapor was released and held close by gravity.

After millions of years, the molten surface cooled. As it cooled, the water vapor condensed into rain. The rain fell for millions of years. Oceans formed, and barren landmasses rose from the waters, marking the beginning of a world that would one day be called Earth.

Over time, the continents of the Earth shifted and collided, separating and rejoining repeatedly. Vast landmasses rose and were worn down. At one time, a single supercontinent formed, later to be called Pangaea. In its center, enormous mountain ranges were thrust upward by the collision of land. When Pangaea finally split apart, those mountains were divided. One portion would become the Appalachian Mountains of North America. Another would become the ancient mountains of Scotland. Both moved into the northern waters, one becoming part of North America, and the other, part of the British Isles.

The more northern land was shaped by ice. Massive glaciers carved valleys and lochs into the stone, grinding mountains down and leaving behind a rugged, broken landscape. When the great Ice Age retreated, there came a brief period of warming, followed by another sudden cold reversal known as the Younger Dryas. The climate of the northern lands shifted back and forth between temperate and bitterly cold. The ground became saturated, and peat bogs formed across wide stretches of land. Life was hard, and survival demanded resilience.

The wind off the high ground carried wet cold even when the sun broke through. It was a cold that lived in bone and stone, not the clean bite of winter but the constant damp that seeped into everything—wool, leather, hair, and skin. Smoke from peat fires curled low inside their shelters and clung to the throat. At dawn, the world smelled of soot, wet earth, and animal breath.

Life here did not reward softness. A man measured his day by what he could secure: the turning of soil that resisted the blade, the gathering of heather and bracken for bedding, the careful splitting of driftwood that would burn without wasting. Women moved with quiet efficiency, hands red and cracked, drawing water, scraping hides, and keeping infants wrapped tight against the wind. Children learned early to watch the sky, to read the change in birds and the sudden shift in cloud that meant rain would arrive before midday.

A boy—no older than ten—followed an older man along a line of stones that marked the edge of a grazing patch. The older man paused and pressed his palm to the earth as if listening.

"Feel that?" he asked, voice low.

The boy nodded, not because he understood, but because he sensed the seriousness behind the gesture.

"The ground tells you what it will give," the man said. "And what it will take."

The boy looked out at the hills that seemed to have no end. He would grow into that lesson—into a people that did not seek comfort, only survival, and learned to make a kind of quiet pride out of endurance.

From this harsh land emerged a people later known as the Picts. Their ancestors learned to live with cold, damp winds and thin soils. During warmer periods, they became herders and farmers. During colder times, they adapted again, clinging to whatever the land could provide. Far to the south, conditions were less severe, but in the north, endurance shaped character.

When the Romans pushed north into Britain, they encountered these people and called them Caledonians. The Roman legions found the land itself to be an enemy—cold, wet, and unforgiving. The cost of occupying the north proved too high. Defensive walls were built—first Hadrian's Wall, later the Antonine Wall—to separate Roman-controlled territory from the wild lands beyond. Though Roman culture and religion took hold in the south, the northern people remained tied to their own pagan customs and ways of life.

To the west, across narrow stretches of sea, Gaelic peoples began to move outward from Ireland. They settled, raided, and intermarried, pushing into the western isles and coastal regions of what would become Scotland. These movements were often violent. Villages were taken, men killed, and women absorbed into new communities. Over generations, language, customs, and bloodlines blended. A new people slowly emerged from conquest and survival.

The Isle of Mull was nameless at the time, or its name had been lost to the annals of history. The people who lived there may have been Picts, but history cannot be certain. Around the early sixth century, Gaelic raiders—Scots—set sail from the coast of Jura to make conquest on Mull. It was an expansion party. The Gaels had been raiding northward from Ireland for generations, expanding through occupation.

They were looking for wives and new places to settle, and what better way than to conquer existing villages—kill the males and take the rest for themselves. For years, various Gaelic raiding parties had been making conquest across what would one day be called the western isles of Scotland.

After several days of sailing in their currachs—wooden-ribbed, skin-covered vessels, the raiders reached the northern coast of Mull. On a cold, rainy night in late April, just before dawn, they landed in one of the island's natural ports beside a small fishing village. The village was small, poorly defended, and suited the raiders' purpose.

They crept through the pre-dawn darkness and caught the village off guard. The slaughter was quick and furious. There was almost no resistance. Most were still asleep or only waking to the commotion as they died. Once the men were slaughtered, the women were gathered together. As dawn broke, the older women and infant children were killed. Two older women were spared for a time—kept alive for their skills and to help control the younger women in their grief and fear. Those capable of childbearing were kept. All others were discarded.

By full daylight, only the women the raiders deemed useful remained alive.

Some of the men later sailed back to Ireland, returning with older Gaelic women to instruct the captives in Gaelic customs and ways. Once that purpose was served, the final purge followed. The village ceased to be what it had been. Language blended. Customs changed. Names were lost. From conquest and bloodshed, a new people began to emerge—one day to be called Scots.

That morning, the surviving women were forced to stack the bodies of their dead and burn them. When the fires died down, the raiders selected their brides. Fights broke out among the men. The strongest chose first.

Galan was seventeen years old and strong. He chose fourth. He pulled a thirteen-year-old girl into one of the huts, and there his line began. Over the next three hundred years, his descendants and those of his comrades spread across Mull. Inland movement was restricted by the island's rugged terrain, forcing settlement along the coasts. As the land filled and suitable village sites disappeared, the pattern repeated—expansion through conquest.

Raiding parties set sail across the Sound of Mull into Loch Linnhe, moving along its eastern shores, conquering villages as they went.

In the spring of 839, new raiders arrived. Norse longships cut through the western seas. Their raids were driven by wealth rather than land, but land often followed. Villages were pillaged. Those deemed useless were killed. Women of breeding age were taken. Others were sent south to slave markets as far away as Constantinople.

In one small village, later called Druimarbin, the women were raped repeatedly. Nine months later, children were born—children of mixed Norse, Gaelic, and Pict blood. Again, a new people were forming, bound to the land as if by design.

One of those children was born to a fourteen-year-old girl who died in childbirth. Before she died, she named the boy Brendan Fóxi, marking him as the son of the Norseman, Breidi the Fox, Breidi Fóxi. Orphaned at birth, Brendan was tolerated but never embraced. He was raised without affection, treated little better than a slave. He learned early to fend for himself. He learned endurance. He learned silence.

Brendan was beaten often. He was forced to fight. No one explained who he was or where he fit. He had no understanding of family, yet his heart ached for it. From his earliest days, he looked east toward a mountain that stood in the distance. He was told savage people lived there, that wild beasts roamed its slopes, that no one who went there ever returned. Still, the mountain called to him.

When Brendan was twelve, after a beating he thought might kill him, he ran.

He ran as hard as his legs would carry him, never looking back. When he finally slowed, he found he was still moving—steady, relentless. Two Norsemen followed for a time but soon gave up. They were sailors, not forest men, and they feared the mountain as much as they feared losing him.

Brendan ran until the village behind him began to fade from his memory. He had no reason to return. No good-byes. No attachments.

He walked for days. He drank from streams and ate what he could forage from the forest. He learned quickly. He learned how to cross water safely by finding shallow, slow-moving places. He learned to spear fish in pools, fashioning points from broken branches sharpened with stone. He ate them raw when he had to. He learned which berries to eat by tasting slowly, cautiously.

At night, he built shelters from branches and moss, lifting himself above the cold ground. He packed sod over the frames to keep out rain and wind. The nights were cold, but he learned to stay warm. For the first time in his life, he felt content.

Near a waterfall he built a more permanent shelter. He remembered watching the Norsemen strike stones together to make fire. Through trial and error, he found the right stones, the right angle, the right patience. When flame finally came, everything changed. He learned to cook his food. He learned efficiency. He learned confidence.

On another of his long explorations, he found a second waterfall feeding a deep pool—a place that would later be known as Steall Waterfall—where the forest opened into a cleared swath of land and smoke rose from stone dwellings.

It was there, during one of his explorations, that he found people again—a village of Picts living along a stream beneath another great waterfall. He watched them from the forest's edge for days. They were different. Their language was different. Their ways were different. There was no brutality in what he saw.

Brendan had learned to move like a shadow. Even when he stood still, he listened as if his life depended on it—because it did. He kept to hedgerows and the edges of trees, where the light broke unevenly and a man could be missed if someone weren't looking hard. Hunger had hollowed him in a way that made him older than his years. It was not only the ache in his stomach, but the constant calculation: how far to go before resting, how close he could approach a home before a dog sounded the alarm, whether the smell of cooking meant safety or bait.

The village he saw that day looked ordinary in the way danger often did. Smoke rose from low roofs. A woman shook out cloth and hung it where it might dry. Somewhere a child cried, then quieted. There were animals—goats, perhaps—close enough that he could smell them, that rank, living smell of bodies and dung that meant food existed here, even if it were not meant for him.

Brendan's instinct was to retreat. His legs wanted to take him back into the cover of brush, back to the places where no one looked twice. But the hunger pushed him forward a step, then another, until he found himself watching a man carry water as if that simple act were the most precious thing in the world.

He told himself he would not beg. Begging invited humiliation, and humiliation invited cruelty. Yet he could not stop his eyes from tracking the smallest details, the hands, faces, the set of shoulders. He looked for weapons. He listened for shouting. He waited for the sudden turn of attention that would expose him.

Instead, what he heard was work. Ordinary work. The low murmur of voices. The scrape of a tool. A dog barked once and then settled. No one ran. No one shouted a warning. No one pointed.

Brendan stood on the edge of the village like a man suspended between two worlds—one that had already tried to kill him, and one he did not yet trust. He tasted the air again and realized, with a strange, almost painful clarity, that the scent he was smelling was bread.

An old man, widowed and childless, noticed him first. There were no threats, no words. The old man simply allowed Brendan to follow. They fished together. They worked together. Slowly, without ceremony, Brendan was taken in.

The old man held up a strip of dried fish and spoke a single word, gentle but firm, "eat." Brendan hesitated, then took it with both hands, "thank you," he said in the only tongue he knew. The old man only nodded, as if the meaning mattered more than the words.

He learned their language. Their customs. He became a herder of Highland cattle. He worked the land. At seventeen, he married one of the village girls. In the foothills of Ben Nevis, he raised his clan.

Brendan Fóxi had been born of violence and abandonment, but the mountains claimed him. His blood would remember it long after his name was forgotten. The land remained harsh in Scotland. Poverty and hard labor were the norm, and resources were always scarce. Over generations, the people became more alike in language, dress, and customs. The land itself was becoming Scotland, shaped as much by struggle as by blood.

Wars were fought with neighbors to the south. Victories won and lost, and borders shifted with time. During one of these conflicts, the now named Mac Fhocsa clan was forced from its mountain home. Brendan's name had long since faded from memory, but his heritage lived on. Britton Mac Fhocsa, his great-great-grandson, settled in the lowlands of Scotland. He told his children stories of the mountains—of endurance, freedom, and belonging. The stories endured even as the land changed.

Christianity had taken root across Scotland, and by the sixteenth century, Protestantism spread quickly among a people inclined toward independence of thought. By 1560, the Mac Fhocsa family had become Calvinist, their faith shaping both belief and discipline.

In 1603, Glendon Mac Fhocsa sailed for Ireland seeking opportunity. He and his family landed near Larne in Ulster. Hope traveled with them, but it faded quickly. The land was already claimed, and the welcome was cold. The predominantly Catholic population viewed the newcomers with suspicion, and life proved as hard there as it had been in Scotland.

Generation after generation worked the land, but prosperity remained elusive. Though five generations passed, and with the family being illiterate and with the misunderstanding of official record keepers, the now Fox clan never felt at home. They remained outsiders. The mountains of Scotland lived on in memory and story, passed down to children who had never seen them.

James Fox listened to those stories. He heard of a land across the ocean where mountains stretched endlessly and where a man might claim land of his own. In 1743, James and Elizabeth Fox set sail from Larne aboard the James and Mary, carrying their two children with them. They landed in Charleston, South Carolina, on a hot summer's day. Stories were not the only inheritance passed down in the Fox home. There were nights when the lamp burned low and the wind worried the seams of the house, and a man's voice became quiet—not because he had nothing to say, but because he did not want fear to be louder than reason.

James remembered one such evening. A plate of simple food sat untouched, cooling as the adults spoke in measured tones. No one wanted to say the word aloud at first—leave—because saying it made it real.

His father held a worn Bible in one hand, thumb resting on the edge of the pages as if the book itself could steady him. His mother sat opposite, hands folded so tightly her knuckles shone, her gaze fixed on the tabletop.

"We can stay and be pressed smaller every year," his father said at last, eyes lifting to meet hers. "Or we can go where a man's work has room to breathe."

"And if the sea takes us?" she asked. The question was not dramatic. It was practical—like asking whether a roof would hold under snow.

His father glanced down, then back up. "Then the sea takes us. But if we stay, something else will."

Silence settled in. James stared at the flame in the lamp, watching it bend with every small current of air. He felt, without fully understanding, that he was witnessing the moment a life is divided into before and after.

His father opened the Bible, not with flourish, but with the familiarity of habit. He read a line softly—enough for those at the table, not enough for the night outside the walls.

Then he closed the book and said, "We will carry what matters."

From there, the family moved inland to York County. They settled, farmed, and endured, but the call of the mountains persisted. Their son Jonathan followed it westward into the southern Appalachians, settling near what would one day be known as Bryson City, North Carolina.

Jonathan's son, Britton, carried his family farther still, crossing the mountains into a hollow in what would become Blount County, Tennessee. On a south-facing slope where the sun shone long and steadily, he set stakes and claimed the land. He and his eldest son felled trees, cleared fields, and built a one-room cabin. As the family grew, so did the cabin, the farm, and the community around it.

Over six generations, the Fox family spread through the hollow. Cabins multiplied. Fields expanded. Jonas Fox, a descendant of Brendan, inherited the original homestead. There, in the mountains once again, the Fox family became what they had always been—mountaineers.

The mountains had claimed them once more.

The Fox bloodline belonged to these ridges and hollows now—shaped by cold stone, thin soil, and the stubborn economy of mountain life.

Half a world away, with no shared name and no shared blood, another lineage was being shaped by a different bargain—not with rock and frost, but with river silt, monsoon rain, and the disciplined labor of rice. This is the ancestry of the Phạm family.

In East Asia, another people were forming far from the mountains of Scotland. South of the Chang Jiang—Trường Giang—in the southern mountains of what is now China—Trung Quốc—a distinct people began to emerge, pressed and pulled by larger powers yet refusing to disappear. Through time, they moved toward the Red River Valley—Đồng bằng Sông Hồng—where seasonal floods could destroy a village or make it rich, depending on how well a community learned to manage water and soil.

They learned to farm the land, cultivating rice—cơm—as their principal crop. They domesticated the water buffalo—trâu—to plow flooded rice paddies—cánh đồng lúa. They built dikes and levees to control seasonal floods and terraced hillsides to increase production. They lived simple agrarian lives, supplemented by fishing along rivers and coastal waters.

In 111 B.C., armies from the Han world swept south and brought the Red River region under foreign rule. Resistance never ceased. Rebellions flared repeatedly, not always successful, but always remembered. Over centuries, the people learned a critical truth: they could not defeat larger empires by meeting them head-on. They learned instead to fight by using the land—rivers, forests, swamps, and mountains made into weapons. They dug pits and planted sharpened bamboo stakes—chông tre—sometimes smeared with filth so that even the smallest wound could kill.

They used rivers the way other people used walls. In the autumn of 938, on the Bạch Đằng River—Sông Bạch Đằng—Ngô Quyền planted thousands of sharpened stakes in the riverbed, tipped to tear open hulls when the tide fell. He lured an invading fleet upstream at high tide and struck as the water receded. Ships grounded, impaled and broke apart. It was not only a victory; it became a lesson passed down for centuries: the land itself could be made to fight.

To the south lay Champa—Chămpa—a chain of coastal principalities whose people spoke a different language and whose culture was deeply influenced by Hinduism. Their towers rose from the plains as if the earth itself had been marked. For centuries, Vietnamese history was not only resistance against the north, but also pressure toward the south—a long movement of settlement and conquest known in later memory as Nam tiến.

There were turning points that the land never forgot. In 1471, Đại Việt forces struck Champa's northern heartland, sacked the Cham capital at Vijaya, and broke the kingdom's power; Champa survived afterward only as a diminished remnant in the south—Panduranga. Centuries later, in 1832, that final remnant was absorbed under the Nguyễn state, and Cham autonomy in the south was formally ended.

Even before Champa's final contraction, Cham communities had moved inland from the coast into river valleys that opened toward the highlands. They chose the same things every farming person chooses: reliable water, workable soil, a slope that caught the sun, a hollow protected from wind. Then, over generations, settlers from the north pressed into those valleys. The names changed. Authority changed. What had been Cham became Vietnamese—Bình Định by the new tongue—and families that arrived later built their lives atop the work of those who came before.

Centuries later came the French. Then the Japanese during the Second World War. Scarcity tightened into catastrophe. In the famine of 1944–1945—Nạn đói Ất Dậu—estimates vary, but hundreds of thousands and possibly more than a million died in the north, not from drought alone, but from war, requisitions, and collapse of transport and governance. In 1954, at Điện Biên Phủ, the French built a fortress in a remote valley, believing it impregnable. The Vietnamese dismantled artillery and carried it by hand through jungle and mountains, hauling it up surrounding hills. Trenches crept closer each night. The valley became a trap. The French were defeated. An empire collapsed.

Yet the land still did not belong to those who worked it. Through dynasties, colonial administrations, occupations, and wars, the Phạm family remained on a small parcel along the west tributary of the Côn River—Sông Côn. The river kept its schedule: flooding, retreating, silt, and the slow reshaping of banks. The family learned early that land is not truly possessed; it is negotiated with water every year.

A father showed a son where to cut a channel so it would not collapse in the first heavy rain. "Angle it," he said, pressing his heel into the wet clay. "Let the water work for you, not against you."

The lesson was not given in speeches. It was given in mud and water, in the angle of a blade and the patience to do it twice if the first cut wandered. The father stood barefoot in the field, pant legs rolled, toes sinking into the cool soft earth. He pointed with the handle of the tool, not with his finger.

"Here," he said—quietly, as if loudness would disturb the work itself. "If you cut too shallow, the water won't carry. If you cut too deep, it will steal the soil."

The boy nodded and set the blade where he was shown. His hands were small, but he put his weight into it the way his father did. The water moved reluctantly at first, then began to follow the line, obedient to the new path.

From the edge of the field, an older woman watched without interrupting. When the boy glanced up, seeking approval, she did not praise him. She only said, "Remember this. Water does not forgive carelessness."

The boy returned to the work, face serious. He was learning more than irrigation. He was learning the quiet discipline of a people who honored what came before them—not with grand ceremony every day, but with the steady respect of doing necessary things well, so the family line could endure.

The parcel was not born as a farm. It began as edges—scrub cleared back by blade, grasses burned in controlled strips, bamboo cut and replanted to serve as windbreak and boundary. A hut came first. Then a storage shed raised off the ground to keep rice dry during hard rains. Then the first shallow ditch, cut by hand, to guide spring water toward a low patch where rice could survive.

One generation learned how to build dikes that held. The next learned which clay packed tightest and which grasses anchored best. In the wet months they reinforced dikes; in the dry months they deepened channels and repaired collapsed edges. They kept fish in ponds because a pond could feed children when a paddy failed. They planted gardens because rice alone could not carry a body through sickness. They harvested bamboo because bamboo was wall, roof, basket, trap, tool-handle, and fence—an entire hardware store growing out of the soil.

A trâu entered the family story the way all useful things enter a peasant story: as an answer. When labor outran human backs, the family acquired a water buffalo and, with it, the ability to expand production without expanding hunger. The plow line lengthened. The paddy line widened. The farm became less fragile—not safe, never safe, but less fragile.

There were years when the outside world arrived as taxes and levies. There were years when it arrived as soldiers passing through. In those years, the Phạm family learned concealment as a second craft: rice sealed in jars and buried under floors; tool hidden in bamboo thickets; livestock moved before dawn to safer ground. When violence flared in the countryside, survival depended on reading small signals—unusual quiet in a market, unfamiliar faces at a crossroads, the sudden absence of birds along a tree line.

They brought Buddhism into the valley and honored their ancestors not as ceremony, but as discipline: remember what was paid for this land. Remember who died so the parcel remained. Remember that the farm was never created in a single lifetime. It was assembled—one repair at a time, one harvest at a time—by people who understood that endurance is not a virtue. It is a required skill.

They asked little of the outside world—only the freedom to live and work their land, but freedom never came. There was always an overlord. A magistrate. A government. A war. The names changed. The burden did not.

Chapter 1

Phương

April 4, 1968

Hebrews 13:2 (KJV)

> "Be not forgetful to entertain strangers: for thereby some have entertained angels unawares."

Phương was disturbed; it rained through the early part of the night. She lay for those first few hours of darkness and listened to the heavy drops. She knew her small hut would protect her from the downpour. The artisans who maintained her thatched roof protected her by their skill. Even in this river valley, she would remain dry, even in the heaviest rain. Yet, as the rain poured, she worried about those things she was there to protect. Rain was essential, but this heavy rain worried her. The incense and lone candle offering comfort to Buddha only gave her flickering loneliness as they began to dim. She lay on her mat and looked over to Buddha (Đức Phật). She prayed that all would be protected and the rain would end soon, but then she thought of the comfort—the muffled silence of the war the rain brought. She started slipping in and out of sleep. As she did, the rain began to ease.

It was the first moments of dawn. The night breeze drifting down from the surrounding mountains put a chill in the air. Soon a steady flow of air brought coolness to the entire valley that early morning. The old woman could hear the crowing of roosters and the sounds of the surrounding jungle coming alive over the babbling headwaters of the west branch of the Côn River (Sông Côn). Birds of all sorts, silent during the night, started chirping their morning songs. The night birds and the night stalkers were going to sleep. Monkeys cackled to the new day. In those days, those first few moments of morning were the most silent, even with the sounds of the new dawn. It was also the loneliest. Her eyes opened to the emptiness of the lonely hut.

Phương lay still for a few breaths, letting the first light find its way through the palm-leaf seams. The air smelled of wet earth and smoke that had long since cooled—yesterday's fire, yesterday's labor, yesterday's grief. Even when the valley was beautiful, the mornings could feel cruel. In the daylight she could work and survive. In the darkness she could only remember.

She listened again—roosters, the river, the waking jungle—yet the sounds did not comfort her the way they once had. In years past, those sounds meant family would soon move about the hut: Dũng shifting on the mat, Liên whispering to her mother as she braided her hair, the small clatter of bowls and a child's bare feet on wood. Now the same dawn arrived to an empty space that answered her with nothing.

Her gaze returned to Buddha (Đức Phật). The small figure did not change, did not flinch at artillery, did not fear helicopters, did not bury children. It simply endured—like the mountains. Phương wanted to believe endurance meant something. In her youth, she had believed the prayers could hold a household together the way a good roof held out rain. But war had a way of making a person feel foolish for hoping too much.

She pressed her palms together, not yet praying, only steadying herself. A mother was supposed to carry burdens. A widow was supposed to keep her household alive. She had done those things. Yet the morning still came, and with it the ache that she could not set down.

Outside, mist clung to the valley floor and drifted through the trees in slow, pale ribbons. It softened the world, made the riverbank seem gentler than it was. For a moment she let herself imagine that the mist was a curtain drawn across violence—an old trick of the land, hiding what it could not stop. But the quiet would not last. It never did.

The palm-leaf thatched hut had existed for a thousand years, reworked by the endless generations who had occupied it, first the Cham, and then the Việt as they migrated south from their original home in southern China. The hut lay isolated at the far end of a valley cove that ran into the base of the surrounding mountains—the Central Highlands (Cao Nguyên Trung Phần) of Việt Nam. The Americans referred to the valley as "Happy Valley," but there had been no happiness in the valley for years. This valley and her isolated farm were beautiful by anyone's standards. The valley remained green all year. The cultivation of crops, even in the rainy season, continued year-round. The valley stayed lush and green, providing an abundance of food. The cool breezes and the shading from the surrounding mountains brought a freshness to the air. Her home place was like a picture book.

Her hut was situated on the west side of the valley at the eastern base of a mountain, Hòn Xum, rising high above the valley to its west. At the north end and to the east of the valley rose additional mountains. The mountain springs and streams fed the river below. She had three fish ponds, each growing a different variety of fish, and a garden that contained all the herbs and vegetables a person could want. The once-clean waters were now being contaminated by defoliation chemicals—chemicals the Americans called Agent Orange. How could a place be so beautiful, and yet be so hard and raw? How could a place that sprouted so much life also contain so much death?

Lying on the woven mat, she stared at the bamboo frame of the roof, seeing the first glimpses of the morning light. She rolled across her mat, her feet against the wooden floor. She looked and saw her only companion, the Buddha (Đức Phật), in the corner. The incense had extinguished itself during the long night. The bowl of rice offered was stale, with the insects and rodents of the night taking their fill.

Once the rain stopped, her night had been restless, punctuated with the continuous sounds of war. Every night she listened to the crack and pop of small-arms fire. Machine guns would open up. Then there was the thundering boom of artillery, along with the distant k-thoop of mortars. Now all was quiet, except for the waking of nature.

She sat and listened to the silence of war—the silence that came with the first rays of sunlight. The silence meant the warriors of the night were now tired and getting their rest. As she sat there, she could feel the dampness of the morning air. The cool mist of the morning fog crept through the valley like a ghostly apparition, filling her hut with the dampness of death. Her body shook with the chill. The emptiness of her soul was heavy. The loss of those she loved weighed her down more crushingly than the bundles of rice she would soon harvest in the blistering sun.

Her body ached, but she willed herself into a sitting position. Phương was forty-two but had rapidly aged in this land of war, despair, and continuous toil. Her body felt ancient, and she had to force herself to move. As she lifted herself on her frail, but unusually strong legs, she realized there was an emptiness of sound coming from the rice paddies just a few hundred meters north of her home. The creatures of that area had suddenly grown quiet. There was an absence of birdsong and monkeys cackling.

She wondered if a mountain predator was about.

She stood for a moment, listening to the silence. Silence was disconcerting at the break of dawn when the world should be coming alive. What had brought about the silence, she wondered? She listened for a few more moments but then set aside her concern to focus on her morning ritual.

Her first duty was to attend to Đức Phật. Her old legs carried her to his bowl, and then to the opening of her hut. She eased down the steps to the valley floor and carried the bowl a few yards, tossing the stale rice to the hungry chickens. Then she hobbled to the thatched canopy where each day she dutifully prepared both her and Buddha's sustenance.

She bent down to the fire pit, took an ash scoop and broom, and swept the previous day's ashes from the pit, placing them in a storage pot. The ashes would later be used to make lye for soap and for parboiling. She placed a few small sticks of wood into the fire pit and lit them. Once lit, Phương added a few small chunks of charcoal—charcoal she had made from the hardwoods of the surrounding mountain jungle.

Over the fire pit was a metal grate, and on top of the grate was a ceramic pot. She added water to the pot and allowed the flaming kindling to slowly warm it. She would add or remove kindling to control the heat. The process took nearly thirty minutes to bring the water to a boil. It was necessary to go slow so as not to crack the pot, which had existed for generations.

When the water began to boil, she took a cup of rice harvested from the nearby paddies. She placed the rice in a woven bamboo basket, set the basket into the mouth of the pot, and covered it with a bamboo lid. She allowed the boiling water to steam the rice. Every day she followed the same procedure, cooking enough rice for the day. She would eat in the morning and again in the early evening. Eating alone always brought her sorrow. The emptiness of her life weighed heavily on her.

Phương watched the steam rise and fall beneath the bamboo lid. The rice was ordinary—always rice—but even ordinary things required vigilance. Too much heat and the pot could crack. Too little and the grains would remain hard, wasting fuel she could not spare. She adjusted the kindling with a practiced hand and felt the familiar sting in her fingers where old burns had thickened the skin.

Her hands were the story of her life. The palms were calloused from cutting bamboo, hauling water, packing dikes, and pulling weeds that fought to reclaim the paddies. The knuckles were swollen from years of grinding and carrying. The backs of her hands were darkened by sun and scarred by small cuts that never fully healed before the next cut came.

The pot began to rattle faintly as the boil strengthened. The sound should have meant comfort—food coming, the day beginning in order—but it did not. Order was something she created with effort, not something the world gave her. War had taught her that.

Her mind drifted, as it often did when she waited for water to do what water always does. She thought of Liên's hair, straight and black, and how her daughter used to twist it between her fingers when she was worried. She thought of Dũng's shoulders, still boyish even as he tried to stand like a man. She thought of the way the hut used to feel crowded and alive, and how she had once wished—only for a moment—that she could have one hour of quiet. Now she would have given anything to hear a child breathe beside her again.

A cough rose in her throat and she swallowed it down. Tears were dangerous. Tears blurred vision, and a woman alone in a valley at war could not afford blurred vision. She leaned closer to the pot, letting the steam warm her face, and told herself what she always told herself.

Eat. Work. Live.

As the rice steamed, she turned to another morning task. It was still quiet in the direction of the rice paddies—too quiet for Phương. Her hearing was keen, not dulled by the sounds of the industrial age. The absence of sound from the paddies troubled her. Typically, when a predator moved through an area, the creatures would go quiet at first. Some would cry out alarms to warn others. Once safe, they would begin again their songs and cackling. That morning, they remained silent for too long.

Phương held still, listening again—this time not as a lonely woman, but as a farmer who had survived years by noticing what others missed. Silence had a shape. It gathered in pockets. It spread like spilled oil. When the birds stopped and the monkeys did not cackle, it usually meant one of two things: a predator was moving, or men were moving.

A mountain cat could slip through grass without bending a blade. A snake could pass beneath leaves without stirring them. But men disturbed the land in ways even the jungle resented. Men broke twigs and shifted stones. Men carried metal that clicked softly when they breathed. Men brought unfamiliar smells—sweat, smoke, fuel, the sharp bite of chemicals. And men brought consequences that lasted longer than a claw mark.

Her eyes went to the edge of the paddy where the grasses thickened. Mist still lingered there, thin and low, blurring distance. In the fog, a human body could be close and still seem far. Phương felt the hair rise on her forearms.

She did not rush. Rushing made noise. She moved with the slow care of someone who had learned patience as a form of protection. Her mind began sorting possibilities the way it always did: if there had been fighting in the night, there might be wounded left behind. If Americans were close, there might be helicopters soon, and then soldiers on foot. If there were Việt Cộng moving through, they might also be wounded, and they might also be dangerous.

She glanced toward Buddha (Đức Phật) and felt no comfort there—only the reminder that the world turned regardless of her fear. She went to the small place where she kept what she needed for the day—tools, cord, a knife worn smooth from use. The motions were ordinary, but her body had tightened, readying itself.

Then she listened again, one more time.

Nothing.

That was what frightened her.

The sun was beginning to brighten the day. Layers of morning mist still filled the valley.

Phương raised chickens and pigs. Neither did she eat unless one died prematurely. Otherwise, she ate only the eggs from the hens. She kept her breeding stock, and surplus chickens and pigs were bartered to a man named Hùng. He was the principal leader of the village of Láng Cây Tre. On a monthly basis, except during the rainy season, he took the stock to Quy Nhơn to sell or barter. He would bring back items that the people of Láng Cây Tre and that end of the valley needed.

Láng Cây Tre—Bamboo Tree Village—and the north end of the valley were known for the abundant growth of bamboo along the Côn River (Sông Côn). Bamboo was used for many purposes. A house could be built solely from bamboo. It could be made into hoes, shovels, water wheels, pipes, surgical instruments, cooking utensils, fencing, and much more.

Phương went about feeding the chickens and pigs. She felt no attachment to any of the animals. To her, they were simply food or trade goods. Her emotions toward them were no different than those of an American looking at meat in a grocery store. Even so, she cared for them well. She kept them healthy and well fed, but without sentiment.

At this small homesite, everything was used. Phương swept the dung from the chickens (con gà) and pigs (con lợn) and dumped it into the fishponds fed by mountain streams. The dung fed the fish, which were her primary source of protein. She trapped fish, gutted and salted them, then laid them out on drying racks to bake in the sun. During the rainy season (mùa mưa), she smoked the fish to draw out moisture. Once dried, they were hung beneath the roof of the cooking canopy.

She cut portions of the fish to steam and eat with rice. Additional fish were prepared to be taken by Hùng to the markets (chợ) in Quy Nhơn. Along with fish, Phương supplemented her diet with snails, mussels, grubs, and any other source of protein she could gather from nature.

Once the fish, chickens, and pigs were fed, she returned to the steaming rice. She knew it would be ready by then. She took the bowl used to feed Đức Phật and wiped it clean, then filled it with enough rice for the offering. Phương carried the bowl up the steps into her hut and placed it before the Buddha.

She removed the old incense that had burned out during the night and replaced it with three new sticks. She lit them with wooden matches kept on a small shelf behind the Buddha. Once the incense was burning, she began to pray.

She first prayed for her mother and father. Her father had been killed by the Japanese in 1943. Her prayers then moved to her husband, Bảo, whose death came at the hands of the French in 1953. It was followed by prayer for her son, Dũng, who had died just over two months earlier in combat against the Americans near An Khê.

She had been told he died bravely on the eve of Tết—Tết Mậu Thân, the Year of the Monkey, 1968. Knowing that did nothing to ease her pain. Dũng had joined the Việt Cộng two months before his death and moved into the Central Highlands (Cao Nguyên Trung Phần) for training. He and the others in his unit were excited. They would be fighting alongside the North Vietnamese Army—the People's Army of Việt Nam (PAVN).

Their mission was part of a nationwide effort to drive the Americans out of Việt Nam during the night of Tết. His unit's role was not to take and hold the base at An Khê, but to help keep it pinned—harassing it, confusing it, and drawing Americans into defensive positions while larger, more visible attacks struck the cities, especially Sài Gòn and Huế, and major installations elsewhere. At An Khê—Camp

Radcliff, the "Golf Course"—the attacks that night were often felt first as incoming: mortars walking across the base, striking fuel areas and open ground, forcing men into bunkers and throwing the whole compound into alarms, flares, and shouted orders.

His unit was engaged by an American patrol on the eve of Tết. When the fighting began, Dũng was not even able to raise his rifle before a bullet struck him below the right rib cage, knocking him off his feet and stunning him. The bullet missed his vital organs. When he regained enough strength to try to run, another well-aimed shot struck him in the back just below his left shoulder blade, destroying his heart and killing him instantly.

He was one of four Việt Cộng soldiers killed.

None of that mattered to Phương. She only knew that he was dead—like the other men in her family.

She then prayed for her beautiful daughter, Liên. Whether Liên was alive or dead, Phương did not know. It happened to many young girls throughout Việt Nam. They disappeared. Some were taken to the sex markets that served American soldiers.

She prayed that Liên was alive and would soon return.

Her two children—Dũng, seventeen, and Liên, who was fifteen—were both gone. It left her unbearably lonely. Even here, a mother was not meant to outlive her children.

Phương and her husband Bảo had married in 1941. Over the next ten years she lost three children at or near birth before Dũng was born in 1951. Liên followed in 1953. Dũng was still a toddler, and Liên was in her mother's womb when Bảo was killed.

It had been difficult for Phương to raise the two children alone, but she had done it. She grieved for them as any mother would. Yet she also missed them for their labor. With both children gone, she had been forced to dramatically reduce the amount of food produced on her farm.

Her thoughts remained with Liên. What had happened to her? Scenarios rushed through Phương's mind.

A week after Dũng left with the Việt Cộng, Liên went out in the morning to attend the small school in the village. That evening she did not return home. Phương waited long past Liên's usual time of arrival. When night came and Liên had still not returned, Phương started walking quickly toward the village and the school.

The path crossed three mountain streams, each forded by a narrow bamboo footbridge. The village lies more than a mile to the south. When she arrived, the teacher—Miss Bình (Cô Bình)—told her that Liên had never arrived at school that morning.

There had been no fighting that anyone knew of. Liên could not have been accidentally killed, as others had been in the past. Miss Bình said she had heard a motorbike go up the valley and return minutes later. Motorbikes were uncommon in this rural area, but since the Americans had arrived there had been more traffic. They were usually ridden by young men, often handsome, smooth-talking. They searched for older girls and young women.

Age rarely mattered.

It was their job to recruit.

There was high demand for the services the girls and women could provide. It was possible Liên had left on the motorbike. Some villagers said they had seen a motorbike heading back toward Highway 19 with a man driving and a young woman riding behind him.

If it was Liên, who had taken her—and for what purpose?

Phương had heard rumors that many village girls were now in An Khê, in the Central Highlands, or in Quy Nhơn on the coast. She was told the young women worked in sex markets serving American soldiers. The girls were seduced by promises of money—more money than their families could earn in years of hard labor.

Phương thought of her daughter, only fourteen, and hated the thought of her being used that way. Yet as she considered the day that lay ahead—heat, insects, and backbreaking labor—she could not help but believe Liên may have made the right choice if that were where she was.

Phương herself had married at fifteen, common in the rural countryside. The thought of Liên having sex did not trouble her as much as the thought of her daughter being forced to service several men a day.

Once her prayers were complete, Phương returned to the thatched canopy that covered her cooking area. She sliced a section of dried fish hanging from the roof supports and squatted beside the boiling pot. She placed the fish in the basket with the steaming rice. In this land, with no refrigeration, food had to be cooked hot and kept hot until eaten.

As the fish steamed, she reached for a leather pouch containing betel leaf and areca nut, wrapped together in small chewable wads. The combination produced a stimulating effect, like coffee but stronger. Phương chewed the mixture throughout the day. Her body needed the stimulation to endure the long hours of labor ahead. One effect of chewing betel and areca was the staining of her teeth to a dark mahogany. Americans unfamiliar with the habit often assumed those who chewed it had rotten teeth, which some did—but not because of the stain itself.

As she squatted and chewed, the fish (cá) and rice (cơm) continued to steam. Her thoughts drifted. A rare calm settled over her, a blankness of mind—a small refuge from the world. Her body relaxed. Comfort, seldom felt, crept into her bones.

K-thoop, a sudden explosion.

The blast hurled her several feet and slammed her to the ground. Thatch and framework from the canopy collapsed onto her. Pain shot through her body, along with burning stings across the left side of her face, neck, and arm. Fear surged through her as machine guns erupted and small-arms fire cracked nearby. Men screamed in both Vietnamese (tiếng Việt) and English (tiếng Anh).

More k-thoops followed—mortar rounds firing and exploding. One round, overshot from a hastily set 60-mm mortar tube, landed no more than forty feet from her. She was just outside the killing zone. As she lay there, shaking, artillery rounds whistled overhead, followed by heavier explosions. They were landing roughly one hundred and fifty meters away.

The ground bucked violently. Her small body was thrown back and forth as the blasts shook the earth. There were several heavy explosions in rapid succession. Poles that had stood in the ground for generations worked loose. The canopy frame broke apart, palm thatch falling over her. Inside her hut, the Buddha fell, a small chip breaking from his marble head. A clay bowl of unknown age shattered, along with much of her pottery. Chickens cackled wildly. Pigs squealed and ran in panic.

The artillery barrage lasted only minutes, but it felt endless. As suddenly as it began, it stopped.

Then she heard helicopters approaching—the deep whop-whop-whop of rotor blades. They flew fast and low. The prop wash lifted dust and debris into the air. Rockets fired. Machine guns chattered. Her body cramped in terror. She screamed aloud and bowed her head in prayer, knowing prayer would not stop the killing. It never had.

More helicopters came. She pushed the thatch off her body and looked up as two aircraft with red crosses painted on their bellies flew overhead. She knew what they were—medical helicopters bound for the hospital in Quy Nhơn. She also knew Vietnamese wounded would be carried away through the jungle if they were carried at all.

The fighting was in the rice paddies she tended. She knew death lay there now, along with destruction of her labor. She knew weeks of work lay ahead to repair what the war had shattered.

Phương thought of the Americans and how they must be demons. Only demons could bring so much hurt. Her body shook—not only from the violence of the war, but from the anger, pain, and fear that filled her. Her soul ached and tears flowed. She screamed, as loudly as she could, though only within herself. Only the gods could hear her screams, yet she knew they would not answer. They had not stopped the death this day.

She knew only the valley in which she lived, yet she could not help but wonder if all people suffered this way. Did all lands know this kind of death, generation after generation? Why did the gods hate her people so? It had to be hatred for the gods to punish them in this way. What sin had the Việt committed to deserve such suffering?

For a thousand years they had fought the Chinese, then the French, followed by the Japanese during WW II. The French returned, only to be driven out. Now the Americans—the Người Mỹ—had come. What had her people done to deserve this? She knew nothing of politics. She only knew that men killed one another and that her soul suffered with every loss.

Communism (chủ nghĩa cộng sản), socialism (chủ nghĩa xã hội), and capitalism (chủ nghĩa tư bản) meant nothing to her. They were empty words spoken by cadre who came into her village. They seemed no less foreign than the Americans. She had watched those men bring harm, even death, to anyone who opposed them. They spoke of freedom for the Việt yet imposed their will with the same cruelty as any other power.

She did not care about ideology. In those moments after the battle, her life felt emptied forever.

The minutes dragged by. Time lost its meaning. She prayed only that the fighting would move north, away from her home.

Her prayers were answered.

She could hear the battle moving farther away, helicopters firing at a distance. She knew the Americans were pushing the Vietnamese fighters deeper into the mountains and jungle. Again, she heard artillery screaming overhead, followed by explosions. She wondered how many had died—or would die—that day. She thought of Dũng and wondered if these were the same men who had killed her son.

She heard the helicopters with red crosses again, now heading southeast. She looked up and saw them flying low. She knew Americans lay wounded or dead aboard. A part of her wished death upon them, but another part recoiled from the thought. They were being carried to hospitals. Dũng had never had one—only a cave or a tunnel, if even that.

How could some have so much while her people had so little?

As the medevac helicopters disappeared, more gunships flew northwest, unloading rockets and machine-gun fire into the jungle. Other helicopters descended to retrieve American troops. She knew there would be no victors—only death. Soon the helicopters lifted off again and flew toward Quy Nhơn.

For another hour she heard artillery chasing Vietnamese fighters farther into the mountains. She knew it was the Việt Cộng and the North Vietnamese Army's way to disengage once enough damage had been done. The sight of the red-cross helicopters told her that some Americans had been wounded or killed. It also meant many Vietnamese had fallen.

Eventually the valley grew quiet again. Helicopters still passed overhead, but the immediate terror had lifted. What she felt was not peace, but the absence of imminent death.

Finally, her thoughts returned to what remained to be done.

She pushed the fallen thatch and bamboo away from her body. Pain screamed along her left side. She forced herself upright. Her left sleeve was singed and peppered with holes. The skin of her face and neck burned. Small fragments of hot metal had embedded themselves from below her elbow to just beneath her cheekbone. There was little blood. The heat had cauterized the wounds.

Her hut was damaged, but the cooking canopy was nearly destroyed. Two-thirds of it lay on the ground, the remaining section leaning and ready to fall. She knew she had to tend her wounds.

Beneath the fallen canopy was a small leather bag of cloves. In her garden grew aloe. Thatch had fallen into the fire pit and smoldered from the heat. Her ceramic cooking pot lay shattered beneath the debris. Despite the pain, she worked methodically, pulling thatch away until she found the bag of cloves and her mortar and pestle, still intact.

She went to the garden and cut a sprig of aloe. Back under the canopy, she crushed the aloe and cloves together into a paste. She unbuttoned her singed blouse (áo), pulled her left arm (cánh tay) free, and applied the paste to her arm, neck (cổ), and face (mặt).

The pain was immediate and intense.

Phương screamed aloud and wrapped her arms around herself, shaking as she fought to control it. Slowly, the pain subsided until it became bearable. She moved back toward the cooking area and set the mortar and pestle down.

She returned to clearing debris. As she leaned over, a voice spoke.

She straightened suddenly, heart pounding. No one was there.

She dismissed it as imagination and bent again to her work. The voice came again, clearer now, from the direction of the rice paddies. She felt drawn to it. In her mind she heard, "Mẹ, giúp tôi!"—Mother, help me.

She told herself it was not real. She thought of Dũng. Had he called for her as he lay dying? She tried to force the voice away, but it returned repeatedly. Without realizing it, she began walking toward the paddies. Her body ached with every step. Her left side burned. Still, she walked, faster now. What if it was her son? What if he was calling her?

Her legs carried her down the path toward the place of death.

She arrived at the paddies and stood on the outer dike of the four fields she tended. She looked over the land. What she saw was the destruction of her labor. Each paddy bore the scars of exploding mortar rounds. One had a section of the dike blown away entirely, leaving a gaping hole and a large mound of mud hurled back into the field. Water was draining out steadily.

She listened again for the voice. She was certain she had heard it. Now there was nothing—only the soft sound of water escaping and the distant echo of war moving away. Whoever called was not there.

A deep emptiness settled over her, heavier than before. She turned back toward her hut. Sadness was always with her, but this was deeper.

As she walked away, a body fought silently for its life beneath the mound of mud.

Phương was exhausted when she reached her hut. Only then did she feel how badly she was hurt. Pain radiated through her body. She cried—not loudly, but with the quiet release of someone who had reached the edge of endurance. The horror was over, yet those who caused it were gone, leaving her with the wreckage.

The weight of it all pressed down on her. Her legs weakened and she could no longer stand. She sank to the ground at the entrance of her hut. Dizziness swept over her. Darkness crept into her vision. Though still aware, she could not stop herself from slumping forward.

When her head struck the ground, the world went black.

She lay there beneath the rising sun.

Two hours passed. It was near midday. For that time there was nothing—no awareness, no thought. Then the dream came.

The voice returned, urgent now, pleading. Her frail body jerked as she struggled in the dream, trying to reach it. "The mud—dig the mud," the voice urged.

Heat burned along the left side of her body where the sun beat down on her wounds. She awoke suddenly, confused, her head spinning. She lay still, trying to understand where she was. Her mouth was dry. Her face burned. When she tried to sit up, her strength failed her.

She waited, then tried again. With effort, she pushed herself upright. The world swayed around her. Nausea churned in her stomach. She steadied herself with slow breaths until the spinning eased.

Gradually clarity returned. She remembered the battle. The explosions. The voice.

She was desperately thirsty.

She looked toward the water storage barrel beside the steps leading into her hut. It had been made long before she was born and had stood in the same place for generations. She took a hesitant step toward it, feeling weak, but continued until she could place both hands on the rim and steady herself.

She took the ladle hanging from the side of the barrel and dipped it into the water. Slowly she raised it to her mouth. Her stomach churned in protest, but she forced herself to take a small sip. The water came back up almost immediately. She bent forward, retching, gripping the rim of the barrel to keep from falling.

She waited, breathing slowly, until the weakness eased. She dipped the ladle again and took another small sip, holding it in her mouth before swallowing. Her stomach churned, then settled. She waited and took another sip, then another, slightly larger. Gradually she began to drink more freely, gulping the water until she felt life returning to her body.

With the water came hunger. She realized she had not eaten. Her eyes moved toward the cooking area, then to the drying rack beneath the canopy supports. The rack was still intact. She took another drink and walked to it, removing a dried fish. She ate slowly, chewing carefully, then returned to the barrel for more water.

Strength returned little by little.

Yet her thoughts remained fixed on the voice. She remembered the words urging her to dig the mud. The memory unsettled her. She looked toward the paddies. Hunger no longer ruled her. The voice did.

Chapter 2

The Voice

Isaiah 30:21 (KJV)

> "And thine ears shall hear a word behind thee, saying, This is the way, walk ye in it, when ye turn to the right hand, and when ye turn to the left."

Phương knew the breach in the dike had to be repaired quickly. If the paddy dried out, the crop would be lost. The rice was near harvest, and the next planting had to be completed before the coming dry season. It was near the end of the Đông Xuân—winter–spring—growing season.

She turned toward the small storage shed where her tools were kept. Inside was the hoe she used for the paddies. She took it and began walking back toward the fields. She was still weak and leaned on the handle as if it were a cane.

As she walked, the voice returned. She was certain she heard it now, calling for help. Even if it was only in her mind, she had to be sure. She could not silence it any other way.

She moved as quickly as her battered body allowed, back toward the paddies and the broken dike.

When she reached the paddies, she walked the length of the dike until she came to the breach. The explosion had torn a hole nearly four feet wide through the earthen wall. A large mound of mud lay just inside the paddy, blown back by the blast. The water had drained away, leaving a shallow layer of thick, slowly drying mud.

She stopped and listened again. The voice seemed close now. Whether it came from her mind or somewhere beneath her feet, she could not tell.

She loosened the buttons of her brown shirt (áo nâu) and slipped it off, laying it on the dike. She rolled the legs of her black trousers (quần đen) well above her knees and stepped out of her rubber sandals (dép xăng đan), leaving them beside the dike. Barefoot, she stepped into the mud. It was cool and slick between her toes.

She positioned herself between the mound of mud and the breach in the dike. Gripping the hoe, she reached into the mound and gently pulled a blade of mud toward the opening. She worked carefully, not only repairing the breach but listening—searching—for the voice.

With the third pull of the hoe, the blade struck something firm.

She froze.

She held the hoe steadily, afraid to drive it deeper. At the point where the blade rested, the mud darkened. Slowly, it turned red. She watched the color spread.

Blood.

She inhaled sharply and withdrew the hoe. She tossed it up onto the dike and dropped to her knees. With trembling hands, she began pulling the mud away. Her fingers worked slowly, deliberately, pushing the thick earth aside.

There—beneath the mud—an arm emerged.

It was covered in green cloth.

An American uniform.

She staggered backward and rose to her feet. She stared at the arm, at the torn sleeve where the hoe blade had struck, and at the blood seeping into the mud. Her first instinct was to grab the hoe and make certain the American was dead.

Her hand hovered.

She hesitated.

Under that mud, the American must already be dead.

She stood there for several long moments, then dropped to her knees again and continued pulling the mud away.

She worked quickly now, her fear giving way to urgency. The mud was heavy and clung to her hands and arms, but she dug with determination, pulling it away in large clumps. As more of the body was exposed, she saw that the man lay on his side, his legs twisted unnaturally beneath him.

She reached the head last.

The helmet was still in place.

Mud had packed tightly around it, but beneath the rim she felt a hollow space. An air pocket.

Her breath caught in her throat.

She cleared the mud from around the helmet and placed both hands beneath it. Slowly, carefully, she lifted it away. As she did, the man's head rolled slightly, and his face emerged from the mud.

The right side was mangled—torn flesh, burned skin, and blood matted into the dirt. One eye was swollen shut. The other was open, unfocused, staring past her.

His mouth opened.

A shallow breath escaped.

He was alive.

Phương recoiled, scrambling backward through the mud until she reached the dike. She sat there, stunned, staring at the broken man lying half-buried before her. Her mind raced. Everything in her told her to leave him. He was American. He was the enemy. He was part of the force that had killed her son, destroyed her home, and stolen her daughter.

How could he have called her? He was American—buried under mud, half dead, his mouth filled with earth. And yet she had heard it as clearly as if someone stood beside her: Mẹ, giúp tôi—Mother, help me.

She stood frozen in the thought. Maybe it had not been his voice at all. Maybe it was the voice of God—speaking to every heart in a language it could understand.

She looked at his chest. It rose and fell, barely.

She looked at the torn uniform, the shattered helmet in her hands, and the blood pooling beneath his head.

She thought of Dũng.

She thought of Liên.

She thought of the voice that had called her.

Slowly, she stood.

She returned to the man and knelt beside him. With trembling hands, she brushed the remaining mud from his face and neck. His skin was hot. His breathing was rapid and shallow. She placed her fingers at his throat and felt a faint pulse.

So small, she thought. Still alive, but already half gone.

Her stomach turned. The smell of wet earth and blood filled her nose. The mud clung to her fingers like glue. The open eye did not see her. It stared past her into nothing.

She knew he would die if she left him there.

She also knew that if she helped him, she might die as well. She sat back on her heels, staring at him, weighing the choice she never expected to face.

If she walked away, the valley would swallow him by nightfall. He would become one more body in the mud. The earth would take him, the insects would take him, and she could tell herself it was not her doing. It was war. War did this.

But if she helped him—if she dragged him into her hut—then the war would not stop at the paddies. It would come back to her doorway. Americans with rifles. Men who did not ask questions, only searched. Vietnamese cadre who would punish mercy as betrayal. Either side could kill her for what she did.

She felt the burn on her face throb. She touched the edge of her singed sleeve and remembered the canopy collapsing, remembered the heat, the screaming, the way her own body had been thrown like a sack of rice. He belonged to the force that did that. He belonged to the sky that rained metal.

Her hands clenched into fists. Rage surged through her—hot, overwhelming. This man was American. His people had killed her husband's brothers. They had killed her son. They had destroyed her home. They had taken her daughter, directly or indirectly. Everything she had lost seemed to lie there in the mud before her.

She wanted him dead.

She picked up the hoe and stood over him. The blade hovered above his head. One blow would end it. No one would ever know.

Her arm trembled.

She stared at the hoe blade and saw, in her mind, not metal but the clean certainty of a cut. She knew how to kill. Life in the countryside demanded it. Hunger demanded it.

But this was not a chicken. This was not a fish.

This was a man.

She looked at his face again—what remained of it. Half of it was ruined, burned and torn. The other half was strangely young beneath the mud, as if the war had not had time to finish writing its cruelty there.

A sound escaped him. Not a word—only a faint exhale, like a child sighing in sleep.

Phương's grip tightened on the hoe handle.

For an instant she imagined Dũng in the paddies, the same way—broken, helpless—calling for her in his last breath. She imagined herself arriving too late, standing over her son with a tool in her hands and being unable to change what had already been done.

"Đủ rồi," she whispered before she could stop herself.

Enough.

Her arm remained raised, but the strength drained out of it. The hoe blade dipped lower, hesitated, hovered again.

If she killed him, she would be safe—for a day. For a week. Perhaps longer. She could hide the body under mud and let the paddies swallow the evidence. She could tell herself she had protected her home. She could tell herself she had honored Dũng.

But her hands would remember. Her dreams would remember. The Buddha in her hut would remember.

Her arm shook harder.

She lowered the hoe.

She could not do it.

She looked down at the man again. He was no warrior now. He was broken, helpless, barely alive. She thought of Dũng lying alone as he died. She thought of how she would have given anything to reach him, to hold him, to keep him from dying alone.

She dropped the hoe onto the dike.

She went back into the mud and began digging again.

She freed his legs first, then his torso. His right leg was bent at an unnatural angle. The left lay still, buried deeper beneath the mud. She worked carefully, afraid of worsening his injuries. When she pulled his torso free, blood flowed more freely from beneath his uniform.

She could see then how badly he was hurt.

Metal fragments had torn into his body. His right side was severely damaged. His uniform was soaked with blood at the hip. His face—what remained intact—was pale and gray.

She dragged him free of the mound and rolled him onto his back. He groaned faintly. The sound startled her. She froze, then continued.

She looked around quickly, expecting to hear helicopters or voices. The valley remained quiet.

She picked up her blouse from the ground and tore it into strips. She pressed the cloth against his wounds, trying to slow the bleeding. She knew little of battlefield medicine, only what life had taught her. Pressure stopped bleeding. Cleanliness mattered. Beyond that, fate decided.

She washed his face with muddy water, clearing his mouth and nose. He coughed weakly and took a breath. His chest rose again.

She leaned back, exhausted, staring at him.

The voice had been real.

Phương rose slowly to her feet. Her body trembled with exhaustion. The man lay motionless in the mud, his breathing shallow and uneven. She knew he would not survive the night if left there.

Still, she turned away.

She began walking back toward her hut. Each step felt heavier than the last. She told herself she had done enough. She had freed him. She had given him a chance. What happened next was no longer her burden.

After only a few steps, she stopped.

Her chest tightened. The thought of leaving him there—alone, helpless—pressed down on her like a physical weight. She imagined the night falling, the chill settling into his broken body, the animals that moved through the paddies after dark. She imagined him calling out, unheard.

She thought again of Dũng.

She turned around.

She walked back to the American and knelt beside him. She placed her hand on his chest. It still rose and fell, faintly. She leaned closely and listened. His breath rasped softly, uneven and fragile.

She spoke aloud, though she did not know why.

"Đừng chết," she said quietly.

Do not die.

She looked around the valley once more. There was no movement. No sound of helicopters. No voices.

Decision settled over her.

She stood and looked toward her hut. It was not far, but the distance felt immense. She knew what she must do.

She would not let him die alone.

Phương knelt beside the American and used her hands to scoop water from the paddy. She poured it gently over his face, washing away mud and blood. Much of what remained would not wash away. She realized then that it was not dirt, but torn flesh and burned skin.

The damage to the right side of his face was terrible.

She straightened his head and eased his body into a position that allowed him to breathe more freely. His right arm lay twisted beneath him. When she tried to move it, she felt the unnatural looseness of broken bone. His leg was no better. The femur was shattered just below the hip. She had set broken bones before, using bamboo splints, but injuries like these were beyond what she could treat in the paddies.

She poured more water over him, clearing his mouth and nose. He coughed weakly and swallowed. His eyes fluttered, unfocused, then closed again.

She stood and looked toward the path leading to the village. She needed to tell Hùng what she had found. The American would surely be dead by the time she returned. There was no other choice.

She looked down at him one last time, then turned and began walking away.

She forced herself to face away, because if she looked again she would already be undone. The man's breathing was so shallow it seemed impossible that it could continue. Phương told herself what was true: he was American, and Americans brought helicopters, bullets, and defoliation. Americans brought death into valleys that once only feared flood and famine. Saving him could bring danger straight to her hut, and then to Hùng's village, and then to anyone who still had something left to lose.

She took three steps, then five.

Her stomach clenched—not with fear alone, but with the old, familiar fury of helplessness. War took men and boys and called it duty. War took daughters and called it fate. War took a mother's labor and left her with empty mats and quiet mornings.

And now war had left this man, broken in the mud, to die without anyone even knowing his name.

Phương stopped.

She had seen bodies left in the open before. She had seen the way dogs circled once the smell turned. She had seen the way the jungle accepted flesh and erased identity. She thought of Dũng, and the unbearable idea that her son's last minutes might have been like this—alone, the world going quiet around him, no hand on his chest to feel whether he still breathed.

Her throat tightened. She whispered, not loudly enough for the valley to hear—only enough for herself.

"No… not like that."

She did not pray for the American. She did not bless him. She simply refused the thought of another human being dying the way her mind imagined Dũng had died. She stood in the mist with her jaw clenched, as if the decision were something she had to bite down on to keep.

Then she began walking again—toward the village, yes—but with the knowledge already forming inside her: she would not leave him to die alone. Not tonight. Not in her valley.

Her steps were slow at first. She passed her hut, the narrow path familiar beneath her feet. From her home to the village, the trail was meant only for foot traffic, crossing three mountain streams by narrow bamboo footbridges. No carts or motorbikes could pass this way. Only beyond the village, where the path widened and joined the road toward Highway 19, could carts and motorbikes travel. The village lay more than a mile away. The moon had risen over the mountains to the east, half full, casting faint light across the valley floor. It was April 4, 1968.

In the distance she heard artillery and the crack of small-arms fire.

As she walked, her thoughts returned repeatedly to the man she had left behind. She thought of Dũng lying alone as he died. Grief tightened around her chest. When she reached the point where the village came into view, she stopped.

Without understanding why, she turned and went back.

She walked faster now, driven by something she could not name. She could not let the man die alone—not after all she had seen.

She passed her hut and stopped at the storage shed. From inside she took a length of hemp rope. Without hesitation, she turned back toward the paddies.

The American lay where she had left him. He was still breathing. She went back to the spot where she had pulled him out of the paddy. She uncovered his helmet and pulled it free from the mud. She pushed her hand and arm into the mud and searched. It did not take long, and she felt the barrel of his rifle. She pulled it free from the mud. She laid both the rifle and the helmet on the man's chest.

She wrapped the rope around his chest and under his armpits, securing it tightly. She tied a loop at the far end, turned away from him, and slipped the loop around the back of her neck and beneath her arms. Facing away, she leaned forward and began to pull. The tightening of the rope lifted the man's head off the ground.

The first steps were difficult. His body dragged heavily across the ground. Then, as the rope tightened and her footing steadied, the weight seemed to lessen. She pulled steadily, breath rasping in her chest. Along the way, she would have to stop and reposition the helmet and rifle onto his chest. It took nearly half an hour to reach her hut.

She dragged him up the steps. The helmet and the rifle fell to the ground. After several hard pulls, she had him in the hut, dragging him to her sleeping mat.

The interior was dark. She had an oil lamp and candles. They were seldom used. There was rarely reason for her to be awake after nightfall, and she was usually asleep by this hour. She lit the oil lamp and two candles and set them near the wounded man.

The only sign of life was his shallow breathing.

She decided then to wash him, to prepare him for death. That he was American slipped from her mind. In this moment, he was only a broken man.

She removed his uniform. There were no groans, no cries. He was too near death to feel pain. His boots and clothing lay in a heap beside the mat. He was naked.

She took one of the candles and stepped back into the night. At the water barrel she filled a bucket and returned to the hut.

In the center of the hut stood a small fire pit, built of stones and used only during heavy rains. The wooden floor had been constructed around it. It was safe but seldom needed except during the monsoon. She built a small fire and placed the bucket on a grate above it.

As the water began to warm, the pain from her own wounds returned in force. She realized that she had no shirt on. Soap was a luxury for most Vietnamese, but one of Phương's small sources of income was making it during the rainy season. All the ingredients she produced herself—pressed coconut, palm leaf, aloe, crushed limestone for pumice, and lye made from ash.

She took one of the precious bars and washed her own wounds with the hot water. Pain surged through her body. Over the coming days she would dig the remaining metal fragments from her flesh. For now, she endured.

She finished tending herself and turned back to the man on the mat.

Phương left the bucket of water on the fire and let it continue to heat. She dipped a coconut-shell ladle into the water and carried it to the mat. Squatting beside the wounded man, she took the bar of soap and began the slow work of washing him.

She cleaned his body carefully, repeating the process repeatedly. The right side of his body bore multiple wounds, with pieces of metal lodged deep beneath the skin. His face was the worst. The right side had been torn and burned. There was a gaping wound in his cheek, and above his right temple a deep gash where skin was gone entirely. Bone was exposed, metal embedded in it.

She believed he would die.

Yet something within her would not let her stop.

Like most peasants, she kept a small medicinal kit made mostly of bamboo. Inside were tweezers, picks, needles, thread, a knife, and a razor. With the bamboo tools she began removing the metal, starting with his head and face, then working downward. Burned flesh surrounded many of the wounds. She knew the dead skin would rot if left, inviting infection. She used the razor to cut it away.

She worked slowly, methodically, stopping only to dip the ladle again and rinse blood and debris from the wounds. Where she could, she pulled torn tissue together and sutured it. She knew that if he lived, his face would be terribly scarred.

As she worked, she realized he needed water. She took a mouthful herself and carefully fed it into his mouth. His body responded. He swallowed. She gave him only a few drops at a time, waiting between each. Other than that reflex, there was no sign of awareness.

She continued through the night. As the night before, sometime in the dark, the rains came, and they came heavy. In the rice paddy, other than a gaping hole in a dike, all signs of digging were being washed away.

By the time the sky began to lighten, she had removed most of the metal—nearly all of it. Only the smallest fragments remained. She fashioned splints for his broken arm and leg from bamboo and bound them tightly. She had done all she could.

Exhaustion claimed her.

She lay down beside him on the mat, pulled the thin night sheet over them both, and fell asleep at once.

April 5, 1968

A sound broke her sleep.

Phương awoke to the distant thudding of helicopters—low at first, then swelling until it felt as if the roof beams themselves vibrated. She sat upright at once. Her eyes went immediately to the pile of clothing beside the mat—the American's uniform, and boots.

Her mouth went dry.

The thudding grew louder, then split into multiple engines. She could hear the deeper chop of gunships and the heavier, steadier rhythm of troop Hueys. The sound pressed down on the hut like a weight.

She swung herself off the mat and moved too fast. Pain flared along the burns on her cheek and neck. She ignored it. She gathered the uniform, rifle and boots in a trembling armful and hurried outside.

As she descended the steps, four helicopters passed overhead—two gunships and two troop carriers. The gunships flew first, raking the paddies and the surrounding jungle with rockets and machine-gun fire. The sound was sharp and tearing, nothing like thunder. The other two descended toward the valley floor.

Rotor wash hit her like a hot wind. Dust and ash lifted into the air and stung her eyes.

Dũng had once built a small cache bunker beneath the firewood pile. Phương ran to it. Thatch and bamboo poles still lay scattered over the wood from the earlier destruction. She pulled them away with frantic hands and uncovered the bunker. She shoved the uniform, and boots inside, forcing them down until they disappeared into darkness. She hurried back to the steps and grabbed the helmet and rifle lying on the ground. She went back to the bunker and placed them inside. Then she covered the bunker again and piled debris back over the top, tamping it until it looked like nothing more than ruined firewood.

She rushed into the hut.

Only then did she see the chain around the American's neck. Metal tags rested against his chest.

For a moment her hands froze. If they saw those tags, they would know. They would take him. They might take her. They might tear the hut apart until they found the uniform buried outside.

She slipped the chain over his head as gently as she could and crossed to the corner where the Buddha lay broken. Beneath the cracked marble and ceramic shards, she tucked the tags deep into the shadowed hollow and slid a fragment over them as if sealing a wound.

She returned to the mat, pulled the sheet up over the man's body, and turned his head so that only the damaged right side of his face showed. She remembered she did not have a shirt on. Each of her family members had one extra pair of clothing, which was kept in a pile in the corner. She quickly grabbed a shirt and covered herself. She then returned to the man laying on the mat.

She forced herself to kneel beside him, as a mother would.

She knew the Americans were searching for the one they had left behind.

Minutes passed—perhaps half an hour—before she heard voices approaching along the path. Boots stopped short of the homesite. Through the open doorway she saw an American officer standing below, looking over the destruction.

He did not come up immediately.

He stood still and read the scene like a map.

He took in the collapsed cooking canopy, shattered pottery, scattered thatch, and the shallow crater where a mortar round had struck near the hut. His eyes moved along the burn marks, the churned earth, the broken poles. Whatever had happened here, it had happened close.

Behind him, men spoke in English, low and urgent.

"Spread out. Watch the tree line."

"Easy—don't step where you can't see."

"Tripwire's everywhere in this damn valley."

A voice farther out called, "Clear left!"

Another answered, "Clear right!"

The officer spoke without raising his voice. His tone was controlled, the tone of a man who had already seen too much.

"Keep it tight," he said. "We are here for Fox. Nothing else. Do not make it worse."

A Vietnamese voice called up the path, warning Phương that soldiers were coming to search the hut.

Footsteps climbed the steps.

An American soldier leaned into the doorway and shouted something she did not understand. His rifle was angled down but ready. Another soldier followed him inside, scanning corners, roof beams, the floor, as if the hut itself might attack.

A Vietnamese soldier stepped in behind them. He was young, his uniform damp at the collar. His eyes moved from Phương to the man on the mat and back again.

"Ai đó?" he asked.

Who is that?

"Dũng," she replied immediately. "Con trai tôi."

My son.

Fear tightened in her chest until it hurt to breathe. She felt her heartbeat in her throat. She kept her hands in her lap so they would not see them shaking.

The Americans spoke again. The Vietnamese soldier translated the question with a glance at the officer.

"Sao bị thương?" he asked. "Bị gì?"

How is he injured? What happened?

Phương answered slowly, choosing her words with care.

"Nó bị thương nặng," she said. "Con trai tôi đang chết."

He is badly wounded. My son is dying.

She gestured toward the shattered canopy and the churned earth beside the hut.

"Đạn cối rơi gần nhà trong lúc đánh nhau," she continued. "Chúng tôi bị thương ở đây."

A mortar fell near the house during the fighting. We were wounded here.

The Vietnamese soldier translated.

The officer's eyes moved again over the damage outside—the collapsed canopy, the blast mark near the hut—then back to Phương's burned face. Finally, he looked at the man on the mat.

The injuries made sense.

But Phương knew "making sense" was different from being believed.

The officer asked another question. The Vietnamese soldier translated, his voice careful.

"Hôm qua… con trai chị có bắn người Mỹ không?" he asked.

Yesterday… did your son shoot Americans?

Phương felt the hut narrow around her. Her throat tightened. She could see, in her mind, the tags beneath the Buddha and the uniform beneath the woodpile. She imagined them digging. She imagined hands pulling everything apart.

She lifted her eyes and met the officer's gaze.

She did not look away.

Her face became a wall.

For a long moment, the officer watched her. He could not understand her words, but he could read the battle's signature on the place and on her body—the burns, the soot, the torn cloth, the crater near the hut. He looked at the man on the mat again.

Then he spoke, quiet but final, as if he were deciding the limits of the day.

"He's no threat," he said. "We move."

Outside, a sergeant called, "Sir—area's clear!"

Another voice answered, impatient, "Let us go. Stay on line."

The officer gave the order to move on.

The soldiers filed out of the hut and continued down the trail, their boots fading into the distance as they resumed the search for the missing American—Sergeant Gabriel Fox.

Phương remained motionless until she could no longer hear them. Only then did she let herself breathe. Her lungs burned as if she had been underwater.

She returned to the man on the mat and knelt beside him. Her voice came out thin and shaking.

"Dũng, chúng ta an toàn," she whispered. "Người Mỹ đã rời đi."

Dũng, we are safe. The Americans have left.

She stayed there, watching his shallow breathing, praying for him to live.

A short while later, an explosion echoed from the direction of the village.

Phương did not know that two American soldiers had been killed by a booby trap, or that the young officer who had stood below her steps and spoken quietly to his men had been severely wounded. The trap had been hastily placed after helicopters had landed at the paddies and lifted off again. The same unit of North Vietnamese Army and Việt Cộng soldiers that had fought the Americans the previous day had moved farther southeast along the wooded edge of the valley floor.

They had reconnoitered the area and anticipated the Americans' movement.

The helicopters that had dropped soldiers at the paddies had flown southeast to Firebase Thunderhead, near the mouth of the valley. They remained close in case of contact. Once the booby trap was set, the NVA and Việt Cộng withdrew back into the mountains, avoiding further engagement after the losses they had already suffered.

Ten minutes after the explosion, two helicopters returned—both Hueys configured to carry troops and evacuate wounded. The injured officer, Captain Sean McMurtry, was flown first to the field hospital in Quy Nhơn. From there he was sent to Sài Gòn, then on to Japan, and eventually to Fort Campbell, Kentucky, near his home in Dover, Tennessee.

Captain McMurtry lost his left arm and left leg due to the injuries. After months of recovery, prosthetic fitting, and therapy, he was separated from the Army on medical grounds and returned home to Tennessee. A Tennessee Tech mechanical engineering graduate, he later earned a master's degree in biomedical engineering at Duke. He worked through the VA system with amputees and prosthetic clinics, learning realities that never appeared in textbooks. In 1980, he entered Vanderbilt's doctoral program in biomedical engineering. He devoted his life's work to improving prosthetics, convinced there had to be better replacements than those he had been given.

He often wondered about the missing soldier—Sergeant Gabriel Fox—and whether he had ever been found. The Army called off the search later that same day. Sergeant Fox was listed as Missing in Action and presumed dead.

On April 11, 1968, a black Ford Custom bearing U.S. Government plates turned onto a mountain road outside Townsend, Tennessee. A young corporal drove the vehicle, his eyes fixed forward. In the back seat sat a First Lieutenant. They were on their way to deliver the news to a family living high in the hills—that their son, Sergeant Gabriel Fox, was missing in action and presumed dead. His body could not be found.

Neither the driver nor the passenger knew the terrain or the driving conditions they would face climbing into the mountains to inform a family that their son was gone. This was their first assignment. The lieutenant and the corporal both understood that their time delivering this kind of news would be short-lived. They had been sent down from Fort Knox for this duty. The lieutenant would navigate as the corporal drove. There was little conversation between the two as they both thought about their assignment, and the corporal concentrated on driving.

The driver was from Abilene, Kansas, of all places. Ninety-nine percent of his driving had been on the flat plains of Kansas. He had never been more than fifty miles from home—not until he was drafted. People cautioned him that morning before they left, but he still did not have a clue what the roads would become.

Neither did the young officer from New Jersey, who had spent little time outside Edison, not until he enlisted and signed up for OCS. He had been working at the Edison Assembly Plant, but he believed he would be drafted soon. A family friend advised him to enlist and try for Officer Candidate School instead of waiting to be drafted. He took the advice. It had put gold bars on his shoulders, but it had not prepared him for this.

They left the city limits of Knoxville and headed toward Maryville. Just outside town, the road began to wind. The driver and his passengers thought they understood what they had been warned about. They did not realize they were still on the straight portion—excluding the stretch where they passed McGhee Tyson Airfield. It was not much in size, but it was being enlarged to make room for military aircraft and passenger planes. Many smaller airports were transitioning from the prop era into the jet age, and this one had already been expanded during World War II.

The road ran straight in front of the airfield, but once they were past it—and past the streets of Maryville—it only grew more winding. They passed the ALCOA plant and continued into town. They stopped at a filling station to top off the tank and confirm their directions.

The attendant told them they could stay on the road they were on, reach Townsend, and ask again there. Townsend was a place the attendant had heard of but had never seen. The lieutenant and the corporal both had trouble understanding the attendant's accent. They felt, suddenly, as if they were in a foreign country.

The lieutenant asked how long it would take. The attendant shrugged and said, "Three hours or so."

It was only about forty miles away, the corporal thought. That could not be right.

Shortly after they left Maryville, the drive became a test of skill for the young corporal. The lieutenant sat in back, as was proper, but within miles he began to feel nauseated. The turns came sharper and more frequent with each mile. The corporal drove no more than forty miles per hour, often fifteen. His hands stayed tight on the wheel. The cab felt cold with nerves, despite the heater.

The worst came when they reached a stretch where a rock-faced wall leaned out over the roadway. The corporal dropped to ten miles per hour through those curves. Sweat formed at his hairline. His shirt clung to his back. In the rear seat, the lieutenant swallowed hard and prayed for a place to pull over. He did not think he could hold out much longer.

Finally, they found a small turnout on the opposite side of the road. A boiled peanut stand sat there like a place of mercy. The corporal pulled in. The lieutenant was out of the car before it fully stopped. He dropped to his knees and vomited the morning's breakfast onto the gravel.

The peanut vendor watched without surprise. He had a cooler full of drinks—mostly Coca-Cola, plus grape sodas. In that part of the woods, you either drank a Coke, a grape, or an orange soda. Pepsi existed, but to people there it was all "Coke," whatever color it came in.

Once the lieutenant regained himself, he and the corporal each drank a Coke, swigging like men who had crossed a desert instead of a county line. They rested for thirty minutes, then got back on the road.

When they finally arrived in Townsend, they stopped at the general store. The owner and clerk knew the Fox family and knew they lived up in the hills. The man gave the two the best directions he could, pointing with his whole hand, naming roads as if they were relatives.

Two more hours passed. They made several false turns and stopped twice to ask again, the lieutenant writing notes on a folded map that seemed to grow less helpful with every mile. At last, they reached the Fox cabin.

Jonas sat on the porch as the evening approached. Esther came to the door when she heard the vehicle grind to a stop. The corporal stayed with the car while the lieutenant stepped forward and delivered the news: their son, Gabriel, was missing and presumed dead.

Jonas and Esther were stoic mountain people. They accepted the words as graciously as they could, as if grief were another hard season a family had to live through. The lieutenant kept his voice steady and formal, as he had been taught, though he felt the weight of every syllable. When the words were finished, the lieutenant returned to the car. Both the lieutenant and corporal hoped they would be out of the mountains before dark.

Three months later, the Fox family received a check for ten thousand dollars. It was more money than they had ever seen. It meant nothing.

Gabriel's father, Jonas Fox, placed the check inside the family Bible—one that had been passed down for generations. He tucked it carefully between the pages where Gabriel's name would have been written among the deaths. Jonas believed his son would need the money when he came home.

In the years that followed, after everyone else in the family was gone, Jonas would open the Bible to that page. Gabriel's name was still not there. Below the empty space were the names of Gabriel's mother, his older brother, and his two older sisters. The check remained folded and waiting.

Jonas never believed there would come a day when Gabriel would not return.

The check, long since worthless, waited for him.

In the coming months, a family in Abilene, Kansas, sat on their couch as they received the news that their son and brother had been killed in an ambush outside Tam Kỳ, Việt Nam. Weeks later, a widowed father in Edison, New Jersey, was told that his son had died in a mortar attack on a firebase outside Tuy Hòa. The man drank a pint of whiskey that night, but he still made it to work at 7:00 a.m. the next morning, slapping the control buttons on a stamping machine as if the world had not ended.

In the mountains of East Tennessee, the work continued on the small mountain farm that had been in the same family for generations. Grief had settled in at the loss of a son, a son missing or dead in Vietnam. Jonas and Esther neither had a clue where Vietnam was when their son Gabriel was sent. Jonas went into Townsend, the small town about five miles from their cabin. The owner had a world map on a wall. The owner showed Jonas where Vietnam was on the map.

Jonas stood, staring at the map and the place called Vietnam. On occasion, he would look at the opposite side of the map at a place called France. He looked at the coast on the map, and he thought about the sand on a beach and the hills in the not too far distance. He could hear the sound and feel the pain, and most of all the fear. Then he would look back at that place called Vietnam, and he would quietly pray for his son, Gabriel.

Chapter 3

Tết Mậu Thân

Psalm 144:1 (KJV)

"Blessed be the LORD my strength, which teacheth my hands to war, and my fingers to fight."

Gabriel crouched low. His gaze was focused from five to fifteen yards out. He would bring his vision close and scan the area nearest to him. He could see things, smell things, and hear things that the other men could not. He would scan in and then out in five-degree increments. The turn of his head was slow and deliberate. He seemed immune to the gnats and flies, never a swat or a twitch of the eye.

He had learned long ago that the jungle rewarded the man who acted like the jungle—still, patient, and unwilling to announce his presence. The gnats were nothing. The itch was nothing. Pain and discomfort were only signals, and he had trained himself not to answer them. The woods back home taught him the first lesson: if you move, you can be seen. Vietnam had taught him the second: if you move at the wrong moment, you can be killed.

He let his eyes work the way his father taught him—soft focus first, letting motion reveal itself, then hard focus, picking out shape and color. Nothing in nature was truly still. Leaves shifted with air currents. Insects jittered. Light moved across bark. A man trying to hide always betrayed himself by being too still in the wrong pattern—or by being still while everything else moved.

Gabriel's breathing was slow enough so that he could hear it inside his own chest. He kept his mouth slightly open so the air could pass without the louder drawing through his nose. He had discovered early that the body made noise when it was afraid—little involuntary sounds. He did not allow himself those.

Behind him, men waited, every one of them watching his shoulders as if his posture itself were the radio. They had learned that if Gabriel froze, they froze. If Gabriel dropped to a knee, they dropped. If Gabriel raised a fist, it was the same as an order.

He did not enjoy that kind of authority. He simply accepted it because it kept them alive.

He watched for any movement or out-of-place color. He would watch for the flickering of an eyelid, the white of an eye, or the movement of a hand. He drew in deep, slow breaths, trying to catch a hint of nước mắm, the fermented fish sauce that the Vietnamese loved. They ate it with everything. With time, the smell saturated their skin and clothing. If there were a small group of Việt Cộng or NVA (Quân đội Nhân dân Việt Nam) soldiers, the smell of nước mắm would often fill the air with its aroma. The smell could be faint—so faint a man might mistake it for the natural rot of the jungle. But Gabriel had learned the difference. The jungle had its own odors: damp leaf mold, sap, stagnant water, and the sharp mineral smell where stone had been broken. Nước mắm rode over those smells like a thin film of oil, not strong enough to overwhelm everything, but strong enough to change the air.

He did not just smell for "enemy." He smelled for proximity, direction, even mood. A small group that had been moving hard and sweating would carry the scent differently than a group that had been lying still for hours. Wet clothing held it. Dry cloth released it. If the wind shifted, the scent shifted. And if it disappeared suddenly, Gabriel took that as information too—because men who realized they might be detected often stopped moving, stopped breathing hard, stopped being human for a moment.

He had tried explaining this to one of the lieutenants early in-country and had regretted it. The officer had looked at him like he was telling ghost stories. Gabriel learned to keep his reasons to himself. He gave signals. The unit obeyed. That was all that mattered.

A bead of sweat ran down his spine. He ignored it. The jungle was always wet. Men were always wet. What mattered was whether the wet air carried something it should not.

He pulled in another slow breath and held it a heartbeat longer than comfort allowed.

There it was again—just a hint.

He would pull the air in slowly, taking in the smells. More than once, the scent of fermented fish told him the enemy was nearby. That smell was the reason for his unit to halt.

Gabriel was the point man, the place he most wanted to be. It was not common for a sergeant to have that position, but in this unit, it had become evident that in the mountains of the Central Highlands, it was the most appropriate place for Sergeant Fox to be.

He was patient, with a patience learned in the forests and mountains of the southern Appalachians, along the slopes of the Smoky Mountains. He was born in those mountains, the Unicoi Mountains, in a log cabin nestled on the south bank of a mountain hollow known by most as Fox Hollow. From as early as he could remember, he was in the mountain forests with his father, being taught the art of hunting.

As a child, he would tote a bolt-action, single-shot .22. His father taught him the importance of making one shot count. He also taught him how to watch and listen, how to recognize the ever-so-slight movement of game. When it was time for the shot, he knew that for larger game, the chest was the place to aim. Placed properly, the shot would take out the heart and lungs, and the game would die instantly.

For squirrels, partridge, and other small game, it was the head, and he seldom missed. You did not want to ruin the meat with a gut shot.

By the time he was twelve, unless he was hunting small game, he would tote the single-shot, breech-loading long rifle that had been in his family for generations. Today, though, his weapon was an M-16. He had qualified expert with both the M-14 and the M-16. He was deadly accurate with them, just as he was with those rifles back home.

Shooting a gun did not bring him any pleasure. He viewed it as a tool, just like a saw or a hammer. His dad taught him that if you were going to use them, then use them well. His father taught him that every draw of a saw blade or swing of a hammer needed to be accurate and count, and every pull of the trigger was the same.

He could hear his father's voice as plainly as if Jonas were standing beside him in the brush—low, steady, never wasting a word.

"You don't point a rifle at anything you ain't ready to kill," Jonas had said when Gabriel was still too small for the rifle to fit his shoulder right. "That ain't fear talk. That is respect talk."

Gabriel had nodded then, trying to understand something larger than hunting. Jonas didn't speak much about right and wrong in the abstract. He spoke about it through work.

"If you take a life," Jonas had said, "you make it quick. And you make it clean. You don't play with it."

Gabriel had learned the lesson in the field behind the cabin, aiming at a tin can nailed to a stump. He had missed the first shot, embarrassed, wanting to rush the second. Jonas had stopped him.

"Breathe," his father said. "Ain't no hurry. The can ain't goin' nowhere."

Now, in Vietnam, everything could go somewhere—fast. But the lesson stayed: slow was smooth, smooth was fast. Panic spent bullets. Discipline saved lives.

Sometimes he wondered what Jonas would say if he could see this—his son crouched in a jungle on the other side of the world, using the same calm meant for squirrels and deer on human beings. Jonas would not praise it. Jonas would not condemn him either. Jonas would only ask if Gabriel was doing what he had to do and whether he was doing it well.

And Gabriel would have answered honestly.

"Yes, sir."

As he crouched in the heat on the northwest corner of Hòn Cong Mountain (Núi Hòn Cong) above An Khê in the Central Highlands, his mind would roam back to his home. At home, today, January 30, 1968, it would be very cold. Most likely there was snow in the mountains around his cabin home. His father would be gathering split wood for the fireplace.

Every winter, Jonas, his father, and he would cut logs for firewood. They would cut them to length and let them cure for a few days for natural splitting to occur. Then they would split the firewood and stack it to dry for the following year. They rotated the split logs often to allow for proper drying. If the logs had too much moisture, they would not burn as hot, and creosote would form inside the flue walls of the chimney. Neither Jonas nor Gabe's mom, Esther, would ever tell Gabriel that their supply of firewood had grown short with him not there.

He then thought of his mother cooking smoked ham and eggs, or some other morning feast, such as brains and eggs, biscuits and gravy, or cornmeal and flour pancakes. They grew their own corn but had to trade for flour, so Esther would always mix finely ground cornmeal in with her flour to make it go farther.

After breakfast, his father would be in the woods felling trees. He would drag the logs with their two mules back to their mountain sawmill. If not cutting lumber, then Jonas would be working one of his many moonshine stills, which he had scattered throughout the mountains along different creeks. He would tell Gabriel, "Never put all your eggs in one basket." If the government people found one of his stills, he would still be in business with the others.

He and others living in the surrounding hills, ridges, and hollers would go together and build sacrificial stills. They would not make them easy to find, but easier to find than the others. The mountains had numerous streams, creeks, and springs to feed a still. They found the most difficult access points alongside creeks. The stills they intended to make a living off were put in difficult spots to access and never in the open.

Jonas was known to be an expert distiller. His corn whiskey was clear and clean. It always produced at about 180 proof. A sip of Jonas Fox's whiskey would spin a man's head. Jonas always marveled at why anyone would want to drink "that darn stuff." Jonas would always taste his liquor but would also spit it out. Jonas was not a drinker and did not understand why anyone was.

It was turning toward early afternoon in the Central Highlands, just after 1:00 p.m., which meant it would be morning at home in about five hours. Gabriel thought of those early lessons his father taught him. They suited him well in this foreign country.

Those behind him had learned quickly of his abilities. At first, he seemed like such a foreigner to them. The language he spoke, even though English, sounded so different. It was the language of the southern Appalachians—a language formed by isolation from the rest of America. Electricity was late in coming, and so were radio and television, neither of which his family possessed. The mountain people very seldom ventured far from their isolated existence. A trip to Townsend, a town of less than three hundred people, was rare.

The history of the clans of the Scots-Irish still hung tight. Strangers were to be avoided because one never knew what harm they might bring. Hunting, farming, logging, and moonshine distilling were the trades of his father, and each he was taught well.

Gabriel had no fear of the forest or this jungle. He had spent untold hours on his own in the mountains of his home. He was often sent on his own to graze their few cows in the upper meadows called balds. He would spend days, and even nights, with just a knapsack filled with cornbread pones, cracklings, deer jerky, and homemade preserves.

He always carried his .22 rifle with him, and when the opportunity arose, he would venture out from his mountain camp and hunt for small game. Most of the time he was successful. The nights alone would be spent cooking the game and listening for an unwelcome intruder, most prominently the black bear. Many times, he had to stand his ground against the hungry intruder. He would pop a round into the fatty shoulder, and the beast would screech in pain and run off. In those cases, Gabriel always aimed to put the bullet just under the skin for it to hit and pass through, exiting the other side. Unless he was hunting an animal, he never meant to cause it more harm than necessary.

He never felt glee about killing an animal, but satisfaction in providing food.

In this distant jungle, he never let the thoughts of home distract him from what might be in front of him and waiting. Yet those thoughts constantly ran through his mind. The thought of home never distracted him from the dangers. It helped guide him. His lifelong education in mountains, finding game, hiding spots, and staying safe suited him well in these mountains.

As he crouched, gazing ahead, he thought of the irony of such a poor boy now hunting other poor boys. When his company searched villages, he often noted the similarities between his life and the lives of those poor people. They might live in huts rather than cabins, but their lives were so much alike. Nothing was wasted.

He assumed this war was worth the killing and the dying. There could be no other reason for being here unless it was worth it.

Once, in a village, he saw an old man hobbling, and it reminded him of his father, Jonas. He wondered if this old man had gotten his limp from a war wound, as had his father. Jonas never spoke of that day—the day he nearly lost his leg on that stretch of beach on the French coast. He never spoke about the dead and dying around him, or the fear that drove him on. He never talked about running in the direction of the oncoming fire, or the sudden jerk of his leg out from under him.

Not once did he talk about the fear he felt, lying on that beach for hours with bullets slamming into the sand all around him. Not once did he tell Gabe about that day, or the long months that followed in military hospitals. Only his mother had told him why his father limped; otherwise, Gabriel would never have known.

Gabriel was happy about his unit's new assignment. The first three months in country were spent outside Biên Hòa, just north of Sài Gòn. Then, in November, they were transferred north to the Central Highlands. The Central Highlands were hot, but refreshing compared to the south. Though different, the mountains reminded him of home. This was his unit's third month in the Highlands, and he was glad to be there. It was here that he really began to prove himself.

Moving through the mountains was an easy task for him. The unit had been on constant patrol since arriving, operating out of different firebases in the region. They had been sent to Camp Radcliff at An Khê for a bit of rest and relaxation. They were to spend three to four days at the base and then move out again to remote firebases. It was only their second day at Camp Radcliff when Army intelligence reported there was a lot of enemy movement around the base. Gabriel's unit, along with others, was pulled to take on a one-day search-and-clear mission to clear the mountain above the camp.

Deuce-and-a-half trucks hauled them early that morning from their temporary quarters to the northwest perimeter of Camp Radcliff. It was strange—they could not load their weapons until they were offloaded from the deuce-and-a-halves and lined up along the perimeter fence. Once they lined up, they crossed over the fence and were given the order to lock and load.

Gabriel thought of the first time in the field when he and the others were given the order to lock and load. Gabriel's hand shook violently as he attempted to place the magazine in the rifle, but once inserted, a calmness came over him. That morning, there was no fear as he loaded his weapon.

His unit was told that these search-and-clear missions were routine operations to protect the base and that seldom was there any contact. However, due to the intelligence, his unit was being pulled to help rout out any NVA or Việt Cộng that might be setting up on the mountain above the camp.

Gabriel looked up the side of Hòn Cong Mountain (Núi Hòn Cong). The first two hundred yards were stripped of any vegetation except for low-growing grass and an occasional shrub. Gabriel had seen planes and helicopters spraying defoliant along the perimeters of camps, firebases, and LZs. All military encampments of a somewhat permanent nature had a stripped patch of earth between the camp and the jungle.

He thought of the time he and others were digging a perimeter trench around a firebase. It was blistering hot. The heat was oppressive. He heard the engines of a C-123 approaching. A cool mist fell on Gabriel and his fellow soldiers. The cooling mist was welcomed. Gabriel looked up and saw nozzles along the wings of the aircraft spraying the mist. As the C-123 flew on, Gabriel and the others wished it would return to spray them one more time.

His unit spread an arm's distance apart along the perimeter fence. They would traverse those first two hundred yards parallel to each other. They were given the order to move out, and they headed up until reaching the jungle growth. Once at the edge of the jungle, Gabriel took point.

The unit began to travel up through the jungle. The undergrowth was thick and heavy. The unit was forced to travel in single file while men took turns with machetes, hacking their way through the dense undergrowth. The farther they moved up the side of the mountain, the lighter the undergrowth became. After an hour or so, the jungle floor cleared well enough to move with ease.

They spread out in a V-shaped formation with Gabriel in the lead. It was just after midday when they reached the ridge of Hòn Cong Mountain. They were to move along the ridge for a quarter mile heading north and then start down the west side of the mountain, connecting with a mountain road that would lead them to a plain stretching for miles west of An Khê. Deuce-and-a-half trucks would be at the base of the mountain to take them back to camp.

Most in the unit felt this would be an easy day. Even Gabriel felt relaxed as they moved through the mountain jungle.

It was along the ridge that Gabriel's senses heightened. He detected a faint hint of nước mắm. It was here that he went to one knee and began his search. The relaxation the others felt instantly disappeared when they saw Gabriel drop. They knew there was something ahead of them. What it was, they did not know, but they knew Gabriel had detected something. They had all learned to respect his instincts. He was seldom wrong.

Then he saw it—the slight turn of a head and the sudden silhouette of a pith helmet.

His hand slowly moved, forming a locked fist, then palm down. Those behind him knew the meaning, and fear crept in. They understood the prey was ahead.

The lieutenant, Lieutenant Russell Davenport, began easing the men forward as stealthily as they could move. Gabriel detected the movement behind him. He clenched his fist as tight as possible. The lieutenant saw the sudden grip of Gabriel's fist. He knew he had just been scolded by Gabriel. The others had seen the gripped fist and stopped their movement.

The lieutenant was new, and it was going to take Gabriel a while to train him. The lieutenant kept his eye on Gabriel, waiting for another signal.

Gabriel searched the area more quickly now, trying to detect if the enemy had any awareness of their presence. A mixed unit of NVA and Việt Cộng was moving in the opposite direction toward Gabriel's unit. It was their intent to be in the jungle just above Camp Radcliff prior to nightfall. There, with several other units moving in from various locations, they were to wait until the early morning hours of January 31, 1968, to mount a mortar attack on Camp Radcliff.

The point man of the enemy unit was not as adept as Gabriel. Both the NVA and the Việt Cộng in this combined unit were new to combat. The North Vietnamese were training soldiers quickly to send south, and the Việt Cộng had recruited heavily, training new personnel. This combined unit was made up of those freshly trained men.

The NVA soldiers had been en route for three months, traveling down the infamous Ho Chi Minh Trail (Đường mòn Hồ Chí Minh). This contingent of NVA and Việt Cộng had been led into the mountain above Camp

Radcliff by a master NVA scout. Once he had led the inexperienced unit onto the mountain, he left to guide another unit into position. The scout who took over did not have the experience to lead men through the mountain jungle. He had not detected Gabriel and his comrades.

Gabriel watched the lone NVA soldier moving slowly forward. The helmeted soldier scanned the forest of Hòn Cong Mountain. Gabriel watched him raise his hand and signal those behind him to move forward. He saw the collective movement of foliage and shadows. He knew the game was on.

Those behind him sensed the same and were ready when they saw Gabriel's M-16 pop to his shoulder.

"Contact front!" someone shouted.

With his weapon on fully automatic, Gabriel unloaded a full magazine in a sixty-degree arc. Those behind him were doing the same.

"Move! Move! Move!"

From the jungle ahead came frantic shouts in Vietnamese.

The words snapped through the trees—high, urgent, layered over one another so fast they sounded like argument and command at the same time. He did not understand Vietnamese, but fear was its own language.

"Nằm xuống!" (Get down!)

"Tản ra!" (Spread out!)

"Rút lui! Rút lui!" (Fall back! Fall back!)

"Bắn! Bắn!" (Shoot! Shoot!)

"Mỹ! Mỹ!" (Americans! Americans!)

Branches shook. Leaves fluttered in sudden unnatural patterns—bodies moving, men trying to become smaller. The jungle that had been a wall a moment earlier became a living thing, full of direction and panic.

Gabriel's world narrowed to mechanics: front sight post, trigger squeeze, recoil, re-acquire. His hearing separated sounds the way his eyes separated color—M-16s cracking sharp and bright, AKs popping with a harsher rhythm, the deeper, steadier voice of the M-60. Somewhere in that noise was the thin, human sound of screaming. Somewhere else was the heavier sound of a body hitting ground.

He did not let himself think about any single man. Thinking made hesitation. Hesitation made you dead.

He moved forward when the enemy broke, not running like a boy, but advancing like a hunter closing distance on wounded game—fast enough to keep pressure, slow enough to see the trap.

There was constant fire in the direction of the enemy. The enemy had been caught off guard. The cacophony of noise from the Americans filled the jungle instantly. The sudden burst of firepower stunned the mixed unit of NVA and Việt Cộng.

Once the initial shock passed, the Vietnamese began responding with heavy fire. The distinct pop of AK-47s filled the air, along with the burst of American M-16s and the M-60 machine gun manned by Claude Jarrett.

Gabriel's first burst caught a young Việt Cộng soldier on the left side, just under his rib cage. It threw the soldier back, knocking him semi-conscious. Gabriel heard round after round whizzing by, with the sound of wood popping and splintering as bullets slammed into the surrounding jungle. He could hear sudden screams of pain coming from both sides. Shouts of commands in both English and Vietnamese rang out through the jungle.

He wished he could understand those foreign words as he popped another magazine into the rifle.

It was obvious Gabriel's unit had done a lot of damage quickly, and with that he began to move forward, no longer aiming from the shoulder but with his M-16 held waist-high, throwing rounds into the jungle at belly height. He did not look back but could hear his comrades moving with him. Their charge was effective, with accurate firing. Enemy dead and wounded grew quickly.

Their leader knew they had been outgunned and called for a retreat. Gabriel sensed the sudden change and knew the enemy was pulling back. He dropped to one knee; rifle raised to his shoulder again and flipped to semi-automatic. Those around him followed his lead, even the lieutenant.

Gabriel knew it was better to wait. Often, the sudden retreat of an enemy force was just a ploy to draw them into a trap.

He saw sudden movement just a few yards in front. A Việt Cộng soldier was attempting to run. Gabriel fired a round just to the right of the left shoulder blade of the fleeing soldier, killing him instantly. Gabriel would attempt to kill every fleeing soldier he saw. That was his job. It was his duty.

The soldier he had just killed was the same Việt Cộng Gabriel had hit earlier. The wounded soldier had gained enough strength and awareness to try to make a run. The bullet Gabriel fired was dead on, ripping the heart out.

Gabriel waited, but enemy targets had disappeared. He scanned the jungle patiently, even the trees. After five minutes, the rest of Gabriel's unit began to move forward.

Gabriel moved to the dead Việt Cộng soldier. He looked and saw nothing more than a boy. This was not the first boy Gabriel had killed, and he knew it would not be the last.

He realized they had engaged a mixed unit of NVA and Việt Cộng. He knew the silhouette of the helmet he had seen was NVA. In the south, his unit had never engaged the NVA. It had been purely Việt Cộng they fought, but in the Central Highlands it could be either—or both.

Gabriel waited next to the dead soldier. The soldier looked so young, but only two years younger than Gabriel. The rest watched cautiously as Gabriel began to move forward slowly. He looked intently ahead, waiting again for the sight of movement.

He saw none but still brought his weapon to his shoulder and fired three rounds ahead. There was no return fire. He waited and fired three more rounds. Again, there was no return fire.

He stood in a low crouch and duck-walked ahead ten feet or so. He made a forward motion with his left hand. He, along with the others, started moving forward.

He heard a shot from behind and to his left. He recognized the sound of an M-16. It was obvious someone had seen movement of another enemy soldier. With the sound of that shot, there was still no return fire. The enemy was on the move in a fast retreat.

The lieutenant gave the halt command and was quickly on the radio, calling for a medevac response. Three of the Americans had been wounded. Claude Jarrett, a PFC from Chicago, had been hit badly. When he opened up with his M-60, several of the enemy took aim at him. The medic worked on him furiously, but it was obvious this young Black soldier from the inner city of Chicago was not going to live.

The medic's voice cut through the gun smoke and noise, sharp with the kind of command that came from necessity rather than rank. "Hold this. Hold pressure right here—don't let up." A private dropped to his knees and pressed both hands into Claude's uniform as if he could push the life back in.

Claude lay on his back, eyes half-open, trying to focus on faces that came and went above him. His chest rose in short, ragged lifts. Each breath sounded wetter than the last. The medic tore open a packet with his teeth and slapped gauze into place, then reached again for another. His hands were red to the wrists.

"Stay with me," the medic said. It wasn't prayer. It wasn't hope. It was a demand—an order thrown against the reality of blood loss.

Claude's mouth moved. At first there was no sound, then a thin rasp came out, almost swallowed by the jungle.

"Tell… my granny…" he tried.

The medic leaned closer. "Say it again."

Claude's eyes fluttered. "Tell her… I—" The words broke and did not come back.

A man behind them swore and looked away, blinking hard. Another muttered, "Goddamn," as if the word could cover what everyone could see.

The lieutenant hovered a step back, face tight, wanting to do something and unable to do anything that mattered. He looked toward Gabriel, as if expecting the point man to give him a solution the way he gave hand signals.

Gabriel did not look away from the jungle line. He kept his rifle up and his body angled forward, listening for the enemy to return, because in Vietnam even grief could be ambushed. Yet the sound of the medic's work, the wet struggling breath, and the sudden quiet as that breath thinned—all of it carved itself into him.

The medic's shoulders sagged just slightly, like a man setting down a weight he had been carrying at full extension. He kept working anyway, stubborn, methodical, until the moment came when his hands stopped fighting and began only arranging—closing, covering, making the scene look less like the violence it was.

Gabriel kept an active eye on the jungle ahead, waiting for the return of the enemy. He was quite certain they were gone, but one could never be sure. As he watched, he could hear the distant whop-whop-whop of the Huey medevacs and gunships coming to take the wounded out and to hunt the retreating enemy.

Claude Jarrett died as the medic worked on him.

Word was passed to Gabriel. He moved back just far enough to see the medic kneeling over Claude's body. The medic's hands were slick with blood.

"I'm sorry," the medic said quietly without looking up. "I couldn't stop it."

Gabriel nodded. "You did what you could."

The medic shook his head once. "He was gone before the bird even got close."

Gabriel looked down at Claude, then back toward the jungle. "Thank you," he said. It was all he could manage.

Gabriel thought about Claude and wondered how his family would feel. He wondered how his own family would feel if they were to get the same news. Gabriel and Claude seemed to be complete opposites. Neither could imagine the other's life. Gabriel had never seen the inner city of any city. The closest had been Knoxville, as he took the trip by bus to and from the induction center. Claude had never spent a day in the woods until the first bivouac in basic training.

Like most units in the United States Army, there was a separation between the Black and white soldiers. There was no malice, nor any necessary intention; it just seemed to be that way. Yet Gabriel and Claude had struck up a tacit friendship, one in which they seemed to enjoy learning about each other's lives. It was as though two aliens were learning about life on different planets.

Gabriel did not look back as he and the others set up a perimeter to protect the incoming Hueys. Charges were set to blow down a swath of trees for the medevacs to descend.

Gabriel moved back a few feet, returning to the dead Việt Cộng soldier's body. He glanced down, and the sense of remorse he felt each time he took another human life settled in. He knew that those of his unit who were wounded would be carried away by the medevac helicopters.

Gabriel searched the dead Việt Cộng for any intelligence but found none. There was no identification. Gabriel wondered about the dead boy. Was he from a nearby village? How would his family be notified?

Once the wounded Americans were lifted out, the unit continued its patrol. Their orders were to return to Camp

Radcliff before dark. Gabriel knew it would take about two more hours to make it down the mountain. He wondered why the NVA and Việt Cộng were moving together through these mountains. He did not realize that many NVA and Việt Cộng units were spread throughout this mountain overlooking An Khê.

It was only Gabriel's keen eye and nose that had spurred this engagement. The mixed unit of NVA and Việt Cộng did not intend to engage the Americans. They had other plans for the coming hours. Even though Hòn Cong Mountain was full of enemy soldiers, Gabriel's unit would not meet them again that day.

Gabriel listened to the medevacs flying east toward Camp Radcliff, just a short distance away. He kept his eyes on the jungle ahead. There was a deep awareness and sadness that he would never see Claude again.

As he heard the helicopters leaving, he realized how thirsty he was. He thought about the cold water from a mountain spring, the smell of rhododendron and azaleas that would be in bloom in just a few more months back home. As he stood in the heat, he thought of the snow that must be lying on the ground today at his mountain home.

He then thought of summer days back home. There was a bit of an inward chuckle. He thought he would never complain about the heat back home again. This heat was quite different. Even on this next-to-last day of January, the heat would strip one of every ounce of energy.

The heat in his mountain home seemed to be life-giving, whereas the heat here was just a specter of death. It seemed that all was rotten in the mountains of the Central Highlands, whereas back home all seemed fresh and fragrant. He longed for those mountains. He longed for the hoarfrost on autumn leaves. He longed for a fresh drink of water from a mountain spring.

He longed to be away from this death, but no one would know. No one would ever see it in his face, nor hear it in his voice. He would not complain. He would not voice his desire to be away from this God-forsaken place. No one would hear the grief in his heart as he inwardly cried over Claude Jarrett and the dead Việt Cộng.

He would continue to look forward into the jungle, knowing that for the next few months he would see and bring more death.

It was then that his eye caught the sight of a Buddhist shrine a hundred feet down the mountainside on his left. It sat next to a mountain road—the road they were to take that would lead them off the mountain. These small shrines dotted the countryside, some in the most peculiar places.

The shrine was small—nothing like the churches back home—but it had the same purpose as any place a human being set aside for the holy: it marked a boundary between what a man could control and what he could not. A little roof of tile or cement, darkened by rain. A place for incense. A place for offerings that birds and insects would eventually claim. It looked fragile against the mountain, but it had endured longer than most soldiers did.

Gabriel felt the tightness in his chest rise again, not from fear of enemy fire, but from the weight that always followed killing. He tried to tell himself what he told himself every time—that it was duty, that it was necessity, that if he did not kill, he would be killed. Those things were true. They were not enough.

He thought of Claude's face—how it had tried to hold on, how it had slipped away anyway. He thought of the dead Việt Cộng boy, his body lying in the leaves like discarded clothing, nameless to the Americans who stepped past him. He had searched the body for intelligence like he was trained to do, but he had found nothing human that the Army cared about: no paper, no name, no proof that the boy had been more than a target.

Back home, Jonas would have known the name of every neighbor within ten miles. Back home, a dead boy would have been mourned as someone's child. Here, a dead boy was a number—if he was counted at all.

Gabriel did not know the words to a Buddhist prayer. He did not know the proper gesture. He only knew the posture of humility his mother had taught him at the edge of her bed when she prayed. When the column moved again and he drifted near the shrine, he slowed half a step and bowed his head, just enough that no one would notice unless they were watching for it.

"Lord," he whispered, barely moving his lips, "take care of the ones I can't."

He wanted to ask forgiveness for the dead boy, for Claude, for himself—for what his hands were learning to do too well. But the only words that came were the simplest ones, the ones that had been in his mouth since childhood.

"Have mercy."

He lifted his eyes once more toward the shrine. The jungle gave nothing back. It never did. Still, the brief act steadied him the way a familiar verse steadied him: not by erasing the guilt, but by keeping it from hollowing him completely.

He saw the shrine and wished he knew the name of the dead Việt Cộng. He knew nothing of Buddhism but had the desire to pray. He wondered who would grieve for the young man. Where was his home?

Gabriel had no knowledge of the young Việt Cộng soldier and the others who came from a not-so-distant valley fifteen kilometers east of his current location. He had never heard of the place called Happy Valley, a place he would experience in the coming months.

Four other dead enemies were found. The bodies of the dead enemy were searched. As usual, little information was gathered.

It was time for Gabriel's unit to move out. They were to move down along the road Gabriel had seen and make their way to waiting deuce-and-a-half trucks to carry them back to Camp Radcliff.

As they moved out, Gabriel wondered if he would ever see his mountain home again.

Gabriel led the unit down the mountain, staying fifty feet from the road. He knew there were still enemy soldiers on the mountain, but he and the other men hoped and prayed there would be no more contact that day.

At Camp Radcliff, officers studied intelligence and the contact with the enemy units, trying to digest its meaning. Two hours passed when Gabriel and his unit arrived at the rendezvous point. They waited for the deuce-and-a-halves. The wait was not long.

The unit loaded onto the trucks and headed back along the road skirting the mountain to a good night's rest—or so they thought.

All through the country, intelligence was recognizing the movement of Việt Cộng and NVA units. Senior officers questioned the reason for all the movement. As hidden as the meaning and purpose was, it would be violently evident within eight hours.

Gabriel's unit arrived at their temporary quarters about an hour later. Chow was ready in the mess hall when they arrived. It was strange, but the death of Claude Jarrett and the wounding of two others was almost an afterthought to most of the men. They quickly ate, showered, and some were soon off to Sin City.

Gabriel never ventured that way. He was content spending time in the hooch reading a Western of some sort. Gabriel had never been much of a reader except for what was necessary for school and his nightly reading of the Bible. He carried the tradition of reading the Bible nightly with him to Vietnam. The only time he did not read the Bible at night was on a jungle patrol.

Otherwise, he always read the Bible first and then said his prayers. After that, he would read one of his Western novels. He had gotten into reading the Westerns of Louis L'Amour. He would read until he fell asleep, losing himself in the action of the novels and dreaming of the West and what it must have been like in those olden days.

Most of the guys in the hooch went somewhere, either to an on-base EM Club or into Sin City. Most were going to get drunk, and some were going to get drunk and laid. Gabriel was often asked but never accepted the invitation. He was content with reading the Bible and Westerns and then going to sleep.

There was nothing scheduled for his unit on the 31st, so that night would be a good night of rest.

Gabriel finished his reading and once again prayed. That night he asked God to watch over Claude. He thought Claude was a good person. He did not quite understand him but still found him to be a good friend. Tears came to his eyes as he prayed.

Regardless of the conditions, Gabriel always prayed. He prayed for his family, and then he prayed for himself. He prayed for his soul. He accepted that the killing was necessary but could not rid himself of the guilt.

He thought of the young man he had shot that day. He looked so young—just a boy. He wished he had not taken the shot, but at that moment, it had been his immediate response when he saw the boy rise up.

Gabriel hated the killing. He hated pulling the trigger every time, but he accepted that to live, the killing must be done, and he had a great desire to continue to live. Any time he took a shot, it was intended to kill.

He finished his prayers.

On his cot, the thought of home came to his mind. He was beginning to drift in and out of sleep. A few hours passed.

He heard his father calling him from somewhere beyond the cabin.

"Gabriel... come on now."

His mother sat by the window, sewing. He could hear her voice as well, soft and steady.

"Gabriel, supper's about ready."

Their voices drifted in and out, just as he remembered them. He found himself flying overhead, circling the cabin. Flying—how was he flying? The flight felt so real. He circled above, flying low over the cabin. He saw his brother Jacob sitting on the front porch. His sisters were working in the garden.

He flew high and then swooped down. Then, for no reason, he felt himself falling.

In the dream, he slammed to the ground, and his eyes flew open with the sudden impact.

He immediately realized there was an explosion nearby.

Just as his eyes flew open, the camp sirens exploded with their harshness. He and the others in their temporary hooch responded by dressing immediately. About half were still drunk from all the drinking just a few hours earlier, but they responded as well. All were quickly dressed and out the door.

They were soon on deuce-and-a-halves headed toward the perimeter. It did not matter how often they faced combat; each time they felt the same anxiety.

The perimeter guard towers were already manned by the night's guard detail. Each tower was throwing bullets into the surrounding jungle, and in turn, bullets were flying back at them. Gabriel and the rest of his unit spread along the perimeter and began returning fire from ground level.

Gabriel quickly realized that the opposing force was not large enough to pose a threat of breaching the wire. All along the perimeter, other units were facing the same style of attack. Gabriel could hear firing from all directions. He could hear one specific place in the distance where the firing was much heavier. There were multiple explosions. He knew that was the location where the enemy was attempting to breach the wire.

He moved to find Lieutenant Davenport, not knowing that the lieutenant had just received a radio command to gather his unit together and wait for transport to take them to the place of heaviest attack. Soon they were loaded and on their way.

Enough reinforcements arrived at the location near the main gate to lay down heavy suppressive fire that drove the Việt Cộng units back. They were attacking from the city of An Khê. The battle dwindled quickly but continued until the first rays of dawn. The enemy forces retreated to their safe havens.

His unit quickly took count of their own and realized that none had been wounded in the four-hour skirmish. Gabriel knew they had inflicted damage on the enemy. He knew he had done damage himself, but again he found no joy or sense of accomplishment in it—only the same feeling of necessity.

The next day, Gabriel and his unit were back in the bush, working out of a firebase southwest of An Khê.

A few days later, in the early morning hours, a grandmother in Chicago, Illinois, sat in her rocker. She rocked slowly, rereading the telegram delivered the night before. She wiped tears from her cheeks. She could see Claude as a small boy. She saw his big grin. She knew how much she loved him.

She read the telegram until it was time to dress. She donned her crossing guard uniform. She picked up her STOP sign and headed out the door. She would lead children safely across a Chicago street intersection. She would smile and talk to the children. She would tell them to have a good day at school and that she would see them that evening. She smiled and waved at the cars passing by.

When her morning duty was done, she walked to her church. She told the pastor that Claude was coming home and that she wanted a special celebration for her beloved grandson.

A month later, a wounded Việt Cộng soldier returned to his home in the upper end of a mountain valley northeast of An Khê. He told his family of the killing of his friend, Dũng, by the Americans on the eve of Tết. The father felt the responsibility to inform Dũng's mother, Phương, about her son's death.

He walked the mile or so up the valley and told Phương. The grief was hidden in her stoic face, but the pain was just as real. Dũng's younger sister, Liên, sat on the floor of their hut and cried.

Gabriel's unit was on constant patrol after Tết. They patrolled every sector surrounding An Khê and Hòn Cong Mountain. A large plain encircled Camp Radcliff and Hòn Cong Mountain. Gabriel's unit would spend a couple of weeks working out of a firebase. They would return to An Khê for a few days and then move to another firebase.

In early April, Gabriel and his unit would be sent to patrol a mountain ridge for a few miles and then descend into a valley fifteen kilometers northeast of An Khê. Those familiar with the valley had tagged it as Happy Valley.

Chapter 4

The Men

Psalm 91:1–2 (KJV)

> "He that dwelleth in the secret place of the Most High shall abide under the shadow of the Almighty. I will say of the LORD, He is my refuge and my fortress: my God; in him will I trust."

The morning mountain humidity soaked through the hooch in the early hours of April 1, 1968, as Sergeant Gabriel Fox sat upright on his cot. Mosquito netting was draped all around. He could hear a distant firefight, along with the boom of artillery raining hell down on some enemy position in the distance.

He was spending this supposed quiet time studying the topo maps of a mountain ridge about twelve kilometers east of An Khê. He could hear his comrades in their bunks, sleeping soundly. In the dark, he used his Army-issued flashlight to study the maps.

Gabriel eased the light away from the contour lines and let the beam fall across the small stack of personal things kept close to his cot. His Bible lay there, its cover darkened by sweat and handling, corners softened by months of use. It was the one piece of home that felt immune to distance—ink and paper, yes, but also voice. The words sounded the way his mother read them, the way his father made him read them, slow and certain, as if Scripture itself could build a fence around a man.

He opened carefully, pages whisper-thin beneath his thumb, and the flashlight found the familiar place. He did not choose it at random. On nights when the sounds outside the wire felt too close, he returned to the same story—as if reading it again might keep him from becoming the kind of man who could no longer feel anything at all.

He read of a son who had run out of a good home and come back with nothing but hunger and shame. Gabriel's lips barely moved as his eyes tracked the lines, absorbing the rhythm of the King James words. He could see it in his mind as clearly as any ridge on a map: the long road, the dust, the thinness of the returning boy, and the father who did not wait on the porch to measure what was deserved. The father ran.

The thought struck him harder than the distant artillery. His own father was not the running kind. Jonas Fox was built of endurance and restraint, a man who loved without spectacle. Yet Gabriel could picture him all the same—standing in the doorway of the cabin, one hand braced on the frame, the other holding back whatever would break loose if he let it. And behind Jonas, he could see Esther near the stove, apron on, hair pinned, turning her head at the sound of boots on the porch. She would not run either, but her face would change first—hope arriving before any words did.

Gabriel closed his eyes for a moment, letting that picture settle. He did not know if he would ever walk back into that doorway. But he knew what he wanted his heart to be if he did.

"Lord," he whispered, voice lost beneath the damp hush of the hooch, "keep me fit to come home. Don't let me turn into a stranger."

He looked back down at the open page, held the light steady, and read on until the door creaked.

He traced the contour lines with a blunt fingertip, following the ridges the way he would have followed a deer trail back home—slow, patient, imagining the land before he ever set foot on it. The mountains here were not the Smokies, but they spoke a familiar language: folds and hollows, saddles and draws, places where a man could move unseen or die without anyone knowing exactly where he fell.

The verse from earlier drifted through his mind—not as poetry, but as something practical. Refuge. Fortress. The words sat in his chest the way the weight of his rifle sat against his shoulder: constant, accepted, and necessary. In Vietnam, a man learned quickly what he could trust. Sometimes it was training. Sometimes it was the man beside him. Sometimes it was only God.

He listened again to the distant cannon, the faint crack of small-arms fire, and the steady hum of insects that never seemed to sleep. For a moment he imagined the kitchen at home—his mother's hands, his father's quiet presence at the table, the smell of coffee, grease, and biscuits. He did not let himself linger there long. A man who lingered too much in memories could get someone killed.

He heard the door of the hooch creak open with the yawn of the door spring expanding. The Charge of Quarters stuck his head into the hooch and, in a loud whisper, said, "Hey guys, time to move. Fifteen minutes till chow!"

Gabriel heard the other men stirring from their sleep. The men did not dawdle; each started moving immediately, spouting words of encouragement laced with profanities. Each was well rested. They had gone to bed early and slept soundly. It was amazing how they could sleep so well the night before a patrol, but each of them did.

Sergeant Fox had awakened about forty-five minutes earlier. He had been promoted to sergeant three months before. He was the unit's point man, their lead. He led them everywhere they went in the mountains, except into Sin City, the infamous bordello of the Central Highlands located just outside An Khê next to Camp Radcliff.

His unit worked principally in the field. They would move from one firebase to another, trying to identify enemy movement. Their job put them in constant contact with the enemy. On occasion, they would be brought back to Camp Radcliff for about three days of rest and relaxation. The officers and NCOs would go over plans for their next objectives.

Some of the guys more friendly to Gabriel would encourage him to go with them into Sin City, but he would never accept, telling them he did not have time for it. A few went as often as they could; others went reluctantly. They felt as if it was mandatory. Most stayed in the company area or at least on camp. Some lied about their exploits just to fit in.

Gabriel was born in a strict Baptist home in the mountains of East Tennessee. There was no way he was going to risk his soul doing such things. Gabriel stayed at camp and read cowboy novels while others engaged in other activities, whether it was basketball, baseball, volleyball, or football. Some played cards for hours.

Gabriel participated in none of those activities. He would not go with them to the camp bars. He did not drink, even though he was raised distilling moonshine. He would spend hours reading a Western novel.

The only book in Gabriel's home had been the family Bible, and it was mandatory for him to read every night. His father and mother would listen as he and his sisters read the Bible aloud. There was an older brother, but he was slow, as the people around his home called it. In this case, Jacob was terribly slow.

Occasionally, Gabriel would bring home a book from the small school he attended just outside of Townsend, Tennessee. Most were biographies written for younger students in short novelettes. Gabriel enjoyed reading about George Washington, Abraham Lincoln, and Thomas Jefferson. For a boy who lived in a cabin with no electricity, his favorite story was of Thomas Edison inventing the light bulb.

He read his first Western after he arrived in Việt Nam. He found one in the PX at Cam Ranh Bay (Vịnh Cam Ranh), where he first landed upon arriving in Việt Nam. He bought it and read as much as he could before being deployed to his unit outside Biên Hòa. He kept it in his footlocker next to his cot in the bunker he stayed in at a firebase. He would read it every chance he had. He completed it prior to his unit moving to the Central Highlands.

At Camp Radcliff, he bought two more at the PX. He read them as often as possible, which was only when they had the opportunity to be at Camp Radcliff.

He arrived in country on August 4, 1967. The first three months were spent outside Biên Hòa in one of many firebases. In the south, Gabriel was just another ground pounder and showed no exceptional skills other than his shooting. He was a deadly shot. He was prone to firing his weapon on semi-automatic, taking careful aim and firing one round at a time.

In November, they were sent to the Central Highlands. His unit was not officially a long-range reconnaissance patrol, but that is what they did. His unit was a downsized platoon, comprised of two squads. Personnel had been pulled from the brigade and transferred north.

Each company in the battalion was reduced in size, and the reduction was sudden. Orders came down one morning just weeks earlier, and movement started that afternoon. The place was a mess. Units and personnel were being moved north rapidly. Each company in the battalion took heavy losses in manpower.

Lieutenant Russell L. Davenport had joined the company in early January, and Staff Sergeant Abraham Lacey was brought in five weeks after the Tết Offensive. Gabriel was now one of the older members of the company. He had been in country for eight months and had proven himself quite handily.

In the short time SSG Lacey had been with the company, he had grown to appreciate Gabriel. He thought it was hilarious that he could barely understand a thing Gabriel was saying, even though both were born and raised in the United States. Gabriel's accent could be traced to the Scottish Highlands of three centuries prior. Many of the words he used dated to that time—words even the Scots no longer used. Those words were locked away in the isolation of the Southern Appalachians.

Staff Sergeant Lacey had grown up at the start of the hard times in Detroit. He was born in 1943. The fathers in his neighborhood were off to war, and the mothers were working in factories to support the war effort. His father left for the Pacific six months before Abraham Lincoln Lacey was born. His father was a proud Marine.

Abraham's grandfather and father worked at the River Rouge Plant for the Ford Motor Company prior to the start of the war. After the war began, Abraham's father joined the Marines. He was a transportation specialist. His job was to get food, supplies, and ammunition to the grunts in the field.

En route to deliver rations, his company was engaged by a Japanese force. Though truck drivers, the Americans fought bravely, driving back the enemy. Abraham's father was one of five Americans killed in the battle. He fought hand-to-hand with two Japanese soldiers and killed them both. He was dragging a wounded Marine to safety when a bullet severed a carotid artery. Abraham's father bled out and died on the spot, along with the wounded Marine he was trying to save.

Most of the fathers in the neighborhood worked at the River Rouge prior to the start of the war. Life was good, even though the men had gone to war. The "Big Three" automakers had gone into war production. In most of the factories, the wives went to work in place of their husbands. They lived in prosperous neighborhoods. Like all Americans, they had to go on rations.

Abraham never met his father. He knew his father died bravely at the Battle of Bloody Ridge on Guadalcanal. He had seen the flag and the ribbons awarded to him, but he never felt him—never felt his presence. His father was such a distant part of his life. His grandfather told him how much his father loved the country, but Abraham had a hard time understanding why.

Abraham grew up in hard times. It was rough. By the time Abraham was in his early teens, the good jobs had dried up in Detroit. Detroit was becoming a shadow of its glorious past. So much of the automobile production had been moved out of the city to minimize strike situations and to seek cheaper labor, even if it was organized. The River Rouge had been downsized by two-thirds starting in the mid-1950s.

That magnificent city—Detroit—so beautifully built, started decaying. The decay was sharp and quick. Life just got damn tough for a lot of people. Neighborhoods were split apart and became completely isolated from each other by interstate construction. Those prosperous neighborhoods no longer had the financial means to sustain themselves.

Sergeant Lacey's mother died when he was eleven. He went to live with his widowed grandfather. The old man had been a blacksmith in Alabama. Born in the 1890s, he lived in poverty his entire youth but worked hard. He moved to Detroit in 1929 with his family and went to work for "Mr. Henry." He was a metalsmith at the River Rouge.

For many years, he thought he would always prosper. For a poor boy from Alabama, he sure was living a good life. But things had changed. He lost both of his sons in World War II. His wife died six years later. He had a good retirement income, so the bills were paid, but he was spiritually broken. He grieved heavily for those he had lost.

He and Abraham barely talked. The old man drank some, but he was not a drunk; it just helped ease the pain. He let Abraham do as he pleased.

Abraham Lacey ran the only way he knew. He spent six months in a juvenile detention center when he was sixteen for breaking into a neighborhood store and stealing cigarettes. He dropped out of school upon his return from the detention center and ran rough for the next six years.

He and two of his friends stole a 1964 Impala convertible in late fall of 1965. Abraham was twenty-two. It was only the luck of the draw that he had not been arrested since his juvenile days. Fortune looked his way until that November night in 1965. In less than two hours after the Impala was stolen, Abraham and his two friends were in jail.

That night, after being booked, Abraham and his friends were approached by a lawyer from the Public Defender's Office, a young woman just out of Michigan State, and a lawyer from the Prosecutor's Office. They came to offer the three young men a deal. The young woman was simply following orders from the Public Defender's Office. The military needed men. The buildup in Vietnam had started.

Abraham and the other two were given a choice: military or jail. Like so many, Sergeant Lacey chose the former, while his cohorts chose jail. The old man had died two years earlier, so there was no one who would really miss him.

Abraham was kept in jail overnight. The next morning, he, and a group of young men from Detroit loaded onto a bus for the recruitment center. Late the next day, Lacey was at Fort Knox for basic training.

Those first few moments upon arrival blew him away. Men were screaming in everyone's face as loud and as hard as they could. The men screaming did not look as though they needed to be messed with. Even the smaller guys doing the screaming looked tough as hell. Yet these men were not going to be nearly as tough as the ones he would meet in five more days.

For the next five days, this group of young men went through all kinds of preparation for basic training. The very first thing they did was get a military haircut. It did not matter how short one's hair was—they were going to get a haircut. At the rapid speed the barbers moved, the very sharp electric shears would often draw blood.

That was the first of the very demoralizing, self-esteem-lowering actions taken to condition them to accept orders without ever questioning them.

They were issued uniforms. They were taken through medical and dental exams, with teeth being pulled if necessary. They were inoculated against every form of communicable disease known. They were given instructions on the proper way a soldier should behave. They were given basic instruction on marching, saluting, and maintaining their barracks.

After five days, they were prepped with their gear and ready to be picked up by the Drill Sergeants of their new basic training units.

They were waiting in their temporary barracks, most sitting on their duffel bags. Suddenly, the double doors of the old wooden barracks—built during World War II—came flying open. Drill Instructors came crashing through the doors, screaming like demons.

Abraham was a tall fellow and had been known to be a fighter in his old neighborhood, but these men scared him. He could not help but notice two of the Drill Sergeants—one about five feet nine inches tall, and the other about Abraham's height. Their Drill Instructor hats sat perfectly on their heads. Their heads were held high. Their utility jackets were starched and perfectly ironed. Their boots sparkled, they shined so bright.

Suddenly, a picture he had seen of his father flashed before him. He looked at the two men and thought this must have been what his father looked like. These two men, without ever knowing it, became Abraham's mentors over the next eight weeks.

Basic training was initially hard for Abraham. He had not been an athlete, so he was unaccustomed to arduous training. He was never much of a student and found reading the various slides they were shown to be difficult. The first three weeks were hell, but then his body accepted the conditioning.

Abraham began to excel. He became the fastest runner in his basic training unit. He maneuvered through the obstacle course faster than anyone. He was the fastest on the rope climb. He watched his two mentors and wanted to be like them. He wanted to look sharp in his uniform. He wanted to hold his head high. Neither of those men smoked, so Abraham gave up his smoking habit.

Abraham graduated at the top of his basic training unit. When he received the award, he wished that the man he had never known, his father, could be there. He longed for his father to know.

His two mentors were Airborne, and Abraham made the decision to go Airborne. Five months later, after AIT and the three weeks of jump school, Abraham was back in Detroit on leave. He stayed only a few days. He did not search for any of his old running buddies. He was initially granted a month's leave but volunteered to report early.

Abraham had one principal mission while in Detroit. For the first time on his own, Abraham went to visit his father's gravesite. He knelt and prayed. Once his prayer was complete, he said aloud, "I am your son, Private First-Class Abraham Lincoln Lacey, and I am proud you are my father. May God give me the courage you had. I love you." He stood and saluted the headstone.

Soon he was in the Mekong Delta, exhibiting his father's courage and more. He knew being a soldier was going to be his profession. He worked diligently in his chosen profession. He was an excellent, brave soldier. He soon made corporal, and within six months became a sergeant.

Shortly after being promoted to sergeant, Abraham received his first wound, a bullet through his right thigh. Fortunately, the bullet passed through without causing much damage. He was sent to the hospital at Đồng Tâm Base west of Mỹ Tho. He spent a week in the hospital. Upon release, he was assigned to the battalion headquarters at Đồng Tâm to fully recuperate. He spent five weeks working in the commanding general's office.

The first weekend there, he and others traveled into Mỹ Tho. The cities were relatively safe. He and the others walked the streets, dropping into various bars. Abraham soon tired of the bar scene and left to walk the city on his own.

He found himself walking on Lê Lợi Street (Đường Lê Lợi). The street ran perpendicular to the Mỹ Tho River (Sông Mỹ Tho). He watched the people scurrying about. The street was crowded and busy. He walked by different food vendors. The smell of the food was pleasing to his senses. He wanted to eat but was hesitant. He had no idea what to order from the men and women selling food along the street.

Occasionally, different young boys would run up to him, soliciting him to have sex with the boy's sister. According to each boy, the girl was thirteen and still a virgin. Abraham would decline, but each time the boy would chase after him, almost demanding Abraham go with him.

Other children would run up begging. He saw one young girl, no more than five, that was of half American descent. Her hair was partially blond. It saddened him to see such a young child on the streets begging. He felt sympathy, reached into his pocket, and pulled out several MPC, the military currency. In an instant, the young girl jerked the whole lot of bills out of his hand and took off running.

Abraham started to run after the child but suddenly found himself surrounded by a number of children. Each was grabbing at his pockets. Abraham forced his way out of the herd of children. Fortunately, he still had his billfold.

He continued walking the street, which was crowded with Americans from each branch of service. He saw several exiting one of the buildings lining the street. Above the door hung a sign with the words, "Nhà Hàng Ngon," with "Restaurant" beneath.

He was very hungry and thought if other Americans were eating there, it must be a good place to eat. He entered the door and immediately saw a young woman waiting tables. She had on the traditional Vietnamese silk tunic and pants, áo dài. The tunic was royal blue and the pants were white. She wore a white palm-leaf conical hat, nón lá. She was beautiful.

Abraham had never had a meaningful relationship, but the beautiful young woman took his breath away. He stood in the door. The young woman looked at him and pointed to a small table that two airmen had just gotten up from. He sat at the table, without being able to take his eyes off the young woman.

She handed him a menu, removed the dishes, and cleaned the table. He was still looking at her when she asked in broken English, "What you want?"

She was used to the Americans having no idea what to order.

He just stared at her.

"You want phở gà, chicken soup?" she asked.

He nodded.

"You want cà phê sữa đá?" she asked.

Again, he nodded his head.

He had no idea what he had ordered, but was going to attempt to eat what was brought to the table. Soon, a bowl of steaming soup and a coffee cup with a metal container sitting on top, and a glass of ice were brought to the table, along with chopsticks, đũa, made from bamboo and a metal spoon. Abraham sat for several moments, staring at everything before him. He was lost.

As he sat there, the young woman came to his table again. She looked at him and said, "Give," pointing to the chopsticks. He handed them to her. She picked up the metal spoon, thìa kim loại, and deftly began mixing the ingredients in the bowl. A thick wad of noodles sat at the bottom. She used the chopsticks and spoon to separate the noodles. She stirred the ingredients and handed the chopsticks and spoon back to Abraham.

The smell of the soup floated up to him. He took a deep breath and thought it was the most delicious smell he had ever smelled. He dipped the spoon into the liquid. Again, he thought it was delicious.

He made a few attempts using the chopsticks and had little success. He finally reached in and pulled out a piece of chicken. Again, it was delicious. He struggled some but was able to pull a length of noodles out. They were hot. He bit part of the noodles off and thought they tasted so good.

Within minutes, Abraham was using the chopsticks fairly well.

Again, the young woman returned to the table and stirred and poured the contents of the cup into the glass of ice. She handed the glass to Abraham and said, "Drink, little," while holding her forefinger and thumb close together.

Abraham sipped. The drink was sweet, with a chocolate taste. He found himself fully enjoying the food and drink.

Abraham finished his meal. He thought it was the most enjoyable thing he had ever eaten. The young woman returned to the table. He was completely surprised when she told him, "One MPC." One MPC was a dollar.

He gladly reached into his billfold and pulled out a five-MPC note. He handed it to her and told her to keep it. She looked at him and said, "Cảm ơn bạn rất nhiều." She smiled and bowed.

Abraham had no idea what she said, but he responded, "You are welcome."

He knew it was time to leave the restaurant. It was getting late in the afternoon, and curfew was at dark. He left the restaurant as reluctantly as he had ever left anywhere.

Working out of the battalion commander's office had its luxuries. He found that he was given different tasks that would take him into Mỹ Tho. His daily duties were usually over by about 4:00 p.m., and he found he could catch a ride into Mỹ Tho daily.

On those trips, he went nowhere else except to Nhà Hàng Ngon. During those few weeks of his temporary assignment, he quickly got to know the young woman Hoa, flower. He fell in love with her immediately.

For the first week of his regular visits, Hoa remained straightforward. There was no conversation other than what was necessary to order food and the occasional instruction she gave him. She had difficulty pronouncing "Abraham," but after the first week of his visits, she began to say, "Abraham!" every time he walked through the door. He noticed that she called none of the other customers by their names.

Hoa sensed that Abraham was a good man. Her parents were not happy that she paid so much attention to the black-skinned American.

Hoa spoke little English except for what was necessary to communicate with the Americans about ordering food. To her, the Americans were only customers—except for this one tall man. She found herself looking forward to his visits to the restaurant and was disappointed on the days he did not come. With her few words of English, she would scold Abraham when he failed to appear.

Those few weeks passed quickly. Abraham healed quite well and no longer limped as he walked. He was ready to go back to the bush.

On the last day before he was scheduled to return to his unit, he walked into Nhà Hàng Ngon and told Hoa it was his last day to visit. She understood. Tears came to her eyes as she listened to him say, "Tôi yêu em rất nhiều. Tôi muốn làm vợ tôi. Tôi muốn đưa em đến Mỹ."

"I love you very much. I want you to be my wife. I want to take you to America."

Her reply was simple and straightforward: "Em muốn."

"I want."

They talked for a while, upsetting her parents. He explained that he had to leave but would make arrangements and that they would marry soon. She did not understand everything he said but grasped the meaning.

The next day, he returned to his unit.

In his free time, Abraham began working on the arrangements to marry Hoa. It was a difficult and lengthy process. As soon as he received approval, he would request a few days' leave to return to Mỹ Tho to marry her.

He received notice the night before his unit was scheduled to go on patrol near Bến Tre that approval had been granted. He immediately requested a three-day leave to begin upon his return from the patrol. He had three months remaining on his tour. He wanted to be able to send Hoa to America once he was back in the States.

Early on the first day of the patrol, a bullet caught Abraham in the upper right chest, fracturing two ribs and blowing a hole in the upper lobe of his right lung. Fortunately, no major arteries were hit.

The medic tended to Abraham quickly. He and another man sat Abraham upright and immediately removed his jungle fatigue jacket. The medic retrieved two field dressings and plastic wrap. He instructed Abraham to blow his breath out and hold it. Abraham did so. The medic held one dressing over the entrance wound and one over the exit wound while the second soldier wrapped the plastic tightly around them. Abraham was able to breathe without wheezing as he had been doing moments before.

There was not much of a firefight. It was one lone Việt Cộng soldier who gave up his life to shoot Abraham Lacey in the chest.

Sergeant Lacey was medevac'd to the field hospital at Đồng Tâm. His wound was critical, and from Đồng Tâm he was sent to Sài Gòn. From there, he was flown to a hospital in Japan. He spent six weeks in Japan and then returned to the States.

During his recuperation, Abraham made several attempts to contact his bride-to-be but never received a reply. His wound healed sufficiently. Once healed, he was sent to Germany. He immediately applied for duty in Vietnam. While waiting on orders, he was promoted to Staff Sergeant. He spent fifteen months in Germany and then returned to Vietnam.

Abraham was assigned to the 173rd Airborne Brigade at An Khê in the Central Highlands. Through that ordeal, he lost contact with Hoa. Her family sent her to live with relatives in Cần Thơ, a city seventy-six kilometers from Mỹ Tho.

Abraham spent three tours in Vietnam. On his third tour, he was the Sergeant Major of the battalion headquarters with the 101st Airborne at Phú Bài. On that tour, he met a young woman who remained his wife until the day she died forty-eight years later. They had two sons, one a doctor and the other a retired admiral in the Navy.

Upon returning from his third tour, Abraham—old by most standards—attended Officer Candidate School. He retired after twenty-six years as a Colonel, holding a law degree. He practiced law in Detroit. He was a defense lawyer, always looking for opportunities to give young people another chance with guidance.

He formed a group of successful professionals to mentor those young people. Abraham required a few things: discipline, self-worth, and the understanding that one could always do better. Their success rate was high. They mentored with love. Abraham loved his wife deeply and missed her after her death. Yet he never forgot Hoa.

Gabriel had been awake studying the topo maps to ensure he understood the terrain. He wanted a mental picture of every possible ambush site or place where a surprise encounter might occur. Lieutenant Davenport and Staff Sergeant Lacey had come to trust Gabriel's knowledge of mountain terrain and his ability to guide. They always included him in planning meetings for each patrol.

The men of the unit felt more secure with Gabriel at point. At five feet five inches, Gabriel was the smallest of the men, but each believed he was the toughest in the unit. A boy from the Smoky Mountains near Townsend, Gabriel had been educated his entire life for the tasks he would face over the coming days.

On their first patrol together, Staff Sergeant Lacey recognized Gabriel's skills and understood why he most often led point.

That day, they would begin a six-day patrol along a mountain ridge about fifty-five kilometers northwest of Quy Nhơn and twelve kilometers northeast of An Khê. About halfway along the ridge, they would descend into a remote valley. It and another nearby valley were often referred to as "Happy Valley."

The far end of the valley was remote and isolated. It ran from northwest to southeast, descending out of a series of mountains in the Vĩnh Thạnh District of Bình Định Province. The mountain ranges running south from Kon Tum toward Quy Nhơn formed a perfect corridor for both the Việt Cộng and the North Vietnamese Army.

Army intelligence was correct—there had been significant movement through the area for several days. The Army wanted direct ground observation, and Gabriel's company had proven itself capable through different assignments.

With Lieutenant Davenport and Staff Sergeant Lacey, the patrol would consist of sixteen men. They would divide into two groups: the first led by the lieutenant and the second by Staff Sergeant Lacey.

This was intended to be Lieutenant Russell L. Davenport's last patrol with the unit. He had received orders for promotion to captain and would be reassigned once the unit returned to An Khê.

Initially, Staff Sergeant Lacey's primary mission with the unit was to keep the lieutenant alive and professionally trained. It turned out Lieutenant Davenport was a quick learner. His official home was listed as Pulaski, Tennessee, but his father was a career Army Sergeant Major. The lieutenant attended Tennessee Tech on both a scholastic and an ROTC scholarship, earning a degree in mechanical engineering. After graduating, he immediately went to the infantry officer basic course at Fort Benning. When he graduated, he went directly to airborne school at Ft. Benning.

He had studied military strategy since childhood and was fascinated by his father's profession. He was especially pleased with his real-life instructor, Staff Sergeant Lacey, who understood the logistics of combat, the placement of men, and the orders required in serious situations.

Sergeant Gabriel Fox was their most valuable resource in training and familiarization with combat in the Central Highlands. Although Staff Sergeant Lacey was well versed in combat from his time in the Mekong Delta, the Central Highlands presented a new learning curve.

The unit often divided into two squads. The lieutenant, Sergeant Fox, and six men would lead. Staff Sergeant Lacey, another sergeant, and six men would follow approximately a kilometer behind and several hundred meters to the left of the lead squad.

In the early weeks after Staff Sergeant Lacey's arrival, they conducted shorter patrols to practice pacing and communication methods. Most of their activity was southwest of Hòn Cong Mountain or on the mountain itself, which overlooked the base at An Khê.

During their first four weeks together, they engaged the enemy on three occasions. They suffered several casualties—one KIA and two wounded. One thing became clear: they were now primarily engaging the North Vietnamese Army. The Việt Cộng had suffered significant losses during Tết and were no longer a formidable force.

For the remainder of America's presence in Việt Nam, it would be primarily a war against forces from the north.

Staff Sergeant Lacey would take seven men and follow a thousand meters behind Lieutenant Davenport, Gabriel, and the six others. The two groups would make the fifteen-kilometer journey in three days. Once in the valley, the unit would patrol the east side of the valley for an additional three days. Their movement would be slow and deliberate. Their task was to find the avenues by which the remaining Việt Cộng, and particularly the North Vietnamese Army, were moving through the area.

Lieutenant Davenport's group would scout along the east side of the ridge, while Staff Sergeant Lacey's group would scout the west side. This was strictly a reconnaissance mission. They were to avoid the enemy. Yet, if either squad made contact, they would be in close enough proximity to support one another.

As soon as the charge of quarters awakened the hooch, Gabriel left to meet with Lieutenant Davenport and Staff Sergeant Lacey. They spent the next thirty minutes going over the mission once again, confirming routes, spacing, and contingencies. After the men had eaten, they held a brief meeting with the rest of the unit and were ready for departure at dawn.

The three of them huddled over the map in a cramped corner where the light was weak and the noise of the waking camp could not easily carry. Davenport knelt with one knee down, pencil in hand, the motion of his mind as precise as his engineering training. Lacey stood above him, hands planted on his hips, eyes scanning the lines as if he could feel the ground through paper. Gabriel crouched low, close enough to point without blocking the view.

Davenport tapped the ridge line with the pencil. "If we hold this shoulder, we keep the high ground and we keep the timeline. The drop into the valley starts here."

Gabriel nodded once. "Yes sir, but don't treat it like a road. Them draws'll slow you. Rain'll make it worse."

Lacey gave a quiet grunt. "Say that again, Fox."

Gabriel glanced up at him. "Them draws," he repeated, slower. "Gullies. Hollers. Whatever you want to call 'em."

Lacey shook his head with a half-smile that never fully formed. "Man, I'm going to need a translator for Tennessee."

Davenport almost smiled too, then forced himself back to the map. "Spacing stays the same. Five minutes behind, thousand meters offset. Radio only if it's life-or-death."

Gabriel's finger traced a narrow contour change—subtle on paper, dangerous on the ground. "This here's where you get hurt," he said. "Folks like to sit above a cut and wait. You won't see 'em till you're in it."

Lacey leaned closer. "Where would you put the ambush?"

Gabriel answered without hesitation. "Where you can't run, and where you can't hide. If they make you cross open—paddies, bare slope, anything like that—you're already behind."

Davenport exhaled through his nose. "And if we do make contact?"

"Then we live," Gabriel said, flat and honest. "We don't chase. We don't get pulled. We keep our heads."

Lacey watched him for a moment and understood the simple truth under the mountain accent: Gabriel was not being dramatic. He was speaking in the language of survival.

Before they broke, Gabriel quietly added something he had picked up from listening to villagers near the wire and from the interpreters on earlier missions. He leaned in toward Davenport and spoke low, as if the words themselves needed stealth.

"Couple phrases," he said. "If you ever hear 'em out there."

He held up one finger. "Im lặng. Means be quiet."

A second finger. "Đi chậm. Means move slow."

A third. "Đứng lại. Means stop."

Davenport repeated each one carefully, not wanting to butcher it. Lacey did not repeat them—he only stored them away, like tools. Gabriel nodded once, satisfied, and stepped back from the map.

"Alright," Davenport said, standing. "We move at dawn."

Gabriel's eyes went briefly to the ridgeline outside the camp, dark against a brightening sky. "Yes sir," he said. "We move."

It did not take long for all of this to occur, and soon they were on their way down Highway 19 toward An Khê Pass (Đèo An Khê). Gabriel was fascinated by how much this country reminded him of home, except for the constant heat. The humidity and rains were much the same. At home, there was always rain. On a hot summer day, the humidity could be just as bad. His mountain home had just as many biting insects, and there were poisonous snakes he had dealt with since he was a young child.

The difference was that back home there was fall, winter, and spring. Here, it was just hot summer—always wet.

The two trucks and their escorts made their way down the winding road as quickly as possible. There was essentially no movement on the road at night. Once daylight came, the locals would move out to tend to their business. In rural areas, everything went quiet after dark. As innocent as one might be, death was almost assured if you moved in the open at night. Someone would shoot you. Whether American or Vietnamese, if you were moving after dark, you had better be one of them. Those who moved at night intended to kill someone.

It was only in daylight that the locals went about their business. Most traffic consisted of buffalo-drawn carts, some motorbikes, and a few trucks hauling goods up and down the mountain. Then there was the military traffic, which seemed constant during daylight hours.

Just before Gabriel and his unit left Camp Radcliff, the sweepers headed out. Their mission was to ensure the road both up and down the mountain was safe for travel. The trip took about an hour before the unit reached its drop-off point. The trucks pulled over. Prior to offloading, the group ensured there was no indigenous traffic within viewing range.

Once they dismounted, they moved down the trail a short distance and stopped to make one final readiness check. When Lieutenant Davenport gave a quiet nod, Gabriel took the lead, along with the lieutenant and six other men. Sergeant Lacey waited five minutes and then followed suit.

Their mission was not to engage the enemy, but they all knew there were times when contact could not be avoided—and when it happened, it usually turned deadly.

From their vantage point, they could see the ocean and Quy Nhơn to the east, but they knew this was not a sightseeing tour. Shortly, they would be in the heavy growth of the mountain jungle. Their steps were slow and deliberate. Their pace was set to be as silent as possible.

Their drop-off point was approximately 1,600 feet in elevation. Certain portions of their patrol would rise above

2,500 feet, with constant changes in elevation. Back home, Gabriel could easily cover fifteen miles in a day in this type of terrain if needed. Here, patience and stealth were the greatest virtues.

It was Gabriel's intent to lead the men as slowly and quietly as possible while still meeting the timeline. Throughout the day, the squad moved forward a few hundred paces, spread out, and searched for any sign of recent enemy movement. At times, they found evidence—activity that had occurred within the past week. Each discovery was noted on their maps.

Gabriel set the pace for what turned out to be an uneventful day, aside from their few findings. The hours were long, the heat oppressive, and the pace slow, but every man understood the necessity. This was a good group of men. They had good leaders.

The only oddity was one E-5 sergeant. So far, he had not demonstrated the leadership skills or combat awareness needed in such a unit, nor even the desire to learn them. He resented Gabriel's relationship with the staff sergeant and the lieutenant. Lieutenant Davenport had already requested a replacement, but so far the request had not been approved.

The two-squad unit moved on, separated by a thousand yards and five minutes of movement at that pace. Either group could be back in contact with the other in about two minutes. Lieutenant Davenport's squad skirted along the east edge of the ridge, while Staff Sergeant Lacey's followed behind on the west side. There was no communication between the two, even though both the lieutenant and Lacey had radio operators available if needed.

Gabriel led them on until just before dusk.

They quickly established the two camps. On this patrol, they were issued K-rations, freeze-dried meals sealed in foil packs. Each man hydrated his ration with water from his canteen. While the rations reconstituted, they went about setting up camp. Once ready, they ate the meals cold, knowing that heating them would send the smell of American food into the air.

They formed a perimeter, each man facing outward. When a man needed to urinate or defecate, he moved several yards from camp and dug a hole deep enough to completely cover the waste. The intent was to conceal any scent. When they broke camp in the morning, the only trace left behind would be buried waste. Each man knew how to hide any evidence of their presence.

The watches were divided evenly. Each man knew his responsibility. The final watch began waking the others thirty minutes before dawn. They rose, ate quickly, took turns attending to personal needs, and prepared to move out.

Gabriel took the lead once again. A thousand yards behind him, Sergeant Lacey and his men followed.

The bivouac and departure times were controlled by watches worn by Lieutenant Davenport and Sergeant Lacey. Even without communication, they worked in sync. These two teams were well disciplined—except for the one sergeant. Lieutenant Davenport did not understand why the man had been assigned to his platoon. Thankfully, Sergeant Lacey kept an eye on him.

Unfortunately, Sergeant Lacey did not see the gum wrapper the sergeant dropped on the ground that second morning. What Lacey did see—minutes later, while they were still tightening their formation—was the habit behind the mistake.

The same sergeant lagged half a pace too far back, hands busy at the wrong times. Lacey caught the faint crinkle of packaging and turned his head just enough to confirm what his ears already told him. The man's attention was split between his weapon and whatever he was fussing with—some small comfort, something sweet, something that did not belong in a place where every sound had consequence.

Lacey slid back along the line without breaking the unit's rhythm. When he reached the sergeant, he leaned in close enough that his words were a breath against the man's ear.

"Hands stay on your job," Lacey whispered. "Not on candy. Not on wrappers. Not on anything that leaves sign."

The sergeant's jaw tightened. In another world—back at the company, back in some safe place—he might have snapped back. But the jungle had its own rules, and Lacey enforced them with the kind of calm that told a man the argument would not be entertained.

"You drop something," Lacey continued, "and you don't just make a mess. You make a trail. You make a target. You make us dead."

The sergeant swallowed and gave a stiff nod.

Lacey held his stare a second longer, then let him go without another word. Discipline, in a unit like this, was not about pride. It was about whether the next day had a sunrise for them to see.

Lacey moved forward again, eyes sweeping the ground without thinking—trained to spot anything that did not belong. The rain had washed the ridge clean and made the jungle smell alive. It also made small human mistakes harder to find.

And that was how a single piece of trash remained behind, quiet as a whisper, loud as a flare to the right set of eyes.

The men hoped the entire patrol would be like the first day. They had no desire to engage the enemy—but would if necessary.

Soon, Gabriel was leading the unit north along the east side of the ridge. They found evidence of movement, though none appeared to be within the past day. The patrol took some comfort in that, but their alertness never waned.

As with every patrol, Gabriel allowed his mind to drift home while remaining constantly vigilant. Holding his M-16, he thought of the breech-loading long rifle he had used back home once he was old enough to be trusted with it. The rifle was simple, easy to maintain, and well cared for. As a child, he dreamed of the day he would carry it into the woods. He and his father hunted year-round to supplement their diet.

As they moved along the ridge, heavy dark clouds began to form. One thing Gabriel had noticed about the storms here was the lack of lightning and thunder. Rain often fell hard with little wind. At other times, the wind-driven rain stung like bee stings against the skin.

Recognizing the coming storm, Gabriel halted the unit so everyone could put on their ponchos. Those behind him helped one another, while Gabriel worked his own on. Everyone knew Gabriel preferred the men stay ten yards behind him. He felt safer that way, confident he was unseen—at least by anyone ahead.

Just as the last poncho was secured, the rain came. It was a downpour, one that would last for two days.

There would be no relief for Gabriel or his comrades. No matter how hard they tried, most would develop jungle rot by the time they emerged from the mountains and the valley below. Gabriel glanced back and saw the men were ready. They moved on.

That night was miserable. There was not a dry spot on any of them. The only comfort was the sense of safety the downpour provided. The enemy could see no better than they could and was likely just as unwilling to fight.

Still, the night watches kept a close watch on the jungle. Each man stood his two-hour shift. The middle watches were the worst. Even in the rain, a man could sleep soundly or at least rest—but being awakened in the middle of the night to stand watch was a misery all its own.

Fighting sleep while standing watch, especially in pouring rain, was its own form of hell. All they wanted was to curl up, get warm, and sleep.

At least Lieutenant Davenport and Sergeant Lacey were as fair as possible with watch assignments. The men recognized that and respected both leaders for it.

Lieutenant Davenport, a recent graduate of Tennessee Tech and Army Officer training, was not the typical gung-ho, know-it-all junior officer. His father, a career Sergeant Major, had taught him well. He told his son to respect his men, and they would respect him; to be firm in decision-making, but willing to listen before making a final decision.

Lieutenant Davenport had applied those lessons since arriving in the company. He did not socialize with his men, but neither did he make himself unapproachable. By most accounts, Lieutenant Davenport was all right.

In a place like this, promotions came quickly—sometimes earned, sometimes not.

Russell Davenport had earned his.

The long, rainy night ended without incident. Under the cover of their ponchos, the men took turns eating their K-ration breakfast. Once they had eaten, they were ready to move out. They would descend in a more easterly direction. The jungle was slick and wet, so Gabe searched for the best avenues of travel while maintaining their general course. Even with the misery of the rain, today promised progress. It would be about a two-mile hike down the slopes toward Happy Valley. One more night in the mountains, and then they would enter the valley.

Later in the day, the rain began to slacken. The change brought both relief and caution. Gabe sharpened his senses even further. They had been alert all along, but he knew that with the rain easing, the chances of contact increased. Intelligence had been clear—this ridge was a corridor for both NVA and Việt Cộng movement. The patrol's purpose was to confirm that movement on the ground. The rain had hampered them, but now the likelihood of contact grew. Gabe knew it, and he led the men with that knowledge. They followed, understanding.

By mid-afternoon, the rain stopped altogether. The sun broke through and poured heat onto the mountains. As the temperature climbed into the low nineties, the humidity followed close behind. The heat could drain a man quickly. Insects swarmed constantly. Though each soldier had changed socks and powdered his feet, dampness remained. Some would develop jungle rot, not only on their feet but in the crotch as well—an ailment that could sideline a man for days.

The others swatted continuously at the insects. Gabe never did. Like most mountain boys, he had smoked most of his life, but never while hunting and never on patrol. He knew the smell lingered, and even field-dressed cigarette butts could leave a trail. He spoke only in whispers, and as rarely as possible.

Throughout the day, Lieutenant Davenport and Sergeant Fox checked the topo maps to ensure they held their course. Gabe had never seen a topo map until AIT, but the first time he studied one, the terrain seemed to rise in his mind. He could picture slopes, valleys, and draws almost perfectly. Even though raised as a soldier's son, the lieutenant marveled at Gabe's instinctive understanding of terrain.

When opportunity allowed, Davenport spoke with him about the mountains. His grandparents had taken him to Gatlinburg nearly every year as a boy. He loved the mountains and felt a deep respect for this small, quiet man from East Tennessee. Almost elf-like in stature, Gabriel Fox was tough as nails. The lieutenant admired him.

Back at An Khê, Gabe spent his free time reading or carving. He carved animals and creatures he had seen in the jungle. Davenport often watched him work. More than once, he told Gabe that when the war was over, he wanted to visit those Tennessee mountains and see the places Gabe described. Gabe looked forward to that—showing him the real mountains, far from this place.

As the patrol continued along the ridge, it eventually bent southeast. This was where their descent into the valley would begin. Gabe knew there would be one more night in the jungle, at a position roughly a hundred feet above the valley floor. By his reckoning, they were about sixteen hours from entering Happy Valley. He also knew that at any moment, everything could change.

Earlier that same morning, several kilometers south of Gabe's position, an NVA scout spotted a gum wrapper on the ground—despite the rain. He had been operating in the South since 1965 and was exceptionally skilled. He noticed footprints leading north along the western slope of the ridge. He waited for his unit to close up.

His commanding officer ordered the scout and two others forward to locate the Americans. A company was sent to follow them. The rest of the battalion continued on its original route.

Even in the rain, it took three hours of rapid movement for the scout to locate Lacey's squad. One of the NVA soldiers broke off to guide the following company. The rain provided perfect cover as the scout shadowed the Americans. Later that day, when the Americans turned east to begin their descent, the scout continued to follow. He had traveled these mountains many times over the past three years. He had fought in the Ia Drang Valley in November 1965. On January 30, he had helped lead forces onto Hòn Cong Mountain for the attack on Camp Radcliff during Tết.

It did not take long for him to know where the Americans would exit the jungle into the valley below.

He returned to his company commander. After a brief exchange, they set their pace. By morning, they would be in position.

A single gum wrapper had set them on their course.

Gabriel set the pace so they would reach the edge of the valley just before dark. His movement was slow and deliberate. At the same time, the NVA unit was moving as fast as possible, skirting the northern end of the valley, and shifting along the eastern slope. Those extra miles forced them to move throughout the night, reaching their intended positions only a few hours before daylight. The scout led them down a descending path that brought them to the eastern slope above the valley floor at approximately 4:00 a.m. Mortar tubes were hastily set up. Machine-gun positions were thrown together. Other men spread out through the jungle, facing four rice paddies to the west.

Gabriel's unit had reached its intended position the evening before. They set their bivouac roughly one hundred yards above the valley floor. Three men were sent forward to observe the valley throughout the night. In the early hours, they detected no movement on the opposite side of the valley, where enemy forces were quietly positioning themselves along the jungle's edge. Four large rice paddies lay between the Americans and the Vietnamese.

Heavy rain fell for the first part of the night. Gabriel slept poorly. A sense of unease troubled him. He moved down through the jungle several times to check on the observers. One man slept while two watched the valley floor. All they saw was emptiness. Farther south, they noticed a hut at the jungle's edge—only its silhouette visible in the darkness.

On one visit, a soldier pointed toward the hut. Gabriel stared at it, seeing nothing more than a dark blur. He asked the soldier to describe it. The request puzzled the man, but he complied. Gabriel hoped he could see it better in the morning. He returned uphill, unable to sleep, wondering about the hut's occupants and what the war had done to them.

At first light, he saw dawn creeping over the eastern ridge. He quietly roused the man nearest him. Soon, the remaining five moved down to join the three observers. There would be no breakfast in the field that morning. They scouted the area while waiting for Staff Sergeant Lacey's element to arrive.

From their position at the northwestern corner of the paddies, Gabriel studied the valley. They would need to cross the rice paddies to reach the trail along the west of the west branch of the Côn River. They would then patrol the valley for three days.

Gabriel strained to focus on the hut he had seen in the night. Weeks earlier, he could have seen it clearly, but now it was blurred. His vision was sharp only to about fifty yards. Beyond that, details faded. He had already told Lieutenant Davenport that his distance vision was failing. From that point forward, Alejandro Gomez took point in open terrain, with Gabriel following closely behind, covering the near ground.

Rice paddies frightened Gabriel more than anything else. His height and short legs made movement difficult. Everyone hated paddies. They were exposed, slow, and unforgiving. When possible, they walked the dikes separating them, though Gabriel disliked that even more.

When Lacey's squad joined them, they conducted one last scan. Lieutenant Davenport gave Alejandro the order to move out. Alejandro stepped onto the dike. Gabriel, trusting his limitations, allowed the others to pass and took the rear—one of the few times he ever did.

If his eyesight had been stronger, he might have caught the movement ahead—enemy positions hidden less than a football field away.

The NVA scout and the company watched the Americans emerge from the jungle. They waited patiently. The order had already been given. The mortar crews were ready.

Gabriel was about twelve feet onto the paddy dike, roughly forty feet from the next intersecting dike, when the sharp k-thoop of a mortar tube echoed across the valley. Just as the mortar was dropped into the tube, a private's foot slipped, knocking the tube off target. The round arced high and long, passing over the paddies and slamming into the ground near the lone hut at the edge of the jungle. The explosion sent earth and debris into the air, just yards from the structure. It was the opening shot.

An instant later, machine-gun fire erupted from the eastern tree line. Two guns opened at intersecting angles, stitching the dike and the paddy with deadly precision.

Alejandro Gomez went down immediately, killed before he could react.

Lieutenant Davenport was struck just beneath his right collarbone and thrown backward into the paddy. His .45 disappeared into the muddy water. For a brief second he was stunned, then tried to pull himself forward.

His radioman jumped in after him, grabbing him by the collar to drag him toward the cover of the dike—unwittingly seizing him on the wounded side. Davenport screamed in pain. Staff Sergeant Lacey was right behind, plunging into the water to help pull him clear.

As soon as they reached cover, Lacey had the radio in his hand. He knew they were badly outgunned. He called for artillery support.

At the southern entrance to the valley, the firebase responded immediately. Coordinates were relayed, guns adjusted, and the first 105-mm round thundered into the air. It landed seventy-five feet behind the NVA positions. Lacey corrected the fire, and soon hell rained down.

Mortars answered. The mortar tube previously knocked off target was righted and sent mortars arcing for the paddies.

Gabriel had dropped into the adjacent paddy as bullets cut the air. One round struck the platoon's other sergeant squarely in the chest. He died instantly. Gabriel pushed forward through the mud toward the dike. He was three feet from cover when the mortar struck.

The explosion tore the dike apart. Fire and shrapnel slammed into Gabriel's right side. His leg fractured. His hip dislocated with a break mid-thigh. His jaw was blown open. Teeth vanished. The right side of his face burned. His skull cracked. Fluid leaked. The concussion erased everything.

His body collapsed into the paddy. Mud and debris buried him.

Artillery continued. Gunships approached. Medevacs lifted from Firebase Thunderhead. Alejandro and the sergeant were dead. The lieutenant was wounded but conscious. Suppressive fire continued until gunships arrived and drove the NVA back into the mountains.

Sergeant Lacey and the radio operator loaded Lt. Davenport on the first medevac as it landed. It took off immediately. Moments later, the bodies of Alejandro and the sergeant were loaded onto the second medevac. It was in no hurry, other than to lift off and get out of range of gunfire.

The gunships and artillery rounds, along with the gunfire from the team, drove the NVA back into the mountains. Slicks were on their way. In moments the men were loading onto the helicopters, headed toward Quy Nhơn. Immediately when the choppers landed, SSgt. Lacey was taken to a briefing room. There he spent the next hour going over the details of the battle. As soon as it was over, he headed to the hospital to check on the lieutenant. Lacey knew they had lost two men.

Only later—after intelligence briefings, hospital visits, and exhaustion—did Staff Sergeant Lacey realize that

Sergeant Gabriel Fox had not returned. Lacey immediately rushed to the nearest officer he could find and reported it. Lacey desperately attempted to organize a rescue team. The day was late; it was getting dark. Those in command made the decision to hold off the search and rescue. There was no need to risk the lives of others at that time.

Lacey stood in the doorway of the operations area long enough to force the truth into shape. He had been moving on instinct since the paddies—dragging men, calling fire, hearing the gunships, watching the medevacs lift. In the blur of it all, he had kept counting heads the way he always did, the way good NCOs did when the world went sideways.

And somehow, in the controlled chaos after the shooting stopped, the number had felt correct—until it was not.

He stepped forward to the nearest desk and drove his hand down on the map board hard enough to rattle the pencils.

"Sergeant Fox is not here," he said. Not loud. Not pleading. Only fact.

An officer behind the desk looked up, eyes tired, uniform stained with the day. "Staff Sergeant, we've got wounded. We've got KIA. We've got—"

"We've got my point man missing," Lacey cut in. "We have a man out there."

The officer's mouth tightened. "We're not sending anyone back into that valley at dusk."

Lacey leaned forward, close enough that the officer could smell the wet jungle on him. "Then we're leaving him."

The officer's voice hardened, the tone of command made for moments when emotion threatened discipline. "We are not losing more men tonight. We hold until first light."

Lacey's fists clenched. He had seen too many men become "held until"—held until their blood cooled, held until the jungle swallowed them, held until all that came back was a tag and a story no one wanted to tell. He forced himself to breathe through it, but the anger stayed in his chest like a live coal.

"Sir," he said, controlled now, "Fox is small. He's hurt. If he's alive, he can't move far. If we wait—"

"We wait," the officer repeated. "That is the order."

Lacey straightened. His spine felt rigid with restraint. He did not salute the order. He saluted the rank. Then he turned and walked out before he said something that would end his career and change nothing.

He went straight to the temporary barracks and pounded the floor with the heel of his boot until the wood complained. He did it once. Then again. Not childish fury—something older and more dangerous: the need to act with nowhere to put it.

A captain he did not know well stepped into the doorway, helmet under one arm. "Staff Sergeant Lacey?"

Lacey turned, eyes sharp. "Yes sir."

The captain's name tape read McMurtry. He looked young for his rank, but there was something in his face that said he had already learned what war did to plans.

"I've been given the mission," McMurtry said. "First light. Search and recovery."

"Search and rescue," Lacey corrected automatically.

McMurtry did not argue the word. He only nodded once, as if he understood exactly why Lacey had said it. "Search and rescue," he agreed. "I'm putting the team together now."

"Let me go," Lacey said.

McMurtry's eyes held his for a beat. "I tried."

"And?"

"And they told me no," McMurtry answered, voice clipped with the same frustration. "They want you available. They want you to be steady. They think you'll do something reckless if you're in that valley with Fox on your mind."

Lacey's laugh was humorless. "They finally got something right."

McMurtry stepped further in and lowered his voice. "They're assigning an interpreter and a Vietnamese liaison. ARVN (South Vietnamese Army) has someone who knows the district. It's not much, but it's better than going blind."

Lacey nodded once—accepting the necessity, hating it anyway. "Then make sure your interpreter understands this: Fox may not answer you. He might be out cold. He might be quiet on purpose."

McMurtry absorbed that. "Understood."

A moment later, the Vietnamese liaison arrived with the interpreter—both men in crisp uniforms compared to the mud-smeared Americans. The interpreter introduced himself quickly, eyes wary in the way men's eyes got when they stood near grief.

McMurtry spoke, and the interpreter turned the words into Vietnamese with practiced speed. Lacey listened closely, then cut in with something he wanted said plainly, without polish.

Tell them: don't make noise. Don't spook anyone. Don't turn it into a fight.

The interpreter nodded and spoke, low and direct:

"Chúng tôi sẽ tìm anh ấy. Nhưng phải im lặng."

We will find him. But we must be quiet.

Then he added, gesturing with his hand as if pushing the air down:

"Đi chậm. Đừng bắn nếu không cần."

Move slowly. Do not shoot unless necessary.

Lacey felt something tighten behind his ribs. Those were Gabriel's words—his small list of survival phrases—now echoing in someone else's mouth.

When the meeting broke, Lacey stood alone for a moment in the dim barracks light, hearing the sounds of the camp continuing like nothing had happened. Men laughed somewhere. A radio played faintly. Life moved on because life always moved on.

Lacey did not.

He sat on the edge of his bunk, elbows on his knees, and finally let his head drop forward. He did not cry. He did not have tears to spare. He only closed his eyes and pictured the last clear glimpse he had of Fox—low to the ground, rifle up, eyes searching the near space like he could smell danger before it arrived.

"Lord," Lacey whispered, not caring who might hear, "don't let that man die out there alone."

Outside, night settled hard over the mountains. And in the dark, the war held its breath until morning.

The rain came, and came hard. For the next few hours it poured heavily. Mud and debris flowed into the gaping hole of a rice paddy dike, essentially erasing any signs that there had been digging. At Quy Nhơn, the rain was light, just a sprinkle. Captain McMurtry lay on his cot, studying in his mind the coming day. He did not know what to expect.

Lieutenant Davenport slept soundly from the drug-induced haze. Even in that haze, he dreamed about the mountains of East Tennessee. He was not aware that one of his men had remained behind.

Chapter 5

October 1960

The Boar Hunter

Proverbs 22:6 (KJV)

"Train up a child in the way he should go: and when he is old, he will not depart from it."

Jonas's voice dropped another notch, the tone he used when the lesson was not only about hunting but about living.

"You see snake sign, you give it respect," he said. "You hear somethin' big movin,' you don't get curious."

Gabriel's mouth tightened in a boy's seriousness that already looked like a man's. "Yes sir."

Before first light, Esther had been at the stove, quiet as a shadow, hands moving by memory. Cornbread pones cooled on a plate. A slice of fatback hissed once in the skillet—more for scent than for meat—then she turned it out onto paper to save the grease. The cabin held its usual smells: woodsmoke worked into the logs, coffee grounds waiting in the tin, damp wool hanging near the door.

Gabriel sat on the edge of his pallet and pulled his boots on without a word. Jonas watched him from the table, not hovering, not fussing—just watching the way a man watches what he's trained and prayed over. In those mountains, too many words were a kind of boasting, and boasting was how you got humbled.

Esther handed him the cornbread and an apple, her fingers lingering on his wrist a half-second longer than necessary. "You don't go takin' chances," she said.

"Ain't," Gabriel answered softly, as if saying it louder might wake the whole hollow.

Jonas nodded toward the long rifle. "You keep that muzzle where it belongs. You keep your ears open. And you don't go chasin' what you can't finish."

"Yes sir."

Esther pressed her palm once to the center of his chest, then stepped back. Jonas bowed his head at the table. Gabriel did too—automatic, trained as breathing.

"Lord," Jonas said, simple and plain, "keep this boy's feet under him. Keep his mind clear. Keep his hands steady. Bring him back to this door. Amen."

"Amen," Gabriel echoed.

And then he was outside, swallowed by the cold leaf-smell and the dark creek air, carrying the family's need on his back as surely as the rifle.

His was one of those families locked away from the advancements of society in the Appalachian Mountains, just on the border of the Great Smoky Mountains National Park. They lived much like their ancestors a hundred years earlier. Their subsistence was off the land. What they ate was hunted, raised, or traded for. Their source of income was logging or moonshining.

The young boy—twelve years old now—crept through the low mountain foliage. He could hear boar snorting and foraging along the creek bed. His rifle was as long as he was tall. Though small for his age, he had courage and no fear of the mountains he called home. It was part of his job to hunt these woods, helping to provide for his poor mountain family.

Corn was their most valuable crop. It had multiple purposes. During the harvest season, they would feast on corn on the cob, or his mother would make creamed corn, poured over homemade biscuits and eaten with fresh, sliced tomatoes. Some of the corn was hauled to the mill in the valley and ground for cornmeal or grits. The miller would keep a third to pay for the milling. A portion would be traded for flour. Another portion was dried and stored as feed for their hogs and chickens. The bulk, though, was used to brew their main cash product—moonshine whiskey.

Moonshining, however, was becoming a less profitable trade. With the advent of the national park, logging had dwindled. So, the Fox family did everything they could to survive the changes.

Today, with the first signs of autumn and the impending winter, Gabriel was out to kill a wild mountain boar. These wild boars were a crossbreed of European boar and domestic pigs. The European boar had been brought from Europe and kept at a hunting lodge in North Carolina. Some escaped forty years earlier. They thrived in this isolated part of the country by breeding with domestic stock.

They were a destructive force within these mountains. They plowed large swaths of mountain land in their search for tubers, grubs, and small creatures in their dens. At times they would make it into a mountain garden and destroy it overnight. During the summer months they stayed in the higher, cooler elevations, and now, with colder temperatures settling in, they were making their way down into the lower elevations. They foraged along the creek beds. One would almost think a tiller had churned up the ground after their passage.

Some of the animals of purer stock were slick-coated and pure black. Others carried long, grayish fur. The young males separated from the herd once they reached breeding age and went in search of females. The females could have two litters per year—four to twelve piglets per litter—and could be fertile after six months of age. The males reached breeding age a little later.

The rifle he carried had been passed down for generations. Now of unknown origin, it was heavy and long. It was the same rifle used by his family when they first inhabited these mountains. It had been oiled and well maintained through the years. His father had taught him to respect it. Legend had it had been used a hundred years earlier in the fight for Southern independence.

He had been taught to shoot with a single-shot, bolt-action .22. He had become deadly with it. His father told him he had the eyes of an eagle and the ear and nose of a fox. Gabriel had become a prolific hunter, as capable as any man. His short stature allowed him to move through the undergrowth of these mountains with the stealth of a cat. He was patient. He would listen and smell. His eyes moved in a slow arc, detecting any movement. He kept his rifle in a near-ready position to fire.

Most boys his age would not have been able to handle this heavy piece of iron, but Gabriel was strong—strength built from logging with his father. He would duck-walk through these woods, keeping his short frame even lower to the ground. The snakes of summer were moving into their winter dens, catching the last rays of sun before the cold set in. He kept his eyes on the ground, watching for the movement of a copperhead or timber rattler. He feared neither, so long as he could see them.

Each step was deliberate. He would scan the ground first, then place the outside edge of his toe down and roll his foot into the leaves so slowly that the sound was no more than a squirrel's shuffle. He broke the cadence of his movement on purpose, imitating the stop-and-start rhythm of mountain creatures.

His hunting clothes were never stored in the cabin. Smoke clung to cloth, and smoke warned game. He kept his gear where it could air out, and he went into the woods carrying only the scent of cold leaves and creek water.

Not far away, he could hear boar snorting and plowing the ground with their tusks. They were after succulent roots and grubs. Once they found a good spot, they would tear the earth in wide swaths. Today, he wanted a young juvenile—one whose muscles had not been hardened by age or testosterone.

He crept closer, undetected. He eased forward until they were in sight. Only a few more yards and he would be in range. He slowed his pace. Each step was slow and deliberate. His legs were strong. He could balance on one foot while placing the other with the slightest motion. Any crackle of leaves or ground cover was minimal.

His silhouette blended into the background. If a boar glanced his way, it might see only a rock, a stump, or a rotting log. He watched them all. If one looked toward him, Gabriel froze, almost perfectly still. Any forward movement came in the smallest increments. His shoulders stayed square. His head remained aligned, with minimal up-and-down or side-to-side motion. His eyes moved in fractions. He did not open them wide. He minimized the white, lightly squinting to control blinking.

Once in range, he chose his target—a young male, sleek and black, white tusks curving up from its lower jaw. Gabriel could not help but admire the animal's beauty. He squatted, waiting for it to turn broadside. He knew where to aim—just below the shoulder, at the crease where the leg met the body. A clean shot through the heart would kill it instantly. There would be no running. Nothing was worse than tracking a wounded animal through the woods. He considered it wasteful, and he never allowed it to happen.

He held still long enough for the woods to teach him again what his father had already taught: the mountain did not reward hurry. The boar rooted and snorted, working the earth like it owned it, and Gabriel watched the muscle ripple under the hide—strong, young, full of life. For a moment he felt that old, strange pinch that came every time he was about to end something breathing. It was not softness. It was not weakness. It was a kind of accounting.

He let his breathing slow and his eyes narrow until the world reduced itself to one thing: that crease behind the shoulder. He did not hate the animal, and he did not love killing it. But he loved his mother's quiet relief when there was meat, and he loved the way his sisters' voices sounded lighter when the pantry was not empty. He loved the way Jonas carried worry without talking about it.

Gabriel shifted his weight—barely—until the rifle would rise clean and true. He waited for broadside not because he wanted the easiest shot, but because he wanted the most merciful one. He had been raised to believe that if you took from the mountain, you did it with skill and you did it with respect.

Jonas had drilled it into him with the flat certainty of mountain law. "No chasing," his father would say. "If you pull that trigger, you end it clean. You owe the animal that."

Gabriel remembered those words now as clearly as the weight of the rifle on his shoulder.

He steadied himself and drew in a deep breath. In one smooth motion, he rose to a standing position, the rifle tucked tight to his shoulder. He let half the breath out as he rose, lips clenched. His left foot stepped slightly ahead of the right. His shoulders squared with the target. The crosshairs dropped, crossing the ridge of the boar's back. There was no hesitation. He squeezed the trigger. The rifle roared. The bullet slammed into the animal's side, tearing through lungs and heart. The boar dropped where it stood. The rest fled in panic.

Gabriel slowly squatted back on his haunches and waited. He let the smoke clear. The animal was going nowhere. He allowed the thunder to fade from his ears and waited for the woods to settle. For a few minutes there was silence. Then, gradually, the forest returned—birds chirping, chipmunks and squirrels resuming their movement.

He stood and walked the thirty yards to his prey. The young male lay still, killed instantly. Gabriel leaned his rifle and rucksack against a tree. His father had taught him never to dress an animal near the creek. He did not want to foul the water with offal. He grabbed the boar by the hind legs and dragged it several hundred feet uphill.

He retrieved his rifle and knapsack. From the pack he removed the small digging spade and dug a hole large enough to hold the intestines and stomach, deep enough to be covered with six inches of dirt, leaving a slight mound. He positioned the animal uphill from the hole. From the scabbard on his right side he took a six-inch folding knife. Another knife rested in a scabbard on his left.

A small hatchet rode in a loop on the outside of his rucksack—useful for trimming branches, splitting kindling, or clearing a place to work when the woods grew too tight.

The knives were different. One had a thicker, heavier blade, ground for durability—a utility blade, slower to dull but not as sharp. The second was thin and honed razor sharp, slicing through tissue with surgical ease.

With the sharper knife, he cut the skin down the center of the belly, careful not to pierce the organs. He continued the cut to just above the penis, circled below the anus, and joined it back to the main incision. He opened the cavity and field-dressed the animal, letting the entrails fall into the hole. He pushed the carcass aside and covered the remains with dirt.

From his knapsack he removed a rope and tossed it over a low branch. He tied it around the boar's hind legs and hoisted it into the air. With his knife he slit the throat. Blood poured freely. Satisfied, he went to the creek and washed his hands.

He returned to the tree and retrieved his rifle. Using the cleaning rod and cloth from his pack, he swabbed the bore, blew residual powder from the chamber, and ran an oiled cloth through the barrel. He wiped the firing mechanism, the stock, and the barrel, then reloaded.

He sat against the tree and pulled an apple and a small pone of cornbread from his pack. He ate as the animal drained. The cornbread left his mouth dry. He stepped into the creek, balanced on stones, washed his hands and face, then cupped the cold water and drank deeply.

He was twelve years old and alone in these mountains yet completely assured. When the last drops of blood fell, he knew it was time to go.

He lowered the carcass, untied the rope, rolled it neatly, and returned it to his pack. He took a shorter rope and tied the forelegs to the hind legs. He pulled the knapsack onto his shoulders, checked its weight and fit, then bent and lifted the hog. With a practiced motion, he swung it over his shoulders, threaded his arm through the tied legs, and stood upright, testing the balance. It held.

He picked up his rifle and started the long walk home. The drag back was slow and punishing. The rope cut into his hands through the thin skin at the base of his fingers, and the weight wanted to pull him downhill every chance it had. He stopped when he had to, not from quitting, but from pacing—because Jonas had taught him the difference. He would rest just long enough to get the ache out of his forearms, then he would lean into it again, boots sliding in leaf mold, the smell of blood and iron traveling with him.

When the cabin finally came into view, smoke lifting from the chimney like a signal, Gabriel's throat tightened with a boy's private pride. He did not need praise, but he needed his family to eat.

Esther saw him first. She stepped out onto the porch, apron still on, one hand shading her eyes. "Lord have mercy," she breathed—not drama, just surprise at the size of the thing. Then her face set into work. "Jonas!"

Jonas came around the side of the cabin wiping his hands on a rag, already reading the situation before Gabriel said a word. He walked down to meet him, took one look at the boar, then looked at Gabriel's hands. "You cut yourself?"

"No sir," Gabriel said. He swallowed once. "Clean."

Jonas nodded approval without smiling. "Good. You done right."

Esther came down behind Jonas and touched Gabriel's shoulder. "You hungry?"

"Yes ma'am."

"You go wash up. I'll fix you somethin' quick." Her eyes went to the boar again, calculating meals like math. "That'll carry us."

Inside, Jacob sat near the hearth where the warmth lived, rocking slightly, making a low sound in his throat that was neither word nor song. He looked up when Gabriel came in, eyes bright in a way that did not always connect to what was happening. Gabriel gave him a quick, gentle pat on the shoulder as he passed—habit, affection, family.

"I'm back," Gabriel told him anyway, as if Jacob needed the reassurance.

In the yard, the work began like it always did: not with excitement, but with efficiency. Jonas set the gantry line. Esther fetched buckets and knives. The girls moved where their mother told them, practiced and quiet, the way mountain children learned to be. No one wasted motion. No one wasted anything.

Jonas spoke only when necessary—short instructions, measured as a man's breath. "You hold that. You don't let it slip. You keep your fingers clear."

Gabriel did what he was told, eyes steady, stomach tightening once at the smell and then settling. He had seen enough blood in these hills to know it was part of the trade. Still, as the animal became meat—useful, necessary—he felt that same inward pinch again, the small solemn cost of living this way. He did not tell anyone. In his family, you did not speak every feeling aloud. You carried it and kept working.

When it was done, Esther stood at the washbasin, cleaning her hands, and looked at Gabriel like she was taking his measure. "You did good," she said.

Jonas did not add much, but he did add something. He met Gabriel's eyes and gave him a single nod. "You're learnin'."

To Gabriel, that was praise enough to last all winter.

That was in the fall of 1960. Gabriel knew nothing of life beyond these mountains and felt no need to. This was his world. From the genetic memory of the Scottish Highlands, he had been born for it. He never imagined a time—or a reason—to leave.

He would eat as well as any man. There was not an ounce of fat on him, his body burning enormous amounts of calories each day. His muscles absorbed the protein, and with every passing day he grew stronger than the one before.

As he moved through the woods, he listened carefully to every sound. His thoughts drifted to what it must have been like when his Scots-Irish ancestors first settled this land, fighting the native people who already lived here. In his mind's eye, he pictured battles for this ground. He imagined that if he were an Indian, he would fight with everything he had to protect it. He thought about how ambushes would be set, how the natural terrain would be used to counter men armed with rifles and muskets. He imagined how he himself would deploy—how he would hide, strike fiercely, then vanish back into the woods. Then he thought of how his ancestors would have tracked and hunted their enemy. There were times he wished he had been born in those days. In his mind, he saw the worth on both sides. If he had been an Indian, he would have fought just as hard to stop his ancestors as he would have fought to conquer the land.

Throughout the long trek home, his eyes never stopped scouting. As well as he knew these woods, he constantly discovered new places hidden from the view of the "revenuers," as they called them—ideal spots for a still. He found dens where bears would soon hibernate. Along the creeks that flowed down the mountains were natural footbridges formed by fallen trees. There were shelters shaped by nature itself where one could hide from an approaching storm.

He learned to recognize the movement of men through the forest. He could tell the footprint of a store-bought boot from one made by the cobblers in Townsend. If revenuers had been through an area, he knew it. The soap his family used was made from lye they produced themselves—no perfumes, no artificial scents. Daily bathing was unheard of. The men from the cities who came searching for stills carried a distinct smell, one entirely different from mountain people. Even in Townsend, Gabriel could smell the difference between those who lived in the mountains and those who did not. Outsiders thought the Fox family carried an odor, and they did—but it was the smell of the mountains, one that blended seamlessly into its surroundings.

For a time, deer had been scarce in these mountains, but with the creation of the Great Smoky Mountains National Park, they were returning. Still, wild boar was the preferred game. His family liked the taste better than deer, and the boar were far more destructive. More than once on trips like this, Gabriel had the chance to take additional game. When that happened, he would kill it, dress it, and hang it in a tree to retrieve the next day.

He often found signs of revenuers on these journeys. Once he reported it back home, it would not be long before other mountain men were quietly trailing them. The government men were rarely aware they had been detected. In these mountains, Gabriel earned what could only be called a doctorate in tracking game and men. His father, Jonas, bragged about him to the other mountain men, and they knew Jonas spoke the truth. The boy was exceptional.

Jonas himself seldom traveled far on foot. The limp from his war injury made long distances difficult. When logging, he rode the mule-drawn wagon along mountain roads as close to the site as possible. The mules dragged the logs back to the road and awaiting wagon. Though limited physically, Jonas constantly passed his knowledge on to Gabriel.

Gabriel began venturing into the woods at an early age. He carried his father's lessons with him and put them into practice. He was given his .22 bolt-action rifle at six and hunted small game constantly. The only thing that slowed him was his mother, who only wanted to cook squirrel so often. Though Jonas could not hunt bear, Gabriel joined other men on his first bear hunt at eight. He carried his .22, but the purpose was learning how to track, not kill.

By ten, he was trusted with the long rifle. The mountain men joked that the rifle was bigger than the boy, but they admired his seriousness. At eleven, Gabriel became something of a legend when he went into the woods alone, tracked and killed a bear, dressed it, quartered it, and hauled it back to the cabin over two days. In most hunts the meat was shared, but in this case there was only one hunter, and the bear fed his family.

He reached home around two in the afternoon and immediately set to work finishing the processing of the boar. He had learned from watching his mother and sisters. The meat was portioned, salted, and hung to cure. He cut a slab of ribs for supper.

The Foxes had an outdoor pit for cooking larger cuts. Gabriel burned short slabs of hickory into coals. When ready, he placed the ribs on the steel grate and cooked them slowly. They would be ready by supper.

Esther stepped to the cabin door and watched her son at work. There were no games in these mountains—no football or baseball—only work, and Gabriel was good at it. He never saw it as labor. To him, felling a tree was an adventure, splitting firewood a game. He challenged himself to split a log with a single swing of the axe. He raced himself against older, bigger men, determined to match or surpass them.

"Gabriel," she called softly, not wanting to break the spell of his concentration. "Wash up before you come in. And don't you track creek mud across my floor."

He looked up just long enough to grin.

"Yes, ma'am," he said, and went back to turning the ribs as if the world depended on doing it right.

If it involved mountains or survival, Gabriel excelled.

He had no concept of the outside world. Townsend seemed like a metropolis. He could not imagine anything larger. The first television he ever saw amazed him—it sat in the general store where the family shopped. The Fox cabin had no electricity or plumbing. Light came from the fireplace, candles, or oil lamps. The cabin had two rooms: a bedroom for Jonas and Esther, and a combined kitchen and living area. A ladder led to the attic where the children slept. The roof was shingled with hardwood. When the wind was right and snow fell, a fine dusting would sometimes settle on the children's blankets. Heat came only from the fireplace and the wood stove. Candles and lamps were lit briefly at dusk and extinguished by Jonas at bedtime.

Bathing was occasional. A galvanized tub was brought inside, a curtain hung for privacy. Water was pumped by hand. Gabriel carried it in two-gallon buckets, fifteen trips in all. Jonas bathed first, then the girls, then Gabriel, then Jacob. Esther bathed last. No one thought twice about sharing the water.

Jacob had been a bright boy until kicked in the head by a mule at four. From then on, he required constant care.

Esther washed clothes once a week using the same tub. In winter, laundry dried indoors by the fire.

There were no luxuries in the cabin, save photographs. A photographer from Maryville occasionally set up in the Townsend general store, hanging a painted backdrop of a church or countryside. Individuals were photographed, then families together. Though the photographer urged them to smile, the mountain people never did.

The pictures hanging on the walls were Esther's greatest possessions. Other than the pictures, there was nothing else beyond the necessities that Esther could call her own. She had clothes. She had shoes. She had a coat, scarf, and hat for winter. There were the necessities for cooking, sewing, and quilting. There were the few items for taking care of the medical needs of the family.

She did have a Singer sewing machine. It was built into its own cabinet and had foot pedals to drive it. Jonas bought it for her just after he returned home from the military. Everything the Fox family wore, for the most part, was sewn on that machine. The general store sold sewing patterns. Even though she had little education, she could follow a pattern. Most of the patterns had been bought years earlier. As the children grew, she adjusted the size of the cut cloth. She always made sure she adjusted the cuts to accommodate growth. So, every time she sewed a new outfit for one of the children, it would be baggy on the child. New clothes were made only when the old were worn out. Patching clothes was one of Esther's regular activities. The clothes would be patched until there was no good material remaining, and then she would go about the process of sewing new.

Every family in these mountains lived essentially the same way. They worked what tillable land they had, growing what crops they could. They raised stock of different kinds—

most for eating. The Fox family raised four hogs every year. They had a smokehouse where they would cure the meat from the animals.

Each fall, with the first hard, cold day, they killed hogs. Typically, they killed four hogs. They had a gantry made from locust, a strong wood. From the cross member of the gantry hung a pulley system made from cast iron and operated by a chain pull. They would lead one hog at a time to the gantry. Jonas would shoot the hog behind the ear, not necessarily killing it, but knocking it unconscious. The hog would fall to the ground. They would quickly place a harness around the hog's hind legs and hoist it in the air. A bucket was placed under the hog, and then its neck would be slit, cutting the windpipe and the carotid arteries of the beast. They would remove the full bucket of blood and replace it with a larger bucket beneath the hog.

Then they would gut the animal, removing its stomach and intestines, making sure they did not puncture either. They would remove that bucket and place another bucket under it. Then they went about removing the other organs of the hog. If it were a female, they would save the uterus, cervix, and ovaries. If it was a male, they saved the sexual organs, along with the penis and scrotum. Once all the organs were removed, they finished cutting the head off the beast.

Gabriel's mother and sisters would go about the task of rendering the blood into a gelatin mass. They would remove the brains, eyes, and tongue from the hog's head. They cut the ears and snout off. They would cut the remaining meat and tissue away from the skull. The skull was thrown into a boiling pot. One of the girls would squeeze the feces out of the intestines, then wash them out by filling them multiple times with water.

Next to the gantry was a large boiling pot, capable of holding enough water to boil the hog for a few moments. The boiling loosened the hair on the skin. Once boiled sufficiently, they would pull the hog from the pot and strip it of hair. Once the hog had been cleaned, they would move it to a table covered with white waxed paper bought from the store in town. The men would slice the skin along each leg and finish slicing from the belly to the neck. The boiling had also loosened the skin from the underlying meat and tissue. One person on each side would start peeling the skin from the hog. They then would flip the skin over and, with special scraping knives designed for that purpose, begin stripping away the attached fat.

Esther and one of the girls would cut the hog into shoulders, hams, loins, ribs, and slabs for bacon. They would strip most of the fat. Once all the fat necessary was stripped away, they would dump it into a larger rendering pot. The pot would boil the fat away from the tissue. The tissue would curl up into what they called cracklings. They had a perforated scoop with which they fished the cracklings out of the rendering pot. They placed the cracklings in a wire basket hanging over the rendering pot so grease would drip back into the pot. They would scoop out any unusable debris and place it in a trash bucket.

Once they were satisfied with the rendering, they had special sealable buckets that they would cover with cheesecloth and begin filling with grease. The cheesecloth filtered it as they poured. Soon several buckets would be filled and set aside. The grease would begin to cool into lard. Throughout that day and the next few, they would go about the same process four times.

The women took every usable part of the hog. Eyes, snout, lips, ears, and the sexual organs were ground to make souse. The cartilage was ground to a fine powder to blend with the other ingredients after they had been thoroughly pickled. The mixture was poured into a form to make a gelatin loaf. It was quick and easy to slice off a portion for a snack. When all the work was done, the family would celebrate by having fried pork loin, eggs, and brains.

Their first bear hunt would be in the early fall, just before hibernating season, when the bear would be at its fattest. They always hunted yearling males, before testosterone had invaded their bodies. They never hunted females. A few males could breed many females to keep the population strong, but a female could not be replaced. The only exception would be a mature female past her prime.

Once the first heavy frost set, they would hunt both boar and deer. From any kill there would be fresh meat the first few days. They would strip much of the meat, soak it in brine, and then hang it either to smoke or air-dry.

Along the north slope of their mountain home, fields were terraced to grow hardy crops that could withstand mountain conditions. Corn was their principal crop. They ate fresh corn in season, but most of what they grew was for other purposes. Some, after being air-dried, would be taken to Townsend to have it milled. The miller got thirty percent of what they brought in. He would mill his third, along with all the other thirds he had gathered, and sell it in Maryville and Knoxville.

Another part of the corn crop went to feed the chickens, guineas, and pigs. Most of it, though, went to moonshine. It was the major source of income for the Fox family from the earliest days of their migrating into the mountains. They could make four times as much by shining as they could by trying to sell the corn.

The rest of the cultivated land went to raising wheat for flour and straw, hay for the two mules and two cows, sorghum for molasses, and the remainder of the terraced land for vegetables of all kinds.

As poor as these people were, they ate as well as anyone. Esther had learned to cook from her mother. Cakes and pies were not out of the question, even by the rudimentary means of cooking with a wood-burning oven. Esther could control the heat in her wood-burning oven as well as anyone could in a gas-fired or electric oven. There was always food on the table at the Fox cabin. Very few would stop by, but if one did, there was food to eat—and it was good food.

The family worked hard. There were no luxuries in their lives. Anyone from the outside would think they were extremely poor. The Fox family never felt that way. Each day was a struggle, but a struggle they were born to bear. They inherited their nature from the generations that had preceded them. Much of their nature was pure animal instinct, bred into them from the Icelandic waters of northern Europe and the hills and ridges of Scotland. They were true mountaineers, not by force, but by their nature.

Years later, Jonas and Esther would eat alone most evenings, except for Jacob, who had to be fed. The two girls would be gone from the mountain, making lives of their own. Their youngest, Gabriel, would be lost in a faraway place—Vietnam.

They would bow their heads over the same plain table and pray together at every meal.

"Lord, thank You for what You've given us," Jonas would say.

"And bring our boy home," Esther would whisper, as if saying it quietly could keep it from breaking.

Neither of them would accept that he was dead.

In earlier years—before the girls grew restless for whatever lay beyond the ridges, before age pressed heavier on Jonas's shoulders—Esther's whisper would have been different. It would have been for protection when Jonas was out in the woods, or for Jacob to have a good day, or for their children to be protected from harm. Back then, the prayer was still shaped like the present.

But even then, the Fox family carried a quiet understanding of what it meant to lose and what it meant to be given back. Jonas would read by lamplight when there was kerosene enough, his finger moving slow across the thin Bible pages, his voice steady as creek water over rock.

Sometimes the reading would land on a story that made Esther go still—one of those passages where a family thought something was gone for good and then grace arrived without warning.

On nights like that, Gabriel would sit close enough to hear the words and close enough to hear his mother's breathing change. He would not always understand why a verse could make a grown woman swallow hard, but he could feel the weight of it.

And Jonas, who never talked much about fear, would close the Book, set it down like a tool, and say simply, "Ain't nothin' too far for the Lord to reach."

Esther would nod, eyes lowered. Then she would get up and tend the fire, keeping the heat alive in the cabin the same way she kept hope alive in her chest—quiet, constant, and stubborn as the mountain itself.

The children, with the exception of Jacob, would climb the ladder to the loft. There were two beds, one a double bed for the girls and a single bed for Gabriel. The mattresses had been in the family for ages. One generation after the other had sewn patches on the heavy material, originally used for flour sacks. Each was stuffed with feathers. At times, a spine of a feather would poke through, causing one to receive a slight prick. A person would sink into the mattress. Heavy quilts would cover the occupant on a cold winter's night. It could be well below freezing, but still a person could sleep soundly.

The girls would giggle and talk till both drifted off to sleep. Gabriel often stayed awake longer, studying the words he had heard his mother or father read from the Bible. Sometimes they read about David or Joshua and the battles they fought. He was always amazed that David, just a boy, could kill Goliath with a slingshot, or how Israel could defeat a larger army. It could be only through God they could achieve such victories.

At school, there was always a reading hour. There were books on a shelf. Each student was required to pick one out and read it completely and give a report when finished. Gabriel was reading about Davy Crockett. He was proud to know that Davy Crockett was from Tennessee. It told the story of Davy killing a bear and catching a rattlesnake. Gabriel had done both. He thought he must be just like ol' Davy. He could not imagine the amount of sadness he felt when he reached the part where Davy died at the Alamo. He thought of how closely he and Davy were alike. Could it be possible that one day far from home, he would die like Davy. Gabriel closed his eyes and prayed. In his dreams, he was in the forest, just like Davy, hunting some foe.

Chapter 6

Life Again

Isaiah 43:2 (KJV)

> "When thou passest through the waters, I will be with thee; and through the rivers, they shall not overflow thee: when thou walkest through the fire, thou shalt not be burned; neither shall the flame kindle upon thee."

Day after day, Phương maintained the same routine. She would awaken with the coming of the dawn. The sounds of the jungle and the distant war were ever present. Her hut was still intact. Her fishpond still provided food. Her livestock were still alive. She still had rice. She still had vegetables. She still had work. She still had purpose. Yet the war had changed everything. The canopy over her cooking area had been repaired and strengthened. She now kept an extra pot of water ready. She now kept food hidden in a way she never had before. The valley was still beautiful, but it was no longer safe.

Her daughter Liên weighed heavy on her mind. It had been more than six months since her disappearance. Phương had accepted she was gone. She had pushed herself to accept it. Yet acceptance did not lessen the ache. Some mornings she woke thinking she had heard Liên's bare feet on the packed earth, or her soft voice from the cooking canopy. Then the truth settled back in—quiet and final. The dying man on the mat in her hut, and her full day's labor, kept her from sinking fully into grief. Still, grief waited. It waited in the pauses—when the fire had burned down, when the rice was set to steam, when the jungle quieted for a moment and the war felt far away.

Once she had completed caring for Buddha and completed her prayers, she would check on the man. She would kneel beside him and place her hand on his chest to feel the rise and fall of his breathing. She would touch his forehead to see if fever had come. She would check the cloth covering his eyes. She would wipe his mouth and nose. She would look for any signs that his body had given up during the night. Then she would rise and begin the work of the day. She did not linger. She did not allow herself to hope. She simply did what had to be done.

Once she fed him, she would go about the task of cleaning him. She washed him with a cloth and warm water. She cleaned his wounds. She changed the bandages. She checked for infection. She did everything she could with the limited resources she had. He did not speak. He did not move much. Yet she sensed something had shifted in him. The way his breathing held. The way his body fought to remain. The way his eyes, even covered, seemed less empty. She knew this meant something after the past months and years she had endured.

Grief in the valley was never loud. It did not come as wailing unless death had just occurred and neighbors were gathered. What Phương carried was older and heavier than a single day's sorrow. It lived in her bones. It lived in the way her hands kept moving—because if her hands stopped, her mind would wander into places she could not afford to enter. She could not afford to picture Liên alone on a road at dusk. She could not afford to imagine a frightened girl calling for her mother where no one answered.

Sometimes, when she stood at the cooking canopy, she caught herself setting out a second bowl without thinking—rice and a few vegetables, the way Liên liked them cut small so she could eat quickly and get back outside. More than once, she reached for the extra bowl and held it for a moment, staring at it as though the food might explain why her daughter had vanished. Then she would quietly return it to the pot, as if the movement itself could erase the mistake.

The man in the hut—Dũng, as she now forced herself to call him—pulled at her attention in a different way. He was not her son. He was not Liên. Yet in the hardest moments her mind insisted on making him familiar, because the alternative was unbearable: an unknown young man, broken nearly beyond recognition, left on her mat by the war. Calling him Dũng was a kind of stubborn defiance against the chaos. If she named him, if she fed him, if she kept him breathing, then the war did not get to claim everything.

She lit incense again that afternoon—too much, perhaps, for a small hut—because smoke gave her something to do with her hands, and because the smell steadied her. She spoke to Buddha in the same quiet tone she used when she spoke to the air where she imagined Liên still lived.

"Con ơi… nếu con còn sống, hãy về nhà."

(My child… if you are still alive, come home.)

Then, as if the words might invite punishment for asking too much, she turned toward the mat and softened her voice further.

"Dũng… chỉ thêm một ngày nữa. Mẹ sẽ làm được."

(Dũng… just one more day. I will manage.)

She did not know whether the young man heard anything at all. But speaking kept her from drowning in the silence.

Once she had completed caring for Buddha and completed her prayers, she would return to her cooking area. There was a new daily task she performed. She would take her mortar and pestle. She would add a small handful of rice to the mortar, along with medicinal herbs, roots and berries, and a small portion of fish. She pounded the mixture of ingredients into a fine pulp. While doing that, she would boil tea. She would add the tea to the pulp, making a soup. She would take her concoction into the hut and sit beside the near-dead body.

His eyes were fixed in a permanent stare. They remained wide open. Every night she would place a folded cloth over the man's eyes to shut out any light. She thought it would help him rest better. In the morning, she would remove the cloth and move her body into position and place her left leg under the man's head. With his head tilted up, she would begin talking to him. "Dũng, ăn ngay." (Dũng, eat now.) She would take a small spoonful of the soup and put it into his mouth.

From the beginning of his arrival in her small hut, feeding him this fine soup mix, she would have to massage his throat for him to swallow. Days earlier, though, she was surprised when his throat swallowed voluntarily, and it had been doing so since. She would now feed him and watch his throat swallow with each spoonful. Feeding him was much quicker now. Still, throughout the feeding process, his eyes stared ahead. There was never any hint of awareness on his part. There were no signs that suggested he knew anything.

Once she fed him, she would go about the task of cleaning him. She kept large cloth diapers on him. She would remove the diaper and its contents. She would wash him and put a clean diaper on him. On this morning, after she fed and cleaned him, she started to stand when she looked at him.

His eyes, those blank eyes, had moved. Rather than being pointed straight to the roof, they were pointed toward her. She moved closer to his head. The eyes followed her. The eyes did not move instantly, but they moved. She moved back from him. The eyes followed her. There was no other reaction from his body other than his eyes moving.

That morning, she stayed inside the hut for a longer period than normal. Each time she moved, his eyes moved with her. She knew this meant something after the past months and only his blank stare, but what it meant, she did not know. "Con nhìn mẹ sao?" she said softly, more to steady herself than to question him. There was no answer. Only the slow tracking of his eyes. She finally forced herself down the steps to begin her daily chores.

She first fed the livestock and the fish. Then she went to the garden, hoed, and weeded the earth around the various vegetables and herbs. She picked what was ready for picking. She spent about two hours in the garden. After the garden, she moved to the rice paddies. It was essentially the same process as the garden. She would spend several hours ridding the paddies of any unwanted growth. She inspected the dikes and made any necessary repairs. She would add water from the irrigation dam, as necessary. She was successful four months earlier in making repairs to the paddies. She lost a minimal amount of the crop at that time.

When she was done at the paddies, she would hike up into the jungle above her hut. She would hunt for additional roots, leaves, berries, snails and grubs, or anything else that could be used for medicine or food. She carried a basket for placing the items in, and her hoe to dig with. She would also bundle fallen branches suitable for burning. She spent an hour in the woods.

She was hungry when she returned home. She always cooked enough food in the morning for the day. She would add coal to the fire so the pot would stay hot. In the evening, she would add a portion of the freshly picked vegetables from the morning harvest. This routine went on day after day, with a different set of chores being added on different days.

On rainy days she would fire hardwood in the pit to make charcoal. She would also smash limestone into a fine powder and bake it at extremely high temperatures. The charcoals were used for that purpose. When at the proper temperature, she would add ashes she had collected. She would bake the ingredients to make lye. With the lye and other ingredients, she would make soap.

On other rainy days, she would take bamboo she had cut from the lush growth. She would cut the bamboo to length, then split it to make chopsticks, đũa, which she would send with Hùng to be sold in the markets in Quy Nhơn. Along with the chopsticks, she would make bamboo knives, forks, and spoons. She would make large spoons for cooking. She would split bamboo, making slats for weaving the conical hats, nón lá, that were common throughout Việt Nam.

Throughout the valley, the same chores were repeated by the citizens of the valley, even during the war. The war brought constant struggle and death, but the day-to-day life stayed the same for so many, just with the added burden of the war.

Hùng would often come by. He and Phương's husband, Bảo, had been friends since youth. They were in the same Việt Minh unit when Bảo was killed by the French. Hùng was wounded and never understood why he was not killed. When he returned home, he always looked after Phương and her two children, Dũng and Liên. For months now, he knew that something occupied Phương's mind. He was not sure what it was. He did not pry and ask questions, but he knew there was some secret Phương was keeping.

He came by that morning and talked to Phương just a short while. Hùng stood beneath the edge of the cooking canopy, careful not to step closer to the hut.

"Phương," he said quietly, "tuần tới, cô có gì cho tôi mang xuống Quy Nhơn?" (Phương, next week, what will you have for me to take down to Quy Nhơn?)

Phương kept her hands busy, tying a bundle of bamboo strips. "Đũa," she said. "Và muối. Và ít rau khô." (Chopsticks. And salt. And a little dried vegetables.)

Hùng nodded. "Tôi sẽ ghé. Như mọi lần." (I'll stop by. Like always.)

He hesitated, then added softly, "Cô... ngủ được không?" (Are you... able to sleep?)

Phương did not look up. "Ngủ được." (I sleep.)

The answer was short and final. Hùng studied her face, searching for something she was not saying.

"Nếu có chuyện gì," he said at last, "cô nói." (If there is anything… you tell me.)

Phương paused only a moment. "Tôi biết." (I know.)

Hùng's mouth tightened as if he wanted to say more than manners allowed. He had known Phương since she was younger, since before the war had turned every conversation into something careful. He had known her as a woman who carried her burdens without complaint—and that was exactly what frightened him now. When Phương withdrew into silence, it was never because she had nothing to say. It was because what she carried could not be spoken safely.

He shifted his weight and lowered his voice. "Cô đừng giấu hết trong lòng." (Don't hide everything in your heart.)

Phương's hands did not pause. Bamboo strips slid through her fingers with practiced speed. "Nếu tôi nói, có giúp gì không?" (If I speak, will it help anything?)

Hùng exhaled through his nose—one short breath that sounded like frustration held in check. "Không biết… nhưng tôi không muốn cô ở một mình với tất cả." (I don't know… but I don't want you alone with all of it.)

Phương finally looked up. Only for a second. The look was not anger. It was warning—gentle, but unmistakable.

"Trong chiến tranh, một lời nói sai có thể giết người." (In war, one wrong word can kill people.)

Hùng nodded once. He understood that warning was not only for him. It was for her. It was for anyone who came near her hut, near her secrets, near the quiet, broken young man she tended.

He did not press again. Instead, he did the only safe thing: he stayed practical. He asked about salt, dried vegetables, rice, and what she needed him to carry. And in the careful way he repeated her requests, as if memorizing them, Phương heard what he could not say aloud: I will come back. I will keep coming back.

They made plans for what she would deliver to him to be taken to Quy Nhơn in another week. When Hùng left, he carried with him a quiet certainty that Phương was hiding something, and an equal certainty that whatever it was, she would never speak of it unless forced to do so.

Throughout the day, Phương continuously thought about Dũng, the man in her hut. The transformation in her mind was complete. The American had become her son. She cared for him as well as she would have Dũng. She did not see an American soldier lying there, but her son, Dũng.

As she had in the morning, she prepared Dũng's evening meal. She would talk to him as she cared for him. She was mother, mẹ, and he was son, con trai.

She would ask softly, "Con trai có đói không?" (Is my son hungry?)

Or "Con trai có khát không?" (Is my son thirsty?)

As she worked, she would tell him about her day. "Mẹ đang làm việc trên cánh đồng lúa." (Mother is working in the rice paddies.)

Sometimes she spoke of small things. The weather. The chickens. What she had planted and what was growing well. There never was any response, no sign of awareness.

Until that morning, his eyes had stared straight forward. But as it had happened earlier that day, when Phương approached him that afternoon, his eyes moved to her. Again, she walked around within his view, and his eyes followed her. She did not know what it meant, other than it was a change.

That night, as she was about to place the cloth covering over his eyes, she saw that his eyes were closed.

Over the next two weeks, the ritual continued. Each new day, there seemed to be more movement in his eyes. Where there had been a constant stare, there now was blinking. Occasionally, his eyes would be shut, as though he was resting. When she moved about the hut, his eyes followed her, each day more connected to her movements. When she talked, his eyes seemed to be studying her. The eyelids squinted, like a studying pup. It appeared he was listening.

It was mid-August 1968, early morning. Phương was sitting before Buddha, saying her morning prayers. She was praying for Dũng when the silence of the hut was broken.

"Mẹ ơi, con khát lắm." (Mother, I am very thirsty.)

For half a heartbeat, Phương could not move. The words were so ordinary—so human—that her mind refused to accept them. For months, the hut had been filled with only the sounds she made: the scrape of a spoon against a bowl, the soft slap of cloth as she cleaned him, the hiss of rice steaming, the distant thunder of war rolling along the mountains. And now a voice had risen from the mat—thin, ragged, but unmistakably alive.

Her throat tightened. A hot sting filled her eyes. She swallowed hard and forced herself to act, because if she allowed herself to feel, she might freeze. "Đừng nói nhiều," she whispered as she hurried to him. "Đừng cố." (Don't talk much. Don't strain.)

His gaze struggled to find her face. The eyes were not vacant now. They were searching—confused, frightened, and strangely young. He tried to lift a hand, but it trembled and fell back to the mat. His mouth worked again, shaping the words with effort.

"Khát... quá." (So... thirsty.)

Phương slid her arm under his shoulders, careful of the stiffness in his joints, careful of skin that had been injured and healed poorly. He was lighter than he should have been. The weight of him felt wrong—like holding a body that belonged to the dead. She pulled him close anyway and steadied his head against her leg.

When the water touched his lips, he jerked as if startled by the sensation. Then he drank too fast and coughed hard, the sound tearing out of him. His fingers clenched once around her wrist—not strength, not violence—only a reflex, an instinct to hold on to whatever was keeping him from slipping away again.

Between coughs, something flickered behind his eyes. Not a memory he could name, but a flash of panic. His gaze darted past her shoulder to the hut opening as if expecting men to appear there. His lips moved, and for a moment Phương thought she heard a sound that was not Vietnamese—something broken, unfinished, like a word half-remembered. Then it vanished, swallowed by his breathing.

She leaned close enough for him to feel her presence even if his hearing failed him.

"Ở đây. An toàn." (Here. Safe.)

He stared at her as if trying to understand the meaning behind the sounds. The fear in his eyes eased by the smallest measure, replaced by exhaustion so deep it looked like surrender.

Phương gave him another careful sip.

"Chậm thôi," she repeated. "Từ từ." (Slowly. Little by little.)

He swallowed, and this time the water stayed down. His eyelids fluttered. His lips formed one more word—soft, almost childlike.

"Mẹ…"

(Mother…)

Phương felt her chest tighten again. The word cut two ways—toward Dũng, toward Liên, toward every child she had ever fed from her own hands. She blinked hard, pushed down the ache, and kept her voice steady.

"Phải. Mẹ đây." (Yes. I'm here.)

He had become mentally aware about a month earlier. For three and a half months, his world was totally dark. There was no connection to the outside world. There were no dreams, no visions, no thoughts. The world was dark. He felt none of the pain of his injuries. He felt no thirst, no hunger, no heat or cold.

After those months, sound started creeping in. At first, all sound was the same. Then Phương's voice began to inch through to his brain. It was as though a baby was hearing sounds from its mother's womb, the brain beginning to digest noise, synapses starting to fire, signals searching for alternate pathways. Along the way, bits and pieces of information from a time past came creeping through, attaching themselves to the new information.

For so long, there had been no information at all. Swelling and damage blocked the movement of signals. The roadways inside the brain were damaged and in need of repair. Just another few ounces of concussive force and the brain would never have functioned again. Just another ounce or two of pressure, Gabriel Fox would have died instantly in the rice paddy. The brain had been on the cusp of destruction, and with it, the body.

The fate of his helmet created a dam and, in turn, an air bubble. The fact that the woman who could have easily hated him and left him lying in the mud to die instead poured her love onto him. The long hours of cleaning and sanitizing wounds. The daily nurturing and refusal to let him die. The food formulated from what the earth provided to nurture and heal. The ancient instructions passed down.

All of it came together, bringing life back into a nineteen-year-old body—a new person, tied to two worlds. The old world still connected by the weakest of bridges. The new world carrying instincts and training from the old. There appeared to be no clear connection between the old world and the new. Things once taught now seemed to come naturally.

Phương had his head propped on her leg. She kept a bucket of water beside the mat. She grabbed a small ladle of water and put it to his lips. For the first time, he sipped the water. His mouth and lips pulled it in.

He choked, his head jerking from her knee with each cough.

"Chậm thôi," she whispered. (Slowly.)

She tilted the ladle cup, and again he sipped. In an instant, he retrained himself to drink. She pulled the ladle away, not wanting him to choke again.

He looked at her. "Nước." (Water.)

She placed the ladle to his mouth again. More sips. He looked at Phương as he drank. He finished the water. His eyes began to close. Soon, he fell asleep. She laid his head back on the mat.

Phương knew nothing of celebration. She had never celebrated a day in her life. Every day was the same as long as she could remember. Her first memories were of work. It may have been a simple task, but it was her task, and she had to do it. There were no dolls, no play sets, no birthday parties. Holidays were observed, but there were no celebrations in her home. Still, the woman's heart was celebrating.

Every morning, the task of assisting Dũng was added to her daily chores, but somehow she managed. Not only did she manage, but she also became more productive. The same amount of work at the paddies was completed in less time. She walked faster. She dug quicker. She did everything at a faster pace, allowing time to care for Dũng.

She began exercising his arms, stretching his legs. He initially screeched in pain as long unused limbs were forced to move and bones once broken were flexed again. Each day over the following weeks, she pushed him to push past the pain, and each day he did. She helped him reach for things.

It took a week before he could sit with his back in a corner. At first, he could only hold his head up for a short while, but each day he grew stronger. It took six weeks before he could stand. Stand he did, for short periods, over the next four weeks. During that time, she helped him take small steps around the hut. Each day, he walked a little farther.

By mid-November 1968, with her help, he eased down onto the valley floor. He held a cane in one hand, Phương supporting him with the other. He was an inquisitive child. He looked all around him. He did not feel emotion, only understanding the images he saw. Land. Green all around. He looked to his right and knew they were at the base of a mountain. He looked to his left, eastward, and saw more mountains. He heard the river—the splash against rocks, the ripple of current—and knew it was nearby.

He saw chickens and pigs and immediately knew what they were. He had heard Phương calling them by name. He understood their purpose. Some things he had to relearn. Others connected instantly.

They stepped onto the valley floor. Phương led him to the cooking canopy. His legs were strong enough to walk and stand, but he would never be able to squat on his haunches as the Vietnamese did. His right leg would not bend enough.

Phương went about preparing their morning meal. Dũng leaned against a rail placed there for him. She had also made a stool from bamboo so he could sit with his right leg extended. As he leaned against the rail, he watched Phương's every movement. In many ways, he was like a newly hatched bird watching its mother.

When she took a wad of betel nut to chew, she handed one to him.

"Thử đi," she said. (Try it.)

She had introduced him to it a few weeks after he regained consciousness. He quickly became dependent on it. It helped him. It sparked his energy.

Other than the distant sounds of war, this end of Happy Valley had been peaceful for the past few months. Still, any explosion in the distance would cause Dũng to jerk his head and tremble. Dũng showed little reaction with his face. To suture his wounds, Phương had been forced to pull the skin tight. The undamaged portions of his lips were drawn to the right, twisting his mouth. His nose had been pulled in the same direction.

Phương taught Dũng to keep his face covered, especially when outside. She tried to keep his presence secret for as long as possible. Few people ventured near her hut, but there was the occasional fisherman, or sometimes Hùng. She taught Dũng to remain quiet whenever anyone was nearby.

Even though his vocabulary was limited, when he did speak the words carried a hint of a dialect not heard in the valley. She was not concerned about people seeing his scars; it was the American side of his face that worried her. That side was always covered.

With his first venture onto the valley floor, Dũng's progress accelerated. Within two weeks, he was able to descend the steps on his own. He began taking on small chores around the homesite. When Phương left to tend other work, he returned to the hut and waited patiently.

His thoughts were limited. In the quiet of the hut, when he was alone, his mind would sometimes drift back into a level of darkness. That condition lingered for months. When Phương was present, or when he was outside the hut, his mind moved more quickly—absorbing his surroundings and learning the skills necessary to survive in this land.

Each day he grew stronger, gradually taking on more work. At first, the tasks were simple. Over the coming months and years, his abilities expanded. He seldom spoke. He never asked questions. He did not wonder who he was. He had no youth to remember. His life had begun in a fog, and he accepted it as it was.

He knew he looked different from other people, but he did not ask why. Phương told him he could not show his face to anyone or speak to anyone else other than her. The pain he felt each day had existed for as long as he could remember. Pain was normal for him. He accepted it without question. There was nothing in his mind searching for answers. He simply existed, and that was enough.

On occasion, patrols from either side passed through the valley. Sometimes questions were asked of Phương. To anyone who inquired, the young man was her son, Dũng. Anyone could see that he had been gravely injured. She would explain that Dũng could not speak and could do little because of his impairments. A brief look was usually enough for people to accept her story and move on. Even those who were members of local Việt Cộng units and had heard that Dũng had died would look at the gravely injured man and ask no more questions.

Just days after Dũng's first venture outside of the hut, Hùng came by. Seeing the young man quickly answered his wondering about Phương's secret. Hùng knew Dũng had been reported dead, killed by two bullet wounds. Hùng was a good man. His daughter, the village schoolteacher, had been killed in 1966 along with several children when an artillery round fell short. The shell had been intended to strike near the top of the mountain above the school, but the casing had been loaded light. There had not been enough force to reach the target.

Hùng did not react the way most men in the village would have reacted. He did not shout. He did not step closer and demand answers in front of the hut where any passerby might hear. Instead, he waited until Phương moved toward the cooking canopy with a pot in her hands, and he followed at a distance that looked casual to any watching eyes.

When she set the pot down, Hùng spoke without greeting, his voice low and tight.

"Cô nói với tôi… đó là ai?" (Tell me… who is that?)

Phương did not turn. She kept her eyes on the fire pit as if studying the coals.

"Con trai tôi." (My son.)

Hùng's jaw worked once.

"Dũng đã chết. Cả làng biết. Người ta đã nói." (Dũng is dead. The whole village knows. People said so.)

Phương's hands stilled. Only for a second. Then she picked up a stick and nudged the coals the way she always did when her mind needed something to control.

"Người ta nói nhiều thứ." (People say many things.)

Hùng glanced toward the hut. Dũng stood with his head down, cane in hand, shoulders tense beneath the cloth that covered his face. He looked like a man trained to shrink away from attention. The sight unsettled Hùng more than any wound.

"Cô đã giữ bí mật này bao lâu?" (How long have you kept this secret?)

Phương finally faced him. Her expression held no apology. Only determination.

"Đủ lâu để giữ anh ấy sống." (Long enough to keep him alive.)

Hùng's eyes narrowed. He searched her face for the kind of lie he could expose. What he found instead was something harder: a truth she would defend even if it destroyed her. Hùng looked again at Dũng—at the way the young man's weight favored one leg, at the tremor that ran through him when a distant crack of gunfire echoed down the valley.

Hùng lowered his voice further.

"Cô biết nếu sai… họ sẽ giết cô."

(You know if this is wrong… they will kill you.)

Phương's answer came without hesitation.

"Họ đã giết nhiều thứ rồi."

(They have already killed many things.)

The two of them stood in silence, listening to the valley—birds, distant war, the small sounds of a life still being lived. At last, Hùng nodded once, slow and grim.

"Vậy thì nghe tôi," he said. "Anh ấy không được nói. Không được bỏ khăn. Không được ra khỏi đây một mình." (Then listen to me. He must not speak. He must not remove the cloth. Must not leave here alone.)

Phương's gaze did not soften, but something in her shoulders eased—just a fraction.

"Tôi biết," she said again, quieter this time. "Tôi đã dạy anh ấy." (I know. I have taught him.)

Hùng looked toward the hut one last time.

"Được," he said. "Tôi sẽ nói với người ta... Dũng sống. Nhưng họ không cần biết nhiều hơn." (Alright. I will tell people... Dũng lives. But they don't need to know more than that.)

Hùng questioned Phương carefully. He studied the young man. Dũng was about the same size as the boy he remembered. The injuries were severe, but they were not the injuries Hùng had been told killed Dũng. Hùng did not know who the young man was, but he knew he was not Dũng.

After a while, and seeing the agitation it was causing Phương, he asked no more questions.

When he returned to the village, he gathered several people around him. He told them that Dũng had returned home. It was a miracle—Dũng had survived and had been injured in an explosion while fighting the Americans. The villagers accepted his explanation. Hùng was known as an honest man. Some would wonder who brought Dũng back to Làng Cây Tre, but none of them had the time to think about it with more than brief thought.

Eventually, Dũng was strong enough to walk into the village with Phương. He never spoke and kept his face covered at all times. No one asked questions. The village accepted that he was Dũng. Hùng had convinced them so.

Often, when Hùng saw Phương and Dũng together, he studied the young man quietly and wondered, who are you? He never spoke the question aloud. There had already been too much sorrow in the valley, in Làng Cây Tre. For Hùng, the young man would remain Dũng.

The new teacher, Cô Bình, originally from Quy Nhơn, was also curious about Dũng. Dũng had once been her student, along with Liên. When Dũng left to join the Việt

Cộng, Bình had feared for his life. When the village was told he had died, she grieved deeply. She also grieved for Liên and felt great pity for Phương.

She could not imagine the depth of Phương's sorrow. Yet sorrow was everywhere. Việt Nam was a land of sorrow—from North to South—and that sorrow spread beyond its borders, to Laos, Cambodia, South Korea, Australia, and the United States. How such a small country could produce so much suffering was difficult to comprehend.

Bình was only twenty years old and had only a high school education. Still, in a village where most adults were illiterate—with the exception of Hùng—she was qualified to teach. She was determined to give the children of Làng Cây Tre the ability to read, write, perform basic mathematics, and understand something of their country's history.

When she heard Dũng was alive, she went at once to see Phương and Dũng. She knew quickly that Dũng was not the man he appeared to be. The injuries were not consistent with the story. She kept that knowledge to herself. She did not question Phương.

Bình approached the hut the way she approached frightened children—slowly, hands visible, voice gentle. She was young, but the war had aged her in ways she did not yet have words for. She had seen too many widows. Too many hungry mouths. Too many boys pressed into roles they never chose."Cô Phương," she called softly from a respectful distance.

Phương emerged from the shadow of the hut opening, her expression guarded. Bình saw the new lines around her eyes, the tightness around her mouth—the look of a woman who had learned that kindness could be costly.

Bình nodded toward Dũng, who stood near the cooking canopy with his face covered. His posture was careful, as if he expected pain from the air itself.

"Em nghe nói… anh Dũng về rồi." (I heard… Dũng has come back.)

Phương answered with the barest nod. "Về." (He is back.)

Bình took one step closer, then stopped. She did not want to crowd the space.

"Anh ấy có bị sốt không? Có ho không?" (Does he have fever? Cough?)

Phương's eyes narrowed—not hostility, but calculation. Every question was a door. Some doors could not be opened.

"Không."

(No.)

Bình hesitated, then tried a different approach—one that sounded like a teacher offering help with a lesson.

"Nếu cô cần... em có thể đem lá thuốc. Hoặc muối. Hoặc vải." (If you need... I can bring medicinal leaves. Or salt. Or cloth.)

For the first time, Phương's gaze softened slightly—not enough to be called warmth, but enough to show she understood the intent.

"Cô tốt," Phương said. "Nhưng đừng hỏi nhiều." (You are good. But don't ask much.)

Bình nodded. She had already seen the answer in what Phương did not say. Dũng's injuries—and the way he held himself—did not match a village boy wounded in the paddy or hurt by a fall. The shape of his shoulders, the length of his limbs, the way his silence felt trained rather than shy—none of it belonged neatly to the story being told.

But Bình also saw something else: the way Phương positioned herself so her body could block Dũng from view if anyone came too close; the way her hand hovered near his arm when he shifted his weight, ready to steady him without making a show of it.

Bình lowered her voice. "Em hiểu," she said simply. "Em sẽ giúp như em có thể."

(I understand. I will help as I can.)

Phương studied her a moment longer, then gave the smallest nod. It was not trust—not yet. But it was permission for kindness to exist without questions.

Dũng never spoke in Bình's presence. His silence, his covered face, and his manner left no clear proof. Bình simply knew. She never shared that knowledge—not even with Phương.

Within two years, Dũng was working alongside Phương in the rice paddies and performing the necessary chores of survival. Phương was able to expand the productivity of their small farm.

The war continued, but it was changing. The Americans were growing tired. Troop levels were reduced. Battles were fewer, but no less violent—sometimes worse. Phương knew nothing of American politics, protests, or division. She knew nothing about riots or demonstrations. She knew only the destruction the Americans had brought.

As the war shifted, Dũng—her son—grew stronger.

In America, the country was deeply divided, sometimes violently. Protests against the war grew louder. Race relations deteriorated. The nation was weary, facing the reality that victory might never come—only stalemate. While young men suffered and died in Việt Nam, movies were made, music played, and dances held. The war appeared on television nightly. For brief moments, people felt the pain—then life continued.

In a mountain cabin in East Tennessee, an elderly couple grieved daily for their son. They held onto the belief that their son still lived and would someday return home. Much of their lives now was prayer. Every night, Esther read from her old King James Bible. Jonas would sit by the fire and listen. Some nights he would pray aloud. Some nights he would just stare at the fire and hold his wife's hand.

Esther kept the Bible wrapped in cloth when she was not reading it, as if the covering could protect the words from the damp that crept into the cabin and the grief that lived there year-round. The pages were thin from use, the corners softened by her fingertips. She did not read quickly. She read the way mountain women did when they believed the reading itself was a kind of labor—steady, faithful, and necessary.

Jonas did not speak much during those evenings. He listened; eyes fixed on the fire as if the flames might show him something he had missed. Sometimes, when Esther reached a verse about sons returning, or about the Lord hearing the cry of the afflicted, she would pause. The pause was never theatrical. It was simply the moment when both felt the same thought, and neither could bring it fully into the open: Gabriel should be here.

On the mantle above the fireplace sat the photograph from basic training. Jonas had straightened it so many times the wood beneath it was polished by his hands. He would look at the face in that picture and feel the old anger rise—anger at distance, at war, at the way men in offices could sign papers that moved boys across oceans. Then he would force the anger down because anger did not bring a son home.

Some nights, when the reading was done, Jonas would stand and face the dark window as if he could see through the mountains and across the world.

"Lord," he would say, voice rough, "I don't know what You've done with my boy. But I ain't forgot him. And I ain't quittin' on him."

Esther would rise and place her hand on his arm. The touch was simple, familiar—like the weight of a quilt in winter.

"Amen," she would whisper, and they would stand together in the quiet until the fire burned low.

Jonas and Esther were alone now. They continued their daily chores. They never stopped working. Jonas walked with increasing difficulty from his war injuries, but he walked. The pain in his leg had been with him for fifty years. The pain had become normal. It made life difficult, but it was his life. As bleak as life seemed, they did not give up.

Over nine thousand miles away, in a remote valley, an old woman and a young man were building a new life. The young man forced himself through pain. He pushed himself through the confusion of his damaged mind. He forced himself to do things, to learn things, and to accept the condition of his life. The old woman, who had lost so much, who could have surrendered to despair, pressed on. Neither of them gave up.

The people in the valley and in the village of Làng Cây Tre worked through the harshness of the war. They continued to plant and to harvest. They saw death too often. They suffered too much, but even in all the grief that the war brought, they continued to push forward. Politics meant nothing to the people, only the repercussions they experienced from all the political forces surrounding them. After countless sorrows, the humble people of Làng Cây Tre continued to push forward. They never gave up.

Chapter 7

Bình and Liên

Matthew 18:6 (KJV)

> "But whoso shall offend one of these little ones which believe in me, it were better for him that a millstone were hanged about his neck, and that he were drowned in the depth of the sea."

The school lay nestled at the foot of the mountain range. One could hear the flow of the not-too-distant river that fed the valley between the surrounding mountains. Springs and creeks flowed from the hillsides, feeding into the river along the length of the valley. This was a true valley, held between two mountain ranges. The natural draft of cooler air dropping out of the surrounding hills brought a continuous breeze to the valley floor.

The students could listen to the sounds of nature in the one-room school. Nature had provided an idyllic place for the students to learn. Unlike the village itself, the school was a stucco-walled building, built by the Việt Minh twenty years earlier. There were no adornments to the school. It had no electricity. A large chalkboard covered a portion of the wall on the north end of the building. Six tables filled the room, three on each side. Three students could sit at each table.

Ngô Ngọc Bình was the teacher. Bình was twenty years old. Her only qualification to be the teacher was that she had graduated from high school in Quy Nhơn. Both her parents worked in one of the busy markets in Quy Nhơn. Her mother cooked all day, squatted in the same position. She and her husband would buy whatever ingredients they could afford for the day, and she would cook rice in one pot and stir-fry vegetables in a wok, chảo, over a wooden fire. She had a second pot to clean her dishes and utensils, consisting of chopsticks and lacquer spoons. Her husband hauled fish from the beachfront fish market.

They had worked hard to see Bình educated and were happy to see her leave Quy Nhơn and away from the chaos the war had brought. Attached to the back of the school was the hut Bình lived in. Her pay was the staples that the villagers brought to her. In this fertile valley, she lacked no provisions when it came to sustenance.

Her life was a lonely life. She was not the prettiest of Vietnamese girls, and she knew she wasn't. She was pragmatic in nature and long ago gave up the idea of romance and love. As modest as her life was, she loved teaching the children of the village and was thankful for the opportunity.

In her little home attached to the school, she cooked all her meals. As with most Vietnamese, hers was a rice-based diet, but unlike some, she always had some form of meat to cook with her rice. The village farmers, which everyone in the village was a farmer or a member of a farming family, provided her with vegetables and the best herbs to garnish her food. She had four hens and a rooster. The chickens were not for eating, but for supplying eggs. When one of the hens or the rooster got too old to produce, then it would be cooked.

Bình was content with her life. The only things that troubled her were the war and missing her mother and father. All the young men were gone, and so many of the older girls had left as well. She taught for only four hours each day, but four hours was enough to make a difference. All the children were eager to learn. Their parents had taught them the necessity of education. Universal education was a goal of the independence movement, and all the villagers were engaged in one way or another in that movement. Politics itself did not enter their thinking. Their only goal was to be free people.

Before dawn, Bình would wake to the same sounds every morning—the small stir of her hens, the first cough of a rooster, the river's steady voice beyond the trees. Her room was little more than a sleeping space attached to the school, but it was hers. She would sit on the edge of her mat and listen for a moment, letting the quiet settle her mind before the day filled with children's questions and chalk dust.

She washed from a basin, combed her hair back tight, and stepped outside to gather eggs while the air was still cool. The war felt farther away at that hour. The mountains held their breath. The valley breeze ran down the river corridor and across the schoolyard as if it had its own purpose.

Some mornings, when loneliness pressed harder than usual, Bình would take out her one prized possession—thin paper folded into a square, a letter from her mother. The ink was faded in places from how often it had been unfolded and refolded. She would read it quickly, as if reading too slowly might make the ache worse. Then she would put it away, set her face, and become the teacher again.

Cadre for the NLF (National Liberation Front), Mặt trận Dân tộc Giải phóng miền Nam Việt Nam, the Việt Cộng, would come into their village frequently and talk about the necessity to support the independence movement. For a poor people who lacked a formal education, they were well versed in the history of Vietnam. They knew the legends of those that fought the Chinese for a thousand years to win their independence. Many of the older villagers had fought with the Việt Minh against the French and the Japanese during World War II, and again against the French after World War II.

The Việt Minh were formed in 1941. After defeating the French at Điện Biên Phủ in 1954, they thought they had won their independence, but now the Americans were here. Again, they were willing to make sacrifices to fight the Americans. They encouraged their sons and daughters to fight with the NLF forces against the Americans. The Americans called them the Việt Cộng, describing them as communist, but communism had little to do with their thinking, especially in the rural areas. It was a matter of freedom for them, and for the Vietnamese to determine their own destiny. Their thinking may have been at odds with the direction the North Vietnamese government had in mind for them, but still, their intent was freedom.

The school was no different than any one-room school anywhere. Bình had fourteen students, ages from six to fifteen. Every student participated in the lessons. The younger students sat in front, while the older ones were at the rear. She would start each day with the students reciting the alphabet. All the children would recite, and they would sing their recitation. The sound of the children would float through the open windows of the school and fill the surrounding area with joy. The Vietnamese language is a tonal language, and the singing recitation would almost sound like birds singing.

Once the recitation of the alphabet was complete, then each student, one at a time, would get up to the chalkboard and write a portion of the alphabet and recite it to the class. Once that was done, Bình would write sentences on the board, and the students would read the sentences aloud. The younger children quickly picked up the ability to read as they read aloud with the older students. Each student had his or her own personal chalkboard at their desk. Each would write what was being written on the large chalkboard in front of the class.

After reading came math, and the structure was the same. The class would count one to a hundred, then thousands, ten thousand, hundred thousand, and then millions. Each child would get up to the board and write the number

Bình instructed them to write—the younger children the smaller, less difficult numbers, and the older students the more difficult. Again, the younger children learned quickly in that environment.

After math came history. Unfortunately, the only books available were the books Bình had for instruction, and they were her personal books brought with her from Quy Nhơn. She would read to the students the history lesson for the day. Bình would read the lesson in such a way that the students found it interesting and exciting. Reading, writing, math, and history were the only subjects Bình taught, but for the students in this rural, farming community, it was enough.

Bình tried her best to protect her students from the horrors of the war. She knew there was nothing she could do about the war itself, but she would not allow the students to talk about it. She hated it when either the Americans or the NLF came to this section of the valley. This village was lucky that it did not have the frequent number of battles between the Americans and the NLF that other places had, but still, it did occur.

She had been teaching in the valley for twenty-one months, and she was beginning to see a change—not necessarily in the students, but in her ability to teach them. Thùy, the previous teacher, had taught them well.

Hùng had brought her from Quy Nhơn in May of 1966. It was not long ago, in January 1968, that she saw her first NVA soldiers in the valley. It was frequent that she saw NLF soldiers moving through, looking for food and support, but the NVA were new to the valley. The Americans made regular patrols through the valley, and she and the students often heard helicopters flying over. During the day the war seemed remote; there was little combat action in or around the valley. At night there was a constant fire of artillery and explosions up on the mountains above them.

On two different occasions, one before Bình came to Làng Cây Tre, and one after, artillery rounds hit in the village. The one before she came landed near the school just as children were arriving for the day. The teacher, giáo viên, and two of the students were killed. The teacher was Thùy, the daughter of Hùng, the village leader. Thành, a male student, lay dying next to her. Another male student, Dũng, rushed to his fallen friend's side and held him as he lay dying. From that moment on, Dũng swore vengeance against the Americans.

After Bình's arrival, another artillery shell hit on the south side of Làng Cây Tre, killing an entire family. Two of those killed were Bình's students. For most of her life, and all her students' lives, there had been war—maybe not to the level it had become by then in 1968, but still, there had been war. Being isolated from the rest of the world, and not knowing, she wondered if this was how other people lived. Did all people face war constantly, the way she and these children did?

Liên, her oldest student, had just lost her brother, Dũng, in combat. He was the same young boy that held his dying friend back in 1966. He was only seventeen, but dying in this country from war could come at any age. At least he was fighting, not an innocent victim.

That morning, Liên did not act like the oldest student in the room. She kept her eyes down, shoulders slightly rounded, as if she were trying to make herself smaller. When Bình began the alphabet recitation, the younger children sang with bright confidence, but Liên's voice stayed buried in her throat.

Bình watched her while the class read from the board. When it came time for Liên to stand and write, her chalk hovered an instant too long before she formed the first letter. The room had gone quiet in the way children become quiet when they sense something is wrong but do not know what to name.

Bình stepped closer, lowering her voice so only Liên could hear.

"Liên... em có khỏe không?" ("Liên... are you well?")

Liên's eyes did not lift.

"Dạ... không." ("Yes... no.")

Bình nodded once, as if the answer were expected.

"Em cứ ngồi. Hôm nay cô viết cho em." ("Just sit. Today I will write for you.")

Liên's fingers tightened around the edge of the table. She whispered, barely audible.

"Con không ngủ được, cô Bình." ("I can't sleep, Miss Bình.")

Bình did not touch her—touch could invite tears in front of the younger ones—but she stayed close for one more breath, steady and present.

"Cô hiểu. Em không một mình đâu." ("I understand. You're not alone.")

Then she returned to the front, lifted her chin, and continued the lesson as if the room itself depended on routine to keep it from breaking.

At night, Bình could not help but lie awake and listen to the sounds of war. There were times when she could hear small arms in conjunction with the explosions of artillery rounds up in the mountains. There were nights she heard the movement of soldiers past the school. Sometimes it was Americans and other times it was Vietnamese. She never looked to see, but she could tell by the smell. She could smell the Americans, whereas she only heard the Vietnamese. She emotionally supported her Vietnamese brethren but wished they all would go away.

She would often think of Liên and the evident sorrow she felt when Dũng was killed. Liên's mother, Phương, was pregnant with Liên when Liên's father was killed by the French in 1953. Her father had been Việt Minh. He, along with other members of the Việt Minh, built the school in 1948. He was twenty-four when the school was built and twenty-nine when he died.

Liên was pretty, by anyone's standards. Hers was a hard life, combined with school and hard work. She was nearing the age to marry, but all the young men were gone, either serving in the South Vietnamese army or with the Việt Cộng. Many of the other girls her age had left the village to work in Quy Nhơn or An Khê up in the mountains. She had never been beyond the village. She dreamed of those other places. She wondered what life would be like outside of this valley.

A few days earlier one of her childhood acquaintances, Hả, came back to the village, riding on the back of a Honda motorcycle. Rather than being dressed in the common peasant pajamas, Hả had on a pretty pink silk blouse with a miniskirt and high heels. She was adorned with jewelry and makeup. Liên had never seen anyone look like that. Liên was amazed by Hả's appearance.

The motorbike pulled up to Liên as she walked home from school. Liên immediately smelled Hả's sweet perfume. Her senses were overwhelmed by the sight and smell. As foreign as this was to Liên, she was immediately envious.

Hả and her driver Bùi, a young and handsome man from Quy Nhơn, pulled up beside Liên. Hả immediately went into her practiced spiel about how good her life had been since leaving the village.

"Trời ơi, Liên… em lớn quá." ("Oh my God, Liên… you've grown so much.")

Liên looked down at her own patched blouse and bare feet, then back up at the silk and heels.

"Chị… chị làm gì ở ngoài đó?" ("What do you do out there?")

Hả smiled as if she were letting Liên in on something important.

"Anh Bùi kiếm việc cho chị. Ở An Khê, có tiền. Dễ lắm." ("Brother Bùi found work for me. In An Khê, there's money. It's easy.")

She told Liên how Bùi had gotten her a job in An Khê dancing for the American soldiers, and how she had American boyfriends that wanted to marry her and take her back to America.

Liên was puzzled when Hả told her she had many boyfriends.

"Nhiều… bạn trai hả chị?" ("Many… boyfriends?")

Hả nodded as if it were normal, as if it were modern.

"Người Mỹ trả tiền để có bạn gái. Ở đó là vậy." ("Americans pay money to have a girlfriend. That's how it is there.")

"Có nhiều người, em chọn người tốt nhất." ("With many men, you choose the best one.")

She told Liên that with many boyfriends she could choose the best to marry and go to America with—and she was making lots of money, far more than Liên could ever hope to make in the village.

Bùi then spoke, calm and confident, like a man who knew the road belonged to him.

"Anh giúp em được. Em đi một chuyến thôi. Có tiền liền." ("I can help you. You only go once. You'll have money right away.")

What Liên did not know—and what Hả did not say in front of her—was that Bùi's work was recruitment. He traveled throughout Bình Định Province and up Highway 19 toward An Khê and the highlands, delivering girls into a war economy that profited from hunger, loneliness, and coercion.

Phương did not know this. Hùng did not know this. Bình did not know this. In Làng Cây Tre they saw only what appeared in front of them: a motorbike, perfume, city clothes, and a promise spoken with confidence.

Bùi's access came from his father, a Major in the Army of the Republic of Vietnam assigned in provincial administration. The Major hired Bùi as an assistant, which exempted him from conscription. With the father's credentials, Bùi moved through checkpoints and towns with an authority most young men could not claim. He was known across the region, not only by South Vietnamese officials and Americans, but also by the Việt Cộng, who watched roads the way farmers watched weather.

There was another layer beneath the uniform and paperwork—an allegiance kept quiet, profitable, and insulated. Money moved out of bars and brothels into hands that never touched the labor. In that kind of war, corruption did not respect flags. It fed whoever was positioned to collect.

None of that reached the understanding of a village girl on a footpath.

Bùi was a slick talker. He knew how to woo the girls. So many, like Liên, were innocent when he approached them—just like any young schoolgirl anywhere. They had dreams of love and romance, just like all young girls do.

Hả told Liên she should go with Bùi soon.

"Em đi. Em sẽ mừng vì đã đi." ("Go. You'll be glad you did.")

All of it was a lie, and Hả knew it was. Hả had learned it was necessary to please Bùi and the others who ran the bars and brothels. It was for her safety that she would go with Bùi to recruit other girls. It was better for her to ride on the back of a motorcycle with Bùi than to be ridden by the G.I.s in An Khê.

As pretty as Hả was, she carried sickness in her body that she did not name. There was little or no treatment for the girls who contracted diseases. Still, to so many, it was better to make their living this way than to toil in the rice paddies and heat of South Vietnam.

There was also the fatalism of so many young girls in Vietnam. It was better to get it while you could, because death in this land of war was almost a certainty. Very few did not have a relative or a friend who had died because of the war.

Bùi and Hả talked to Liên for a few more minutes. Then Bùi told her he would be back.

"Năm ngày nữa anh quay lại. Nếu em muốn đi, đứng chờ ở đây." ("In five days I'll come back. If you want to go, wait here.")

Liên walked away, headed toward the hard labor of the day. She could not help but wonder about what she had just been told.

The path home felt longer than it ever had. The smell of Hả's perfume stayed in Liên's nose like smoke trapped in cloth. Every few steps she looked down at her feet—brown with dust, nails broken short from work—and tried to imagine them inside shoes like the ones she had seen on the back of the motorbike.

She told herself she was only curious. She told herself she would not be foolish. Yet Dũng's death had made the valley feel smaller, as if the mountains had leaned in closer. If a boy could die and be carried home wrapped in straw matting, then what safety had any of them?

By the time she reached her mother's hut, Liên had already begun the quiet lying a person does to survive: she kept her face calm, answered Phương's simple questions, and did not speak of Hả at all. The words sat inside her like a stone.

That night, while Phương slept, Liên stared into the dark and listened to the valley breeze. She tried to picture herself in An Khê, in a place where there were lights, money, and men who spoke a language she did not know. She tried to picture herself never carrying baskets, never bending in the paddies, never waking to hunger.

Then her mind snapped back to her mother's breathing beside her. The sound was thin and tired, as if each breath had to be earned. Liên swallowed hard and turned her face to the wall so Phương would not hear the quiet sob she could not stop.

The sadness still was overwhelming about Dũng's death. Liên was a virgin, but she understood what Hả meant by many boyfriends. She continued her walk home, thinking about a change in her life. She felt sad at the thought of leaving her mother, but it would be better to leave alive than dead as Dũng had. It soon would be rice harvest time, and she thought about the back-breaking labor she would endure. The thought of many boyfriends did not seem so bad.

Bình often thought about Thùy and about her death, and the death of the two students. She thought about the terrible reason she had been brought to Làng Cây Tre and the stories she had been told about it.

The morning was beautiful that March day in 1966. The first American combat troops had arrived in Vietnam a year earlier. Within that year, the American bases, firebases, and landing zones had spread across the countryside rapidly. At the entrance to the Sông Côn valley sat a newly constructed firebase named Thunderhead. It sat adjacent to Highway 19 that led up into the Central Highlands from Quy Nhơn.

A unit of Việt Cộng had set up an ambush on Highway 19 at An Khê Pass, Đèo An Khê. Once the ambush was complete, the Việt Cộng retreated north along a ridge. An observation helicopter spotted the unit and called in an artillery strike on the fleeing Việt Cộng. The unit at Thunderhead received the orders. The artillery crew rapidly set up and dialed in the coordinates. Unfortunately, the FDC had miscalculated the coordinates by a few degrees. The crew pulled the trigger lanyard and the shell exploded out the end of the 155 howitzer. The Sergeant in command immediately recognized the sound of a round with a short powder charge.

Up the Sông Côn valley, in the village of Làng Cây Tre, Thùy, the teacher, giáo viên, of the small village school, trường học, stepped out to greet the first arriving students that morning. The teacher and the two students never heard the oncoming sound. The exploding shell, even though not a direct hit, had enough force to kill the three of them. Other students came running to the three.

Hùng, who was a short way away, driving his two water buffalo, trâu, to a nearby field, took off running toward the school, as did all the villagers.

At the school, Hùng and his wife held their dead daughter, con gái. Dũng, one of the students at the school, held his dying friend as he took his last breath. Another set of parents came running up to see their young daughter dead, con gái đã chết, on the ground. Everyone else stood back and looked on in shock and disbelief. Some studied the damage to the school. The mother of two of the school children who lived about a mile up in the far end of the valley heard the explosion and ran toward the village as fast as she could. All could hear artillery shells exploding in the far distance. Eighteen miles south of the village, men worked diligently loading artillery rounds in a 155 howitzer.

Two months later, Hùng loaded his buffalo-drawn cart with goods from the citizens of the valley. He was on his way to barter or sell the goods. It was amazing what all could be loaded onto the cart, from live chickens and pigs to bundles of chopsticks, nearly ripe fruits and vegetables. The trip was over thirty-five miles and would take two-and-a-half days to make. Throughout the trip, he would stop and feed and water the livestock and the trâu. At night, he would pull alongside the road and sleep under the cart. At first light, he would be on the move again.

He would often be stopped by American or South Vietnamese soldiers and searched for contraband. At times he would be stopped by Việt Cộng. He always carried additional provisions to hand out when necessary. The Việt Cộng only took what they considered a fair portion. Hùng did not always agree with their assessment.

Hùng arrived in Quy Nhơn on Wednesday, May 11, 1966. There were multiple markets in Quy Nhơn, but one Hùng would always go to get rid of his goods and acquire more to take back to Làng Cây Tre. He had met a couple who had a food stall in the market. The woman would remain squatted in the same position for about twelve hours every day. Every day she cooked Cơm tấm gà, broken rice with grilled chicken and stir-fried vegetables. The menu never changed, and she had been in the same spot for over twenty years.

Her husband would go through the market in the early morning hours and acquire the goods needed for the day. The wife could count on serving virtually the same number of meals every day, with it only varying by a few on any given day. When the husband had supplied her with her daily needs, he then would go down to the ocean and haul fish in baskets up to the markets. Night fishermen would be coming in just at dawn with their night's catch.

When he was finished with that task and paid, he would then get his cart that was full of all kinds of goods, such as cigarette lighters, lighter fluid, condoms, small bottles of whiskey, and other goods that a G.I. might want. He would push his cart through the streets of Quy Nhơn, selling his wares to whatever passing serviceman was interested in buying something.

Hùng went to see the wife for one purpose only. The couple had a daughter who had completed school and wanted to be a teacher. The village of Làng Cây Tre needed a teacher. The daughter nor her family could afford to send her further on to school to get her teaching certificate, which she would need in Quy Nhơn, but out in the country it did not matter. If Hùng was willing to take her back to his village, then she could teach.

The daughter's name was Bình and she was introduced to Hùng the month before. Hùng immediately recognized that she wasn't a very pretty girl. Even in Vietnam, attractiveness was a plus. After discussion, it was agreed that on Hùng's next trip to Quy Nhơn, Bình would return with him to Làng Cây Tre to become a teacher. Bình had the books she had acquired going to school, which were not very many, but enough to help her instruct the children of that section of the Sông Côn valley.

On Friday, May 13, 1966, Bình loaded onto Hùng's cart. There were short goodbyes between her and her parents. She waved goodbye as the cart pulled away from the market. Bình was nineteen years old and had never been more than a few blocks away from the sheet-metal shanty she and her parents had occupied all her life.

Her parents worked hard to make sure she would be able to finish school, but there was no more they could do for her now. Within a few minutes, Bình was seeing sections of Quy Nhơn she had never seen. She knew nothing of the town other than those few square blocks that had been the center of her life. That day was the first day she had ever traveled by any type of conveyance other than foot. She marveled at the experience.

After an hour, the city started disappearing. The trâu-drawn cart was entering the countryside. This was a new marvel to Bình. She had never seen open spaces other than her view of the ocean. She heard about the countryside in school, but she had no real idea what that meant. As their cart slowly plodded on, she was even more amazed at the speed of the vehicles passing them. There were trucks, jeeps, motorbikes, and even troop carriers.

At the first checkpoint in which the cart was searched, Bình was completely frightened. She had seen Americans from a distance but had never come in direct contact with them. Like Hùng, she did not know a word of English. If not for the Vietnamese interpreter, neither she nor Hùng would have any idea what the Americans wanted. Also, Bình had heard frightening stories concerning the Americans. Fear rushed through her at that initial contact. It did not take long, but they were waved on without any type of incident.

That night the two of them bedded down by the roadside. This was another scary situation for Bình. Even though she had spent every night of her life until that night on the floor of a sheet-metal shanty, this was horrifying for her. She lay next to Hùng and shook under her cover while he fell fast asleep. She could not understand how he could go to sleep under these conditions. After a few hours, sleep finally overtook her. She had no idea how much greater her fear was going to be.

The next day was uneventful. Bình was accustomed to the hustle and bustle of life in her small area of Quy Nhơn. There was constant movement and noise for twenty-four hours a day. That was her norm. With all the noise in the city, sounds of war were seldom heard. Now, out in the country, things were extremely quiet. She heard the sounds of nature for the first time. In the distance she could hear the sounds of war. She was unsettled by this newness to her life.

Hùng spoke little except for describing her new living conditions and the expectations of her job as the teacher in Làng Cây Tre. She had been excited at the prospect of her new life, but now she realized how much she already missed her parents, bố mẹ. She was experiencing extreme culture shock on that long, plodding ride to the Sông Côn valley.

On the third day they had left Highway 19 and were now on not much more than a cart path, worn by the now frequent motorized vehicles. Bình had nodded off that early morning. Her night's sleep had been restless under the cart. She was dreaming of Quy Nhơn when she felt the sudden jerk of Hùng's hand against her arm. He was pulling her off the cart.

It was in that instant of her being awakened that she heard the first shot, and then the many that followed. As her eyes opened, she saw several men in black pajamas running across the path in front of them. Some were turning and firing their rifles in the opposite direction. Hùng pulled her hard to the ground and then dragged her under the cart.

She saw men coming their way and they were firing their weapons. They were spread out across a rice paddy adjacent to the path. They were firing at the fleeing men in black. From the corner of her eye, she saw one of the trâu suddenly slump and fall to the ground. She heard Hùng scream. Shortly, she saw what were obviously Americans crossing the path in pursuit of the men in black. Within five minutes they were all gone from view.

Bình could not move. Hùng could. Hùng crawled out from under the cart and walked to the already dead trâu. Her falling had pulled the other buffalo to his knees. The two were a breeding pair and had been together since their youth, acquired shortly after they were weaned from their mothers. In the twelve years Hùng had owned them, the female had delivered three offspring. He had trained them well. Not only were they purposeful for work, but they were also a part of his family. Hùng had great affection for the two animals, as they did for each other.

Hùng stood over them in the thin, shocked quiet that follows a burst of gunfire—when the ears are still ringing and the world feels as if it has inhaled and forgotten to exhale. The cow trâu lay on her side in the red dust of the road, her legs folded wrong beneath her, her great barrel chest no longer rising. A dark, wet patch spread through the short hair at her shoulder and into the dust. The cart's yoke beam, ách, had twisted when she went down, and the weight of it had wrenched the male into a kneel, forelegs splayed, neck bowed under the strain. The bow on the cow's side, vòng ách, still cinched around her neck, trapping the beam in place. The male's nostrils flared wide and wet; he snorted once, ragged, and his eyes rolled white at the edges.

Bình crouched behind the cart wheel, gripping the sideboard with both hands. Her face was gray with dust and disbelief.

"Hùng—"

"Hùng—"

"Im." ("Quiet.")

Not a request. A command born of habit. He lifted one hand, palm down, pressing the air as if he could make the world lower its voice. Somewhere off to the left, beyond scrub and stunted bamboo, a rifle cracked—single, deliberate. A distant shout in Vietnamese. Another shout that was not. Hùng did not try to decide who was where. He had learned that guessing wrong was worse than not guessing at all. He dropped to a knee beside the male first. Not the dead one—there was nothing he could do there now.

He ran his hand along the rigging by feel, finding what had gone tight when the cow collapsed: a rope trace, dây kéo, pulled hard against the yoke and the cart tongue, holding the male down with her.

"Ê… ngoan… ngoan." ("Easy… good… good.")

"Đứng yên. Không sao." ("Stay still. You're all right.")

The male trembled but held. Another crack, closer. Dirt jumped on the road ahead of them. Bình flinched and ducked lower. Hùng drew his knife, dao, in one smooth motion. The blade was short, ugly, and familiar. He did not cut anything that would lose him the cart. He cut only what was dragging the male into the ground. One slice. Fibers snapped. The tension released with a sigh. The male jerked his head up, startled by the sudden slack, then snorted again, louder.

"Tốt. Tốt." ("Good. Good.")

Now the yoke. He tried to lift the yoke beam off the cow. It shifted only a finger's width—still trapped by the cow's bow. The cow's neck, heavy even in death, pinned the bow against the ground. Hùng's mouth tightened. There was no gentle way. He moved low along the cow's throat and shoulder, making himself small the way old men had taught him—small targets live longer. He slid his fingers to the bow pin, chốt ách, on her side. It should have come free. It did not. The yoke had twisted; the pin was under load. He braced his boot against the yoke beam and lifted the beam a fraction with his knee, just enough to take strain off the hole. He rocked it—small, precise—then tried again.

The pin budged. He worked it out slowly, wincing at every distant crack as if the sound might make the wood seize again. When the pin finally came free, he did not drop it. He shoved it into his waistband without looking. Pins were life now. The bow loosened around the cow's neck, but her head and shoulder still pinned it. Hùng slid the bow upward, forcing it past the thick curve of her jaw. It snagged once at the ear, then came free with a wet, reluctant pull. For a heartbeat he stared at her face. The eye was half-lidded, glassy already. Flies would come soon. She had been with him long enough that he knew the exact pattern of old scars on her flank—the pale crescent where she had once caught herself on a broken stake. He had always thought she would die old, in mud, with her calves near her. Not here. Not in dust. Not from a stranger's bullet.

His throat tightened hard, as if he had swallowed the wrong thing.

Another shout—close now—somebody moving through brush. Hùng blinked once and forced his hands back to work. He lifted the yoke beam up and away from the cow, freeing it completely. The beam was long, meant to span two necks; with only one animal it would jut out like an awkward arm. But a trâu could still pull if the pull point stayed centered and the cart tongue did not yaw.

He swung the beam onto the male's withers and slid a folded strip of sackcloth under it—always, because wood rubs, and rub becomes raw skin, and raw skin becomes infection. He positioned the center ring, vòng kéo, near the midline of the male's neck. Then he did what only a trâu-hand would think to do in a moment like this: he slid two fingers under the bow line at the throat—checking space, checking breath—making sure nothing pressed on the windpipe.

"Bình, giữ dây." ("Bình, hold the rope.")

She crawled forward on hands and knees, staying below the cart's bed rail, and took the rope he tossed. Her fingers fumbled once, then tightened. Hùng brought the remaining bow, vòng ách, up under the male's neck. He chose the inner holes on the beam to keep the animal as close to center as he could and pushed the bow pins through.

Pin through. Tap with the heel of his palm. Check it seats.

"Ê... ngoan." ("Easy... good.")

"Sắp xong." ("Almost done.")

Now the cart connection. With two animals, the pull ropes would split and feed an evener bar to keep the load balanced. With one animal, leaving the evener in place would make the cart yaw with every step—too much side play with a frightened trâu. Hùng reached under the cart's front and yanked the evener free from its crude hook. Wood clacked on wood. He tossed it into the cart bed beside Bình's satchel and the rolled mat she had brought from Quy Nhơn.

He ran the main pull rope directly from the yoke's center ring to the cart tongue attachment point and shortened it with a quick, ugly knot—a farmer's knot that would hold under load and could be cut later if needed. Not pretty. Strong. The cart would still want to drift, pulled from one side. Hùng took another length of rope and tied a stabilizer line from the free end of the yoke beam to the opposite front corner of the cart, then gave the cart tongue a hard tug to test it. The cart shifted but did not swing wide. It would hold—crooked, but workable. He checked the male's legs—no obvious blood, no torn hoof.

The animal was shaking, but standing now, half-crouched, waiting for permission to move. Hùng rose just enough to look over the cart wheel. Ahead, the road dipped toward a stand of trees—cover. Behind them, open ground and the shimmer of paddies. To the left, brush where the shouting came from. To the right, a low bank and a drainage ditch. He did not think about politics. He did not think about flags. He thought about angles and earth.

"Bình, lên xe. Nằm xuống." ("Bình, get in the cart. Lie down.")

"I can't—" Her voice broke.

"Em làm được." ("You can.")

His eyes cut to hers, hard.

"Ngay." ("Now.")

She climbed into the cart bed, pulled herself in like a child, then flattened behind the front plank. Her hair had come loose; dust clung to her cheek like flour.

Hùng put his palm against the male's neck and leaned close so the trâu could feel him.

"Đi.," "Go."

"Đi thôi.," "Go on."

The male took one step—hesitant, testing. The yoke creaked. Rope went taut. The cart shifted, heavy, then rolled a few inches. The male's ears flicked, searching for danger, but the pull made sense to him: forward meant relief.

A rifle cracked again. Something snapped through the bamboo behind them with a sharp, dry sound. The male flinched. Hùng stayed pressed close, guiding the animal's head forward with the rope.

"Đi.," "Go."

"Đi.," "Go."

The male committed. Two steps, then three, hooves thudding into dust and damp patches where the road dipped. The cart followed, lurching once, then settled into a crooked line that still moved.

The dead cow remained behind—still in the road, still and wrong, as if the world had simply dropped her there and forgotten to pick her up. Hùng did not look back. He could not afford the luxury of looking back. He kept one hand on the lead rope and one hand near the yoke, feeling for any shift that might choke the animal or slip a pin. He listened for the cart's alignment—the scrape that would tell him the stabilizer rope was failing.

The male breathed hard, but he pulled.

From the cart bed, Bình's voice came thin and shaking.

"Cô ấy... chết rồi.," "She's... she's gone."

"Ừ.," "Yes."

"Bây giờ im.," "Now be quiet."

He guided the single trâu toward the dip in the road and the promise of trees, toward cover, toward any place where bullets might pass through leaves instead of flesh. The yoke creaked again, steady now, and the rope held. In the midst of war—men trying to kill each other for reasons that never reached the hooves of a trâu—Hùng did what he had always done in the countryside: he made what was broken into something that could still move forward.

They stopped once before dusk at a hamlet where the houses sat back from the road behind hedges of cassava. An old woman watched from a doorway as Hùng led the male trâu to a muddy puddle and let him drink. The animal drank only a little, then stood with his head low, sides heaving, as if he could not understand why the pull beside him was gone. Hùng did not speak to anyone. He sat on the cart's edge and retied the stabilizer rope, tightening the knot until his fingers hurt, then tightened it again.

Bình did not eat. She held a tin cup someone pressed into her hands and stared past it. When a child came near the cart, curious, Hùng lifted his eyes once—sharp enough that the child froze and backed away.

That night, Hùng slept sitting up with his back against the cart wheel, his hand still looped in the lead rope. The male trâu lay a few paces away in the dirt, not in the mud where he usually preferred to bed down. Twice he rose, turned his head toward the dark road, and made a low sound that was not quite a call and not quite a groan. Hùng did not answer him with words. He only tightened his grip and kept watch.

The return trip to Làng Cây Tre took a day longer than would have been normal. Bình remained in shock from what had occurred. Hùng stayed quiet through the remainder of the trip, moving as if he were counting costs with every step: grief, and economic necessity. How would he replace the female? The male trâu plodded along, steady and obedient, but his ears searched constantly at empty space, as if listening for the familiar breath that should have been there.

They arrived in Làng Cây Tre near dark. Dogs barked from under stilted houses. A few villagers came out to the path and stopped when they saw the cart and the single animal under the long yoke. No one asked questions at first. They did not need to.

That night, and for several following, Bình stayed with Hùng until she had settled into her new environment. Only then did she move into the small room attached to the back of the school. Over the coming months she grew more comfortable with her surroundings. It took her time, but she became proficient at instructing the children.

In February of 1968, as Bình instructed the students, she wondered where one of her favorites was—the fifteen-year-old girl Liên. She had heard a motorbike early that morning but did not connect it to Liên not being there.

It was only late that evening, when Liên's mother, Phương, showed up, that Bình became genuinely concerned. She went with Phương throughout the village and to the different huts surrounding Làng Cây Tre in search of Liên. They asked questions, listened to what people thought they had seen, and followed every small lead until there were no more.

When they arrived at Hùng's hut and told him the situation, he listened and asked a few questions of his own. He did not promise anything he could not deliver. He said he would keep his eyes and ears open and ask around in the days ahead. Bình and Phương continued the search without him.

They had no success other than establishing that a motorbike had left Làng Cây Tre with a young woman on the back. It seemed likely it could have been Liên, but nothing was certain. Phương still hoped that Liên would soon be back at their hut. They did not sleep. The village was not large, but in the dark it became a maze of shadows, bamboo fences, and narrow footpaths that all looked the same. Dogs barked and then went quiet again. A baby cried somewhere and was hushed. Each sound made Phương turn her head as if her daughter might step out of the night at any moment.

At one hut, an older woman shook her head slowly, eyes wide with gossip and fear. "Con bé đẹp quá… dễ bị dụ.," "She's too pretty… easy to be lured."

Phương's voice came sharp, the edge of a mother who would not accept a verdict "Đừng nói vậy. Con tôi không ngu.," "Don't say that. My daughter is not foolish."

Bình tried to keep the questions practical—what time, what direction, who saw what, how many people on the bike—but she could feel the village drifting toward rumors. That was how fear protected itself: by becoming stories.

Near the edge of the village, a boy admitted he had heard the motorbike earlier than usual, heard it stop, then heard it take off fast—too fast for a normal ride. He could not say more. He had been afraid to look.

Bình walked Phương back toward the school only when there was nothing else to do. Phương did not want to stop searching, but exhaustion was beginning to make her movements unsteady. At the doorway, she turned and stared into the dark one more time, as if will alone could pull her child back down the path. "Ngày mai… mình tìm tiếp," Bình said gently.
"Tomorrow… we keep looking."

Phương did not answer. Her face held a hope that was already turning into something harder—an endurance that had no choice but to continue breathing.

That morning, as soon as the motorbike took off with Liên on the back, fear shot through her. She had never been on a motorized vehicle, and the sensation and speed were frightening enough. She immediately realized she had made a mistake and began pleading with the driver, Bùi, to stop and let her off. He ignored her pleas. Her pleading continued until he stopped.
"Dừng lại! Cho tôi xuống! Làm ơn!," "Stop! Let me off! Please!"

Bùi got off the bike and turned and slapped Liên across the face with as much force as he could muster. The slap knocked her off the back of the bike. She fell to the ground, and Bùi was immediately on top of her, with a knife drawn and against her throat. "Im miệng!," "Shut your mouth!"
"Nếu mày không im, tao cắt cổ mày và bỏ mày chết ở đây.," "If you don't shut up, I'll cut your throat and leave you dead here."

It was the first time in Liên's life that anyone had hit her. The fear was overwhelming. Bùi soon had her back on the bike.

Shortly, they were on Highway 19 headed up to An Khê. Liên sat on the back, stunned and frightened into silence. Her head spun with dizziness, and she often felt nausea as the motorbike weaved its way up the mountain road through the many curves. The road was gravel, sprayed with waste oil from the many vehicles that the Americans owned. It kept the dust down.

Many military vehicles occupied the road. Liên saw few of them though. Her eyes stayed closed. Even with overwhelming fear, she laid her head on Bùi's back. She felt like she had died and her life was gone. Hopelessness engulfed her spirit, but she had no idea how much more so it would be. She had no idea how much of her humanity she would lose over the coming months and years. Once a child that could love, she would soon become an individual that cared about nothing, except survival.

The mother, the hut, and the school in the valley would become distant memories. In the coming months, she would learn to steal, to lie, and to cheat. She would smile brightly at her paying suitors and tell each one that she "would love them long time." They were "number one G.I." Somewhere in her mind, she still thought that one of them might take her to America. Each one of the Americans, no matter how many, she would tell them, "I love only you, you number one."

Down in the valley, those that loved her grieved. It was accepted that Liên was gone. Phương kept hope. Bình simply had no answers. The good man, Hùng, thought that Liên was gone for good. The only rescue for Phương was the man she now called Dũng. It was his presence in her life that gave her any meaning.

Chapter 8

A Lost Child

Psalm 27:10 (KJV)

"When my father and my mother forsake me, then the LORD will take me up."

With Dũng for company, Phương's mind did not dwell on Liên as often as it had. She had not forgotten her daughter, but her mind no longer sought answers to her disappearance. She accepted Liên was gone and had no expectation of seeing her again.

She and Dũng had made their place productive. Once he had gained strength, she would find him making repairs to anything he found needing repair. He took palm leaf and repaired the roof of their hut. It was difficult for him to climb, and the pain was significant, but it did not hold him back. Their storage shed was in good order. The fish ponds were thriving. He reworked the overflow screens which kept the fish in the ponds when monsoons swelled and threatened to spill them into the grass. New bamboo pipes ran from the irrigation dam to the paddies. New handles for implements were made. Hoes and shovels were repaired.

Her son, Dũng—always quiet, rarely talking—had come a long way from his first conscious moments. As his ability to work grew, his output grew with it. There was no training. He simply took on tasks of his own will, and he was capable. Even though he made no connection between what he knew and his past, it was from his past that he advanced so rapidly. The things he did in his new home were the things he did in his old home. The crops were different, the location different, yet so similar. Memory of his old home never came fully to the front of his mind, but his activities carried memories with them. It was in his old home he was taught these things, and it was in his new home he executed them.

In the valley, the sounds of war were becoming much less. The Americans had reduced their numbers dramatically from over half a million personnel in 1968 to just over one hundred fifty thousand by 1971, and the talk drifting up Highway 19 was that within another year there would be only a fraction of that remaining. Vietnamization had been implemented, and seldom did the ARVN—Lục quân Việt Nam Cộng hòa—venture into the valley or into the mountains above Làng Cây Tre. When soldiers did appear, they stayed closer to the road and the markets, leaving the deep end of the valley to its own silence.

It was mid-afternoon. Dũng sat under the cooking canopy making a woven basket from palm leaf. He was going to set up a trap for crayfish from the mountain streams. Phương was tending the garden. The meals had become a bit more elaborate over the past few years. They ate more vegetables with their rice and fish. Their diet included more chicken. This household of mother and son prospered. The average American would not see it as prosperity, but in this land, Phương and her son were doing quite well.

The valley sounded different than it had in the years when Americans moved like storms across the ridgelines. Now there were days when the jungle held its breath again—only cicadas, the soft chop of a hoe, the far-off call of a bird. It was not peace, not truly, but the sharp edge of fear no longer cut every hour.

Phương worked without looking up, hands sure in the soil. She did not talk much. Words could be overheard. Words can be remembered. But sometimes, when the air was still and the river's voice covered them, she spoke the way mothers speak to sons when they are both alone in the world.

"Con đói không?" ("Are you hungry?")

Dũng did not answer at first. He glanced toward the tree line—an old habit—then nodded once. His face was covered as always. In the early days, Phương thought she would never get used to the scarf, never stop flinching when she caught the wrong angle of light. But she had learned to treat it the same way she treated everything else: as necessary.

"Chút nữa ăn," she said, more to herself than to him. "Nấu canh rau."

"We'll eat soon. I'll make vegetable soup."

Dũng resumed weaving. The palm strips slid through his fingers with a quiet patience, the kind of patience that came from pain. He had grown stronger over the years, stronger than Phương expected a broken man could become, but his movements still carried stiffness—a reminder that the past lived inside bone and scar.

Phương straightened and wiped sweat from her brow with the back of her wrist.

"Đừng đi xa hôm nay," she said. "Don't go far today."

Dũng paused. His eyes met hers briefly. Then he nodded again, as if he understood more than the words. He always understood caution.

They were both hard at their tasks when they heard a motorbike in the distance.

There had never been a motorbike this far up the valley.

Dũng stiffened, frightened by the new sound. Phương, from the garden, looked at Dũng under the canopy and made a quick motion for him to go into the hut.

"Vô trong nhà," "Get inside the hut."

"Nhanh," "Quick."

Dũng's hands moved before his mind finished naming the sound. His scarf came higher, the cloth pulled tight across his cheek and jaw. He pressed back into the shadows as though the hut could swallow him whole.

A motorbike did not belong up here. Motorbikes belonged to roads and towns, to cadres and soldiers and men with papers. Motorbikes brought questions. Questions brought eyes. Eyes brought the kind of attention that never ended well.

His right side ached in the old familiar way—pain that arrived when fear arrived, like they were tied together by a single cord. In his memory there were flashes: boots in mud, voices too loud, the crack of rifles that made the world turn white at the edges. He could not always tell whether the images were true memories or only dreams that had learned to wear the mask of truth, but his body never questioned them. His body remembered.

Phương's quick motion from the garden was not panic. It was discipline—an instinct sharpened by years of surviving. Dũng understood that more clearly than any spoken instruction.

He watched the path through the hut opening, breathing shallow, waiting to see what kind of danger the sound would carry into their lives.

As quickly as he could, he moved up the steps. From the shadows he looked out. In the distance, the motorbike stopped and became quiet. Both Phương and Dũng wondered what the motorbike meant and why it had come this far.

The motorbike carried three people: the driver, a woman, and a baby. The bike stopped just short of the first of three bamboo footbridges leading to Phương's hut. The woman was holding the child.

The woman looked nothing like the women in the valley.

She wore high heels, stockings, a black mini-skirt, and a purple silk blouse. When she stepped off the motorbike she nearly fell with the baby. She found walking the dirt path in her heels next to impossible, stumbling and tripping. She cursed, then pulled off her shoes and walked in her stocking-covered feet. Runs immediately developed in both stockings.

The woman swore at the result, then spoke harshly to the driver and shoved the baby into his arms.

"Bế nó," "Hold him."

The driver looked at the bridges as if they were a trap.

"Cầu hẹp lắm," "The bridges are very narrow."

"Nguy hiểm," "It's dangerous."

"Im đi," "Be quiet."

"Đi," "Move."

The three proceeded on foot, crossing the footbridges on the way to Phương's hut. The bamboo creaked under their weight. The woman's stockinged feet slipped once, and she hissed another curse as the driver tightened his grip on the baby.

Both Phương and Dũng saw them as they entered the clearing.

Neither Phương nor Dũng had ever seen a woman like this. She did not wear the black or gray peasant pajamas everyone at this end of the valley wore. Her face was covered with makeup—lipstick and eyeliner. Her appearance was shocking. The strong smell reached them even before she did, a sweet scent like flowers poured from a bottle.

Phương felt apprehension tighten her chest as the pair approached. She wondered why the man and the bizarre-looking woman were coming toward her. What could be their purpose?

Dũng stood in the shadows of the hut opening. As the two approached, he stepped back further into the hut. He squinted, trying to see what the man carried in his arms. Dũng could see close-up fine, but at a distance everything was blurry.

Phương stepped forward.

She did not understand why, but there was something familiar in the woman's movement, the angle of her head, the sound of her breath. The closer they came together, the stronger the familiarity became.

The woman spoke one word.

"Mẹ."

"Mother."

Phương froze.

Emotions overwhelmed her. The voice was familiar, but it sounded hard—like a familiar song played on a broken instrument. The realization struck her that the woman approaching was her child, her beautiful Liên. Yet there was no beauty in this woman, only harshness, as if someone had taken the softness out of her and thrown it away.

What Phương had imagined would be joy turned immediately to sadness.

Phương's throat tightened.

"Liên… phải không con?" "Liên… is it you, my child?"

Liên's eyes flicked past her as if she could not bear to look directly into her mother's face for more than a moment.

"Đừng hỏi," "Don't ask."

"Mẹ nghe đây," "Listen to me."

Liên's eyes stayed hard, as if softness would break her. Her hand trembled once, then steadied—anger or fear, Phương could not tell which.

"Con không có thời gian," Liên hissed. "I don't have time."

"Con về nhà," Phương pleaded, the words escaping before she could stop them. "Come home."

Liên's mouth tightened.

"Nhà nào?" "What home?"

Phương flinched as if struck. She tried again, quieter, trying to build a bridge with her voice.

"Mẹ… mẹ chỉ muốn biết con sống hay chết."

"I only want to know if you're alive."

Liên's gaze flicked to the driver—one quick look, a warning between them—and then back to Phương.

"Đừng hỏi," "Don't ask."

Phương swallowed. Her throat burned.

"Con… con bị làm sao? Ai làm con ra nông nỗi này?"

"What happened to you? Who did this to you?"

Liên's jaw clenched. For an instant, the girl Phương remembered surfaced in the shape of her eyes—then vanished again.

"Không còn quan trọng."

"It doesn't matter anymore."

The baby whimpered, sensing the tension the way infants always do. Liên shifted her grip, tightening the cloth around the child as if she could keep him from being seen.

"Nghe mẹ nói," Phương tried again, voice breaking. "Con ở lại. Mẹ giấu con. Mẹ—"

"Listen to me. Stay. I'll hide you. I'll—"

Liên cut her off with a sharp shake of her head.

"Không được," "No."

"Vì sao?" "Why?"

Liên's voice dropped, urgent and rough.

"Họ tìm con. Con ở lại là chết. Nhưng đứa nhỏ… đứa nhỏ phải sống."

"They're looking for me. If I stay, I die. But the child… the child must live."

Phương stared at the bundle, heart turning over in her chest.

"Nó… tên gì?" "He… what's his name?"

Liên's eyes flashed with something like shame.

"Không có tên."

"He doesn't have a name."

Phương reached out as if to touch Liên's wrist, to claim her daughter with one small contact, but Liên jerked away like the touch was fire.

"Đừng nói với ai," Liên said, words spilling out fast now, fear finally breaking through the anger. "Don't tell anyone."

"Mẹ biết," Phương whispered. "I know."

Liên leaned closer, the perfume and sweat and dust all tangled together.

"Nếu họ hỏi, nói là con nhặt được. Nói là… bất cứ gì."

"If they ask, say you found him. Say… anything."

Phương nodded once, already understanding the rules of the moment: lie well, lie simply, lie the same way every time.

Liên's eyes flicked past Phương again—always watching the path, always ready to run.

"Mẹ… đừng ghét con," she said, so quiet it was almost lost. "Don't hate me."

Phương's breath caught.

"Con là con của mẹ."

"You are my child."

For a fraction of a second, Liên's face threatened to crumble. Then she hardened again, as though softness would get her killed. She drew back, readying herself to do the one thing she had come to do—leave.

Dũng moved closer to the doorway, trying to understand the events unfolding before him.

From his position it appeared the young woman and Phương were arguing. Liên spoke fast and sharp. Phương's voice rose and broke, pleading.

Dũng stepped out of the hut and headed down the steps. He walked as quickly as possible toward them.

The young woman snatched the baby from the driver's arms and shoved the child into Phương's arms. The baby cried immediately, loud and desperate.

Liên's mouth twisted as she shoved the bundle forward.

"Giữ nó," "Keep him."

"Mẹ nuôi nó," "You raise him."

Phương clutched the child as if she might drop him, as if her arms did not believe what was happening.

"Tại sao?" "Why?"

"Con về nhà đi," "Come home."

Liên's laugh was short and bitter.

"Nhà?" "Home?"

Liên's next words were laced with profanity, words Phương had never heard in her life. Profanity had never been part of Phương's world, and the meaning was lost to her, but the hatred inside the words was not.

Before Dũng reached them, he heard the cries of the child and saw Phương's face go blank with shock.

The couple suddenly turned and started back down the path. Phương walked after them, still holding the baby, her steps unsteady.

"Liên!" "Liên!"

"Liên, đừng đi!" "Liên, don't go!"

Liên did not turn back.

She hurried away, the driver moving ahead of her toward the bridges as if afraid of what might happen if they stayed even another moment.

Dũng reached Phương, and in her arms was a baby—a boy. Dũng had a difficult time understanding the situation. Phương was stunned by the sudden exchange between her and the daughter who had disappeared over three years earlier. She did not know why she was suddenly handed the baby and why Liên and the motorbike driver took off so quickly.

She had thought about what it would be like to see Liên again, but this was never the image she had carried through the long nights.

It was only the woman's voice that had made her certain.

Phương had never seen a woman dressed like that. The woman's face looked painted. Her lips were bright red, her eyelids blue and sparkling. She smelled strongly of perfume. Her words were few and harsh.

Phương looked down at the child for the first time.

Dũng looked too.

Phương realized immediately that this child was half American. His skin was dark, much darker than any Vietnamese. Phương understood immediately that this was the child of a Vietnamese woman and a Black American soldier. She had seen Black soldiers when they had been on patrol.

In the Central Highlands, as the American troop size continued to dwindle, it became more difficult for the women of the night trade to survive. Those women were looked down upon by Vietnamese citizens, and those with half-American children were looked down upon even more. Liên had moved far past the possibility of ever living in a rural farming community again. Whoever controlled her had forced basic humanity out of her. She was cold and hard now.

The brief exchange between mother and daughter was the last time Phương would see Liên.

Over a decade later, in a shack on the outskirts of Kon Tum, Liên lay on a woven mat, burning with fever, suffering from delirium brought on by untreated syphilis. In the final moments of her life, her mind slipped back into the cool breezes of the Sông Côn valley. She heard her mother's voice talking to her quietly, the way it used to sound before the world took the softness away.

Phương and Dũng walked back to the hut. The baby cried without pause. Phương placed the baby on the floor and told Dũng to watch him.

"Canh nó." ("Watch him.")

Dũng had no idea what he was watching for. Phương told him she was going to the village, then turned and headed out the door and down the steps.

Dũng stood looking down at the crying baby on the floor. In this new life, it was the first baby he had seen. He was not quite sure what he was looking at. He had no idea what he was supposed to do. For the first time, he felt anxious. He looked toward the opening of the hut and wanted Phương to return.

Questions shot through his mind. He looked at the child again. He had absolutely no idea what to do, but he walked to the child and reached down and picked him up. The baby continued to cry.

It was hungry, but Dũng did not know that at first.

He was not quite sure what he held in his arms, except for some memory creeping in from a place he did not know. An image of a boy holding a baby, just as he was holding this child. Out of that memory came a feeling—an emotion—one of happiness. Dũng had not felt that. The only things he had felt for the past two years were pain, hunger, and thirst. There had been little emotion beyond survival, but this new feeling that crept into his being felt good.

He did not question where the image came from. It simply was there.

The baby continued to cry. Dũng shifted the child in his arms. The cry changed slightly. Dũng realized the baby was hungry. Again, where that realization came from he did not know, nor did he ask.

Down-valley, Hùng was working a field between the village and the river when he heard the motorbike. From experience, Hùng understood motorbikes often meant trouble. The people of the valley had no motorbikes. Those who came with motorbikes usually brought bad fortune.

Hùng was working a young pair of trâu when he heard the sound. A few years earlier, he had watched what he believed to be a perfectly healthy male trâu grieve itself to death. He had borrowed to buy the new pair, and it took all his effort to pay for them.

Hùng left the pair in the field and started back toward the village. As he reached the village, he saw the motorbike heading back south toward Highway 19.

At the school, Bình heard the bike coming into Làng Cây Tre and heading north outside the village. A short time later she heard it again as it came back through. She stepped to the door of the school just as it passed. The children rushed to the windows to look out.

Bình called out.

"Hùng!"

Hùng stopped at the schoolyard's edge. Bình came closer, keeping her voice low.

"Xe đó đi đâu?" ("Where did that motorbike go?")

Hùng's eyes stayed on the trail.

"Lên trên." ("Up-valley.")

Bình's face tightened.

"Không tốt." ("That's not good.")

The children watched them, sensing something unusual. Bình lifted her voice slightly so it sounded like ordinary schoolyard instruction.

"Mấy đứa, vào lớp." ("Children, go inside.")

Hùng nodded once to Bình, then started walking toward the north end of the valley.

Hùng had crossed the first of the three footbridges leading to Phương's place when he saw her coming his way. She had a concerned, agitated look on her face. They stopped on the bridge where the bamboo flexed under their weight.

Phương spoke quickly, her voice trembling.

"Liên về." ("Liên came back.")

Hùng's eyes widened.

"Liên?" ("Liên?")

Phương nodded once, then the words poured out in a rush—Liên's painted face, the perfume, the harshness, the baby shoved into her arms, and Liên's disappearance back down the bridges.

Hùng listened. In Phương's face he saw sorrow, not only shock. The sorrow of a mother who had dreamed of a return and received only a wound.

Hùng's voice dropped.

"Đứa nhỏ… ở đâu?" ("The child… where is he?")

Phương pointed back up-valley.

"Trong túp lều." ("In the hut.")

Hùng watched her for a moment, then stepped aside on the bridge to let her pass.

"Chị đi làng đi." ("Go to the village.")

Phương nodded and continued her walk into the village as Hùng continued up to Phương's hut.

Hùng walked up the steps and saw Dũng holding the child. Even in the dim light, Hùng could see the child's dark skin. He knew the child would not be welcomed into the village. He thought about what this would bring down on Phương, but he also recognized the care with which Dũng held the child.

It was the first time Hùng had seen Dũng without a scarf covering his face. The side he saw made Hùng's stomach tighten. The skin tone, the shape—it was not Vietnamese.

Hùng did not speak what he thought. In this valley, speaking the wrong truth could kill you.

He looked at Dũng again—at the covered face, the careful stillness, the way the man held his body as if he had learned to live around pain. Hùng had seen wounded men before. He had seen men broken in ways that never showed on the outside. But this was different. This carried the smell of a larger war, one that did not belong in their valley and yet had found them anyway.

Hùng lowered his voice.

"Che mặt lại." ("Cover your face.")

Dũng's hand went automatically to the scarf, tightening it. His eyes stayed on the baby.

Hùng nodded once.

"Đừng đem đứa nhỏ ra ngoài." ("Don't bring the child outside.")

Hùng's gaze moved to Dũng.

"Tôi sẽ nói với Bình." ("I'll tell Bình.")

Dũng hesitated—just a blink of time—then gave a small nod. Bình was careful. Bình had survived by being careful. If anyone could help them build a story that would hold up under questioning, it was Bình.

Later that day, Hùng found Bình at the school, straightening slates and tidying the room as the light faded. He did not speak at the doorway. He stepped inside first—so anyone passing would only see a man visiting a teacher, nothing unusual.

When Bình looked up, Hùng said only:

"Có chuyện." ("There's something.")

Bình's face tightened the way it always did when danger entered her mind.

"Nói đi." ("Say it.")

Hùng leaned closer, voice low.

"Liên về. Chỉ một lát. Để lại đứa nhỏ." ("Liên came back. Only briefly. She left a child.")

Bình did not gasp. She did not ask why. She only closed her eyes for a moment, as if steadying herself against the weight of what that meant.

"Đứa nhỏ ở đâu?" ("Where is the child?")

"Ở với Phương." ("With Phương.")

Bình's eyes opened. They were very calm now, and that calm frightened Hùng more than any panic would have.

"Vậy thì… phải có câu chuyện."

("Then… there must be a story.")

Hùng nodded.

"Một câu chuyện đơn giản." ("A simple story.")

Bình looked toward the open doorway, toward the valley outside.

"Và phải nói giống nhau mỗi lần." ("And it must be said the same way every time.")

Phương knew one of the women in the village had recently lost an infant and would still be lactating. She went to that hut, located up a small stream valley, and explained she needed milk and would need it for a while. She offered eggs as payment.

Of course, the woman was inquisitive.

"Sữa cho ai?" ("Milk for who?")

Phương's mind raced. She spoke quickly, too quickly, words that came out like a clumsy lie. The woman did not believe her, but eggs were eggs, and hunger in the countryside was its own judge.

They made an agreement.

It was well over an hour before Phương returned. Along the way, she met Hùng after he had informed Bình. When they arrived at the hut, they both climbed the steps to the inside. Phương carried a small bucket and a clear glass bottle. She poured a portion of the milk into the bottle.

As she poured, Dũng said one word.

"Milk."

Both Phương and Hùng jerked their heads toward Dũng. The word brought fear to Phương and clearer understanding to Hùng. It was an American word.

Phương forced herself into instruction, as if teaching could push fear away.

"Sữa. Sữa. Sữa."

Dũng repeated, careful.

"Sữa."

Hùng left shortly afterward. On his way back to his field, he stopped at the school and asked Bình to step outside with him, away from the windows and the children.

His voice was low. He again explained how they must guard their knowledge for the safety and welfare of

Phương, the man, and the baby. Hùng stood silent for a few moments. His head hung in deep thought. Bình studied him as he stood there. He raised his head and looked into Bình's eyes, and they both nodded in agreement.

Into the lives of Phương, Dũng, Bình, and Hùng came the child.

Phương referred to him only as "trai," the Vietnamese word for "boy." Another daily task was added to Phương's routine. She walked to the farmer's house with eggs, vegetables, and whatever else she could spare and exchanged them for milk. In the beginning, Dũng was the principal caregiver. He fed the child most often. He cleaned the child. Phương looked on.

Bình came up-valley a few days later with Hùng, walking as if it were an ordinary visit—no urgency, no signs of alarm. In the valley, urgency drew attention.

The baby was in Dũng's arms, fussing and turning his head with hungry impatience. Bình crouched near him, careful not to reach too quickly, careful not to appear too interested.

Phương watched, expression unreadable.

Bình spoke softly, the tone she used with frightened students.

"Nó cần tên." ("He needs a name.")

Phương's eyes narrowed.

"Tên làm gì?" ("For what?")

"So that if someone asks," Bình replied, "you don't hesitate." She kept her voice even. "Do you understand? Hesitation is what betrays people."

Phương stared at the child. The boy's skin was darker than any child she had ever seen in this valley. His hair was thicker, curling slightly even now. The village would notice eventually. A name would not hide him, but a name could steady the lie that would protect him.

Dũng shifted the baby higher on his hip, rocking him in the small, automatic motion of a man who had learned care through doing, not through tenderness.

Bình continued. “If you call him ‘trai’ every day, the word will become his name anyway.” She glanced at Phương. “Let it. Make it ordinary.”

Phương’s jaw tightened.

“Ordinary,” she repeated, as if tasting the word.

Ordinary did not exist for them anymore.

Hùng’s voice came quietly.

“Đúng. Bình nói đúng.” (“Yes. Bình is right.”)

Phương looked away toward the trees, toward the river. A long moment passed. Then she spoke, not to Bình or Hùng, but to the child himself—testing the sound.

“Trai.”

The baby stared up at her, blinking.

Bình nodded once.

“When people ask, you say he is Trai.” She paused. “And you say he has no father anyone needs to talk about.”

Phương’s eyes flicked to Bình—a sharp warning. Bình did not flinch.

“I am not asking you to tell the truth,” Bình said carefully. “I am asking you to survive.”

Phương looked down at the child again.

“Trai,” she said a second time, more firmly now, as if placing a stake in the ground.

The baby’s mouth opened, and he let out a sound that was not a cry—almost a small, surprised breath.

Dũng rocked him, and for the briefest instant, something softened behind the scarf in the way Dũng held the boy—quickly buried again under caution.

Phương was distant in her emotions toward the child. She did what was necessary and nothing more. It was not cruelty. It was fear and resentment tangled together, fear of the village, resentment at Liên, resentment at the burden dropped into her arms without mercy.

Bình and Hùng took an interest. They came as often as they could without drawing suspicion. Rumors spread through the village anyway. Curiosity about why Phương came daily for milk grew sharper with each passing day.

The child was rapidly weaned from only milk to a combination of milk, rice, and fish. Just as Phương had made soup for Dũng, she made a blend of food that was healthy for the child. Strange as it may be, she still felt little affection in the beginning, but she felt obligation, and obligation in the countryside could be stronger than affection.

Dũng learned quickly how to care for the boy. He learned how to feed him, to clean him, and to keep him safe. Dũng wove a basket to carry the child on his back while he and Phương worked. When the boy became a toddler, Dũng took bamboo sticks and formed a pen at the rice paddies so he and Phương could work while the child crawled and later walked safely.

The boy was bright. As he grew, he learned quickly. Dũng did not teach with words, but the boy watched everything he did.

Over the next few years, the war continued, but its impact on this end of the valley became minimal. By 1972 the Americans were nearly gone from Việt Nam, and by 1973 the last of the American combat troops had left. The valley no longer saw combat. In essence, war disappeared from their daily lives. Word would drift in that there had been a big battle somewhere between the armies of the north and south, but it had little impact on them.

Trai continued to grow. He followed his uncle—chú—Dũng everywhere he went. Dũng still could not walk at a fast pace, so it was easy for his nephew—cháu trai—to keep up. Trai watched everything Dũng did. Dũng spoke only when necessary, and then he said only what needed to be conveyed. It was through actions, not words, that he taught the boy.

In April 1975, word spread through the valley that armies from the north had conquered the government in the south. There was celebration throughout the countryside. People were told that things would be better now.

For the next ten years, that was not the case.

Government policies wrecked the economy. Leadership was brutal. Old surviving members of the Việt Cộng moved back into villages and took leadership roles. Communist cadre from the north were sent in to make sure people understood their roles and duties to the new government. Village leaders throughout the country—even those who had not served the government in the south—were treated harshly. Many were sent to "học tập"—re-education camps. Many died.

Spring of 1976 brought new leadership into the valley, men who spoke in strict Communist principles and demanded more production. They told people what to grow and how much to grow. They did not allow people to veer from policy.

Hùng watched the change. It had been difficult during the war, but now, in certain ways, it was more difficult. He went to the new cadre and offered criticism and advice. It was never accepted openly.

A stucco office building was built for the administrators. A generator was brought in, and the building had electricity, the first electricity seen in Làng Cây Tre. Bulldozers were sent down through the valley, and what had once been a cart path began turning into a gravel road. The expectation was to move goods to market quicker. Along the way, gardens and ponds were covered by the new road. The villagers objected to Hùng, and he carried complaints to the new leadership. He was kicked out of the office more than once.

The cadre did not argue with him in public. They simply watched him.

Without Hùng's knowledge, it was determined he needed to be "re-educated."

One day he was summoned to appear before a judge. Hùng arrived and within minutes found himself being conveyed to a re-education camp. He found himself clearing jungle by hand. The food was miserable, the work backbreaking, and punishment severe when it was perceived someone had committed a violation or was simply not agreeable enough.

More than once, he found himself for days in a metal box just large enough to hold him. Food and water were withheld. When he had enough to defecate, he did it on himself, in his pants, because there was nowhere else.

Hùng held out for years under those conditions.

In August of 1983, his trip to the box was his last. Heat, thirst, stink, and pain became more than he could take. For all the years of his life, Hùng—despite all the pain of that life—remained steadfast and strong. He drifted into unconsciousness, but along the way he passed through the Sông Côn valley in his mind. He felt the cool breeze and smelled fresh air. He saw the wife he lost so many years ago. He saw his daughter standing in the doorway of the school. He heard his old trusty trâu grazing on green grass in Làng Cây Tre.

In 1978, Trai was seven.

He had learned much while working with his uncle, but unlike most children in the valley, he was not allowed to go to school. From the time of Trai's arrival, Cô Bình visited Phương's family as often as possible. When Trai was old enough, Bình began teaching him in secret. Trai was not her only pupil. Dũng would sit with them and study also.

Bình found joy in teaching the two of them. Phương would either sit silently or find something to keep herself busy while the three worked on lessons.

Bình kept the lessons small and ordinary, hidden inside ordinary visits.

"Mở ra." ("Open it.")

"Đọc chậm thôi." ("Read slowly.")

"Không ai được biết." ("No one must know.")

Trai learned that his presence in the village was not welcomed. In truth, neither he nor his uncle was welcomed. Long ago Hùng and Bình had figured out the man at Phương's hut was not Dũng, but who he was, they did not know. They guarded their knowledge closely. Hùng had confirmed his suspicion when Trai arrived and when he saw Dũng's face and heard the American word. Bình confirmed her suspicion after hearing Dũng's accent, an accent not born of tỉnh Bình Định.

After the first word spoken—"milk"—Dũng would sometimes have other words come into his mind. They were seldom spoken aloud. He could be using an implement—cái cuốc—and the English word would appear in his mind like a fish breaking the surface of water. A few times the words, or even a sentence, slipped out.

Phương scolded him each time.

"Im." ("Be quiet.")

"Đừng nói vậy."

("Don't speak like that.")

"Người ta nghe là chết." ("If people hear, we die.")

Phương was fearful someone would hear him. She was afraid the authorities would find out she had an American living with her. She was afraid of the consequences.

Dũng began having dreams. In those dreams there were other people, a man and a woman, talking to him in familiar voices. Bình's lessons triggered thoughts in his mind. He dreamed of sitting at a desk with a woman writing on a chalkboard. He never spoke about the dreams. He never questioned Phương about his existence. After years, he began to realize there was a missing period of time in his life. The presence of Trai made him realize that. He knew he had been a child, but those memories were lost to him, with only the occasional dream or thought reminding him of that time. At times, when showing Trai how to do something, he found himself almost talking in a different voice, and sometimes he did. It was a voice from a memory long ago. It brought him comfort.

In 1983, Phương, Dũng, and Trai headed to the rice paddies. As the three walked, Dũng and Trai noticed Phương falling behind, which had become common. They would stop and wait on her. Often Trai would walk back to give assistance.

Even after twelve years, Phương was reluctant to show affection toward Trai. In their isolated life, the lack of affection seemed normal to Trai. He had nothing to compare it to. He had no friends he could speak to about his life. Dũng, though never verbally expressive, gave Trai as much affection as he could in that environment—steady presence, quiet attention, and protection.

Phương had developed a persistent cough over the past months. In this land of constant fatigue, she felt even more fatigued. Dũng and Trai could see Phương losing energy. She treated it with local remedies. Along the way she stopped and coughed heavily. Dũng and Trai encouraged her to go back to the hut, but she insisted on working.

They reached the paddies and stepped in.

Throughout the morning, Phương continued coughing, and each cough became worse than the last. Dũng and Trai were hoeing when they heard a loud cough and a sudden splash. They looked and saw Phương lying face down in the paddy.

Trai screamed first.

"Mẹ! Mẹ! Mẹ! Mẹ!" ("Mother! Mother! Mother! Mother!")

Dũng's shout followed, rough and broken.

"Mẹ!" ("Mother!")

They splashed through the paddy and reached her. Phương was unconscious. They pulled her up from the water.

"Mẹ, mẹ, mẹ…" ("Mother, mother, mother…")

Phương was unresponsive.

Dũng's voice came hard, the only clear instruction he could form.

"Túp lều." ("The hut.")

They laid her on the sleeping mat, the one they had all shared. Dũng stood for a moment, staring at her face as if willing her to return, then he turned to Trai and spoke with force.

"Đi, Bình." ("Go—Bình.")

Trai understood and ran down the steps toward the village to find Cô Bình. He ran as fast as he could without stopping. Crossing the three footbridges, it took him close to twenty minutes to reach the school. He summoned Bình and told her what had happened. She dismissed the school immediately.

"Về nhà." ("Go home.")

"Ngay bây giờ." ("Right now.")

She went with Trai as fast as she could.

While Trai and Bình were making their way to the hut, Phương regained consciousness and began coughing again. Dũng held her, attempting to give her water, but her coughing was too severe for her to swallow. It had been many years since she had held the man who now held her. After a few moments, her cough quieted and she began breathing heavily, gasping for air.

Trai and Bình arrived.

Inside, they knelt beside Phương as her head lay in Dũng's lap. Bình knew little of medicine, but she could feel Phương's rapid heartbeat. Her breathing was rapid and shallow. None of them knew that inside Phương's left lung was a cancerous tumor. It had been growing for a long time. It had reached its end.

Phương lay there breathing heavily. She looked at the three surrounding her. She did not need to be told. She had reached the end.

Her eyes lifted to Dũng.

"Dũng…" ("Dũng…")

"Con trai mẹ." ("My son.")

Then she reached and touched Trai's face.

"Con trai mẹ." ("My son.")

She gathered breath with difficulty and whispered the truth she had withheld for years.

"Hai con trai của mẹ." ("My two sons.")

Bình's eyes filled, and she did not wipe them away.

Phương looked to Bình with the last strength she had.

"Hãy dạy dỗ các con trai của mẹ thật tốt." ("Teach my sons well.")

Phương's hand fell back onto the mat, light as a leaf. Her breathing was no longer steady. It came in shallow pulls, then paused—long enough that Bình leaned forward, listening, watching for the small sign that life was still there.

Trai's face was wet. He did not wipe it. He was past pride, past the need to look strong. He was only a boy again in that moment, watching the only home he had ever known slip away.

Dũng stayed close, shoulders hunched, as if he could shelter Phương with his body the way he sheltered Trai. His eyes were fixed on her face, searching, trying to understand what his mind could not hold. For years he had lived inside the day in front of him. Now the day in front of him was taking his mother.

Bình did not speak a prayer aloud. In the valley, prayers could be interpreted as defiance, as gathering, as religion—dangerous words in dangerous times. But inside her mind, she formed the words anyway, shaping them silently as she watched Phương's chest rise and fall.

Xin Chúa thương xót.

Lord, have mercy.

Phương's eyes opened once more, unfocused at first, then settling—briefly—on Trai. Her lips moved as if she wanted to say something more. Only air came out.

Trai leaned closer.

"Mẹ..." he whispered, voice cracking. "Mother..."

Phương's gaze slid toward Dũng—toward the covered face, toward the son she had kept alive when the world tried to take him. A faint sound escaped her, not a word, more like the last breath of a name held in the heart.

Then her eyes drifted away from them, as if she were looking past the roof and the mountains and the years into a place none of them could follow.

Her breathing stopped.

Bình reached for Phương's wrist, held it gently, and after a moment she lowered her hand. She looked at the two boys—one born of the valley, one dropped into it by violence—and she understood that whatever love meant in this place, it would have to be taught in actions, not speeches.

In the morning, after Phương's body had been cleaned and wrapped, Dũng and Trai carried her to a far corner of their small farm. They dug a deep enough hole to lay her body in. Dũng and Trai covered her over.

There was no ceremony. No prayers.

One would have thought the two burying her had no love for her.

Neither knew the term love. Neither knew how to define what they felt, but as they looked down on the mound of dirt, their hearts poured out love for the woman.

Bình stood silently by.

At the school, children gathered, wondering where Cô Bình was.

After Phương's death, Dũng was responsible for necessary dealings. He found it difficult dealing with village leadership. Bình assisted him, often communicating on behalf of Dũng and Trai. Dũng and Trai worked their small farm and survived, but their lives were not easy. Dũng did not communicate with words other than the simplest instruction or request for Trai to do something.

Trai had no friends.

Even though he was forbidden from attending school, he was educated as well as any child in the valley.

Trai had a great intellect. Bình recognized that intellect, and she also recognized how limited his life was in this valley.

Trai grew tall. He was as tall as his uncle by the time he was twelve and grew well above him in the next few years. As he grew older, he ventured into the village on his own. He understood the taunts of the other children. There were fistfights at times, but soon they stopped as he outgrew his tormentors. Men in the village knew of his size and strength and hired him for hard work that his size made easier. Even as they used him, he could see the disdain they had for him.

Trai recognized the difference between himself and others. He could see the darkness of his skin. Phương had never been open to questions, and Dũng simply did not have answers he could speak.

After Phương's death, Bình gave Trai what answers she could.

It was through their studies that Trai learned about his mother, Liên. Bình's knowledge was limited, but she shared what she had. Through Bình, Trai learned he was the child of an American. She told Trai about the day his mother disappeared and the day she returned to the valley with him in tow.

Dũng listened from the corner. Each time Bình mentioned America or American, something stirred inside him—like a door handle turning in a locked house.

The most perplexing story Bình told Trai was of the time that Dũng left to fight the Americans and was reported killed at An Khê. Only as she finished the story did she fully remember Dũng—whoever he was—sat in the corner listening.

Bình looked over. Dũng's eyes were intent, studying what he had just heard, as if he were staring at his own shadow and trying to make it speak.

That night and the nights following, Dũng dreamed more violently. He dreamed of a place far from the Sông Côn valley. He dreamed of young men speaking in that foreign language, a language he understood in the dream. He heard shouting. He heard shots. One night he heard a sudden explosion that jerked him off the mat.

Trai, lying beside him, felt his uncle's body jerk violently. He saw Dũng sitting up in a cold sweat.

"Chú ơi, có chuyện gì vậy ạ?" ("Uncle, what's happening?")

Thoughts and confusion raced through Dũng's mind. During the day, Dũng quietly reflected on the dreams. At night they came crashing in again.

One morning, under the cooking canopy, Dũng and Trai noticed a small stack of firewood had fallen. Trai walked to it and saw the ground beneath had sunk.

He called to his uncle.

"Chú ơi, hãy nhìn cái này." ("Uncle, look at this.")

Dũng looked over, wondering what caused the earth to fall in. Without further words, Trai moved the wood aside and began digging. He found rotten boards in the ground. He pulled out dirt and boards.

Then he began pulling items out.

The first item was a rifle, long rusted beyond use. Dũng stared. The rusted piece of metal brought a lump to his throat.

Then a helmet.

A pair of boots.

A flak vest.

Rotting pants, a shirt worn and frayed by insects and damp earth.

With each item, a familiarity shot through Dũng. His chest tightened with the revelation of each piece. He could not digest their meaning, but he knew they meant something significant to him.

That night, in a dream, he found himself walking in a clearing. He saw a man standing on a porch in front of a cabin. The man called out one name.

"Gabriel."

Dũng awoke not with suddenness but with quiet calm, and he heard himself say aloud a name he did not know he knew.

"Gabriel."

In this isolated valley, Trai knew he wanted more.

In December of 1986, the government instituted a new, more liberal policy, Đổi Mới. The policy returned greater control to ordinary people. Through liberalization, productivity increased. Dũng and Trai felt the change, yet they were still outcasts in their community.

Bình continued her instruction of them until the spring of 1988. Then the government did not view Bình as a qualified teacher. A new teacher was brought in with a formal degree. It was not long before Bình found herself back in Quy Nhơn after more than twenty years away.

Her parents were old, but still alive and still working in the market and along the beach. Bình soon worked beside her mother, squatting for hours, cooking cơm tấm gà and serving it to people who did not know the valleys and bridges she had left behind.

On a rainy night in 1989, Dũng sat up suddenly from restless sleep. Two names came clearly into his mind—Jonas and Esther. The mountain cabin of his dreams made sense. The buried military gear was understood.

Yet with that understanding, there was no doubt in his mind that he was Dũng, the son of Phương, and his home was in Làng Cây Tre in the Sông Côn valley.

Dũng looked over at his sleeping nephew.

Before Bình's departure, she had spoken of America and how many children of Americans were finding their way there. In Việt Nam there was little opportunity for those people, and in America there was much. Trai was eighteen now, a young man, smart and far taller than the people of the valley. There was little opportunity for him to establish a family in this valley.

Chapter 9
The Soldiers

John 15:13 (KJV)

"Greater love hath no man than this, that a man lay down his life for his friends."

Staff Sergeant Lacey paced the rough plank floor of his temporary barracks in Quy Nhơn. It was the morning of April 6, 1968—less than twenty-four hours since the fight in the valley had swallowed men whole. The boards creaked under each turn, and the sound irritated him because it proved he could do nothing but walk in circles. He had been told there would be a briefing at first light. He would need to give every detail he could to the captain and the sergeant leading the search party.

A captain and a squad of men had been pulled back into Quy Nhơn from an outlying firebase. The captain was new to Vietnam, but the sergeant and the men were familiar with the Sông Côn Valley.

Lacey's frustration grew sharper each time he replayed the fight in his mind. Two tours, and he had seen men killed—too many men killed—but what gnawed at him was not only the dead. It was the way the chaos of a firefight could rearrange a unit without anyone realizing it in that moment. In the valley, every man's focus narrowed to the next breath, the next burst of fire, the next yard of cover.

Lieutenant Russell Davenport had been taken into surgery within minutes of arriving at the hospital on April 5, 1968. The surgeon had spoken plainly afterward, the way surgeons did when sleep and blood had shaved the softness from their voices.

"You're fortunate, Lieutenant," the man had said. "It hurts because it's a shoulder. Everything hurts there. But it missed bone. Missed the major nerves. Minimal structural damage. If you do what therapy tells you—if you don't get stubborn—this should heal without permanent deficit."

Davenport had tried to smile through the haze. "So, I can go back?"

"You can return to duty," the surgeon had corrected. "Let's focus on getting you through the first week without infection. Then we will talk about the rest."

That had been all the comfort Lacey could take from the day. Davenport would live. But out beyond the rice paddies and tree lines, the valley still held what it had taken, and the fact sat in Lacey's chest like a weight.

Near dawn, there was a knock on the door.

"Staff Sergeant," a voice called through the thin wood. "You're up. Briefing in twenty."

Lacey moved fast, grabbing the issued toiletries as if he were back in basic. Cold water on his face. Teeth brushed. Shirt buttoned. Boots tied tight. In minutes he was walking into a meeting room on a base that never truly slept.

Inside, maps were already spread across a table. Red grease-pencil marks cut through the valley like open wounds.

"This is Staff Sergeant Lacey," someone said.

Lacey nodded once, eyes taking in faces and rank insignia as if cataloging a battlefield.

Captain Sean McMurtry stood near the table. The man looked newly arrived—gear still clean enough to show it had not yet surrendered to the red dust of Highway 19. Beside him was Sergeant Oliver, the kind of hard-eyed NCO who did not waste words, and an interpreter introduced as Đặng Long, a former Việt Cộng who had changed sides and lived to regret and defend that choice all at once.

Đặng Long kept his hands folded, eyes moving between the Americans and the map. When he spoke, his English was deliberate—each word chosen like a man stepping over wire. He tapped a point on the paper and said in Vietnamese, "Ở khúc này, ruộng lúa mở trống—không có chỗ ẩn. Nhưng ngay sau bờ tre thì có hầm trú."

He looked up and translated for them without prompting. "Here the paddies are open—no cover. But behind the bamboo line there are fighting holes."

Sergeant Oliver's mouth tightened. He did not comment on the interpreter's past. In the infantry, a man's history mattered, but the present mattered more.

McMurtry asked, "Can you get us close without spooking the whole valley?"

Đặng Long answered in Vietnamese first, then turned the meaning into English. "Nếu trực thăng bay thấp, dân sẽ nghe. Nhưng nếu vào từ phía tây, theo con suối, có thể đến gần hơn."

"If the helicopters come in low, the villagers will hear. But if you come from the west, along the creek line, you can get closer."

Staunton, the Huey pilot, gave a short nod, already converting the words into angles, altitude, and time.

The last man at the table was that pilot—CWO2 Mike Staunton—quiet, professional, and already writing.

Staunton tapped the map with the end of his pen. "You're the one who was there. Walk us through it."

"Yes, sir," Lacey said. He leaned in, pointing with a steady finger despite the fatigue. "This is the trail line. We came in from the west. The engagement broke here—along the tree line near the paddies. Enemy had overlapping positions. We took wounded early. We pulled back in bounds."

Oliver's eyes followed Lacey's finger without blinking.

"Landmarks."

"A bamboo thicket," Lacey said. "And a broken cart path. We crossed a shallow drainage—nothing that shows on your map."

Đặng Long nodded.

"I know that drainage," he said in careful English. "In rain it runs hard. In dry season it is a scar. Men can hide there."

McMurtry looked up from the map.

"How many enemy?"

Lacey swallowed.

"Enough to pin us. They were spread out and moving with discipline. They knew the ground. We were exposed in the open paddy. We fought our way back to cover."

Oliver asked, "And Sergeant Fox?"

Lacey's jaw tightened. This was the part that had changed everything—because in the valley, it had not been obvious at all.

"During the fight," Lacey said, choosing his words with care, "none of us knew he was missing. Not in the moment. It was too chaotic. We were dragging wounded, trying to keep the perimeter from collapsing, trying to keep from losing more men. I did not see Fox go down. I didn't hear him call. I assumed he was moving with us like everyone else—either pulled back under fire or already on a bird."

The room stayed still. Only the ceiling fan moved.

Lacey continued, voice low and controlled.

"It wasn't until we got back to Quy Nhơn—after the medevac, after the debrief—that the roster didn't add up. We started calling names. Fox didn't answer. At first you think he's on another truck, another corner of the perimeter, another aid station. Then you realize nobody saw him leave the valley. Nobody saw him load. Nobody saw him in triage. That's when it hits you."

McMurtry's eyes held on Lacey.

"Last confirmed sighting?"

"I saw him earlier," Lacey said. "Before the worst of it. He was doing what he always did—moving with purpose, keeping his head, reading the ground. Then the firefight turned into smoke and noise. After that, I can't give you a clean moment where I watched him step one way or the other. I wish to God I could."

Oliver's voice stayed flat.

"So, we're not chasing a dramatic 'last stand' story."

"No," Lacey said. "We're chasing a missing man who disappeared inside chaos."

Staunton looked up from his notes.

"If he's alive, what's his pattern?"

Lacey didn't have to think.

"He won't stay in the open. He'll crawl into shadow. He'll go quiet. If he can keep his weapon, he will. If he can't, he'll still hide. He's disciplined."

McMurtry nodded once.

"That helps."

Staunton closed his notebook.

"Two slicks, two gunships," he said. "We go in fast, we don't hover, and we don't linger. If you have coordinates, Staff Sergeant, give them now."

Lacey gave them as precisely as he could. Oliver and Đặng Long exchanged a quick glance. They knew the valley. They knew what the map did not say out loud.

Hands were shaken. A plan was set.

Before they broke, McMurtry motioned Lacey close again.

"Staff Sergeant—when you realized he was missing, what did your gut tell you?"

Lacey's throat tightened.

"Sir, my gut said Fox doesn't vanish by accident. If he's gone, somebody took him—or he's hurt where he can't move. He's not the kind of man who gets lost on a trail."

McMurtry held his gaze.

"Then we treat it as recoverable until it isn't."

"Yes, sir."

McMurtry's voice dropped so only the men at the table heard.

"And if you hear rumors later—if somebody says we didn't go back—ignore it. We're going back. We're going back until we bring him out or there's nothing left to search."

Lacey felt something inside him loosen just enough to breathe.

They headed out together, and for a moment Lacey took two steps with them—pure instinct—before his role ended at the door.

On the pad, four helicopters were already running, rotors beating the air into a constant roar. Staunton climbed into the left seat of his UH-1H. McMurtry and half the men loaded into the cargo bay, their weapons held tight, their eyes hard. The crew chief checked straps and gear; the door gunner sat behind the mounted M-60, scanning as if the jungle might burst from the horizon and sprint across the airfield.

Sergeant Oliver, Đặng Long, and the remaining men climbed into the other slick. Two gunships tucked in alongside them, ready to go in first and hit hard.

Lacey stood back and watched.

The Hueys lifted. The gunships rose with them like guard dogs.

As the ships climbed, Lacey caught a final exchange through the open cargo doors of the two slicks.

Sgt. Oliver gave Captain McMurtry a thumbs up and McMurtry saluted back. Lacey felt confidence in the team being sent.

Đặng Long slid closer to the crew cheif and called a few quick words in Vietnamese—warnings about where men tended to dig and how quickly a paddy could turn into a killing field.

The crew chief didn't understand the language, but he understood urgency. He adjusted his grip on the gun mount and scanned harder.

As the flight pulled away toward the mountains, Lacey's disappointment gnawed at him, but he forced himself to swallow it. His duty now was what it had always been: endure, report, return.

He went to the mess hall and ate without tasting much. Around him, men spoke in short bursts—how bad the trucks would be, how long the road would feel, how Highway 19 could turn into a trap with one ambush.

A convoy was scheduled within the hour: deuce-and-a-half trucks hauling them back up the winding road toward An Khê and Camp Radcliff. None of the men looked forward to the trip—not only because of the discomfort in the back of a truck, but because any one of the mountain curves could slow them to a crawl and make them easy targets.

Lacey finished fast and headed straight for the hospital.

The ward smelled of antiseptic and sweat. Ceiling fans pushed warm air in circles. Somewhere outside, a helicopter landed, and the sound made every man in the building listen for half a beat.

Davenport lay propped up, pale but alert, his right arm immobilized. His eyes turned toward Lacey as if he had been waiting for the door to open.

"Staff Sergeant," Davenport said. "You're back early. How bad is it?"

Lacey pulled a chair close and sat. He didn't rush his words.

"Sir, I just came from the briefing."

Davenport's eyes sharpened.

"Briefing?"

Lacey took a deep breath.

"Yes, sir. I don't know how to tell you this except by coming straight out. Fox is missing."

"What do you mean, missing?" the lieutenant asked, fully alert.

"Well, sir, we didn't realize it until late yesterday. I wanted to go back and look for him, but the brass said it was too late to send a search party," Lacey explained.

"What the hell? Are they sending anybody?" Davenport questioned with urgency. "Yes, sir. They pulled in a search detail. Captain McMurtry is leading the search. He seems like a good man. He's got a sergeant named Oliver, and an interpreter, Đặng Long. They are both familiar with the valley. Đặng Long knew exactly where I was pointing. He has been there before. Oliver had too. They're flying in with two slicks and two gunships. A guy named Staunton's the lead pilot."

Davenport absorbed the names, then repeated one.

"McMurtry."

"Yes, sir," Lacey said. "He listened. Asked the right questions. He's moving now."

Davenport stared past Lacey for a moment, as if the ceiling fan could turn back time.

"Good," he said quietly. "Fox deserves a man who'll go after him."

Lacey nodded once. Then he said what he needed Davenport to understand—because Davenport had been wounded, evacuated, and unconscious for part of the confusion.

"Sir," Lacey said, "I need you to know something. During the fight, none of us knew Fox was missing. Not then. We were dragging you and the other wounded. We were taking fire. In that kind of chaos, you don't count heads—you just keep men alive."

Davenport's brow furrowed.

"I only found out after we got back to Quy Nhơn," Lacey continued. "After the birds lifted the wounded out. After we got hauled in. We did a muster. Fox didn't answer. At first I thought he was already in triage, or on another truck. Then we started asking around—no one had him. No one saw him load. No one saw him inside the aid station. That's when it became real."

Davenport's expression held for a moment, then shifted—like a door being shut quietly instead of slammed.

"Missing," he said, almost to himself.

"Yes, sir," Lacey replied. "Missing in action. And I don't have a clean last sighting after the firefight broke wide. I wish I did."

Davenport's jaw worked as if he were biting down on something bitter.

"Fox talked about home like it was a place you could carry in your pocket."

"He was different," Lacey said.

Davenport's voice lowered.

"And McMurtry is out there looking for him."

"Yes, sir."

Davenport nodded once, a small motion that still carried weight.

"Then pray for him too, Staff Sergeant. Men like that get used up fast."

Lacey held Davenport's gaze.

"Yes, sir."

They spoke for a few more minutes—about the surgeon's estimate, about the ache of a shoulder wound that made sleep feel impossible, about the way the ward never stayed quiet long. Davenport told Lacey the doctor expected him back in action in a few months, and the words sounded wrong in his own ears, as if time itself had become an enemy.

Then they said their goodbyes.

Lacey left to meet his men for the return convoy.

Davenport remained on his bed, staring at the ceiling fan. Each turn of the blades felt like time being spent without permission.

As Davenport lay thinking, two gunships were unloading ordnance into the jungle beyond the rice paddies at the far end of the Sông Côn Valley. Shortly afterward, two slicks dropped low and hard, men spilling out into the heat and brush to begin the search for Gabriel Fox.

Back on Highway 19, two trucks carried Lacey's unit toward An Khê. The men in the trucks were tired and hollowed out. If they had listened closely, they might have heard distant concussions rolling from a valley north of the road—faint, like thunder buried under the mountains.

Most of them did not notice as they passed the entrance to the valley where, just the day before, they had been in a savage fight—losing two men to death and more, including their commanding officer, to wounds.

Lacey noticed. He did not say anything. He simply lowered his head and prayed.

The trucks reached Camp Radcliff around two in the afternoon. Men drifted toward "Sin City," hungry for noise and distraction. Lacey went to company headquarters and delivered his report to the major.

The major listened, nodded, and said, "You'll meet your replacement lieutenant tomorrow. We'll get you replacements for the others in a few days."

Lacey held his temper.

"And Sergeant Fox, sir?"

The major's eyes flicked up.

"Missing in action," he said. "We're tracking it."

That was all.

Lacey walked out, angry at how small the words sounded. He realized the major had no idea what Fox had meant to the unit. Some men were not just bodies in a slot. Some men held the shape of the whole platoon together.

While Lacey was being debriefed, a slick was acting as a medevac, hauling a gravely wounded captain toward the hospital at Quy Nhơn.

Inside the ward, Davenport heard the pattern before anyone told him. The rotor wash. The shouted commands. The hurried footfalls. The sudden change in the air—like the base itself had taken a breath and held it.

Men were coming in.

Davenport's stomach tightened. He knew that rhythm—how it felt when the valley reached back and took payment. The hospital had its own kind of battlefield discipline: no running unless necessary, no shouting unless it saved a life, no wasted motion. When people moved fast here, somebody was bleeding.

Just as he had.

He watched medics run past, faces set, uniforms smeared, and he knew something had happened out there in the valley. Something worse than the ordinary violence.

A nurse moved down the aisle, brisk and tight. Davenport caught her sleeve gently.

"Ma'am," he said. "Who is it?"

She hesitated. Then, because his rank and his eyes demanded truth, she answered.

"A captain," she said. "From the search."

Davenport's hand tightened around the blanket.

"Name?"

She looked away.

"McMurtry."

The sound struck Davenport like a blow. He had heard the name from Lacey that morning—spoken with a soldier's cautious hope. Now it returned with a different meaning.

McMurtry arrived at Quy Nhơn in the Huey piloted by Staunton. The crew chief had applied tourniquets to McMurtry's arm and leg, preventing him from bleeding out. The captain's face was gray, his body shaking despite morphine.

A medic shouted, "Clear!" and the gurney rolled.

Staunton climbed down and stood for a moment with his helmet in his hand, staring at nothing, as if trying to understand how quickly a plan could turn into wreckage. A corpsman brushed past him.

Staunton grabbed the man by the shoulder.

"He alive?"

"Barely," the corpsman snapped, and kept moving.

In triage, the doctors did not waste emotion. They took the facts and made decisions. McMurtry was stabilized—pressure, fluids, airway, pain control—then prepped for onward transfer.

A surgeon spoke quickly to an aide.

"We're not finishing this here. Get him ready for Saigon. Now."

Davenport listened from his bed as the base vibrated with urgency. He could not see McMurtry, but he could hear the cost in the voices outside.

Later, word came down like a hammer: Sergeant Gabriel Fox was declared Missing in Action and presumed dead.

Lacey heard it while he was meeting the new lieutenant assigned to the unit. Davenport heard it while sitting on the edge of his hospital bed, one arm bound, his body intact but his mind cornered.

In the unit area, men would still have duties. There would be orders. There would be patrols. There would be the next assignment that kept them from staring too long into what they had lost.

In the hospital, Davenport had time.

And time, without purpose, turned grief into a heavier thing.

Two weeks later, Davenport was declared ambulatory and assigned light duty. The hospital put him in an office role at first—forms, logs, the mundane administration that kept blood and chaos from spilling into complete disorder.

Two more weeks and he moved into temporary quarters. He was allowed to move about the base freely, even to go into Quy Nhơn city when he had the energy.

He was assigned temporary duty with the 18th Aviation Headquarters.

At first, he told himself it was just paperwork. But he found himself watching the flight line. Listening to pilots talk. Studying the calm way they treated danger like a constant weather pattern.

One afternoon, a warrant officer stepped out of an office and caught Davenport staring at a Huey as it lifted into the air.

"You like them?" the pilot asked.

Davenport did not look away.

"They keep saving us."

The warrant officer snorted.

"They save you until they can't."

Davenport's eyes narrowed slightly.

"How do you do it?"

The warrant officer studied him for a moment—his sling, his posture, the restrained anger that still lived in him.

"You want to fly."

The words were not a question. They were a diagnosis.

"I want to matter," Davenport said, and surprised himself with the honesty of it.

The pilot nodded once.

"Then start your packet. You will need endorsements, a flight physical, and patience. You will also need to stop waiting for someone to notice you. Do not wait until you feel 'ready.' The paperwork doesn't care about your shoulder. The flight surgeon will. But the paperwork won't."

Davenport swallowed.

"My shoulder—"

"Soft tissue?" the pilot asked.

"Yes."

"No fracture?"

"No."

"Then you rehab like your life depends on it," the pilot said. "Because it does. If you want that pilot's seat, you earn it twice—once in therapy, once in the air."

Davenport stood a little straighter.

"What do I do first?"

The pilot jerked his head toward the office.

"Come inside. I'll tell you what to ask for, who to talk to, and what to stop saying in front of the wrong people."

Davenport followed him in.

Inside the office, the warrant officer talked him through the chain of requests—who signed what, who could stall it out, and who could champion it if Davenport gave them a reason. He spoke about flight school in terms of attrition and discipline: men who washed out because they thought courage was enough, men who washed out because they hid injuries, men who washed out because they couldn't take being coached.

Davenport listened, absorbing every word as if it were a new kind of field manual. His shoulder throbbed in quiet protest, but he welcomed the pain. Pain could be worked with. Grief just sat.

When the warrant officer finished, he slid a sheet of paper across the desk with names and extensions written in block letters.

"Start there," he said. "And quit saying you 'want to matter.' You already do. What you want is control. The pilot's seat gives you some of that. Not all. Some."

And for the first time since April 5—since the moment the bullet struck and the world tilted—he felt the faint beginning of direction. It was not hope, not yet. It was something harder and more durable.

Davenport mulled it over for about a week. He would often walk out to the tarmac and talk to the pilots getting ready to take off. In the mess hall, he would sit with the pilots, asking questions and listening to some of their stories. He would study their answers and stories. He wondered if he had it in him to fly a Huey into the thick of battle. Would it be more difficult than being on the ground, in a rice paddy, taking fire?

One morning he awakened and immediately knew the answer. He went to the office, found the warrant officer, and told him he was ready to start the process. He knew he would soon be back in the field, but hoped he could change his mission.

Doctors told him it would be about three more months before he would be released for duty. He followed all their directions in rehabilitating his shoulder. He was often cautioned to take it a bit easier in his exercise routine. He listened, but not to the level they wanted.

Every day, seven days a week, he would jog around the base in the early morning. At lunch, he would work out with light weights, concentrating on his shoulder. Pain was significant in the beginning. After about three weeks, the pain had reduced enough that he moved to heavier weights. He let the pain dictate how heavy they became. He continued the routine day after day, alternating every other day as to which muscle group he worked on.

He borrowed training books from the pilots. There was a small library of books in the office area. He studied the books every night. He waited on word. He waited on the doctors to say his shoulder was capable of fulfilling its requirements to be a pilot.

After a number of weeks, he was called in by the surgeon who had performed the surgery. He maneuvered Russell's shoulder in every direction it could be moved. He had Russell do pull-ups and pushups. He had him lift a five-pound dumbbell and move it into various positions, holding it in place for periods of time.

He passed, and days later he was informed he was on his way back to America.

He was going to be a pilot.

Chapter 10

A New Beginning

Psalm 68:5–6 (KJV)

"A father of the fatherless, and a judge of the widows, is God in his holy habitation. God setteth the solitary in families: he bringeth out those which are bound with chains: but the rebellious dwell in a dry land."

Trai loved his uncle, but there was a loneliness in his life that neither work nor routine could fully quiet. By 1990, Trai had become a man, and as with any man, he had his desires. He longed for a wife and children—someone to sit beside him at the evening meal, someone to speak his name without contempt. Yet in that valley, he was still the boy people called Người Mỹ, still the outcast with darker skin and features that did not match the village faces. Even after the years had passed and the war was only a shadow in old men's eyes, the valley remembered what it wanted to remember.

As the valley grew and became more modernized, Cô Bình was no longer able to meet the newer requirements as a teacher. In 1988, Cô Bình—teacher and friend to Dũng and Trai—was sent back to Quy Nhơn, and a new teacher was brought in. Trai felt the separation deeply. Other than Dũng, there was no one else in Trai's life.

Shortly after Tết, the lunar new year, Trai told his uncle of his longing for a new life. He had heard stories while working with men who traveled—stories of cities with electric lights and real markets, stories of Quy Nhơn, of Sài Gòn, even of America. He did not fully believe them, but the very sound of those names worked in him like an ache.

Dũng listened to the young man, his face quiet, his hands continuing their work as if the talk were only wind. But sorrow lived in him, too—sorrow that never spoke loudly, sorrow that settled into the shoulders and the eyes.

"Con muốn có gia đình," Trai said at last, keeping his voice low as if the bamboo walls could carry his words to the village. "Con muốn vợ… muốn con."

I want a family. I want a wife… children.

Dũng's gaze stayed on the rope in his hands, the knot he was tightening. His Vietnamese was natural now—more natural than any English could ever be for him again—but there were moments when his voice carried something else inside it, something older and farther away.

"Ở đây… khó," Dũng said. "Người ta… không quên."

Here… it is hard. People… do not forget.

Trai swallowed.

"Con biết," he said.

I know.

A long silence followed. Outside, the valley morning moved on—birds calling, water shifting in the fishponds, the faint sound of someone chopping wood far down the trail. Dũng tied the final knot, tested it with a firm pull, and then he looked up at Trai as if seeing him not as the boy from years ago, but as the man he had become.

"Con đi," Dũng said. "Nếu con phải đi… thì đi."

Go. If you must go… then go.

Trai felt his throat tighten at the permission, at the strange mixture of blessing and loss inside it. Dũng did not tell him it would be easy. He did not tell him the world would be kind. He only gave him what he could: the right to try.

A few years after Phương's death, Dũng and Trai were making repairs to the cooking area. The firewood storage had begun to lean, and the palm-leaf roofing needed replacement. They moved the old timbers and lifted stacked bamboo poles from where Phương had kept them dry beneath the eaves. During the work, Trai found a bundle wrapped in oilcloth and tied with twine, buried under older items that had not been touched in years.

He held it up.

"Cái gì vậy, chú?"

What is this, uncle?

Dũng's face changed before he spoke. His eyes fixed on the bundle as if it were something alive.

He took it carefully, as though it might break. When he loosened the twine and peeled back the oilcloth, the smell of old earth rose from it. Inside was a U.S. Army uniform—what remained of it. Much of it had been eaten away by insects and rodents over the decades, but the shape was still there: the coarse cloth, the faded green, the dull brass. There were patches and rank markings that meant nothing to Trai, and yet everything about the bundle felt heavy with importance.

Dũng held it for a long time without moving. Then he carried it inside, to the bench where he sometimes sat when his mind drifted too far.

There, with the uniform in his hands, he reviewed his life. Memories came in sudden, sharp flashes—himself as a boy walking down a mountain road to school, his mother's voice calling him in from the yard, the smell of a woodstove, and the sound of wind in bare trees. Then the jungle returned: the mountains of Vietnam, the wet heat, the taste of fear, and the anguish of killing other human beings. He felt again the instant of pain when his body had been broken and his mind shoved into darkness.

He knew he was an American in this land—the land that had become his home—and the knowing did not change what he had lived. He had spent more time in his new life than he had in the old one. Vietnamese had grown stronger than the part he had left behind, but the uniform—rotting though it was—still held the outline of another self.

After that discovery, Dũng found himself talking more and expressing himself more to Trai. He told Trai that his first life was in a place called Tennessee, in America, where mountains rose like the ribs of the earth and the air in winter could cut a man's lungs. He told him about a cabin. Of a father and mother. Of two sisters. Of a brother who was different—Jacob—who had needed care even before the war.

Trai listened as if his mind were a jar being filled, careful not to spill. The name Tennessee lodged in him and would not let go. The more Dũng spoke, the more Trai began to understand that his uncle carried a home inside him that did not belong to the valley.

And Trai carried it, too—without ever having seen it.

As Trai considered leaving Vietnam for America, he knew he wanted to go to Tennessee. It was not logic. It was not planning. It was a pull, as if something in his blood recognized the word and claimed it.

Yet leaving was not simple. Even in the years after the war, a poor boy from a remote valley did not just choose a new life and step into it. To leave, he would have to walk to the outside world and survive it long enough to find help.

In October of that year, he and Dũng said what they believed to be their final goodbyes. There were no hugs, no handshakes—men in that valley did not talk love into their hands. But Dũng stood with Trai at the edge of the trail, watching him adjust the strap of the small pack on his shoulder.

"Đi thẳng," Dũng said. "Đừng quay lại."

Go straight. Don't turn back.

Trai nodded.

"Con sẽ nhớ," he said.

I will remember.

Dũng hesitated, then added quietly:

"Nếu con sống... sống cho cả hai."

If you live... live for both of us.

Trai bowed his head once, then turned and started down the valley trail toward what he hoped would be a new life.

It took days of walking. Along the way, Trai scavenged for food. It was not that difficult—his uncle had taught him what could be eaten, what must be avoided, and how to find water even when the land seemed dry. He slept in bamboo thickets and under overhangs, keeping himself hidden out of habit more than fear. Still, fear rode him. He had never been alone in the wider world.

As he walked, the scenery changed along with the homes. At the end of his valley, everyone lived in huts. Then he reached hamlets with better roofs, then villages with corrugated metal and concrete. The road grew wider. Motorbikes became common. Trucks roared past, so close he could feel the push of their air.

The traffic became constant, with the road filled with vehicles of every sort. The noise hammered at him. The smells were overwhelming—food, diesel, rotting trash, salt air that did not belong to the river valleys. He kept his eyes forward, not wanting to meet anyone's gaze for too long.

At one point he saw a sign arching over a busy road. Most of the words were unfamiliar, but he recognized Quy Nhơn. He kept walking, his feet blistered, his stomach hollow.

Children ran up to him shouting, laughing as if cruelty were a game.

"Bụi đời! Bụi đời!"

Street-trash! Worthless drifter!

They darted away when he turned his head, then rushed back again, emboldened by numbers. A shopkeeper stepped outside and waved them off, glaring at Trai as if he were the problem.

"Đi đi," the man snapped.

Go, go.

Trai walked on.

As he continued, a distinct smell came to him—stronger—a smell unlike anything he had known in the valley. It was salt, sharp and wet. He remembered Cô Bình speaking once of an endless water, larger than the Sông Côn River, larger than any flood. He kept walking, drawn by that smell as if it were a compass.

Then, suddenly, the sky opened.

The buildings ended.

The world widened.

There it was—the ocean.

Trai stopped, stunned, his mouth slightly open. The horizon looked like a line drawn by God Himself. Waves rolled in and broke, and the sound of it made the ground feel alive beneath his feet. Boats pulled onto the beach and people scrambled toward them, unloading fish with quick hands. The market was alive—voices, baskets, knives, water splashing, money changing hands.

Trai stood there long enough that someone shouted at him to move.

He entered the market area and found himself swallowed by people. Strips of meat hung from stalls. Fish lay piled on crushed ice. He had never seen ice in his life. Women moved through the crowd with the confidence of city people, their eyes quick, their voices firm. Trai did not know what he was looking for, only that he needed help and did not know how to ask for it.

Fear kept him from stopping and speaking to strangers. His accent marked him as country. His skin marked him as something else. At one point, he walked past a food stall. A woman was squatting, diligently serving food to customers. Trai did not look her way, nor did she look his. If either had known, how grand it would have been. Trai walked on, and Bình continued serving food.

There she continued serving food long after her parents were dead. During the day she chatted with the women around her and to her customers, but at night, she went back to the tin shanty she grew up in. There she laid alone through the night. She often dreamed of her former home, of the children and of those that had grown to mean so much to her.

As Trai walked on, he saw two women walking toward him. They were dressed in a way he had never seen—simple clothing, but clean and orderly. Their faces were calm, not predatory. For a moment, Trai thought they might pass by. Instead, they stopped directly in front of him.

One spoke gently.

"Xin chào cháu trai, cháu khỏe không?"

Hello, nephew—are you well?

The use of nephew was not literal. It was a kindness, an opening.

Trai stood stiff, unsure whether to run. The second woman looked at his clothes, his bare feet, and the way he held himself like someone waiting to be struck.

"Chúng tôi muốn giúp cháu. Cháu có đói không?"

We want to help you. Are you hungry?

Trai nodded once, ashamed that his hunger would betray him before his words could.

They guided him away from the market into a quieter street and bought him food. He ate as if he had forgotten how to stop. They did not stare. They did not laugh. They watched with the careful eyes of people who had seen broken children before.

Over the next several days, they learned as much about the young man as they could. They learned of his aspirations. They learned he had grown up in a remote valley. They learned his uncle's name was Dũng and that Dũng was his mother's brother, and that his mother had been named Liên.

It took time, but the pieces began to form a shape that the women recognized.

They were Catholic nuns.

And they had helped Amerasian children before.

Over the past few years, the process for emigrating from Vietnam—especially for Amerasian children—had become easier. Government officials did not always say it openly, but many were relieved to see these reminders of the war leave the country. Paperwork moved faster than it might have once. Doors opened that stayed shut for others.

Trai lived with the nuns in their residence behind Our Lady of the Assumption Cathedral. He had never been formally trained in anything, but he learned quickly, and the sisters saw that in him. They taught him basic city manners, basic schooling, and the structure of a life that did not revolve around surviving the next harvest.

It was on a rainy Sunday morning, just days before Trai was to leave for the Philippines, that he was baptized. In the front pew, the sisters sat like watchful mothers. Trai did not understand every word spoken that day, but he understood the feeling: that he had been received rather than tolerated.

In the Philippines, he was again fortunate. He was under the care of the Catholic Diocese there. He did not have to stand alone in a strange land. He learned English in practical pieces—words for work, words for directions, words for money. He was placed in training that suited the only skill he already possessed: working with his hands.

The first place he was sent was an automobile repair shop. He learned quickly. Engines made sense to him the way bamboo joints and plow handles had made sense in the valley. The cars were older models, so he learned how to tune vehicles by listening, by touch, by feel. The mechanics laughed at his intensity at first, then stopped laughing when they saw how fast he improved.

When Trai received permission to emigrate to America, a family—members of the Church Diocese in Nashville—volunteered to sponsor him. In time, Nashville became his landing place, not because he had chosen it, but because God had placed a hand on the map and said: here.

The first months were hard. The cold was different than he expected. The language exhausted him. People spoke quickly and looked away when they did not understand him. He took any work offered and never complained. Within a few months, he was able to acquire a small apartment. He kept it clean the way his grandmother had kept the hut clean—because cleanliness was one of the few forms of dignity a poor person could control.

It was on a winter day in 1995 when Trai walked into a newly opened Vietnamese restaurant on Charlotte Avenue.

The smell hit him first—star anise, simmering broth, the warmth of fish sauce and herbs. For a moment, he was back near the cooking canopy in the valley, hungry in a way that was not only physical.

A young Vietnamese woman worked there, moving quickly between tables, her hair tied back, her face composed. She too was half-American, born on the streets of Sài Gòn, and placed in an orphanage at birth. Her job was to bus tables and to make sure utensils, spoon, knives and chopsticks were wrapped. She saw Trai standing at the doorway, and pointed to the table she had just cleaned and prepared.

Trai sat alone, as he always did. A waiter approached him and took his order.

A ticket was placed before her. It was for his table. It was not her responsibility to carry food to customers—she was supposed to focus on other tasks—but the owner watched her and pointed.

She approached Trai's table with a bowl.

"Bánh mì bò kho," she said, setting it down.

Trai looked up and froze.

Her name, he would learn, was Phương—just as his grandmother's name had been.

It felt like a sign too sharp to ignore.

The restaurant became a daily routine for him. At first, he said little. He ate, nodded, paid, and left. The young woman's face remained careful and professional, but she began to recognize him. She noticed he always sat alone. She noticed his Vietnamese sounded rural and old-fashioned, but respectful.

One afternoon, as she cleared a nearby table, she asked quietly:

"Anh… người ở đâu?"

Where are you from?

Trai hesitated, then answered simply:

"Bình Định."

Her eyes lifted, curious.

"Quy Nhơn?"

"Gần đó," he said.

Near there.

Even though Trai had lived all of his youth in Làng Cây Tre, he had never heard its name. He had never heard the Sông Côn referred to as anything other than sông, river. When asked, all he could tell anyone was that he was from Bình Định, near Quy Nhơn.

After that, the questions came slowly, like a door opening a crack at a time.

A few months later, one day after Trai left the restaurant, the owner spoke to Phương in Vietnamese, as blunt as an older man who believed he was doing right.

"Phương, cháu kết hôn với anh ấy."

Phương, you marry that man.

Phương's face flushed.

"Ông nói gì vậy?"

What are you saying?

The owner shrugged as if it were obvious.

"Anh ấy là người tốt. Không uống rượu. Không gây chuyện. Làm việc chăm. Luôn đến đây… và luôn một mình."

He's a good man. Doesn't drink. Doesn't cause trouble. Works hard. Always comes here… and always alone.

Phương did not answer, but after that day she looked at Trai differently—not with pity, not with suspicion, but with thought.

Trai continued to work and learn. Within a few years he became shop manager at the repair shop where he worked, as the owner grew older. He saved money the way a poor man saves—carefully, quietly, without celebration.

In time, Phương and Trai married. They built a life that was not loud, not flashy, but steady. It was the kind of life Trai had once believed belonged only to other people.

Trai and Phương had three sons. They named their oldest Dũng, after Trai's uncle. Trai would tell his sons stories about his uncle. They listened attentively, amazed at the stories their father told.

At the repair shop, Trai learned everything he could about being an auto mechanic. His boss was always impressed by Trai's diligent effort. When opportunity came, the owner would send Trai to school to acquire different levels of certification. Trai learned how to operate the most modern diagnostic equipment. He learned how to rebuild engines and transmissions. He could do a full brake job as quickly as anyone. He seldom made mistakes. The owner realized that few customers ever returned angry because of the work Trai had done.

There were three other employees in the shop. Trai watched their work like a hawk. The owner would be amazed watching Trai fully involved in a job, but suddenly stop to show one of the other employees a mistake the employee had made and how to correct it.

Over the years, Phương continued to work at the restaurant. The owner of the shop gave Trai sensible raises all along. He did not want to lose Trai to a competing shop. Trai and Phương saved their money. After a few years, they moved from the apartment they occupied to a house in Charlotte Park on a street named after one of Ford Motor Company's vehicles. All three of their sons were excellent students.

In 2001, the owner of the shop approached Trai and made him an offer.

"I have watched you," the man said. "You are honest. You don't steal. You don't cut corners. You are as good a mechanic as there is. You lead the other guys in the shop like it was your own. I want to retire. I want you to take over my business. It would be a great honor to see you take it over."

Trai stood silently, stunned by the weight of it. Ownership was not something he had ever imagined. In the valley, a man might own a buffalo. He might own a hut. But a business in America?

The owner waited, then pressed him.

"Well?"

Trai's answer came fast, as if it had been waiting in him for years.

"Yes!" he said.

The two shook hands on the spot.

Within a year, the business became Trai's.

That night, after the papers were signed and the keys sat heavy in his pocket, Trai lay awake beside his wife and stared into the dark. He thought of his grandmother Phương by the river, working until her hands cracked. He thought of Bình teaching him—the hours she spent in the hut, out of sight of any prying eyes, giving him an education he otherwise would not have received. He thought of Hùng, the kind but stern man who quietly watched after Trai's family. He thought of Uncle Dũng in the hut, silent, carrying two lives inside one body.

He wondered what Dũng would think if he could see him now—a man from a remote valley, once called Bụi đời, now standing in America with a home, a wife, and a business of his own.

Trai did not laugh. He did not boast.

He only whispered into the quiet, as if speaking to the dead and the living at the same time:

"Con vẫn nhớ."

"I still remember."

Chapter 11

Changing Times

Isaiah 43:2 (KJV)

> "When thou passest through the waters, I will be with thee; and through the rivers, they shall not overflow thee: when thou walkest through the fire, thou shalt not be burned; neither shall the flame kindle upon thee."

The rooster crowed in the early morning hours, just as the first rays of sun began to show over the mountain to the east. Dũng awakened to the sound. The night breezes had, as usual, carried fog into the valley, and the dampness chilled him. The air smelled of wet earth and leaves, and the hut's bamboo walls held the night's coolness as if it were a thing to be saved.

He lay still for a moment and listened. There was no other breathing in the hut. There was no shifting of a mat beside him, no quiet voice asking if he had slept well. Only the small noises of the valley—far-off insects, the occasional flutter of wings, and the soft, steady drip of moisture sliding off the thatch.

He lay in the empty hut with his only companion, Đức Phật, in the corner. It was always difficult to rise from the sleeping mat. His right leg was fixed in a permanent straight position. It always hurt, but he had learned to live with the pain. Pain had become part of morning, like the rooster's crow—something expected, something endured.

He rolled carefully, planted his hands, and pushed himself upright. The movement sent a sharp pulse up his hip and into his lower back, and he stopped until the worst of it passed. He did not curse. He did not complain. In his mind, complaining changed nothing. It only burned breath.

Once he was on his feet, he forced himself through the day's work, even when it meant traversing the mountain slope beside the hut. He moved as he always did—slowly at first, then steadier, letting the body remember what the mind demanded.

His morning ritual never changed. He removed the burned incense from in front of the Buddha and retrieved the rice bowl. He made his way down the steps of the hut and tossed the rice to the hungry chickens. Then he went to the cooking canopy and began preparing his meal for the day, and Đức Phật's offerings as well.

He poured water into the pot and watched the small flames lick at the bottom. The smoke drifted up and clung to the underside of the canopy roof. A thin part of him still watched the smoke the way he had once watched for movement in the forest—alert, instinctive, as if smoke could carry threat. It was a useless reflex now, but it did not leave him.

He looked north, toward the rice paddies. He would spend the day there, hoeing weeds. By stubborn habit and constant labor, he kept the paddies thriving and producing. There was comfort in the repetition. The work did not ask him who he had been. The work only asked him to do it.

It had been just over a decade since Trai had left. Dũng hoped he had been successful in reaching America, but he spent little time wondering about him. What good would it do? Dũng's greatest concern was surviving. In his years in the valley, there had been only a few people he had ever truly associated with—and now there was no one. His life was a lonely one, but he did not dwell on that, either.

Yet even if he did not dwell on it, the absence was real. When he reached for the hoe, there was no second set of hands to lift another tool. When he cooked, there was no quiet movement behind him, no younger body stepping around the fire with familiarity. At night, when wind moved through the bamboo, he sometimes turned his head, half expecting to see Trai's shape near the doorway—only to remember again that the boy was gone. Then he would close his eyes and wait for sleep to take him, because sleep was the only place where time could be ignored.

The food had been prepared, Đức Phật tended to, and the animals fed. Dũng retrieved the hoe from the storage shed and began his trek toward the rice paddies when he heard a sound coming from the south—the shuffle of men moving up the trail. Voices followed, speaking in a language unfamiliar to his ear.

He stopped at once, his body tightening. The hoe suddenly felt too heavy, as if it might mark him as a threat. He shifted it in his hand and stood still, listening.

He looked up and saw a group approaching: two Vietnamese men, hai người đàn ông Việt Nam, and three foreigners. As Dũng watched the foreigners draw closer, images flashed through his mind. Their faces resembled those he had known as he grew up, before he had come to this land, but their language was different—sharper, clipped, strange on the air. The foreign words struck his ears like stones tossed into a still pond.

Instinct rose in him before thought. Dũng immediately made sure the left side of his face—the American side—was covered as they approached. He pulled the cloth higher and angled his head so the unburned skin stayed hidden in shadow. His heart beat harder, and he hated that it did. He told himself it was nothing. Men walking a trail were only men walking a trail. But his body did not listen to reason the way it once had.

"Xin chào ông, chúng tôi là một nhóm khảo sát do chính phủ cử đến," one of the Vietnamese men shouted.

"Hello, sir. We are a survey team sent by the government."

The man's tone was loud, official, as if volume alone could turn permission into authority. The second Vietnamese man smiled, but it was the smile of someone trained to smile at strangers—polite, practiced, without warmth.

One of the foreigners spoke again in his own language, gesturing toward the valley floor. Another answered, and they laughed briefly, not cruelly—only as men sometimes laugh when they are comfortable in their own group.

The Vietnamese surveyor tried again, stepping closer.

"Ông sống ở đây một mình à?"

Do you live here alone?

Dũng's throat tightened. Phương had taught him silence the way other mothers taught children to speak. Silence was safety. Silence was survival. He did not answer.

The surveyor's face tightened a fraction, then softened again, the way officials learned to do when they met people who did not cooperate.

"Chúng tôi cần đo đạc. Làm đường. Ông hiểu không?"

We need to survey. Build a road. Do you understand?

Dũng gave a small nod—barely noticeable—because refusing to acknowledge an official was sometimes more dangerous than speaking.

The man pointed toward the paddies.

"Chỗ đó… ruộng của ai?"

That place… whose paddy is that?

Dũng looked where the man pointed and felt something cold in his stomach. The paddies were his. The paddies were his life.

He kept his face blank and said nothing.

The surveyor waited, then spoke louder, as if Dũng's silence was caused by distance, not fear.

"Ruộng đó có nằm trong đường quy hoạch. Nếu nằm trong đường, sẽ có bồi thường. Ông nghe rõ không?"

That paddy is in the planned road corridor. If it is in the corridor, there will be compensation. Do you hear me clearly?

Compensation. The word meant nothing to Dũng in any practical way. He did not live on money. He lived on what he produced. And he had learned long ago that promises—especially promises attached to officials—were like smoke. They existed for a moment, then disappeared.

He stared at the man's mouth moving. He understood the Vietnamese, but it was as though the meaning had to pass through fog before it could settle.

Little did Dũng know that the team had been working its way up the valley for days. The three foreigners were Russians. They were laying out an access road. Aerial surveys had determined that the far end of the Sông Côn would be an ideal location for a hydroelectric dam. While the young Vietnamese surveyor explained that a road was going to be built, machinery—bulldozers, backhoes, excavators, and drills—was already being unloaded several miles south of them. Steel culverts had been brought in to create earthen crossings over the many tributaries and streams feeding into the Côn from the mountains.

Dũng's hut sat well west of the valley floor, but the paddies lay in the direct path of the oncoming road. He had little realization of how quickly his life was about to change—and not for the better.

Each of the men carried a different piece of survey equipment: tripods, transits, chains, tapes, levels, theodolites, and clinometers. One carried a bag full of survey flags. In quick order, they began setting up. Farther south, another group was doing the same.

The surveyor spoke to Dũng again, his voice patient now, like a man explaining something to a child.

"Chúng tôi sẽ cắm cờ. Đường sẽ đi qua đây. Ông đừng đụng vào cờ."

We will place flags. The road will go through here. Do not touch the flags.

Dũng's eyes followed the small cloth flags as they went into the earth—bright points of color that looked wrong against the green. It was as if the valley had been marked like a carcass.

Then Dũng heard the start of an engine—the pop-pop-pop of a two-cycle motor. A chainsaw. Men began cutting trees farther down the trail to clear a line of sight for the surveying equipment. The sudden commotion and noise left Dũng stunned.

He flinched, and he hated himself for it. The sound of an engine starting—any engine starting—could still make his muscles tighten. Sometimes, in the split second before he recognized the sound, he expected the crack of gunfire. The mind could learn new rituals, but it did not always unlearn old fear.

As Phương had taught him, he said little—if anything—to anyone. He stood without a word. He watched the men work for only a few minutes before turning toward the paddies again.

He did not know the work he put in that day would be useless within weeks. He did not realize how quickly the road would cut up the valley. He could not yet conceive the scale of what was coming—how the valley would soon be flooded with people, machines, and noise; how the mountains would be bitten into for rock and timber; how the village of huts would swell into a small town of stucco-sided homes, shops, and makeshift businesses built to feed the workers.

He worked anyway. He hoed weeds. He moved mud with his hands. He did what he always did because doing it was safer than thinking.

Within weeks, motorbikes, trucks, and equipment would pass his lone hut from dawn to dusk. The ground would begin to tremble with blasting—dynamite cracking the earth—and with the slamming rhythm of rock-crushing machines. Dust would fill the air. The first time the dynamite went off, Dũng shook in fear. Each blast sent his mind racing back to the immediate, searing pain of the explosion that had changed his world thirty-five years earlier.

The first blast came without warning. One moment the valley was loud with machines and voices; the next moment the earth itself cracked, and the sound rolled through him like a fist.

He dropped the hoe. His hands flew to his head, and for a brief second he was no longer standing in a rice paddy. He was back in fire and smoke. He could smell burned flesh. He could taste blood. His body remembered what his mind tried not to.

A man shouted somewhere behind him, laughing.

"Nổ rồi!"

It blew!

Dũng's breath came in hard pulls. He forced himself to stand, to retrieve the hoe, to keep moving so no one would notice how the sound had broken him. He could not afford to be watched too closely. Being watched led to questions. Questions led to answers. And answers, Phương had taught him, could kill.

With the construction and the disappearance of the paddies, Dũng's life shifted rapidly. Workers who drove past day after day spoke of the strange old man in the hut. Dũng was fearful of the crowds, but he kept his garden active and he learned that what he could produce could be sold—daily.

At first, he tried to avoid people. He waited until the noon heat drove them under shade and then carried his produce down to where stalls had appeared like weeds—sudden, crowded, noisy. He kept his head down and said as little as possible.

But hunger did not care about fear. Men needed food, and someone noticed that the old man's eggs were fresh and that his vegetables tasted like they came from real soil, not from hurried gardens thrown together for quick profit.

A young woman with an apron—thin, energetic, city-tough—stopped him one morning and pointed to the basket he carried.

"Trứng hả? Bao nhiêu?"

"Eggs? How much?"

Dũng hesitated. He did not like bargaining. Bargaining required words. Words required exposure.

The woman raised her eyebrows, impatient.

"Ông bán hay không bán?"

Are you selling or not?

He answered with the shortest thing he could.

"Bán."

Selling.

She held up three fingers.

"Ba rổ. Có không?"

Three baskets. Do you have that?

He shook his head once.

"Không."

No.

Then he added, barely audible:

"Mai."

Tomorrow.

The woman looked surprised that he spoke at all. Then she nodded, as if deciding something.

"Mai tôi tới. Ông ở cái chòi kia phải không?"

"I'll come tomorrow. You're in that hut, right?"

Dũng's stomach tightened. He did not want anyone to come to his hut. He did not want anyone to point at his hut. But she already knew.

He did not answer. He turned away.

The next day she came anyway.

She stood at the base of his steps and called up kindly:

"Ông ơi! Trứng!"

"Old man! Eggs!"

Dũng stayed still inside for a long moment, listening. It took him back to times long ago when voices outside a dwelling meant danger. But this voice held no menace. It held impatience, hunger, and ordinary need.

He went down with the eggs, his face covered. He handed them to her. She counted quickly, then pressed money into his hand.

"Ông trồng rau gì nữa?" she asked.

"What else do you grow?"

He kept his eyes down and said:

"Rau thơm. Ớt."

"Herbs. Peppers."

"Tốt. Mai nữa tôi tới."

"Đừng biến mất."

"Don't disappear."

Dũng did not smile. He turned away, but the exchange changed something: he learned that the valley, as it swelled and roared, also created a new kind of survival for him. He could sell. He could trade. He could remain the silent old man and keep his belly full.

Where the edge of mountain jungle had once been, restaurants appeared—many restaurants—each needing food to feed the laborers. Dũng increased the number of chickens, pigs, and fish he raised. He grew more herbs and vegetables. Each item sold as quickly as it was ready.

He worked harder than he ever had before, not because he wanted to, but because the valley demanded it. The new road brought everything closer—buyers, sellers, and trouble. And it brought eyes.

Some days men stopped and stared at him as they passed.

"Ông già đó lạ lắm," one worker said to another.

"That old man is strange."

"Không nói chuyện," another answered.

"Doesn't talk."

"Chắc bị điên," a third muttered.

"Probably crazy."

Dũng heard them, but he did not react. If they thought him crazy, it was safer than if they thought him foreign.

The work on the dam continued at a relentless pace. In 2009, the dam was completed. Suddenly, the abundance of traffic and people dwindled to a few. What had been an explosion of prosperity for many in the valley became hardship almost overnight. Many had moved into the far end of the valley to support the workforce, but now that the workers were gone, so was the money. Some locals returned to farming. The one lasting benefit was the improved ability to get produce to market faster.

For Dũng, the sudden quiet was both relief and threat. Less noise meant fewer eyes. But fewer buyers meant fewer coins, and fewer coins meant less salt, less oil, and less medicine when sickness came. He watched stalls collapse and businesses disappear, the way temporary things always did.

As time passed, industries moved in. Some worked at the dam, operating turbines that produced electricity. For Dũng, what had once been an open view across the valley floor was now crisscrossed with transmission lines. The village was changed forever. A military garrison moved into the valley to ensure the dam was protected. Even after the worker camps emptied, the village remained several times larger than it had been just a few years earlier. Dũng's hut was one of the few remaining huts in the valley.

He noticed another change: the valley was hotter than it had been. During the rainy season, flooding came in ways it never had before. The managers of the dam were not skilled at controlling the pool level; at times they released huge amounts of water into the river below, overflowing its banks. There were occasions when water crept toward Dũng's hut in ways he had never seen. Areas that had once been habitable could no longer be lived in due to the risk of floodwater.

The first time the water came close, it came in the night.

He heard it before he saw it—a low rushing, a sound like something alive. He stepped outside and felt damp air on his skin. The valley floor was dark, but moonlight showed a sheen where there should have been dry ground.

Water moved silently where he had walked a thousand times.

He stood on his steps and watched the flood creep closer, and something inside him tightened. Water and fire—both were things that took without asking. He remembered rivers in another life, cold and clear, harmless. This water felt different. It felt managed by men who did not know the valley and did not care whom it swallowed.

With access to electricity, factories were built that took advantage of local hardwoods for furniture to be exported. Roads were cut into the mountains above Dũng's hut to reach those hardwoods.

The sound of chainsaws returned, day after day, cutting deeper into the hills. Trucks groaned under loads of timber. Dust rose from new cuts in the earth. Sometimes he smelled the raw scent of fresh-sawn wood, and, for a moment, his mind snapped into a different place entirely—mountain air, pine, cold mornings, and a man's voice calling him from the far end of a hollow.

Through it all, Dũng remained alone. His life was filled with loneliness—no companions, no comradeship—only survival. He did the daily things that kept his life going, and the years moved on.

Even with the damage his brain had suffered so many years earlier, it had healed well enough that memories of his life before the valley became more distinct and clearer. Yet confusion remained. His two lives overlapped so completely that he often became uncertain which memories belonged to which life. They would intermingle and distort each other.

He dreamed of snow falling in the valley—though snow never came here, and true cold never came. Sometimes he dreamed of a water buffalo in the mountains of East Tennessee pulling felled timber from the woods. Sometimes, in his dreams, he saw Phương standing at a wood-burning stove in a mountain cabin, or his mother, Esther, kneeling under a cooking canopy. He saw Jonas in rice paddies, or Trai butchering a hog at his mountain home. He saw Cô Bình before the chalkboard at the one-room school outside of Townsend.

There were times he would wake from the nightmare of hunting people in the mountains above. In the dark, he would see the face of a young man he had killed. The pain of what he felt—each time, every time—returned with the same raw edge. He would hear the voices of his comrades. He remembered the screams and the agony etched in the faces of men who were dying or terribly wounded.

The name "Claude Jarrett" came to him in one of his many dreams. With it came the sorrow—the heavy, helpless sorrow—he had felt when his friend died.

Sometimes he woke and could not remember where he was for a few heartbeats. His hands would grope for a rifle that was not there. His ears would strain for English voices that had been silent for decades. Then the smell of the hut would anchor him—smoke, damp bamboo, fish-pond water—and the truth returned: he was here, in a valley that had taken him in and never truly let him go.

In his waking hours, it was often confusing trying to place it all together. He would be hoeing in the garden and suddenly remember hoeing in the garden of his mountain home. He would slaughter one of the pot-bellied pigs to take to a local restaurant and remember killing hogs with his mountain family. When he walked through the mountains above the valley floor, he would recall hunting wild boar. He remembered the long rifle he once carried, and then—without warning—the memory shifted to the pull of an M-16 trigger.

There were times when he caught the scent of nước mắm and reacted as though he were back on a mountain patrol. His body would go still, his eyes scanning, his breath controlled, and then he would remember he was only standing near a restaurant kitchen where a young cook had set out bowls for workers. He would feel foolish—then feel angry at himself for feeling foolish. Instinct had once saved him. Instinct was not something to mock.

In his valley home, time passed slowly. The days were long, and the nights even longer. There was nothing to occupy him except the work he performed each day to survive. There were no visitors to his hut. No friends or loved ones to speak to. He watched the occasional traffic going to or from the dam farther up the valley. He often wished someone would stop and talk, but he also knew that fear would clamp his words shut. He would say little—perhaps nothing at all.

Time moved on, and even after more than fifty years, he remained fearful he would be discovered.

Phương had taught him never to let his voice be heard. She never explained. She never said why. She only taught him to keep his voice quiet. She could hear something in his speech—a dialect shaped by another place—that would make someone immediately aware it was not Vietnamese. Dũng did not understand that. He did not realize she feared the American in him would become evident.

Phương never knew the name Gabriel. She never knew anything about his existence in his mountain home. All she ever knew was that the young man would become her lost son. He would become Dũng—and Dũng he had been for fifty years.

It was only in his dreams that he ever became Gabriel.

In sleep, he would hear his mother, his father, his teacher—and even Phương—calling him Gabriel. There were times he dreamed that Hùng was his father and was calling him Gabriel, too. In those dreams, he grieved for both men, as though his heart could not decide which life to belong to.

In waking hours, he wondered about those he had known. Names would come to him from nowhere. A name, long forgotten, would suddenly rise into his mind, and with it the face of the person, the circumstances, and a feeling—sometimes tender, sometimes sharp. It would be there all at once, unconnected to what he had been thinking only moments before.

Sometimes the memory was fleeting, vanishing as quickly as it arrived. He would stop what he was doing and try to seize it, trying to make a connection with that sudden thought before it slipped away. Sometimes it brought happiness. Sometimes despair. Sometimes he wanted to linger in it. Sometimes he wanted it to disappear.

The work he had done for years was gone. The people he loved, even though he did not know the meaning of love, were gone.

Each day, he would go about the tasks that were necessary to survive, the things that had to be done. He saw people every day, but none were people who had any concern for him, the strange man who lived alone. Even though he had only known a handful of people in the valley, they—and those he did not know but recognized by face—were all gone.

The valley was different. The people were different. Life was different, but somehow, Dũng kept pushing on. Whatever emotions he had were the emotions he had always had. He did not think of sadness because he did not know what sadness meant. The same was true of happiness; he did not know what it meant. He never thought he was weary. There was no definition in his mind that told him what weariness was.

He thought about those he had known, and he knew that he ached for them. There was a feeling he had for those people, but he could not put words to it. At times he dreamed about running happily, but again, he did not understand the emotion he felt in the dreams. At times, there was a level of clarity about the people in his dreams, but then the clarity would disappear in an instant. For moments he would fully know, but he was not able to hold on to that knowledge.

At times, he would sit, trying to bring an understanding to his life. What was it about him that kept him separated from everyone except a few? Inside, he held fear about anyone knowing who he was, but he did not really know who he was. He remembered the instructions he was given by Phương, Hùng, and Bình, but why was he given those instructions?

He knew he had been a child, but where was that childhood in this life? There were hints of it in his dreams, and sometimes they seemed present, but in the waking hours they were gone, except for the brief memory of the dream.

In this lonely life, it was only the memories that kept him connected.

It was only the memories that kept him alive.

Chapter 12

The Names We Carried

Psalm 147:3 (KJV)

> "He healeth the broken in heart, and bindeth up their wounds."

Sean McMurtry had retired to his old hometown of Dover, Tennessee. After he was discharged from the Army due to severe wounds, he went back to school to study biomechanical engineering. He earned his doctorate from Vanderbilt University, then founded a company that developed much of the biomechanical engineering used in prosthetic limbs. Through that work, Sean became very wealthy.

He had been married once, but his wife died early in their marriage, and he never pursued marriage again. He traveled often in those years. He was a wise man—methodical—and his life was well planned, carefully structured without excluding spontaneity, as if even the unexpected had been accounted for. He felt he could live on about five percent of his wealth, and he directed nearly every other penny to proven charitable groups that supported veterans. He also worked with organizations in Vietnam focused on Agent Orange remediation and on treatment for those horribly damaged by exposure to the chemical. Sean had everything he owned willed to those groups.

His house had been purposefully designed and built to serve as a PTSD retreat. It overlooked the Cumberland

River as it flowed toward the Land Between the Lakes. Sean had found one of the most remote parts of Stewart County that still offered a beautiful view of the river. The house served as the retreat's headquarters, with meeting rooms and office space. Outlying housing units had been built for those who came for extended stays. The retreat served those suffering from PTSD, and it also operated as a rehabilitation center for those severely wounded—especially those living with the loss of limbs. Its proximity to Fort Campbell made it an ideal location. The Gulf Wars had created large numbers of soldiers who needed both PTSD support and long-term wound rehabilitation.

In the spring of 2018, Sean drove to Nashville to meet a man coming up from Pulaski. They had served in Vietnam at the same time. Not only had they both served, but they had also attended Tennessee Tech at the same time and graduated together.

Russell Davenport had found information on Sean McMurtry while reading a business journal—an article about the work Sean was doing with veterans. Russell had gone into construction and home building and had caught the wave of growth south of Nashville in the 1990s, building many subdivisions in that area. In recent years, he had become interested in building homes designed specifically for wounded veterans. Once he found the article on Sean, he reached out.

They agreed to meet at a restaurant on Charlotte Avenue on the west end of town. Sean suggested a Vietnamese restaurant he often frequented when he was in Nashville. The suggestion took Russell aback. He found himself uneasy about going to a Vietnamese restaurant. It struck him as odd—after all these years—that he still had a negative reaction to anything or anyone that reminded him of Vietnam. After some hesitation, Russell agreed.

On the trip to Nashville, a lingering thought kept crossing Russell's mind. Could it be possible that Sean

McMurtry was the same Captain McMurtry whose name Russell heard fifty years earlier. From the article he read, he did realize that this was the same McMurtry he graduated with from Tennessee Tech.

Russell arrived about thirty minutes early. Sitting in the parking lot, he found himself anxious. A nervousness came over him, and he literally shook as he sat in his pickup truck. For a moment, the anxiety was overwhelming. He sat there taking deep breaths, thinking how crazy the emotion felt. His hands gripped the steering wheel, then loosened, then gripped again. He stared at the restaurant sign as if it were an objective he could study and defeat.

He reminded himself that the people inside had nothing to do with a war that had ended forty-three years earlier. Nothing would happen in that restaurant. He needed to overcome the fear. And yet his body didn't care what his mind said. His heart kept thudding, hard and fast, like it had the first time he heard incoming rounds crack overhead.

Russell stepped out of his truck and walked toward the entrance. As he neared, the aroma from the restaurant struck him and took him back to a time in Biên Hòa, a city north of Sài Gòn. During his second tour, he had been sent there for training, learning to fly the Cobra gunship. While there, he and others went to a restaurant in Biên Hòa, and the first thing he noticed when entering was the aroma.

This place in Nashville had the same scent.

As Russell entered, a young Vietnamese woman approached and asked, "Just one?"

"No," Russell replied. "I'm meeting someone."

He realized the extreme anxiety had already begun to ease. The young woman pointed toward a table.

"You sit there."

Russell sat down. The waitress brought him a glass of water, and he waited only a few minutes for Sean's arrival. He kept his eyes on the door, then forced them away from it. He listened to the kitchen sounds—metal on metal, voices calling back and forth, a soft rhythm of work.

He told himself again: Nashville. Not Biên Hòa.

When the waitress returned, she asked, "You want cà phê sữa đá?"

Russell gave her a puzzled look.

"It's coffee on ice," she explained, "and it's very good."

Russell nodded. The waitress returned shortly with a steaming metal cup and a glass of ice. She showed him what to do with the cup and the ice. He watched the dark coffee drip down, slow and steady, as if time itself had decided to move in careful drops.

As he took his first sip, he looked up and saw the door open.

He recognized the man from the article immediately.

It was Sean McMurtry.

It was not apparent in the way Sean walked that he had a prosthetic leg, and with his long-sleeved shirt it was not obvious he wore a prosthetic arm. Russell stood, and the two greeted each other with a warm handshake and a hug. It had been well over fifty years since they had last seen each other.

"Russell Davenport," Sean said, his voice calm, steady—older, but unmistakably him.

"Sean McMurtry," Russell replied. "I didn't think we'd ever sit down across from each other again."

Sean gave a restrained smile.

"Life has a way of circling back."

They sat down and began to reminisce. For the first several minutes, the conversation had nothing to do with Vietnam. Russell told Sean about his construction business and about the article he had read describing Sean's work with wounded veterans. Russell explained his hope: to build homes for severely wounded veterans—and that with Sean's guidance he believed he could build them properly.

Sean listened the way he always had in school—quietly, attentively, as if he were assembling a blueprint in his mind. He asked practical questions: door widths, bathrooms, ramps, thresholds, the psychology of space, the small humiliations that came with a house built for someone else's body. Russell found himself grateful for Sean's precision. It gave him something solid to hold on to.

It was only as they were eating that Russell fully realized Sean's left arm was prosthetic. Sean had ordered gỏi cuốn and bún thịt nướng chả giò for them both—Vietnamese spring rolls and a bowl of vermicelli noodles with marinated grilled pork. Russell found both delicious. As they ate, he couldn't help but wonder about Sean's arm.

Finally, he asked.

"Sean, I couldn't help but notice your prosthetic arm. Was that from the war?" Russell asked. A tingling of nerves gripped him suddenly.

"Yes," Sean replied. "I lost it—and my left leg."

"I had no idea," Russell said. "I was shot in the shoulder, but it was superficial. I had no lasting effects from it. In fact, I went on to flight school and flew Hueys and Cobras on my second tour."

Sean's expression shifted as he thought back. The restaurant noise seemed to drop away around them, the present thinning for just a moment.

"Yeah," Sean said. "We were on a rescue patrol, trying to find a guy who had gone missing the day before. We were just outside a small village when one of the guys tripped a booby trap. I was fortunate. Two of my guys were killed. I lost my arm and leg, but I survived. From what I've heard, they never found the guy we were looking for."

Russell shook as he heard the words. The fork in his hand hovered, then lowered, then hovered again.

"The day I was wounded, we lost a guy," Russell said. "He was never found. I don't think there are many days I don't think about him. We were on a reconnaissance mission in April of '68 in the Côn River Valley when it happened."

Sean's head jerked at the words.

April of '68 in the Côn River Valley.

His face tightened, not in anger—something closer to impact, like a blow taken clean in the chest.

"In Bình Định Province," Sean said quietly, "about thirty miles northwest of Quy Nhơn."

Russell stared at him.

"Yes. April 4th, 1968."

"Damn," Sean blurted.

The young waitress and the few other customers jerked their heads toward the table. Sean glanced up, then lowered his eyes again, as if he'd forgotten where he was.

"Was the guy's name Fox?" Sean asked.

Russell was shaking now.

"Yes. Gabriel Fox. Sergeant Gabriel Fox."

The two men sat stunned, staring at each other. The emotion hit them both like a physical force. Each struggled to breathe. Tears filled their eyes.

Sean reached across the table with his good arm and took Russell's hand in his. His grip was firm—steadying, almost corrective, like he was anchoring Russell to the table so he wouldn't drift away into memory.

"Oh wow," Sean whispered. "This is hard to believe. What are the chances? I didn't know Gabriel Fox—but he has lived with me all these years. I've learned to live, and live well, without my arm and leg. I've even prospered because of what I lost. But I've always carried the weight of never finding that sergeant."

Russell sat silently for a moment.

"Gabe was a good man," he said. "A good soldier."

His voice broke. Russell hung his head and began to cry, struggling to hold back tears.

"It was believed a mortar round blew him apart," Russell said. "I'd heard soldiers were killed trying to locate him—and that their platoon leader was severely wounded. I knew his name was McMurtry, but I had no idea it was you."

Sean's eyes closed briefly, as if he were trying to absorb the sentence as something real and not another story told in a hospital ward.

The young waitress watched the two men from across the room. She saw the distress on their faces. It was one of the things she disliked about her job, because it was not the first time she had seen that look settle over older men and women at a table.

Sometimes it was two men born in Vietnam. Other times it was two men born in America. She had seen women meet with men and carry the same heaviness in their eyes. She would overhear fragments of conversation as she moved between tables. Sometimes she heard men telling women they had served with their husbands or loved ones. Other times, Vietnamese men spoke quietly of the war and of years spent in re-education camps.

They always spoke of the land of her ancestors.

It was a land she had never visited, yet one she knew well through stories and silences. Her father had spent fourteen years in a re-education camp. He carried the wounds and sorrow of those years, even when he said nothing. She often heard him and others speak about the loss of their home country—how it still lived inside them like a wound that would not close.

She knew that pain when she saw it.

And she could see it now in the two old men sitting at table number four.

She slowed as she passed them, not intruding, but listening just enough to know this was the kind of grief that did not want to be watched—and yet could not be hidden.

Sean looked at Russell and said, "You know, I'm a strong believer in fate. I believe many things that seem random or coincidental are meant to be. I can't believe our meeting today was by chance. I've got this overwhelming feeling it's more than our common experience.

"For weeks now, the search for Sergeant Fox has been heavy on my mind. I even dreamed about it last night. The day I was wounded, we came across a small hut just south of where Sergeant Fox was lost. An old woman was tending to her severely wounded son. She said he'd been wounded the day before, during the battle your unit and the NVA engaged in. She told me she was preparing him to be buried when he died.

"I couldn't help but feel for her in her grief. I accepted what she said—but for nights now, I've dreamed about that old woman and her son. For all these years, the possibility that the young man was Gabriel Fox never came to me. But lately, in my dreams, that thought has lingered. Each morning, I push it aside, but Russ… the feeling is just too strong."

Russell stared at Sean as he spoke. As the words poured out, Russell felt swamped by the same rising pressure. Could it be possible? Was there any chance whatsoever that the young man Sean described had been Gabriel Fox? And if it were, what were the odds he lived, or could he even be alive now?

Russell's mouth opened once, as if to say no, as if to force reason back into the room. But the word wouldn't come. Not when the dates matched. Not when the river valley name matched. Not when Sean's face—so controlled—looked like it was holding back something raw.

His thoughts were still racing when his phone rang. He started to ignore it, then pulled it from its holster and saw the name on the screen. A surge ran through him as he read it.

Years earlier, he had entered his old friend and mentor simply as "Lacey." Even though he knew Abraham Lincoln Lacey had retired as a colonel, Russell still referred to him as "Sarge."

He answered, "Hey, Sarge."

"Hey, LT. How are you doing?" the voice asked.

"Good, Sarge. How about you?" Russell replied.

"I hope I haven't caught you at a bad time," Lacey said. "But LT, I've been having some crazy dreams the last few nights—and I just needed to talk to you."

Sean could hear Russell's side of the conversation, and a lump rose in his throat when he heard the distantly familiar voice mention dreams.

Russell asked, "Are they about Gabriel Fox?"

There was a brief silence on the line.

"Yeah," Lacey said. "How did you know?"

Russell took a big gulp of air.

"Sarge, I'm sitting with someone you met a long time ago."

On the other end was questioning silence.

"Captain Sean McMurtry," Russell continued.

For a few moments, the silence was stunned silence.

Then, "My God, Russell, are you serious?"

"Dead serious," was the reply.

When Russell finished, A.L. Lacey—as he was known these days—said, "Russell, I don't know what you and McMurtry's plans are for the next few days, but I'm catching a plane to Nashville as soon as I can book a flight. I want to see you both. Is that possible?"

Sean heard Lacey's words and nodded, as if the decision had already been made long before the call.

Russell said, "Come on. We'll be waiting on you."

It was late the next afternoon when Russell Davenport and Sean McMurtry arrived at BNA—Nashville International Airport—to pick up A.L. Lacey.

After the phone conversation the day before, Russell called home and told his wife he would be spending a few more days in Nashville. He explained the situation, and she was agreeable.

Sean made calls of his own—to Pentagon contacts and to his local congressman, who was also a military veteran. To each of them, Sean's story did not sound probable. But each knew Sean well enough to understand he would not be asking for help getting to Vietnam quickly unless he believed—with everything in him—that it was necessary.

Both Sean and A.L. Lacey had been back to Vietnam on several occasions. One of Sean's longstanding endeavors was the support of rural hospitals. Remediation and care for those stricken by Agent Orange was a priority to him—one he pursued with quiet intensity.

Unknown to what would soon become his two traveling companions, Sean McMurtry had been diagnosed with non-Hodgkin's lymphoma a decade earlier. It had been controlled for years, but only weeks before this meeting in Nashville, his doctors informed him it was no longer under control. His time was limited. He had not told Russell that. He had not told Lacey yet either. He carried it the way he carried most things—privately, deliberately—choosing what mattered most to spend his remaining strength on.

A.L. Lacey had returned to Vietnam with his wife and children on multiple occasions, but he had not returned since his wife's death. For Russell Davenport, the thought of returning to Vietnam was initially frightening. Sean and Lacey assured him there would be no issues.

Through Sean's contacts at the Pentagon, in Congress, and through both American and Vietnamese embassy channels, he pushed the visa process through for himself, Russell, and Abraham. Within two weeks, they were on their way.

In support of his charitable activities, Sean visited Vietnam a couple of times per year to check on the hospitals and medical facilities he supported. Through the years, he had focused much of his work in Bình Định and Gia Lai provinces along Highway 19, from Quy Nhơn up to Pleiku.

His base of operations was Quy Nhơn, and from there he traveled to remote facilities.

Years earlier, Sean had hired Tuân, then a young medical student and now a doctor, to oversee the work. When Sean was in-country, Tuân chauffeured him to the various facilities. For all the years they had been associated, Tuân often wondered why there was one valley road Sean always avoided.

Tuân was surprised when Sean called and told him he was coming to Vietnam with two other men—and that they would be traveling up đường tỉnh 637 into the Côn River Valley. That road was the one place Sean had avoided for more than a decade.

It was late in the afternoon when the airplane, máy bay, landed at Phù Cát Airport, Sân bay Phù Cát. Russell was amazed by the modernity of what he had experienced since the three had arrived in Vietnam three days earlier. They had landed late at night and spent two additional nights in Sài Gòn, recuperating from the long flight and adjusting to the time change.

Even though Sean and Lacey had assured him everything would be fine, Russell was still apprehensive when they arrived at Tân Sơn Nhất Airport. Soon he discovered there were no issues going through customs. Sean had arranged for a driver to pick them up. Russell was again surprised by the luxury of the hotel they stayed in during those nights.

While in Sài Gòn, Sean met with local officials and secured the paperwork necessary for their trip. If they had been ordinary tourists, no special documentation would have been required—but due to the reason for their travel, both American and Vietnamese officials wanted the trip properly documented.

On the third morning, the three Americans caught an early flight from Tân Sơn Nhất to Phù Cát. The flight was short. When they exited the terminal, Tuân was waiting in a Toyota 4Runner.

Tuân spoke excellent English, as Russell had discovered was true of many Vietnamese people they met. Russell was surprised that in their brief time in Vietnam he experienced no hostility—none. In fact, while walking from their hotel to a restaurant on Đường Pasteur in Sài Gòn, he was thanked twice by Vietnamese people for having served in the war.

The first time someone approached him and asked if he was American and had served, he hesitated to reply. When he answered yes, the man thanked him. Sean and Lacey had experienced the same on many occasions, so it did not surprise them—but it surprised Russell.

Tuân was a pleasant man with an easy smile. He helped load their luggage into the 4Runner. Rooms had been reserved at the Sài Gòn–Quy Nhơn Hotel, Khách sạn Sài Gòn–Quy Nhơn, in Quy Nhơn. None of them knew whether they would be successful—or how many days they would remain in Vietnam.

As they left Phù Cát, Russell thought back to long ago when he first arrived at the Phù Cát Airfield in a C-130 en route to An Khê, Camp Radcliff. He also recalled boarding a C-130 to fly back to Cam Ranh Bay, Vịnh Cam Ranh, to return to the United States for flight training.

Sean had similar memories—except his journey from that same airfield had taken him to Sài Gòn, then to Japan, then back to America and Walter Reed. After three months at Walter Reed, he was transferred to Blanchfield Army Community Hospital at Fort Campbell. It was there he was discharged.

The drive from Phù Cát to the hotel took about thirty minutes. Again, Russell was surprised by the quality of the accommodations. His room overlooked the ocean. From his window he watched fishing boats, trawlers, and merchant ships moving through the inlet into Quy Nhơn.

They were scheduled to go with Tuân to his home in Quy Nhơn, where his wife prepared a traditional Vietnamese lunch. After lunch they returned to the hotel to rest. Jet lag still clung to them.

Russell found it difficult to sleep. He wandered down to the lobby and sat in one of the chairs for a while. More than once a staff member approached to see if he needed anything. Finally, he decided to venture outside on his own.

He crossed the street toward the beach. A sidewalk ran along the shoreline. He watched boats coming in and people hurrying to offload fish. As he walked, children ran up to him.

"Hallo! Hallo!" they shouted.

Russell smiled.

"Hallo."

The children giggled, laughed, and ran away.

He was to meet the others at 6:00 p.m. for supper at a local seafood restaurant. As he walked and took in the sights, he found himself at peace—pleasantly at ease.

Early the next morning they met for breakfast in the hotel restaurant, and soon they were off toward Happy Valley. Tuân pulled onto Highway 19 and headed west. The four men talked as they drove, but Russell grew quieter, watching the landscape slide past.

There was familiarity—and yet everything was different from more than fifty years earlier. The realization of all those years struck him hard. In this place long ago, he had felt young. Now he sat in the back seat on the right side, looking out the window and realizing he was an old man.

He knew that time was short for all three Americans.

He wondered about the trip. Was it futile? A waste of time?

And yet, as they drove, he realized he was glad to be there. Nothing about what he was experiencing felt connected to the long-ago fear. Tears came to his eyes—both in remembrance and in the realization that there was no fear.

As a young soldier, he had been brave and had led with dignity while pounding the ground in this land. As a pilot, he flew into situations that raised the hairs on the back of his neck—and he did it bravely—but each time he had to push through fear. He could not recall a single combat situation in which he was not afraid.

He did not pray much anymore, but as they drove he reflected on how often he had prayed in Vietnam. The first time he came under fire, he remembered the immediate freezing fear—and how he prayed his way through it. He did not pray not to die. He prayed not to die in fear. And in that prayer, he had felt the fear lift. He regained his ability to fight and lead—and fight and lead he did.

He remembered, after returning as a pilot, being called to support a firebase during the darkness of night. He and his crew arrived to find it overrun by the NVA. From their position he could see hand-to-hand combat below. He was flying a UH-1B gunship with rockets and two M-60 machine guns manned by the crew chief and door gunner. They could not fire for fear of hitting their own men.

Then the call came in. There were severely wounded who needed to be extracted.

Again, Russell prayed.

His hands shook. Tears came to his eyes. He told his crew to hold on, and he flew the helicopter and his men into that onslaught of bullets. He could feel the slap of rounds against the hull, but he kept flying. Smoke popped, and he drove toward the smoke.

The helicopter dropped hard to the ground. Men ran, carrying their wounded comrades. The crew chief and door gunner tossed out cases of ammo to make room. This model of Huey was not designed to carry additional soldiers.

Russell watched as one of two men carrying a wounded soldier dropped—killed instantly by an NVA round. The other continued, dragging the wounded man to the open cargo door. The crew chief and door gunner helped pull the wounded inside. Four men were loaded, and Russell was waved off.

As he lifted back into the air, he watched more of his fellow Americans fall under heavy fire. He knew he could not return. The UH-1 skimmed the tops of surrounding mountains, gaining elevation. The crew chief shouted how badly the men were wounded. Each of those loaded had one or more limbs missing. With limited medical knowledge, the crew chief and door gunner did all they could to keep them alive.

Camp Evans was the nearest refuge. Russell pushed the UH-1 as hard and fast as he could. At Camp Evans, the wounded were offloaded—along with his door gunner, who had been shot in the left bicep but had not said a word until they were safely down. He was more concerned about the men they had brought in than his own wound.

Russell realized he had lost himself in those memories.

When he looked again, up on a hill not far away stood a white statue of Buddha with four Cham towers nearby. He suddenly recalled seeing those towers from the air on the medevac flight that had carried him and two others from the valley to the military hospital in Quy Nhơn.

The day after that flight, Sean McMurtry had taken a similar flight—but he had been unconscious from the searing pain of a missing arm and leg.

Abraham Lincoln Lacey also saw the four towers—Tháp Bánh Ít—and the Buddha. He couldn't help remembering flying over those temples with what remained of his troop, wondering about Lieutenant Davenport and those they had lost.

As Lacey and Russell looked on, the reason they were there tightened again in their minds.

They both thought about the little man from the mountains.

It was midday.

The strange old man had a food stand set up in front of his hut, next to đường tỉnh 637. With the growth in the valley, he had developed regular customers—men who worked at the dam and at factories built downstream. From his stand he could see the large power substation that transmitted electricity down through the valley. Looking toward the river, he could see towers and transmission lines carrying the power away. He constantly heard the hum that rose from the substation.

There used to be a large bamboo stand along both sides of the river. It no longer existed. Flooding had become constant.

In one way, he was fortunate. The initial road had flooded so often that it had been pushed farther uphill, and now it ran close to his hut. His hut and the road sat above the floodplain.

He had lost the ability to earn income from rice paddies and from producing goods made from harvested bamboo, but now he could make a living from the food stand. There was the additional benefit of not having to walk as far or push his broken body as hard. The pain in his right arm and leg—present all these years—had grown worse. He doubted he could ever return to rice work, and he knew he could no longer harvest bamboo. His ability to search the nearby jungle for hardwoods or climb mountain terrain was gone.

He had learned to become a good cook. There were other restaurants in the village, but he kept a steady clientele.

The lunch rush had come and gone—no more than seven or eight people. With those customers, and the occasional stop, Dũng was able to survive.

The older he became, the more he found his thoughts turning toward things that once would never have entered his mind. Sitting under the canopy, he wondered who would bury him when he died. He had no friends. No loved ones. No family. Would he die and be left to rot?

With as much pain as he lived with, he knew a day would come when he could not walk. That fear brought another fear behind it: would he starve because he could not feed himself?

He no longer had a garden. No fish. No chickens or pigs. The road had taken all of it. All he had now was the hut, the cooking area, and the food stand. A vendor in the village brought him what he needed to keep going. He never ventured beyond that little plot of earth. His entire life existed within less than a twenty-five-foot circle.

His eating habits had changed. He ate only at night, only what was left from what he had prepared for the stand. It was not much, but it was enough to keep him alive.

On the road beside his hut there was a constant flow of traffic—mostly motorbikes, but also cars, trucks, and buses. Buses hauled workers from various places to their jobs. Above the dam, where there had once been jungle, there were now houses and schools. Military vehicles moved up and down the road constantly.

Dũng understood there was a large military complex in the village. He had never ventured far enough to see it, but he saw soldiers often. Some even stopped to eat at his stand.

He had a cloth canopy over the stand, with one table and four chairs. The furniture was molded plastic. The table was red. He had two orange chairs, one white chair, and one purple chair.

He sold food. He kept a cooler with beer. He also made rượu Bàu Đá, a potent rice whiskey. Sometimes people came and sat at the table drinking rượu Bàu Đá until they could not move. They would lie beside the road, sleeping off the drink.

It was mid-afternoon when a Toyota 4Runner pulled up in front of the stand. Behind it, a military vehicle stopped—something like a U.S. military jeep. The sight of the military vehicle brought immediate concern to Dũng. He had not had trouble himself, but he had heard stories from customers. Often, those stories were not good.

He watched as everyone got out. There were four men in the 4Runner and two in the military vehicle.

The four men in the 4Runner had stopped, as required, at the military headquarters down the road. The commanding officer had been forewarned of their arrival. There were no hurdles for them to cross. The commander was accommodating—as he always was when his superiors issued the order. He had assured the three Americans and the Vietnamese doctor that there were no Americans living in the valley. If there were, he would know.

And yet, even though he insisted there were no Americans, he remained cordial. Like most Vietnamese, he had been born well after the war. He knew of it but held no grudges toward Americans. As many would say, the Vietnamese would rather have the Americans than the Russians. The commander felt the same.

As proper etiquette, the four men allowed the commanding officer to approach Dũng first.

The commanding officer knew little about the old man beyond the fact that he kept to himself. From maps the Americans had brought, they believed the four rice paddies where the battle occurred—the battle in which Gabriel Fox had been lost—had been near this location. The commanding officer told the Americans that most of that had been erased by the construction of the dam and the access road. He expected there would be little to find.

He had been in this post only two years. The dam had been operating since 2009. In his mind, there was nothing left from the old days but geography and rumors.

The three Americans hoped the old man at the stand could offer something—some detail, some memory, something that had survived the machines. With the dam and road reshaping everything, they feared their search was in vain.

As usual, while the commanding officer spoke, Dũng only nodded in agreement. His face was mostly covered, leaving little visible to identify him. Sean and Lacey knew some Vietnamese, but they found it nearly impossible to understand the dialects of rural areas. And they found that unless they were in a city, few people understood their Vietnamese.

As Lacey listened to the commanding officer speak to the old man, he couldn't help but chuckle inwardly at how difficult it had been to understand Gabriel Fox at times. Even Tuân struggled in conversation with rural locals.

Russell stood listening, unable to follow a single word. Then he saw it: the sudden jerk of the old man's head, and fear in his eyes.

The others saw it too.

The words that frightened the old man were the commanding officer's last ones:

"Chúng tôi đang tìm kiếm một người Mỹ."

We are looking for an American.

Dũng had long ago figured out there was a secret. He could not put it all together, but he knew Phương had protected him so he would not be discovered. It was only after Trai found the uniform hidden under the woodpile that Dũng understood why Phương had guarded him so fiercely.

Russell asked, "What did he just say?" referring to the commanding officer.

Lacey replied, "He said we're looking for an American."

Dũng heard the tall Black American speak. It was the first time he had heard English in more than fifty years—and he understood it.

Abraham saw the reaction on the old man's face as he answered Russell. Then Abraham stepped forward.

"Chúng tôi đang tìm kiếm Gabriel Fox," he said. "We are looking for Gabriel Fox."

"Tôi là Trung sĩ Abraham Lacey," he said, and then pointed toward Russell, "và đây là Trung úy Russell Davenport."

"I am Sergeant Abraham Lacey, and this is Lieutenant Russell Davenport."

The names rang inside Dũng's head like bells struck in a silent place—names remembered in dreams but long forgotten in waking life. Images flared behind his eyes.

Every man present could see the change in him.

Even the commanding officer—who had insisted there were no Americans in the valley—was suddenly aware of what was happening.

Then he heard Abraham ask in English, "Are you Gabriel Fox?"

Gabriel's eyes shot to Abraham Lincoln Lacey—then, with fear, to the commanding officer.

When he looked at the officer, he did not see reprisal. The commanding officer saw the look of terror and spoke gently.

"Đừng sợ."

"Do not be afraid."

Tuân stepped forward and spoke in English.

"I'm with them," he said, motioning to the Americans. "No one will do you harm."

Russell stepped closer, words choking in his throat, tears rising as he spoke.

"Sergeant Fox—Gabriel—I'm Lieutenant Davenport. Do you remember telling me you wanted to show me your mountain home?"

Gabriel looked at Russell, then at Lacey. He saw familiarity in their faces. He remembered saying it—wanting to show Lieutenant Davenport his mountain home.

He looked again at the commanding officer. He looked at Tuân. He looked at the Americans.

For a moment he stood there, staring at them all, as if his body could not decide whether to run or to fall.

Then he looked back at Russell Davenport and said quietly,

"I remember."

Chapter 13
The Old Man

Isaiah 46:4 (KJV)

"And even to your old age I am he; and even to hoar hairs will I carry you: I have made, and I will bear; even I will carry, and will deliver you."

Jonas sat on the front porch in the early morning of that hot July day. The porch was well worn and decaying, just as the cabin was decaying—the cabin of his life. He had been born there, and he would die there. He would soon be ninety-five, and he knew his time was coming. He did not wish to die, but he had no fear of dying either.

The air already carried heat, thick and waiting, and the old rocker creaked under him the way it always had. Somewhere down the slope a bird called once and then went silent, as if even the woods knew to conserve their breath.

Esther had been gone eighteen years already. Oh, how he missed his wife. Even though his mind let him talk to her as if she were there, he still missed her touch and her smell. He could see her headstone from the porch. He visited her first thing every morning. He told her about the weather and about the letters from Mary and Elizabeth. Mary had lived in Ohio for many years now, and Elizabeth in Michigan.

Each year, they would meet and drive down to spend a few days with their aging father—until both sisters died within six months of each other. Jonas loved seeing the pictures of the grandchildren and the pictures of their children. Years earlier, the grandchildren had come for the annual visit, but once they became adults, they no longer came. He wished he could see his great-grandchildren, but he had given up hope of that.

He spoke to Esther the same way he always had—plain, direct, no wasted words.

"Mornin', Ess," he whispered, as if she might answer from under that quiet stone. "It's goin' to be another hot one."

The saddest thing he had to tell Esther after she passed was that they had lost their oldest, Jacob, and the two girls. He was glad she did not have to see Jacob die or know of the girls' passing, for Jonas could still remember her pain when they lost Gabriel. He loved all his children, but the loss of Gabriel always returned to his mind.

At least Jacob had lived a long time, even though he could not survive on his own. Shortly after Esther's death, Jacob was taken to a care facility. Jonas could not care for him once Esther was gone. It was the two sisters who made the arrangement. Jonas knew he could not take care of Jacob, but nonetheless he was unhappy about Jacob being taken away.

Gabriel had been only twenty when he was reported missing. It was hard to believe he had been gone fifty years.

A tear came into the old man's eye as he remembered that young boy scampering up and down the hollows of their mountain home. The boy seemed afraid of nothing. Jonas remembered him standing down a bear in the mountain meadows where they grazed their cows. He remembered him coming home one day holding a timber rattler just under its head, the tail shaking so hard the rattles sounded like a box of nails.

Unlike his other three children, Jonas knew Gabriel would never have left these mountains for good. He remembered the day—after Gabriel had been home a month on leave—when he and Esther drove him to Townsend to catch the bus for Knoxville. He remembered that last good-bye vividly. He could still feel the ache in his heart as he and Esther watched him board the bus and roll away toward Knoxville. Jonas never said a negative word to Gabe, but still he wondered why in the hell his son was going to that damn place—Vietnam.

That morning, as Jonas knelt beside Esther's grave, he remembered her last words.

"Jo, you tell Gabe when he comes home that his momma loves him."

She always held such hope—a hope that had stayed strong in both her heart and Jonas's.

Jonas bowed his head again and let the words come out the way they always did when he was alone.

"Ess… I'm still here," he said softly. "And I'm still tellin' him."

Jonas felt the first pangs of morning hunger. He looked at the small basket of three eggs he had gathered from the henhouse. Little had changed in his life from the time he was born. As much as he could, he still held to the old ways. When doctors advised him to change his diet, he politely declined and told them he knew of no other way to eat.

Each morning, after visiting Esther, he gathered his eggs. Once inside, he sliced either ham or bacon and fried it in the old iron skillet. Then he used the grease to fry his eggs—straight out of the shell into the pan. Even though the ham or bacon was cured in salt, he always added more salt to his eggs. His coffee was black and strong and extremely hot. He used the same heavy porcelain cup he had used while learning to drink coffee as a pup.

Jonas sat at the breakfast table with the quiet discipline of habit, shoulders relaxed, the morning light laying a clean stripe across the worn wood. A plate of eggs and toast steamed faintly beside his coffee, but his attention kept returning to the open Bible propped near his right hand. The thin pages lay flat beneath his fingertips, the familiar cadence of the King James Version moving through him as he read of the father who ran to meet his lost son—of mercy that did not wait to be earned.

He took a slow bite, chewed thoughtfully, and looked down again, his lips barely shaping the words as his eyes tracked the lines.

He was reading from Luke, and the words settled into the room like something living:

"And the son said unto him, Father, I have sinned against heaven, and in thy sight, and am no more worthy to be called thy son."

"But the father said to his servants, Bring forth the best robe, and put it on him; and put a ring on his hand, and shoes on his feet: And bring hither the fatted calf, and kill it; and let us eat, and be merry: For this my son was dead, and is alive again; he was lost, and is found."

"And they began to be merry."

Jonas read it again under his breath, slower the second time, as if repetition might make it truer.

Even though his hearing was not good, he heard the car coming up the long gravel drive well before he could see it. It was too early for the postman, and it was not Wednesday, so he knew the preacher was not coming. It was also too early for Carl, the neighbor who came every day to check on him.

Jonas continued to eat slowly until he saw the car come around the bend into view.

It took his mind back to so many years ago—to the day a strange car arrived to tell them Gabe was missing in action and presumed dead. Apprehension spread through the old man's body as he saw the car stop. Three men got out, all three in uniform.

The driver was the local sheriff, John Brinkley. He recognized him at once. The other two wore different uniforms, and he did not know either man.

Jonas stood and held the edge of the table for a moment, steadying himself. The room tilted, not from weakness alone—something in his bones recognized this pattern. Visitors. Uniforms. Bad news. He reached for his cane and headed to the door.

Just as they started up the steps to the porch, Jonas opened it.

"Hello, Mr. Fox," said the sheriff. "I'm Sheriff Brinkley."

"Yes sir, I knowed who you be. Can I help you?" Jonas replied.

"Well, Mr. Fox, these two men would like to have a conversation with you—something I think you will want to hear. This is Lieutenant Colonel Parent, and this is Major Balthrop, both with the United States Army."

Jonas's mind raced. He had heard that remains of American servicemen had been found in Vietnam and returned home for burial.

He looked at the two men and asked, "Did you find my son, Gabe?"

The lieutenant colonel answered, "Well, yes sir. That's what we would like to talk to you about."

Jonas's whole body quivered as he heard the words. His knees went weak, and he nearly fell. The three men rushed up the steps and caught him before he hit the floorboards.

"Mr. Fox, let us take you inside so you can sit down," the colonel said.

They helped Jonas into the cabin. The only chairs were at the kitchen table. The house was sparse by their standards—very few furnishings, no luxuries, not even a television. Yet all three noticed how clean it was. Nothing was out of place.

The major noticed the homemade bookcase cut from poplar wood. On the shelves were a few books and framed family photos. Lieutenant Colonel Hastert saw the picture taken of Gabriel during basic training and a few more sent from Vietnam. He wondered how this old man would take the news.

They helped Jonas into a chair, and each of them took a seat. Sheriff Brinkley stayed standing near the door for a moment, as if unsure whether to be official or simply neighborly.

"Mr. Fox," the colonel said, "I want you to listen carefully."

Jonas nodded. His hand tightened around the cane handle until his knuckles looked like pale knots in an old root.

"We have found your son Gabriel."

Jonas whispered, "When will his body be brought home?"

The colonel's expression tightened.

"Well, Mr. Fox... that's the thing. Your son is not dead."

Jonas's eyes widened. He stared at the colonel.

"What is it you are saying?"

"Mr. Fox, your son has been found alive. He was seriously injured long ago, but he's alive."

The words had to be untrue. Jonas was certain he wasn't understanding. All he could do was look at the colonel with questioning, tear-filled eyes.

"Mr. Fox," the colonel said softly, "your son is alive. He's been living in a small farming village for all these years."

Jonas swallowed hard.

"Didn't my boy want to come home?"

"Mr. Fox, for many years he didn't remember who he was. He was injured so badly. From what we can understand, he was saved by a woman in the village after he was hurt, and he has lived as though he were Vietnamese all these years. It has been so long since he has spoken English that it's difficult for him to speak it—and to understand it."

Jonas's voice was thin.

"Is my boy coming home?"

"Yes, Mr. Fox. He is coming back to America. For many years he has had dreams about a life other than the one he has known in Vietnam, and now he understands where those dreams came from."

Jonas sat, his old mind trying to absorb it. Then a thought struck him like a hammer.

Lord, don't let me die before I see him.

"When will he be here?" Jonas asked.

"In just a few days, Mr. Fox. He is in flight from Vietnam to Japan as we speak. He will stay in a military facility for a few days to make sure he is healthy enough to travel before he comes home. And if you have no objection, Mr. Fox, we are going to send one of our mobile medical units up here for a few weeks to make sure your health remains good."

The colonel explained it carefully, but he had the old man in mind. At his age, the news might be too much.

Even as he spoke, the medical unit pulled into the yard and began setting up. It would be at least a week before Gabriel would be released to come home. The order had come directly from the President: Jonas Fox was to be cared for until Gabriel arrived—and for a while afterward.

Jonas sat for a long moment without speaking. The colonel watched him, concerned. Sheriff Brinkley's face had changed too—caught between disbelief and the plain relief of seeing the old man still breathing.

In Jonas's mind, a bear-cub of a boy ran up and down the hollows of the mountain. No one could keep up with him. Skinny, but strong.

Then Jonas remembered what the colonel had said.

Gabe was seventy now. But it didn't matter.

Gabe was still his boy.

Finally, Jonas said, “I don’t mind.”

“I don’t mind what?” the colonel asked.

“I don’t mind them medical people,” Jonas said. Then, as if to steady himself by making it practical, he added, “If they’re here, they can keep the preacher from fussin’ at me about salt.”

The colonel gave a small, careful smile. It wasn’t laughter exactly—more like permission for the room to breathe again.

Jonas told the men he wanted to go back out on the porch. The two soldiers helped him—not because he could not do it, but because it took time. Jonas sat in his rocker and stared out into the distance, waiting for his son.

Occasionally, he would glance at the medical team setting up. The team consisted of three people—a female doctor and two male medics. They went about leveling the van and RV and setting up equipment.

While they worked, the colonel told Jonas that Gabriel had been injured badly and had suffered severe injuries to his face and the right side of his body. It had only been in the past few years that Gabriel had begun to remember pieces of his past. He told Jonas about the three Americans who had traveled to Vietnam in search of Gabriel.

Jonas listened without interrupting. Once, he cleared his throat and said, almost to himself, “So he lived… and we didn’t know.”

The sentence was not an accusation. It was the stunned statement of a man trying to make a world fit back into place.

The old man sat, taking it in, trying to digest it. It rolled through his mind like a movie. He saw Gabe in Vietnam. He saw a life he could not imagine.

At twilight—when Jonas was usually in bed watching the last rays of daylight fade—he was still sitting on the porch.

Earlier, the doctor and medics had taken him into the medical van for a complete physical. The doctor was amazed at the health of a ninety-five-year-old man. The colonel, major, and sheriff left about an hour before dark. The two Army officers stayed at a motel in Townsend and planned to remain there until after Gabriel came home.

That evening, Jonas sat on the porch well after dark. The doctor sat with him. Carl came by as he always did.

Carl was new to the mountains. He was a widower, too. After his wife died, he bought property adjacent to Jonas's land. The first day he owned it, he drove up the gravel road to see what was there. He met Jonas and took to him immediately.

Jonas invited him into the cabin. Carl saw the picture of Gabriel and asked about him. Jonas told the story of his son being lost in Vietnam. Carl stared at the picture and felt his own memories shift.

He had flown UH-1s over Vietnam. As a member of the 1st Cavalry Division, he knew he had flown in the same country, near the same valleys where Gabriel had been lost. Carl had no children. His parents were gone. He was essentially alone. That first day, Carl decided he was going to look after Jonas.

That night, with the doctor sitting nearby, Carl stood at the edge of the porch and removed his hat. He didn't say much at first. Then he murmured, "Jonas… if this is true… I'm glad you lived long enough to hear it."

Jonas stared into the dark, and for a moment his voice nearly failed him.

"I been livin' long enough to hear a lot of things," he said. "But not this."

Carl stayed until dark, then went home.

The doctor stayed longer and finally persuaded Jonas to go to bed.

Jonas slept poorly that night. The initial shock had faded, but the truth remained—impossible and solid.

Gabriel was coming home.

Jonas knew he had to be patient.

And patient he was.

The days passed slowly, but they passed.

The medical team and Carl looked after him. Jonas gained weight with constant care and regular meals. He grew stronger with company around him. On the final day, he woke up early. The military had told him it would be afternoon when Gabriel returned to the mountains.

They were allowing three news organizations to film—along with military coverage. Filming would be limited to the few moments when Jonas and Gabriel met again.

A week earlier, Russell Davenport, Sean McMurtry, Abraham Lacey, and Tuân had traveled with two Vietnamese military members to the hut beside the road. None of them truly expected to find anything of consequence. The three Americans only knew they had to make the trip—to ease what each carried.

They never expected to find Gabriel Fox alive.

Not quickly. Not at all.

Yet they did.

When word first reached officials in Hà Nội, a level of panic set in. Whether true or not, they wanted to dispel the belief that Americans from the war were still alive in Vietnam. They also wanted to dispel the suspicion that Americans had been held deliberately in POW camps after the end of the war.

The American ambassador was summoned. Hours of discussions followed. The ambassador convinced Vietnamese authorities that this could benefit both nations if handled carefully.

The President of the United States was informed early that morning. He quickly spoke with the President of the Socialist Republic of Vietnam. They agreed the news would be presented in the most favorable light possible. Along with the Vietnamese ambassador to the United States and the Secretary of State, a press release was crafted—language both governments agreed upon.

News networks were notified that the President would speak at 10:30 a.m. Vietnam released its statement simultaneously, but without the fanfare of the American broadcast.

Meanwhile, medical personnel—American and Vietnamese—were sent to the village along the Côn River. Operatives from the Vietnamese government also arrived to ensure the flow of information was controlled. They were in place by the time the President spoke. The moment the statement was made, the story flooded twenty-four-hour news coverage in America.

Gabriel was transported to Phù Cát with the three Americans who had found him. From Phù Cát they flew to Sài Gòn—Thành phố Hồ Chí Minh. Along the way, Gabriel was treated for parasites and inoculated against communicable diseases. The inoculations gave him fever and chills, and he remained in bed for nearly thirty-six hours until the reaction wore off.

Once he recovered, he, Sean, and Russell boarded a military transport plane and flew to Japan.

Sean thought of the irony. More than fifty years earlier, he had traveled nearly the same route home.

From Japan they flew to America and then to Walter Reed. Sean and Russell intended to accompany Gabriel all the way back to his mountain home. Lacey told the others he would remain in Vietnam for a while. He did not explain, only said there were a few things he needed to do.

Over the ensuing days, Gabriel regained some clarity. After fifty years in Vietnam and a fog of memory caused by his injuries, he struggled to fit the pieces together. He would never fully return to being Gabriel Fox. Dũng held most of his memories.

Yet once he was told he was going back to America, he felt an immediate desire to see the mountains in Tennessee.

He did not ask many questions. He did not seek answers for the long years. He never asked about his injuries. He felt no regret over the absence from his Tennessee home. Leaving the Côn River Valley did bring sadness. As the 4Runner pulled away from the hut, Dũng looked back one last time. He thought of Phương, Hùng, Bình, and Trai—gone for so long.

He did not show the grief that tightened his chest.

That night he was in a hospital room in Sài Gòn. In his dreams he saw a man limping and calling his name. He saw a woman standing in a place that felt familiar, but it was not the hut in the valley. He saw animals that did not live in the mountains around Làng Cây Tre.

The words spoken earlier—"Gabriel Fox"—had created an instant bridge from long ago to the present. No one had to explain to him that he had lived two lives. No one had to tell him that Làng Cây Tre was not the place of his birth. No one had to explain that his life started somewhere else, and his name was not Dũng—even though he would always be Dũng, too, for however long he lived.

It was knowing without fully comprehending.

His damaged mind attempted to reach through fog and make conscious sense of it. For fifty years, his mind had functioned only in the present. It did not ask questions. It did not analyze. It never questioned how he knew certain things but could not remember learning them. The dreams at night did not cause him to ask why they came. Often the dreams slipped away during the day, only to return in sleep.

But now those two words had set his mind searching while awake.

In Nashville, a man sat in the office of his automobile repair shop going through paperwork. The television played a twenty-four-hour news network. He was not paying attention until he heard the anchor say, "In the village of Làng Cây Tre in Vietnam, a soldier missing for fifty years has been found alive."

The name he did not recognize, but the story itself pulled his full attention.

He listened as the anchor said an American soldier from the Vietnam War had been found alive. Then a short video appeared. Trai sat back in his chair. Emotions overwhelmed him. After twenty-seven years, there was chú Dũng, a man he dearly loved.

Trai thought of his uncle Dũng and his grandmother Phương.

His uncle Dũng never talked, only worked. His grandmother explained things when necessary, but with little emotion. He did not understand until later that "Trai" simply meant boy. His past came flooding in. His mind was full of memories.

The boy called Trai was highly intelligent. He figured things out even when no one instructed him. Even though he was not welcomed in the village, Làng Cây Tre, once old enough he walked into the village anyway. He was chased off, fought the village boys, and still went back.

He knew he was different from everyone else, including his uncle and grandmother. His skin was darker. His facial features were different. He saw it in the reflection of streams and ponds. He knew he did not belong—not in the eyes of those around him. The village children taunted him.

They called him "Người Mỹ," American.

They called him "đen, Trai," Black boy.

Finally, he convinced Phương to explain. She gave only what she had to give. His mind processed it and made its own connections.

After years, hostility in the village faded. He even found work. He helped people. He learned quickly. He did not back away from hard labor.

He knew he would leave the valley one day.

First Quy Nhơn.

Then America.

At every step, he gathered information like a man collecting tools.

Now, sitting in Nashville, he pulled out his phone and began searching for more information.

One hundred eighty miles east, a military vehicle and a medical unit pulled out of McGhee Tyson Airport, heading toward a log cabin in the mountains.

Trai left his desk and walked into the repair bay. A young man named Scott was the assistant manager. Scott took over whenever Trai was away, which was rare. Trai told Scott he would be leaving for a few days—he did not know exactly how long, but he would be gone.

Then he called his wife and told her to pack a suitcase. He explained what he could.

Back in his office, more details came in. Video appeared. There was footage of the hut beside the road. When Trai left his home long ago, the valley had been open fields and thick tropical growth. Now the footage showed change. Roads. Buildings. A world that had moved on.

Ninety miles south, Sarah Davenport watched the same news outlet. She already knew most of the details. When Russell called earlier, his voice had changed. A melancholy that had always lived in him had lifted.

A.L. Lacey called his two sons and told them he would be gone for a number of days. He said there were a few other things he needed to do in Vietnam before he returned home.

Over the next days, things moved rapidly.

Gabriel stayed in Japan for thirty-six hours, then flew with a stop in Seattle before arriving at Walter Reed. He continued treatment for parasites. They fed him a high-calorie diet, but none of the food appealed to him.

He underwent X-rays, CT scans, and MRIs. Old breaks, wounds, scars, and the damage to his brain were studied. Dental work was performed. Two teeth were pulled. A few moles were removed and tested for skin cancer.

In their zeal, some doctors wanted corrective surgeries, including plastic surgery.

Gabriel struggled to take it all in.

Finally, Sean stepped in and convinced them to back off. He told them to make sure Gabriel was healthy enough to travel; the rest could be addressed later.

Gabriel still insisted on covering his face. He felt no shame, only the ingrained need to remain hidden. His scars and burns had never bothered Phương. She had not feared others seeing the burns. She had feared the unburned side of his face—the American side. To protect him, she taught him not to speak to others and never to show his face.

It was not embarrassment that drove him. It was instruction. Obedience. Habit.

His first full bath in Sài Gòn had been quietly pleasant. Phương had taught him to wash his hands and face daily, but a full-body bath had been rare. Medical staff assisted him, washing him with strong antibacterial soap, cutting his hair, and shampooing it.

As apprehensive as he was, for the first time since his injury, he realized how good it felt.

In the mountains of East Tennessee, Jonas Fox received the best care. He gained weight. The companionship helped him as much as the medicine.

One day after the news broke, a Dodge pickup truck drove up the mountain road to the Fox cabin. Visitors had come daily since the story hit the world, and most were turned away. Security was handled by the sheriff's department and the state highway patrol. There was concern someone would try to take advantage.

The Dodge stopped at the checkpoint. The man in the truck said he was Gabriel Fox's nephew.

The officer looked at the man's dark skin and heard the foreign accent.

He called his superiors.

Soon the FBI was involved. Agents from Knoxville arrived by helicopter. At each level, the man repeated his story. At each level, it sounded plausible. He gave no hint of ill intent.

Back in Làng Cây Tre, people began asking questions. Had a half-Black, half-Vietnamese child grown up with the man now known to be American—Gabriel Fox?

Confirmation came.

The man's story was legitimate.

He was escorted to the cabin to meet Jonas. He sat with Jonas and told him the story. When he finished, Jonas looked at him and simply said, "Welcome to my home."

Trai told Jonas how Phương and Dũng had raised him, and how Dũng—limited in memory—had spoken of Tennessee and mountains as something he could feel but not fully name.

By coincidence, Trai had rented a room at the same motel where the Army officers stayed. At the cabin they became acquainted. Trai met Carl, the preacher, and members of the church Jonas and Esther had attended all their married lives.

As Trai walked around the property, he felt echoes of his valley home along the Côn River. Mountain and valley were different worlds, but some things—hollows, ridges, creeks, the feel of green—spoke the same language.

Trai spent the rest of the day with Jonas, becoming acquainted. Jonas asked many questions about Gabriel's life.

During the conversation, Jonas took Trai's hand and said, "You know, for a long time I have been without family around me. My wife and children are all gone, but now I have you—and soon Gabriel."

Trai looked at the old man and felt a quiet certainty. He would bring his wife and children to meet their uncle and grand-uncle.

They talked late into the evening. That night, Trai called Phương and Scott and told them both he would be away for several days. For the next six days, Jonas and Trai became family.

Finally in the morning, Trai returned early. He ate breakfast with Jonas. Gabriel would arrive later that afternoon.

Jonas rose early. As he always did since Esther's death, he started a fire in the stove. He percolated coffee—strong and hot—and poured a cup for himself and Trai. He cooked his usual breakfast, and they ate together.

Then they went to the front porch.

Jonas sat in his rocker.

Trai sat beside him.

They waited.

Gabriel had been told his mother had died. He understood, but the information carried little outward emotion. He was told he would see his father—the man in his dreams. He was told his father was old, and they might not recognize each other.

Gabriel accepted what he was told.

Again, there was little visible emotion.

His plane landed at McGhee Tyson at about 11:30 a.m. Cars waited. Cameras were set up. He was placed in a wheelchair and taken to one of the vehicles. The commotion confused him. He did not fully understand what was happening.

He sat in the back seat on the right side, wrapped and covered. Those around him had learned he did not talk much. He answered questions sometimes but often remained silent.

There was no excitement on his face. No visible anticipation.

In his mind there were questions, but they did not spark emotion. He stared out the window without much thought. He did not count the minutes. He did not measure distance.

Then the car rounded a curve.

Mountain ridges came into view.

Gabriel sat up, trying to see more. Another curve stole the view, blocked by a rock wall cut into the hillside. The car dropped into a valley. The ridges appeared again.

Suddenly Gabriel's heart began to pump harder. He found the window control and lowered it. Air rushed in.

Smells flooded the car.

They struck him like a blow.

Familiarity surged through his body. Thoughts flooded his mind. He did not recognize the buildings, but he recognized the land—the hills, the river to the left.

He began searching for a road to the right. He knew it should be coming.

His heart raced.

"There," he said aloud. "Up there."

The others in the car stared. It was the first voluntary words he had spoken since returning to America.

The driver turned.

In Gabriel's mind the road should have been gravel, but now it was paved. Still, he recognized the direction. The car climbed.

They crossed a creek over a bridge. Gabriel remembered fording it in the family's mule-drawn wagon.

The road began to ascend. Gabriel saw the mouth of a hollow.

A shot rang in his mind.

A black boar falling. He remembered carrying it up the hollow on his shoulders, Esther laughing at the mess of him, Jonas pretending to scold while pride sat plain on his face.

Then—without warning—another memory struck, softer and more dangerous.

Esther at the stove, flour on her hands, turning to look at him with mock severity.

“Gabriel Fox, if you track mud in my clean kitchen—”

But the words dissolved into the warmth of her smile and into the smell of biscuits so real his mouth filled with saliva.

Mary and Elizabeth flickered next—girls on the porch steps, bare feet, hair in braids, arguing over whose turn it was to pump the swing. He heard their laughter, high and sharp. He saw the way Esther shooed them out the door, apron flapping, telling them to quit tormenting their brother.

And then Jacob.

A bigger boy’s body with a child’s eyes, standing in the yard with a stick in his hand, staring at a butterfly as if it were the most important thing in the world. Gabriel’s chest tightened. He remembered taking Jacob’s hand and guiding him gently, showing him how to step over roots, how to follow without fear.

The images came like lightning—bright, brief, undeniable—then vanished.

Every turn brought another memory. Sounds and smells unlocked scenes he had not held in waking life for decades.

Love for the place crashed over him.

Then he knew.

The next turn, and he would be home.

Even before the turn, the cabin came into his mind with sharp clarity—porch boards, a stovepipe, the slope of the roof, Esther’s voice calling him in.

And then he saw it through the windshield.

His body could not run the way his mind wanted to. But the need rose in him anyway. He could not wait to get out of the car.

On the porch, Jonas saw the vehicle coming. Beside him stood Trai. Jonas’s hands gripped the arms of the rocker so hard his knuckles went white. The doctor hovered behind him, ready.

The car stopped.

Gabriel looked out and saw his mountain home. He saw Jonas rising from the rocker with the help of the man next to him. He saw the man standing beside him—Trai.

Before anyone reached the door, it flew open.

Trai held Jonas steadily as they watched.

Gabriel stepped out.

His legs carried him as fast as they could up the hill toward the cabin. Others moved after him, ready to catch him if he fell. His damaged leg dragged slightly, but it did not stop him. The smell of the mountains. The cabin. The man in his dreams. His nephew Trai standing next to him.

And then—without warning—he found himself looking for two women.

Both his mother.

The grief came fast: burying Phương, the weight of the shovel, the quiet afterward. Then the words he had been told in America—that his mother had died. Esther. Another woman he could barely picture, yet felt like a missing limb.

Even with that realization, he did not falter. He kept moving.

He could hear shouts from reporters cordoned off at a distance. Cameras clicked. A helicopter thumped somewhere beyond the trees. None of it mattered. Memories were flooding into him. He did not fully understand the years between, but he understood this: this had been home.

The old man on the porch was his father.

Jonas stood waiting, arms ready, eyes locked on the shape of his boy coming home. His lips moved without sound.

"Lord," he breathed, "you let me see him."

As Gabriel neared, the face covering he always wore loosened and slipped. It fell to the ground in the dust.

The crowd saw the terribly scarred face and reacted—shock rippling through them. A few turned away. Someone gasped.

On the porch, Jonas did not flinch.

And Trai did not flinch.

Aides moved toward Gabriel, ready to steady him at the steps.

Gabriel reached the base of the porch and stopped, frozen, looking up. His chest rose and fell too fast. His hands trembled. The sight of Jonas—older than a man should ever have to be while still waiting on his son—hit him harder than the cameras or the uniforms.

Jonas trembled too, one hand lifted, unsure if he was allowed to touch what might vanish.

A nurse came to Jonas's side and took his arm. Trai let go of Jonas's other arm and eased down the steps to his uncle. He took hold of Gabriel's forearm, and the others stepped back, giving the moment room.

Gabriel turned his head and looked at Trai's face—older now, broader across the shoulders, a man with a family, a man who had crossed an ocean.

"Chú Dũng," Trai said softly.

The words landed like a stake in the ground—naming him, anchoring him.

Gabriel's eyes watered, and for a moment he looked away, as if ashamed to be seen breaking. Then his eyes went back to Jonas on the porch.

Trai nodded toward the steps.

"Slow. I got you."

Trai helped his uncle climb—one step, then another. Gabriel's right side resisted him, stiff and uncooperative. His breath came in short pulls. The doctor watched, hands ready, but she did not interfere. This part belonged to them.

At the top step, Jonas stepped forward. With an aged, frail hand he took Gabriel's—both hands trembling.

Jonas tried to speak and couldn't.

Gabriel tried to speak and couldn't.

So Jonas did the only thing left.

He pulled his son in.

They held each other, chest to chest, the way they had never been allowed to do in just over fifty years. Jonas's arms were thin, but the grip was fierce. Gabriel's arms were uncertain at first, then tightened, as if his body finally remembered what his mind could not fully explain.

No words were said.

None were needed.

Jonas lifted his face and looked at his son's scars, and he saw past them as if they were nothing at all. He saw the boy running the hollows, the boy with the rattler, the boy boarding the bus in Townsend.

"My boy," Jonas whispered at last, the words breaking. "My boy."

Gabriel's breath hitched. A sound came out of him—not language, not yet—just something raw and human, like a door that had been locked too long finally giving way.

Jonas held him tighter, as if he could anchor him to the porch boards themselves. Then Jonas's gaze shifted—just once—past Gabriel's shoulder, toward the edge of the slope where the graveyard lay.

Where Esther's stone caught the afternoon light.

Jonas's lips moved again, barely more than air.

"Mama," he whispered, his voice breaking into a smile and a sob all at once. "He's home."

Gabriel felt Jonas's body tremble, and something in that tremor—something older than pain—pulled at him. His eyes followed Jonas's glance.

He saw the white headstone.

A name in his mind, not fully formed, rose anyway.

Esther.

The memory came not as a picture at first, but as a sensation: the soft press of a hand on his hair. The sound of a woman humming while she worked. The faint scent of soap and warm bread. Then, like a curtain lifting, he saw her—standing in the doorway in a faded dress, wiping her hands on her apron, eyes fixed on him as if he mattered more than the whole mountain.

He did not know how he knew.

But he knew.

A second flash: Mary and Elizabeth running across the yard, skirts swishing, laughing as they chased each other around the porch posts. One of them—Mary, he thought—sticking her tongue out at him. The other—Elizabeth—ducking behind Esther's legs, giggling.

And Jacob again—older now in the memory, sitting in the grass with a stick, pushing a line into the dirt, focused like a man building a railroad. Gabriel remembered kneeling beside him, speaking softly, guiding his hands, and Jacob looking up with a sudden bright smile that made Gabriel's chest ache now.

The memories were brief, fragile, like sparks in dry leaves.

But they were his.

Gabriel swallowed hard. His mouth opened. For a moment no sound came.

Then he managed, barely audible,

"Daddy..."

Jonas's head jerked slightly, as if the word had struck him.

Gabriel's voice was rough, unused, the syllable shaped by years of another language, another silence.

But it was the right word.

Jonas pressed his cheek against Gabriel's temple and shut his eyes.

"That's right," Jonas whispered. "That's right."

Gabriel's arms tightened once more, and he leaned into Jonas as if the porch and the mountains and the years might finally hold him.

Behind them, the cameras kept rolling. People kept watching.

But on the porch, the world narrowed to three things: an old man's breath, a son's shaking hands, and a white stone in the yard catching the light—silent witness to a promise kept too late, but kept.

Epilogue

Revelation 21:4 (KJV)

> "And God shall wipe away all tears from their eyes; and there shall be no more death, neither sorrow, nor crying, neither shall there be any more pain: for the former things are passed away."

Abraham Lacey rode with Sean McMurtry and Russell Davenport to Tân Sơn Nhất Airport in the vehicle behind the ambulance that carried Gabriel Fox. The city moved past the windows in a blur of mopeds, heat, and exhaust—Sài Gòn alive as ever, indifferent to the quiet grief in the convoy.

At the military terminal, Abraham stood with them as they said what had to be said, the kind of goodbye men learned to speak in fragments because full sentences carried too much weight.

Sean clasped Abraham's hand.

"You did right by him," Sean said, his voice low. "You brought him back to us."

Abraham swallowed.

"We brought each other back."

Russell nodded once—his way of agreeing, his way of blessing the moment without making it dramatic.

When the aircraft lifted off, Abraham watched until it vanished into the humid sky. For a long time, he remained where he was, as if leaving the runway would make the last weeks feel final.

Shortly afterward, he caught a flight north to Phú Bài, just outside Huế. He spent several days with what remained of his wife's family—faces lined by years, voices softened by loss and survival. They fed him, fussed over him, and asked him the questions families ask when they do not know how to ask about pain.

He showed them pictures of his children and grandchildren. An elderly aunt traced a fingertip along a photograph and whispered a blessing. At night, the house quieted, and Abraham lay awake listening to distant traffic and the faint sound of rain on tin. The visit was gentle and unexpectedly comforting. It did not erase grief, but it steadied it.

Then he flew back to Sài Gòn.

From the airport, he took a taxi to the bus terminal on Phạm Ngũ Lão Street. He bought a ticket to Mỹ Tho. With nearly two hours to wait, he walked to Bến Thành Market. He ate a bowl of phở gà at one of the food stalls—chicken broth and rice noodles steaming in the crowded heat, the fragrance of ginger and scallion cutting through the press of bodies. The market pulsed with noise and movement: bargaining voices, clinking spoons, the rhythm of a city that had endured too much to ever slow down for one man's memories.

After he ate, he wandered through the aisles and then returned to the bus terminal.

The bus arrived in Mỹ Tho late in the evening. Abraham caught a taxi to Lê Lợi Street. It had been fifty-two years since he had been in Mỹ Tho—and fifty-two years since he had walked down Lê Lợi.

The street was crowded and bright, as was common throughout Vietnam now. He passed shops of every kind: storefronts glowing with modern electronics, small stalls piled with goods, families gathered at sidewalk tables, eyes flicking down to cell phones as they walked. There was little familiarity in anything he saw. He did not expect to find the restaurant he had known so many years before. The city had changed too much. Memory could not keep up with time.

Then he saw a sign hanging out over the sidewalk:

Nhà Hàng Ngon

He stopped and stared at it. His breath caught. Could this be the same place?

He stepped to the door and went inside. Immediately he caught the aroma of food cooking—garlic, fish sauce, char, broth, heat. The sounds were different than he remembered, but the heart of the place felt the same: a crowded room, laughter rising and falling, the clatter of bowls, and the comfort of food made with practiced hands.

A young woman approached him with a bright smile.

"Welcome to Nhà Hàng Ngon," she said in perfect English. "Is it just you tonight?"

"Yes," Abraham replied, and his voice sounded older than he felt.

She guided him through the busy restaurant.

"Please sit here," she instructed, and placed him at a small table where he could see the kitchen door.

Abraham sat down. He could not help noticing the resemblance—something in the young woman's face and carriage that pulled at his memory. The impression of Hoa, the young Vietnamese woman he had loved so long ago, rose in him so sharply that it felt like an ache.

When the young woman returned with a menu, Abraham asked, "How is it that you speak English so well?"

"Oh," she said with an easy laugh, "I was born and raised in America. I grew up in Westminster, California."

"How did you end up back in Vietnam?" Abraham asked.

"As a child, we came back to visit relatives—especially my grandmother," she said. "She owns this restaurant. I always loved it here. I returned four years ago and just stayed to help her."

Her smile softened.

"My grandfather died six years ago. She needed help. And..." She lifted her shoulders slightly, as if the rest were obvious. "Here I am."

Again, Abraham couldn't help noticing the similarity—the voice, the cadence, the way her eyes held his just a second longer than politeness required.

He asked quietly, almost afraid of the answer, "Your grandmother's name wouldn't happen to be Hoa, would it?"

"Yes," the young woman said. "And that's mine also." She smiled again, but now it carried curiosity. "Do you know her?"

Before Abraham could answer, the young woman's gaze drifted toward the register near the kitchen door. Abraham's eyes followed.

A woman stood there, watching him.

Time did something strange in that moment. The restaurant noise faded, and Abraham could hear only his own heartbeat. The woman's face was older—lines at the eyes, a steadiness in the jaw—but the eyes were the same. The posture. The stillness. The way she looked at him was as if she had never stopped looking.

Their eyes locked, and fifty-two years of separation thinned to nothing.

Abraham stood. His hands trembled slightly at his sides.

"Hoa," he said, and it was not a question.

She did not rush him. She walked toward him slowly, as if afraid that sudden movement might break the fragile reality of the moment.

"Abraham," she answered, and his name in her voice carried everything—youth, war, loss, survival, and the quiet endurance of love that had never found a clean ending.

For a long moment, neither spoke. They simply stood close enough to touch, as if both were learning whether the other was real.

Finally, Hoa reached up and pressed her fingertips against his cheek, gentle as a blessing.

"I wondered," she whispered. "All those years... I wondered."

"I tried to find you," Abraham said. His voice cracked. "I didn't know how. I didn't know what was true anymore."

Hoa's eyes shone, but she did not let the tears fall.

"Life happened," she said softly. "And then it kept happening."

They sat together at his table, and the young woman—Hoa's granddaughter—watched them with dawning understanding.

"Grandmother," the young woman said carefully, "is this...?"

Hoa nodded once, and her composure finally shifted, just enough to reveal the girl she had once been.

"Yes," she said. "This is him."

In the days that followed, there was no hesitation. Within weeks, they began the process to be married—two people unwilling to waste any more time pretending that love, once found, could be safely set down and forgotten.

Other than frequent trips back to the United States, Abraham and Hoa established their home in Mỹ Tho.

Six months later, Abraham Lincoln Lacey, Russell Davenport, Gabriel Fox, and Trai stood under a canopy that protected them from falling snow at Arlington National Cemetery. Russell and Trai steadied Gabriel when the Honor Guard began to play "Taps," and the casket of Captain Sean McMurtry was lowered into the ground.

Only two months earlier, Sean had stood with them as the casket of Jonas Fox was lowered into the earth beside his beloved Esther. In a short period of time, these men had become family. Their care and love for one another were beyond measure.

Gabriel did not always grasp the full extent and power of his return. He knew he was alive, but he often felt as though he had stepped into someone else's life—one already filled with grief that should have ended decades ago. Yet in Jonas's final moments, there had been peace, and Jonas had been certain that Esther rejoiced at Gabriel's return.

After the ceremony at Arlington, the four men drove into downtown Washington, D.C. They parked near the Lincoln Memorial. Both Gabriel and Trai marveled at its size. They stood for several minutes looking out over the Reflecting Pool, watching the Washington Monument mirrored on its surface like a memory held steady in water.

From there, they walked the short distance to the entrance of the Vietnam Memorial.

Gabriel had no idea what to expect or what it would mean, but when they reached the black granite wall, standing in the snow, he froze—not from cold, but from what rose in him all at once.

Russell spoke gently, as if in a church.

"You don't have to say anything," he told Gabriel. "Just stand. Just breathe."

Abraham had been there many times, but it did not matter. The wall did not become easier. It only became familiar in its weight.

Trai looked at the other three men and saw the tears they did not bother hiding. Then Trai turned and looked at his chú Dũng. He had never seen tears in his uncle's eyes—not even when Phương died, not even when Jonas died. Trai knew his uncle carried grief like a stone in his chest, but he had never seen it spill over.

Now it did.

They stood and stared at the V-shaped black granite that drew their gazes down into the hollow earth.

Russell knew the names Gabriel would recognize—some Russell knew himself—yet the list was too long for any of them. Abraham had many of the same names and many of his own.

They proceeded down the quiet path of that hallowed place. Trai helped his uncle down the slope, careful with each step.

A warm breeze moved across them—impossible in the snow—and for a moment Gabriel smelled smoke and wet jungle, heard rotor blades and distant gunfire, heard men shouting names into chaos. The wall did not merely display the past. It summoned it.

Russell stopped and pointed out a name to Gabriel. Gabriel nodded faintly, as if the name were a bell tolling in his mind.

Then Russell stopped again and pointed lower.

"Claude E. Jarrett," Russell said.

Gabriel's body shook. The name opened a door in him, and the memories came rushing through—Claude's face, Claude's grin, the way two boys from two different worlds could become brothers in the mud and terror of war. Gabriel remembered looking down at his friend lying dead on the ground. He remembered the terrible thought that near them were other dead boys—boys he had never known—and that he had been responsible for some of those deaths.

He pressed his palm against the stone.

"I'm sorry," he whispered, and it was not only to Claude. It was to a lifetime.

After Jonas's death, Trai took his chú Dũng to live with him and his wife, Phương, in Nashville. Their three sons had moved out long ago. Once each month, Trai took his uncle back to the mountains, and they spent a couple of nights in the cabin.

At the cabin, Gabriel would hobble around the yard, reminiscing about his youth, sometimes smiling at nothing, sometimes going quiet for long stretches. His return brought celebrity to both him and Trai. Reporters sought interviews. Offers came—book deals, movie rights, speaking engagements. Someone even set up a GoFundMe in Gabriel's name.

Through it all, there were sufficient funds to keep the mountain property in the family, to hold on to what Jonas had built with his hands and heart.

It was in the spring, following Sean McMurtry's funeral, that Trai and Dũng took their monthly trip to the mountains. Trai knew his uncle was not feeling well, but Dũng insisted.

"I'm going," Dũng said. "Don't argue with me, cháu."

So they went.

It was the second morning of their stay in the cabin. A mountain chill lay in the air. Frost clung to the ground and glittered in the trees. Trai cooked breakfast while Dũng took his coffee to the front porch and sat in the rocker Jonas had occupied for all those years.

Dũng looked out at the hoarfrost in the branches. He closed his eyes and heard Jonas's voice telling him to fetch wood for the fire. He heard Esther's voice calling that breakfast would be ready soon.

Then he felt a warm breeze.

He heard the Sông Côn flowing in the background.

He saw Phương in the rice paddy, hoeing weeds. He saw Trai as a boy running along the dike. He heard Hùng's voice, and beside him stood Bình with her kind face.

He heard familiar laughter and turned to see Claude with a huge grin on his face.

Then he heard Captain McMurtry's voice, clear as day: "I'm glad I found you."

Trai stepped onto the porch.

"Chú?" he asked softly.

Dũng did not answer. The coffee cup slipped from his hand and tipped gently onto the boards, as if even gravity had decided to be kind.

Trai rushed to him, dropping to his knees. He touched his uncle's wrist, then his cheek. Dũng's face was peaceful, as if he had finally exhaled a breath he had held since childhood.

Trai bowed his head and whispered, "You're home," though he did not know if he meant the cabin, the mountains, or something beyond this life.

The memorial service was held in the mountain home. The narrow road clogged with vehicles. Honor Guards came. Politicians came. The curious came.

None of that would have mattered to Dũng.

Trai, his wife Phương, their three children, and his two friends—Russell and Abraham—were the ones who mattered.

A local Baptist preacher spoke. A Buddhist monk and a Catholic priest—both from Nashville—also conducted prayers. Three traditions, one truth: a life mattered, and a family grieved.

Two urns sat on a table as each man spoke.

When they finished, the crowd fell into a hush so complete that the wind in the trees sounded like a whisper.

Trai stepped forward first. He held the urn with both hands, as if it contained not ashes but the full weight of a man's life. Russell and Abraham moved to either side of him—not crowding him, simply there, steady as they had learned to be. Trai took a step back, supported by his eldest son, his eyes fixed on the ground between Jonas and Esther.

A shallow grave had been prepared in the earth that Jonas had chosen long ago, the place where the family gathered when words were not enough.

Trai knelt and lowered the urn into the hole with careful reverence. For a moment, he remained there with his hand on the smooth surface, head bowed.

Then he rose.

Russell straightened to his full height and brought his hand up in a crisp salute. Abraham did the same, his palm firm at his brow, his posture rigid with discipline and respect. In the background, a bugler began playing Taps, crisp and clear.

The motion traveled outward like a wave.

One by one, then in clusters, men and women throughout the crowd who had served lifted their hands to salute—older veterans whose bodies had stiffened with age, younger soldiers in dress uniforms. Civilians lifted their hands to their hearts. Inexplicably, many found tears flowing freely. A forest of raised hands stood still in the cold mountain air, offering honor to a man who had carried war inside him and still loved fiercely.

Trai's throat tightened. He looked at the salutes, then down at the urn, and whispered, so softly only those closest might hear, "Thank you."

Taps ended.

Hands throughout the crowd slowly fell to their owners' sides. Russell and Abraham hesitated, both holding their salutes, with tears pouring and gulps of air as they both wept. They slowly lowered their arms and each took a shovel held by a uniformed sergeant. Trai took one also.

Together, Trai, Russell, and Abraham each placed a couple of shovelfuls of dirt into the grave, the sound dull and final, the way earth always sounds when it returns to itself. Then they stepped back and let the family finish.

When the mound was formed, Trai pressed his palm into the soil as if to seal a promise.

A week later, Trai, Phương, and their three sons rode with Tuấn up the Sông Côn Valley. Along đường tỉnh 637, beside the river and its familiar bends, Trai asked Tuấn to stop.

It had been more than twenty-seven years since he had been in that valley, but he knew where he was. The hut of his youth was gone, but he knew the ground where it had stood. Some places were burned into a man, regardless of time.

Trai, his family, and Tuấn walked into the forest at the base of the mountain. Trai led them to the place beneath a tree where, long ago, he and his uncle had buried his grandmother Phương.

He knelt and laid a hand on the earth.

His wife stood beside him, steady as always. One of their sons asked, "Is this where you lived?" and Trai nodded.

"Yes," Trai said. "This is where I learned what it means to endure."

With a shovel he had brought along, Trai dug a hole just above that spot. There he buried the second urn and put his uncle Dũng to rest beside Phương—back in the soil that had shaped him, back in the valley that had held the earliest pieces of his life.

Trai covered the urn carefully and packed the earth down with his hands. He stayed there a long time, his family silent behind him.

When he finally stood, he looked out toward the valley and whispered, "You're home."

And in the quiet of that place, it felt true.

Gabriel Fox and Dũng Phạm were home.

Post Script

On the trip back to Quy Nhơn, Trai told his sons of his long trip to America, a story they had never heard. They marveled with greater understanding.

That evening in Quy Nhơn, the family walked through a busy market. As they walked, Trai suddenly felt a sensation, and was drawn to look down to his left. A young woman, squatted, worked diligently before a gas stove. Trai, stood for a moment, curiously looking at the young woman. The young woman had taken over from the old woman who had held that spot for many years and had died two years earlier. Trai stood for a moment and then walked on. He traveled a few feet and then suddenly turned back and looked again. He never understood why.

www.ingramcontent.com/pod-product-compliance
Lightning Source LLC
LaVergne TN
LVHW100515110826
845146LV00002B/642

* 9 7 9 8 9 9 5 5 0 2 2 0 3 *